"Your manner is way
much too stylish for r...

Margaret leaned closer. "In short, Mr. Cutler, you don't belong here. And I don't want my pa to get dependent on a city man like you. You'll only let us down when the going gets tough."

She would make a good detective. Josiah reached out and touched her cheek. She flinched but held her ground. He grinned at her glare. "I think you need to be tamed as much as the broncs in the corral," he said.

"Of all the nerve!" She wheeled to leave, but Josiah caught her in his arms.

She stared up at him, her green eyes wide with alarm. He touched her cheek with his fingertips, surprising himself as much as he did her. He wasn't one to toy with women—his life had been too busy to spare any time for a woman. But he realized he could feel strongly about this woman. Her skin was warm as sunshine.

In a moment, he realized Margaret O'Brien was a danger he couldn't afford. She attracted him too much, and he couldn't allow himself to get close enough to risk exposing his plans. He released her, and she stepped away.

Her green eyes snapped with anger. She drew back her hand to slap him, and he caught the blow in midair. But he wasn't expecting attack from another quarter. Margaret kicked him in the shin, and he bent double with the pain.

"Yee-ouch." He rubbed his shins. "It was only a touch, Ma'am, not an attack on your person."

She panted with the passion of her emotions. "You are despicable!" she raged.

COLLEEN COBLE and her husband, David, make their home in Wabash, Indiana, where they are restoring a Victorian home. They have two grown kids, David Jr. and Kara. Though Colleen is still waiting for grandchildren, she makes do with spoiling her "grandpup" Harley and her "grandcats" Spooky, Damien, and Alex. She is active at New Life Baptist Church where she sings and helps her husband with a young adult Sunday school class. A voracious reader herself, Colleen began pursuing her lifelong dream when a younger brother, Randy Rhoads, was killed by lightning when she was thirty-eight. She now has numerous fiction titles in print. Colleen's books have appeared on the CBA best-seller list, and they also make frequent appearances on the **Heartsong Presents** readers' favorites annual poll. Visit her website at www.colleencoble.com

Books by Colleen Coble

HEARTSONG PRESENTS
HP271—Where Leads the Heart
HP327—Plains of Promise
HP360—The Heart Answers
HP395—To Love a Stranger
HP417—From Russia with Love
HP429—Love Ahoy
HP456—The Cattle Baron's Wife
HP487—Maggie's Mistake

Red River Bride

Colleen Coble

Heartsong Presents

A note from the author:
I love to hear from my readers! You may correspond with me by writing:

Colleen Coble
Author Relations
PO Box 719
Uhrichsville, OH 44683

ISBN 1-58660-681-6

RED RIVER BRIDE

one

Margaret O'Brien strode down the boardwalk in front of the feed store. Pa should be around here somewhere. She nodded to the ladies clustered in front of the general store, the familiar regret washing over her. Why couldn't she look like them? No matter how hard she tried to imitate their dress and walk, she remained what she was: tall, gangly, and more at home with her hands gripping horse reins than a teacup.

Of course they had no idea she felt inferior every time she was in their presence. She held her head up and made her competence known in the community. But the longing to be like other women never left her.

This town of Henrietta, Texas, was beginning to burgeon, and Margaret was proud to be part of it. More cowmen had come to the Red River Valley, drawn by the lush grazing land and the water in the Red River. The O'Brien spread was only one of many now, but Margaret was determined to make the Triple T brand one that lived up to its reputation of quality beef. At least her skills with horses and cattle gave her a sense of pride and purpose.

Cattlemen had driven herds of cattle through here more than an hour ago, but the dust and odor still lingered in the air. Her father waved to her from in front of the stagecoach station. Margaret had started toward him when the man beside him arrested her gaze. He was tall, even taller than her father, which meant he had to be at least six feet three or four inches. The man's Stetson hat was pushed back on his head, and his bronzed face was chiseled with planes and angles that spoke of confidence and determination.

Immediately, Margaret's hackles rose. That kind of self-assurance—arrogance really—always reminded her of her uncle. She'd had to assert herself strenuously with him around the ranch because he thought a woman's place was in the kitchen, not in the stockyard. This man was the same type, the sort of man who would demand to be catered to and obeyed. No one who looked that strong and proud would listen to a woman.

She forced such thoughts away. This man was probably nothing like her uncle. But her instant antipathy slowed her steps. Let Pa talk to him—she wanted nothing to do with him. Her father motioned her forward, though, and she reluctantly moved to join the two men.

Who was he? She didn't recognize him, and she thought she knew everyone in town. He was not the type of man anyone forgot.

Her father's face beamed with pride as Margaret approached. "Here's my daughter, Margaret."

The man's dark-eyed gaze swept from the top of her head down to the dusty boots just peeking out from underneath her serviceable skirt, and Margaret's lips tightened in a grim smile. The men had come after cattle feed, and she had work to do when she got home, so she hadn't bothered to change. People in Henrietta were used to her working attire, but this man's eyes widened, and she knew he'd probably never seen a woman dressed for ranch work. She wore a man's chambray shirt, and her hair hung over her shoulder in a long braid. The bits of cow manure on her skirt and boots didn't add much to the general picture either.

Let him stare. He was nothing to her. She lifted her head and stared him down. His dark eyes betrayed none of his thoughts. She didn't think she'd ever seen eyes that shade of brown. Like a buckeye nut they were, a rich brown color. Heavy brows accented the strong planes of his face, and Margaret thrust out her hand.

"Pleased to meet you," she said. "And you are—?" Attractive men tended to look right past her, and this one could have stared over the top of her head without taking notice of her at all. But he didn't. He gazed straight into her eyes, and her breath caught in her throat as she felt the magnetic pull of the man.

"Josiah Cutler." His handshake was firm and as self-confident as his appearance.

Margaret pulled away her hand. "You been in town long?" He'd given his name but not his business here in town. Pa seemed almost proprietorial toward him, but she clamped her teeth against the questions clamoring to escape.

"He just got in today," her father put in eagerly. "He's our new foreman."

"New foreman?" Margaret's heart dipped like a bronco about to arch his back to the sky. "We don't need a new foreman, Pa. I can handle things by myself." Hadn't she spent the last ten years of her life proving just that? Her dislike for this Cutler guy grew.

"Now, Margaret, I told you I think it's time you let go of some of these notions about running the ranch by yourself. I'm getting too old to be of much help, and I'd sure like for you to set your mind to finding a husband and giving me some young'uns to dandle on my knee." Her father's gaze traveled over Margaret's apparel, and displeasure shone in his eyes. "Though what man would have you when you make no attempt to look like a woman is another concern altogether," he said under his breath.

Margaret had begun to find her composure, but at her father's words, the blood rushed to her face. They didn't need to be airing their disagreements in front of this stranger. Pa had never understood how his words burned her spirit like a brand. She never let on how he hurt her, and she didn't now. Narrowing her eyes, she glared at this stranger who was set to disrupt her life.

Josiah Cutler seemed to be taking it all in with interest, and a small smile played around those firm lips of his. Margaret wanted to slap that knowing expression from his eyes. An expression that seemed to laugh at the notion that anyone would want to marry someone who looked like her. He probably agreed wholeheartedly with her father's assessment. Like all the rest of the men in her acquaintance, he would be looking for some dainty young thing with a simpering smile and golden curls.

She tossed her head and stared him down. His smile faltered, and she felt a stab of satisfaction. "I'm sorry you've come all this way for nothing," she told him. "But we really don't need a foreman."

"The thing's done," her father said with a reproachful

glare at Margaret. "Toss your belongings into our wagon, Josiah. We'll head back to the ranch as soon as we get this feed loaded."

Josiah nodded, then tossed his valise into the wagon. He didn't wait to be asked but went to the pile of feed sacks and began loading them. His muscular arms handled the heavy bags with ease. For a moment Margaret stared at the muscles in his back as they rippled beneath his shirt. In spite of her dislike of the man, he was a fine specimen of masculinity.

She helped load the sacks, but he seemed to do so twice as quickly, with not even a labored breath. She bristled at his strength, annoyed he should show her up in front of her father. She'd teach him she didn't need his help—not for loading feed and not for running the ranch.

She and Josiah worked side by side for several minutes. Josiah tossed the last of the feed into the wagon and turned to her with a grin. "What now, Boss?" he asked.

Boss. The way he said the word with a hint of mockery made her grimace. She opened her mouth to put him in his place, but before the hot words could rush out, shots rang out down the street. Five men, their guns blasting at anything that moved, rushed out of the bank and mounted their horses. The horses came thundering toward Margaret.

"Get down!" Josiah tackled her and threw her to the dusty ground.

The breath puffed out of her as he fell on top of her. She struggled to free herself, but his muscular arms and strong body kept her pinned beneath him. Never in her life had she felt so helpless and dependent. And protected. The word whispered through her brain with a gentle allure. She shook her head and struggled even more. She didn't need protection. For more years than she could count, she had taken care of herself. She wasn't some squealing miss who ran at the first sign of gunfire. The sooner this bear of a man learned that, the better.

It wasn't until the danger was past that Josiah let her up. He grabbed her arm and hauled her upright as though she were a fence post. Margaret glared at him, but he ignored her as he stared down the street. Several men came running from the bank. Margaret recognized the bank president, Orville Meyer. Orville's cravat was awry, and his black hair stood up in spikes.

"Help! We've been robbed!" he cried. "Come on, all of you, we have to catch them."

The sheriff, freeing his gun from his holster as he ran, came rushing from the other side of town. "I need all the men who can ride and shoot," he said. "We might be able to catch them."

Margaret turned to stare at Josiah, but he just stood there placidly as men all around him grabbed horses and guns. She narrowed her eyes at him. Maybe he was a coward in spite of his hefty size.

Then he nodded at her pa. "I reckon I'd best ask your leave to join the posse," he said.

Her pa shook his head. "They have enough men, and we need to be getting back to the ranch."

Was that relief on Josiah's face? Margaret's lip curled with disgust. He must be a coward. Why else would he not want to join the chase? If she were a man, she would have been the first one to volunteer. She turned abruptly and began to clamber onto the seat of the wagon, but before she could climb up, Josiah's large hands spanned her waist and lifted her as though she weighed no more than a feather duster.

Margaret jerked away from his grip and would have tumbled to the street except for his steadying hands. "I've been climbing in and out of this wagon for years by myself," she snapped. "I don't need your help."

"Just being mannerly, Ma'am," Josiah said. Curls had escaped his hat and lay plastered against his broad forehead.

The merriment in his dark eyes set her teeth on edge like fingernails against a blackboard. She would see him fired and gone from her property if it were the last thing she did. She didn't want him laughing at her every day. Laughter behind her back was something with which she was quite familiar, and she didn't need any more of it from a mere foreman.

"Margaret, quit fooling around. We need to get on the road," her father said, climbing up beside her. Josiah bounded up next to him, his bulk causing the springs of the wagon to groan.

Her father's voice held a trace of petulance, and she knew he was tired and needed to rest. Contrite, she settled herself on the seat and leaned forward to grab the reins, but before she could seize them, Josiah had them in his large fists.

"Giddup." He slapped the reins against the backs of the horses, and the wagon lurched forward.

Caught off guard, Margaret nearly tumbled into the back of the wagon with the feed sacks. She scowled at Josiah, but he didn't seem to see her angry stare. Gripping the side of the wagon, she pressed her lips tightly together. This was going to be a long ride home.

⠶

She was a mighty prickly woman, this Margaret O'Brien. Josiah glanced at her from the corner of his eye, then stared straight ahead. Fine figure of a woman, though. She'd give some lucky man sons and daughters worth having if they had her fire and determination. Her red hair and green eyes betrayed her spirit and passion for life. She had no use for him, though, and Josiah couldn't say as he blamed her. He wouldn't cotton to someone waltzing in and taking over a job he had all picked out for himself, either.

But he had a purpose for being here, and not even a woman like the rancher's daughter could be allowed to distract him from it. His mission was too important. Lucky for him that Paddy O'Brien hadn't let him go with the posse. That could have ruined everything if he were recognized. He'd just been glad Willy wasn't among the robbers who rushed past him. If Willy had seen him, Josiah's whole plan would have been jeopardized.

Paddy O'Brien pointed out the lane to the ranch, and Josiah turned the horses down it. From here the rolling meadows of Triple T ranch spread before him. Lush grass for the cattle intermingled with rugged red buttes under the blue skies. The beauty of the place tugged at Josiah's heart, almost as though he were coming home, although he knew that was ridiculous. He'd never been in this part of Texas. But this Red River Valley was beautiful, no doubt about that. He thought he'd heard a song about it once, but he couldn't remember the words.

The ranch house and outbuildings came into view. A low, stuccoed home crouched beneath two cottonwood trees. Several barns and corrals surrounded the home, and he could see herds of longhorns grazing on the hills around the ranch.

"Mighty pretty place," he told Paddy.

Margaret must have gotten her statuesque figure from her father. Paddy was a big man, though age had stooped his shoulders and shriveled his skin, and he lifted his head high, clearly pleased by the compliment to his life's work. And rightly so. The Triple T spread out before them in all its bustling glory.

Josiah cast another glance at Margaret. She intrigued him. A smattering of freckles shimmered on her nose, and her chiseled face with its high cheekbones gave her a regal bearing as she glanced around at the Triple T. He didn't doubt she had helped make the ranch a success and had earned that look of proud ownership.

Her hair was bound in a thick, red braid nearly as big around as her wrist. Josiah wondered what it would look like released from the confines of the braid, gleaming in the sunshine. Like red fire, most likely. He dragged his thoughts away from the intriguing woman and pulled the team to a halt. His job didn't entail casting longing eyes at Margaret O'Brien.

"Margaret, show Josiah to his quarters," Paddy said.

Margaret glared at Josiah; then she jabbed a finger at the bunkhouse behind the house. "It's in there."

"Margaret," her father said in a warning tone of voice.

Her lips compressed, Margaret wheeled, and her braid flipped Josiah in the face. He suppressed a grin as he followed her across the yard. Her stiff back proclaimed her outrage, but she didn't say anything. Josiah was sorry for that. He would have liked to listen to her voice some more. Low and throaty. He liked the sound of it.

She shoved open the door to the bunkhouse and stepped inside. Josiah followed her. It took a moment for his eyes to adjust from the bright sunshine outside to the dim coolness of the room inside.

Margaret stepped to a door on the left side and pointed. "This is the foreman's room. It's got a private entrance off the back of the bunkhouse to the privy."

She turned and started to brush past him, but Josiah reached out and gripped her arm. "I'm not a threat to you, Ma'am. From what I can see, this is a pretty big spread, and you can use the help. I'm not quite sure how I managed to get your back up, but can we call a truce?"

Color bloomed along her cheeks, and she narrowed her eyes. "I've fought all my life to be respected as competent to run this ranch, Mr. Cutler. I thought my father recognized my ability, and it was a shock today to realize he doesn't trust me any more than the rest of the county does. I would have thought he'd have taken one look at you and realized the person he needed to be wary of was you."

She waved in his direction. "Look at you, with your fancy pants and shirt. No self-respecting foreman would be caught dead in that shirt. The thorns and briars would puncture your skin right through those clothes. And those boots look like you just bought them before you boarded the stagecoach. You're no brushpopper, that's for sure."

Josiah glanced down. She wasn't far wrong. He *had* bought them just for this job.

"Your manner is way too cocky, and your hair is much too stylish for ranch work." She leaned closer. "In short, Mr. Cutler, you don't belong here. And I don't want my pa to get dependent on a city man like you. You'll only let us down when the going gets tough."

She would make a good detective. Josiah reached out and touched her cheek. She flinched but held her ground. He grinned at her glare. "I think you need to be tamed as much as the broncs in the corral," he said.

"Of all the nerve!" She wheeled to leave, but Josiah caught her in his arms.

She stared up at him, her green eyes wide with alarm. He touched her cheek with his fingertips, surprising himself as much as he did her. He wasn't one to toy with women— his life had been too busy to spare any time for a woman. But he realized he could feel strongly about this woman. Her skin was warm as sunshine.

In a moment, he realized Margaret O'Brien was a danger he couldn't afford. She attracted him too much, and he couldn't allow himself to get close enough to risk exposing his plans. He released her, and she stepped away.

Her green eyes snapped with anger. She drew back her hand to slap him, and he caught the blow in midair. But he wasn't expecting attack from another quarter. Margaret kicked him in the shin, and he bent double with the pain.

"Yee-ouch." He rubbed his shins. "It was only a touch, Ma'am, not an attack on your person."

She panted with the passion of her emotions. "You are despicable!" she raged. "Are you in the habit of accosting women who find you repugnant? I am a believer, Mr. Cutler, a Christian woman. My—my caresses will be saved for the man who will one day respect me enough to marry me. They are not to be bandied about like currency on the open market."

Josiah felt like a heel when he saw tears sparkling on her lashes. And for the first time in his life, he thought that marriage might not be such a bad proposition with the right wife. Someone like Margaret O'Brien.

He reached toward her to reassure her that his intentions were honorable, but she flinched and ran from the bunk-house. Great. She would probably tell her father that he'd gotten fresh, and he would lose his job before it started. He squared his shoulders. He had to stop that from happening. Too much depended on this central location.

He rushed after her, but her tall form wasn't running for the safety of the house and her father. She was hurrying toward an orchard grove behind the barn. She disappeared into the trees, and he followed. He found her facedown on the grass, her shoulders heaving with her sobs.

Josiah knelt beside her and hesitantly touched her shoulder. She buried her head farther into her arms. "Go away."

He drew his hand away. "I'm sorry, Miss O'Brien. I was way out of line," he said.

Her sobs began to slow, and finally she shuddered and fell silent. "Go away," she said again. This time her voice was resigned and full of sadness.

Josiah didn't understand why one touch should have

produced this reaction. He reached to pat her shoulder, but she quickly sat up and shrugged away his hand.

"Don't touch me." Her face was red and blotchy from weeping.

Josiah fished a handkerchief out of his pocket and handed it to her. "I'm sorry, Miss O'Brien. Truly. I don't know what got into me. All I can say is you're a beautiful woman, and I've wanted to touch you from the first minute I laid eyes on you. I won't touch you again, I promise."

The color ran from her face, and she stared at him as though he'd just grown horns. "Do you take me for a complete fool?" she whispered. "I know I'm not beautiful. The only possible reason you would say so would be to mock me. Well, I'm an O'Brien and we don't give in to mockery easily. Keep your hands to yourself, Mr. Cutler. Or find a town girl who likes to dally in the moonlight."

He frowned at her. "I wasn't mocking you. And if no one has ever told you you're beautiful, then I have to wonder about the men in this valley." He rose and brushed the twigs from his trousers. "But believe me, I would rather hug a polecat than you after that display of female hysteria. You can be sure it won't happen again."

The color came back into her pale face, and she rose to face him. "It certainly *won't* happen again," she snapped. "I understand the type of man you are now, Mr. Cutler, and I won't let my guard down again."

"I suppose you'll go running to your father," Josiah said. "You're not woman enough to face your problems on your own."

Her eyes flashed and she tilted her chin. "If I was going

to tattle to my father, I would have gone to him at once. You're not a problem, Mr. Cutler. You're no more important than a rogue bull that has to be put down. I can handle you with one arm behind my back."

For one crazy moment, Josiah was tempted to show her that he wasn't to be underestimated, but sense reasserted itself and he politely stepped away from her. "We shall see, Miss O'Brien, we shall see."

He felt a stab of satisfaction at the way her cheeks colored and her eyes darkened with trepidation. Her emotions showed so readily in her face. She had translucent skin that colored easily, and it would be tempting to spend his time provoking a reaction out of her. She was a match for him in more ways than one. He would do well to tread warily.

When this job was done, he would woo Margaret O'Brien in earnest. But until then, he'd better keep his distance.

two

Margaret didn't know which was worse: to think about the way the new foreman had touched her or to know it wouldn't happen again. She told herself she hated him, but in spite of her silent protests, he intrigued her. His apology had been sincere, but his assertion that she was beautiful had left her nonplussed about his intentions. Over the next few weeks, she found herself watching Josiah. There was a mystery to the man, and she longed to probe beneath the surface and discover his secrets. And secrets there were, she was sure.

At least he was no slacker. His broad shoulders easily muscled his way into milling cattle, and he wielded a hammer with authority as he tackled the repairs to the barn. But she still had a sense this was not his usual type of job. Margaret couldn't imagine what had brought him to the valley. His smooth-edged veneer hinted he would be more comfortable in a fine hotel than the rustic bunkhouse he now called home.

Oh, he was comfortable on a horse; that much was obvious. But he didn't ride like a cowboy. She couldn't put her finger on what the difference was, but it plagued her just the same. Margaret wasn't one to let an idea loose. Eventually, she would discover where he came from and what he was doing here.

The weather had been hot and dry for days. The sun beat down on Margaret as she worked with the men cutting out cattle. Dehorning was a job she hated, but it had to be done. The cattle bawled and thrashed as they were divested of their horns, and Margaret felt half sick by the time it was over. Her head thumped like an Apache drum. Josiah had worked alongside her without a complaint, taking the brunt of the wrestling of the cattle. For the first time since he'd come, she'd been glad of his help.

"Calling it quits?" he asked when she took her hat off and used it to fan her hot face.

For some reason the question made her decide not to go inside like she'd planned. She didn't want it said that she was a quitter. With all the men watching, she couldn't let it get back to Pa that she'd fizzled out on the job like some greenhorn fresh off the stage from New York. He knew all her inadequacies as it was, and she didn't need to give him more reason to wish for a son instead of a daughter.

She raised her chin and shook her head. "Just taking a break."

"You look tired," Josiah observed. "We can finish up here. Cookie will be ringing the supper bell any minute."

"I'll stay until the work is done." She slapped the dust from her hat, then tossed her braid over her shoulder and put her hat back on her head. He could keep his sympathetic glances to himself. Born and bred to this life, she could outwork him any day. He was a city man, and she would do well to remember that. He'd soon tire of this life and go back to the bright lights.

"Anyone ever mention you're as stubborn as Percy?"

Margaret's face burned at the reference. Percy was her pa's old mule that had been put out to pasture for being so purely cantankerous as he aged that it was impossible to deal with him. Josiah would like to put her out to pasture the same way, she was sure. But he wouldn't get the opportunity. This was her land, her ranch. He might want to take it over, but he would do so over her dead body.

"I get the work done," she snapped. Her headache thumped again, and she was afraid she was going to be sick right on Josiah's boots. His face wavered before her eyes, and she swallowed. Swaying, she put a hand to her head, and a small groan escaped her clenched throat.

His fingers gripped her arm, and he propelled her toward the house. "I thought you looked like your head hurt. Get out of this sun."

Margaret protested feebly, but she knew she was finished. Humiliation added to the sick feeling in the pit of her stomach. What must he think of her? He'd likely use this to secure his position with Pa, more proof that she was too weak to be running the ranch.

Josiah opened the front door and ushered her inside. The cool darkness of the house welcomed her like a soothing balm. At least the bright sun no longer stabbed daggers behind her eyes. She sank into the rocker by the fireplace and leaned forward with her face in her hands. She hated feeling so weak and—and *vaporish*. The next thing she knew, she'd be fainting or fanning herself with an ostrich feather fan. The thought stiffened her spine, and she raised her head.

Josiah was regarding her with sympathetic eyes, and the

kindness in his gaze nearly brought tears to her eyes. Even Pa never looked at her that way, as though he wished he could take her pain away. Pa had no patience for womanly weakness, and she tried never to allow any hint of weariness or sickness to show to him. He'd said often enough that he had wanted a son. She knew she was a poor substitute in Pa's eyes.

"Want a cold rag?" Josiah asked. "My sister swears it helps."

Margaret hesitated.

"I'll get it. Where would I find some cloth?"

Margaret directed him to the buffet that held the linens, and he soon returned with two wet compresses. He gently moved her braid out of the way and pressed a cold cloth to the back of her head, then handed her another. "Put that one on your forehead."

She did as he asked, and the relief was indescribable as the pounding began to ease a bit. "Thanks," she whispered.

"Go lie down," he ordered. "I'll handle the rest of the dehorning."

She wanted to protest, but she still felt too wobbly to object. As she went down the hallway to her room, she heard the front door shut as Josiah went back outside. The window in her bedroom was open, and she lay on the bed with a breeze wafting across her. Josiah's voice drifted through the open window.

"What did you find out?" he asked.

Another voice answered, one Margaret didn't recognize. "Willy wants to meet with you. He'll be in touch in the next few days, so you'll have to be ready to move. He's probably having to help stash the loot somewhere. The posse is still on their trail. This one from Clarendon."

She put a hand to her mouth. They were talking about the bank robbers. There had been a rash of robberies lately, everything from banks to the Butterfield stage line. All her doubts about what Josiah was doing here came flooding back. That explained why he hadn't wanted to join the posse the day he arrived: He was one of them.

She squeezed her eyes at the sharp disappointment. No wonder he'd made up to her—he wanted to allay any suspicions she had. His sweet words and flirtatious ways hid the heart of a criminal. The disappointment she felt in Josiah surprised her. Why should she feel disappointed? She'd known all along he wasn't what he seemed. But she hadn't expected something like this.

She had to tell Pa. Pain stabbed her head when she sat up, and she sank back weakly with a groan. Nothing was going to happen for a few days. Maybe she'd better find out more information before she involved her father in the mess. He was likely to go straight to Josiah and tip their hand. No, it would be best to ferret out the truth herself. When she knew enough, she could go for the sheriff.

She closed her eyes and willed the headache to go away. There was too much to do to take time for this weakness, but her body didn't seem to want to cooperate. She napped fitfully until the supper bell rang. When she sat up, she discovered the pain in her head had subsided to a dull ache, and she felt full of purpose. Her disappointment was gone with the headache. This would prove she was right all along, that Pa had been taken in just as she'd thought.

She shook her hair loose from its braid and quickly plaited it again. The men were all seated around the table by the time she got to supper, and the only place left to sit was beside Josiah. Perfect. Maybe he would let something slip. She slipped into the chair beside him.

"Feeling better?" He scooped mashed potatoes on his plate, then handed her the bowl.

"Yes, thanks." She took the potatoes and deposited some on her own plate. Josiah fell silent as they passed the food around, and she wondered how she could get him to open up. She needed proof, not just some overheard snippets of conversation. If she could foil a bank robbery attempt, that would be vindication for her.

"Hey, did you hear there's going to be a barn dance tomorrow at the Stantons'?" her pa said from the head of the table. "Everyone is invited."

Margaret felt a rush of pleasure. She hadn't seen Lucy in several weeks and had been longing to see how she was doing. The men began to joke and talk about seeing some of the single girls in the area, and her initial rush of happiness faded. It was always the same. No man thought first of her as a possible partner. Even as tall and conspicuous as she was, it was as if she were invisible. She was too much like one of the men to even be considered as an eligible mate.

Josiah said something, but she'd missed his words. "I beg your pardon." She turned toward him. "I must have been wool-gathering."

Josiah's dark eyes probed her gaze. "I said I'd be proud to escort you, Miss Margaret, unless you already have an escort."

Elation lifted her spirits for a moment; then crushing disappointment swamped her as she remembered what she knew about him now. A refusal hovered on her lips; but after a moment, she forced herself to smile and nod. What better way to find out more? If she could get him to trust her enough to let down his guard, maybe she could get enough information to go to the sheriff. "I reckon I can put up with your company for one evening, Mr. Cutler."

"Why are you so formal? I think we've gone way beyond that. My name's Josiah."

Margaret's face burned at how accurate his words were. But the last thing she wanted was to get closer to him now that she knew he was in cahoots with the bank robbers. A moment of unease assailed her. What if he tried to shut her up—permanently? Bank robbers were desperate characters, and she would be alone with him on the drive to Lucy's. Maybe he would arrange an ambush that would ensure she didn't tell anyone her suspicions.

She gave herself a mental shake. Melodrama—that's what she was indulging in. Pure melodrama. Josiah wouldn't hurt her. Everyone would know she was with him, and they would expect him to take care of her. She was perfectly safe with him, she told herself. Then why didn't she feel safe? He made her feel as though she were in danger every minute she spent in his company.

It wasn't the physical danger that frightened her. Her thoughts were way too bound up in this man. His pleasant facade hid his true nature.

"Very well, Josiah," she said finally. It would be best not to give him any reason for suspicion. She would be courteous and lull him into a false sense of security. But why did she feel so bad about the thought—so dishonest? A bank robber didn't deserve anything more. Pushing away the feelings of guilt, she turned her attention to her supper.

❧

The next day dragged by as Margaret attended to her ranch duties and waited for the evening to come. She was looking forward to the outing with a real sense of anticipation. She tried to tell herself it was because of seeing Lucy, but her innate honesty forced her to admit that the thought of spending so much time with Josiah was the thing that appealed to her most.

Five o'clock finally came, and she rushed into the house to get ready. Their housekeeper, Maria, already had the tub filled with hot water, and Margaret thanked her as she rushed into her room and began to peel off the smelly clothes of the day.

Maria scrubbed Margaret's back for her and helped her rinse her long, thick hair. "Señorita Margaret, no," she protested when Margaret began to braid it again. "Is a party tonight. You must wear it in more attractive way. Let me." Maria pushed Margaret's hands out of the way and brushed her hair out again. "We let it dry while you get dressed; then I arrange it for you. What dress you wear?"

"Oh, anything will do," Margaret said. She swung open the door to the wardrobe and stared at the contents. "I don't have much worthy of a party, do I?" The pang of disappointment made her bite her lip. What was the matter with her? She usually didn't care what she wore. Tonight should be no different. She'd long ago quit trying to compete with other women.

"I know just the dress." Maria gave a serene smile. "I will be right back." She rustled from the room.

While Maria was gone, Margaret stared at herself in the mirror. It was no wonder men didn't find her attractive. Her red hair was too wild and untamed, she was too tall, and she hated her freckles. She wished again God had made her differently. The Bible said He had formed her in her mother's womb and created her just the way He wanted her; but when she met Him, she intended to ask what He'd been thinking of to make her so uncomely. A heavy sigh escaped her lips. This evening was a mistake. She should have been born a man. Maybe then her form would have been a source of pride, not dismay.

Maria came hurrying back into the room. From her arms draped a dress in a deep shade of emerald. A triumphant smile played about her lips. "Your *madre* looked lovely in this dress, just as you will. She wear it to a party in Boston before she marry your *papá*. Every man in the room look at her."

That certainly wouldn't happen to Margaret. She wished she'd known her mother. People said she looked like her mother, but they also talked about what a lovely lady she was. If she really looked like her mother, why hadn't she inherited her mother's beauty? "Where did you get it?" Margaret stroked the silken fabric with one finger.

"I keep in special place in attic. These many years I save it for you, for just the right occasion. Today it is right when I see the stars in your eyes for Mr. Cutler."

Heat crept up Margaret's cheeks. "Mr. Cutler means nothing to me. I intend to get rid of him. We have no need for his help."

"My señorita says one thing, but her eyes say another," Maria said with a smug smile. "I press this, then you try it on."

It was useless to argue with Maria. Margaret sighed and sat on the bed to wait. Her hair was drying quickly in the breeze through the open window. The lovely spring weather would soon give way to summer's heat.

"Now we try this on." With a flourish, Maria held the dress out for Margaret.

Margaret stood and allowed Maria to drop it over her head. Maria buttoned up the back. The whisper of silk made Margaret feel like a princess. She smoothed the fabric over her waist. Never had she worn such a lovely garment. Why dress a pigeon in clothes meant for a peacock?

"Your madre, she had your lovely form as well. You are maybe a bit taller, but daily you grow more like her. There now, see how beautiful you look." Maria drew Margaret to the full-length mirror.

Margaret stared at her reflection in awe. Once she'd tried to dress like the other girls, and Pa had bought her a ruffled blue dress she'd coveted. She'd looked ridiculous in the flounces. But the simple lines of this dress looked elegant on her tall figure. "I guess it will do," she said.

"It is lovely. Now, you sit and I arrange your hair." Maria pressed her down onto the bench in front of the dresser and picked up a brush. With a few artful twists, Maria pulled the front of Margaret's hair back and secured it with a tortoiseshell comb. She left the back fall free.

The ends of her hair had curled as it dried in the breeze. "I don't know, Maria. It will probably get in my way all evening." Margaret sighed. "I should probably just braid it." She panicked thinking she might draw attention to herself by leaving her hair down. In school, kids had called her Carrottop or Red. She'd found it best to make herself as inconspicuous as possible.

"No, you must not. This style, it suits the dress. Come, it is time to meet Mr. Cutler." Maria tugged Margaret to her feet and pointed her toward the door. "You go and have good time. You will see—Maria is right."

Margaret felt like an ostrich in a ball gown as she hurried out to meet Josiah. What if he thought she had dressed like this to impress him? She gave a mental shrug. Maybe it would serve her purposes if he thought she was interested in him as a man. But it still didn't feel right. She tugged at the skirt of her dress a bit. Her initial anticipation faded a bit as she worried about what people would think. She breathed a prayer for courage to face the ridicule. Others would probably think she looked as ridiculous and out of place as she felt.

She should have just worn her usual serviceable skirt and braided her hair. Standing out in a crowd and having others laugh at her didn't sound appealing. But there was no help for it. She could hear Josiah and her pa talking in the parlor, and there was no time to change or back out.

She stepped silently into the parlor. At first neither man noticed her standing in the doorway. Then her pa turned his head and saw her.

For a moment, the color leached from his face; then he blinked and smiled. "Margaret, for a second I thought it was your mama standing there." He gave a gruff laugh. "You look lovely, my dear."

Her father's praise brought tears to her eyes. His approving words came far too infrequently. Was her appearance all that mattered to him—to anyone? It seemed to be the way of the world. No one cared about who she was inside. No one saw the heart longing to be loved and to give love in return. She sometimes even doubted God's love for her.

Josiah's chocolate eyes studied her, and a wave of heat stung her cheeks. What did he think? He said nothing, just raked her with a gaze that made her feel self-conscious and gangly.

He stood and held out his hand. "I'd better take my gun," he said.

Confusion thickened her tongue. "Your gun?"

"I'm going to have to protect you from the other men." He grinned, but the admiration in his gaze was clear.

Margaret's heart gave a funny hitch in her chest. She was way out of her league with this man. He was a bank robber, she reminded herself. For a moment she wished it wasn't so, that she could accept his attentions and hope they might lead somewhere. Then reality raised its cold head again, and she knew even if he were who he claimed to be, it wouldn't matter. His head would soon be turned by some pretty little thing in lace and ruffles, and Margaret's heart would be broken. It was a good thing he was someone totally unsuitable. But that reality did little to stop the yearning in her heart. She should turn tail and run.

"Have fun," her father said.

"Aren't you going, Pa?"

Her father shook his head. "Maria has promised me a supper fit for a king. I'm going to enjoy the peace and quiet."

For the first time Margaret wondered why her pa had never remarried. He was still attractive, with his rangy height and bearing. Maria would make him a good wife. Maybe Margaret should talk to him about it sometime. She stifled a smile. Like she had any business talking to anyone about romance. It wasn't something with which she had any personal experience.

Josiah took her hand and slipped it over the crook of his arm. His warm fingers pressed against hers, and she could feel the bulky muscles of his arm under her hand. "I have the buggy waiting outside." He led her to the door and out to the waiting buggy.

She started to clamber into the buggy, but he spanned her waist with his big hands and lifted her easily into the seat as though she weighed no more than a doll. For the first time in her life she felt feminine and cosseted. It was a feeling she could get used to. She pushed the thought away and reminded herself he was not what he seemed.

He went around the buggy and climbed up beside her. "Why did you decide to go with me?" he asked. "I thought you had decided to hate my guts."

"Who says I don't?" she asked lightly.

He grinned. "Do I take that as a challenge to prove you wrong?"

"You decide," she said airily. Her breath caught in her throat at his nearness.

"I reckon I will."

He reached out and touched her cheek with one finger. She knew she should step away, but she closed her eyes and lifted her face. He kissed her soundly, and all thoughts of his nefarious ways flew from her head like thistledown from a cottonwood tree.

He lifted his head. "I reckon you don't hate me at all."

The smugness in his voice brought her to her senses, and she jerked away. "You flatter yourself," she snapped. "I suggest you keep your kisses for someone who wants them."

"I thought I was doing just that," he said.

She hated him for the laughter in his voice. But could she blame him? She'd encouraged him by allowing him to kiss her. Her face flamed with heat, and she wished she didn't have to turn him in to the sheriff.

three

Josiah glanced around at the trim fences and barns. The Stanton ranch was well tended. Several dogs barked and chased chipmunks in a field to the right of the house, but the main noise came from the laughter and voices drifting from the brightly lit barn closest to the house. He was eager to meet the family.

He'd heard the story from other cowpokes on the payroll. Margaret had fancied herself in love with Caleb Stanton until his father had brought home a mail-order bride for his son. That had been five years ago, and Margaret had withdrawn even more since then. Josiah wanted a look at the only man who had caught Margaret's eye. He didn't want to face why he was so interested. She despised him, so why did he even care about what kind of man she found attractive? Though for a moment, when she lifted her face for a kiss, he'd thought there might be some hope for him.

"Nice place," he told Margaret. She'd gone cold on him again. What had possessed him to kiss her? All her earlier warmth was replaced with a wall of ice he found impossible to melt. It was as though she was determined to pretend she hadn't wanted him to kiss her.

She didn't answer, and he glanced at her from the corner of his eye. His first sight of her tonight had been overwhelming. That glorious hair was finally down like he'd imagined it, and he wanted to plunge his hands into those shining curls. How would it feel beneath his fingers? It looked heavy yet silky. He had never touched a woman's hair, not since he was in diapers and used to grasp his mother's black curls. He clenched his fists against the need to touch Margaret's now. He must be loco to let a woman get to him like this. Especially when he was only here to do a job and get out.

Josiah halted the buggy at the hitching post and got down. He tied up the horse, then went around to help Margaret, but she had already clambered to the ground by herself. She was the most aggravating woman. It was as though she were afraid to let herself be a woman. He offered her his arm. She shot him a look of disdain from eyes as clear as glass but took his arm anyway.

He led her inside the barn. Women dressed in their finery and men tricked out in their best vests spun by in a reel. Their laughter floated on the air, and Josiah felt himself relax. Margaret would get over her snit, and they would have fun. Maybe he should apologize. But he didn't feel sorry for that kiss. Not one bit. The only thing he was sorry about was that it had put the wall between them again.

"Margaret!" A young woman waved from near the dessert table. Blond and pretty, her roundness announced the imminent arrival of a baby.

"Lucy!" Margaret waved back and started toward the woman.

This must be their hostess. Josiah followed Margaret's tall figure through the throng. A man stood beside Lucy, obviously her husband by the way he looked at her. Pride and worry warred for possession of his face.

That had to be Caleb. Josiah looked him over. Strong and handsome, he supposed, though he was no judge of what women found attractive. Good humor and contentment radiated from his face. One thing was certain—he adored his wife even after five years of marriage.

Margaret and Josiah reached the other couple, and Lucy hugged Margaret with enthusiasm. "I've been watching for you," she said. "I've missed you."

"I've been meaning to get over here, but you know how it is on a ranch. Never enough time to get anything done." Margaret linked arms with Lucy.

"I've told Caleb he should have married you. I'm not much use other than in the house."

Caleb grinned down at his wife. "I'm not complaining." He turned to Josiah and thrust out his hand. "Caleb Stanton. You must be the new foreman at Triple T I've heard so much about."

"That would be me," Josiah said. "Josiah Cutler."

"Where you from, Mr. Cutler?" Lucy put in.

"Call me Josiah." He could sense the way Margaret grew suddenly still as though his answer mattered to her. But why should it? She had never shown the least interest in his background and future. She just wanted to get him out of her life.

He smiled at Lucy and spilled out the story he'd rehearsed. "Born and raised in Texas, Ma'am. My pa owned a ranch near Houston, and I worked with him until he died about five years ago." He just prayed she wouldn't ask any more questions. Since he'd become a believer, he hated falsehood; he didn't want to lie, but he'd avoid the rest of the story if he could.

"I'm sorry," Lucy said.

The gentle expression in her eyes proclaimed her sincerity. To Josiah's relief, she turned and directed a question at Margaret. "It must be wonderful to have some help."

Josiah couldn't hold back a grin. "Not so you'd notice, Miss Lucy. She wants to see the back of me in the worst way."

Lucy's blue eyes widened, and she stared at Margaret. Margaret flushed and shot Josiah a glare of intense dislike. He grinned back at her. See how she liked being on the defensive. He had to admit to himself that he rather enjoyed getting her back up. Those eyes of hers flashed like green fire, and the color came into her face when she was angry or upset. It was a bit like watching fireworks, and he'd always loved a show like that.

"We don't need a foreman," Margaret said. "I can handle the work."

"Sure, you can handle it, but why should you?" Caleb asked. "It's hard work even for a man."

"And I'm a weak female, right?" Margaret glared at Caleb, and he held up a hand.

"Whoa," he said. "I meant no disrespect. You can work any man I know under the table, Miss Margaret."

She gave a shamefaced smile. "I'm sorry. I'm a little prickly tonight. It's this ridiculous dress. I feel like I must look like a little girl playing dress-up."

"You look wonderful," Lucy said.

"I've been trying to convince her of that since we left the Triple T," Josiah said.

Lucy gave him a smile. "Maybe if you danced with her, she could believe it."

"Don't talk about me as if I weren't here," Margaret complained.

"That's a great idea, Miss Lucy." Josiah grinned, then gripped Margaret's arm and pulled her toward the dance floor as the fiddler struck up a square dance. He winked at her, and Margaret began to smile. His heart leapt at the way she was looking at him. She might not want to admit she was attracted to him, but he could see it in her face. *Careful,* he reminded himself. This job wouldn't last forever, and his way of life wasn't conducive to a family.

They stomped and spun their way around the floor. Margaret was laughing up at him as she dipped and twirled. They were both breathless by the time the dance ended. He led her to a secluded alcove. "Wait here and I'll get us something to drink." She nodded, and he went across the room to the refreshment table.

Lucy was sitting in a chair beside the table. "Hello again," she said. "Did Margaret run you off already?"

"No, I'm getting us something to drink."

She patted the chair beside her. "Sit down a minute. I want to talk to you."

Josiah arched his eyebrows. Now she had him curious. He sat in the chair she'd indicated.

"Caleb told me not to interfere, but Margaret is my best friend and I don't want to see her hurt," she said.

"I won't hurt her." Josiah was a little tired of his motives always being called into question, first by Margaret and now by her best friend. Usually people took him at face value, and he didn't like this constant suspicion.

"She's more fragile than she appears," Lucy said. "She puts up a brave front, but she's really a little girl looking for love. Are you a Christian, Josiah?"

"Yes, I am." Not many people cared about that, and his respect and liking for Lucy Stanton grew.

Lucy's face lit in relief. "Then maybe you can guide Margaret. She needs to know God's unconditional love. She's a believer, but she can't seem to grasp the fact that God is the only One we can turn to for that love. I think her father's high expectations have made her doubt his love for her. And the loss of her mother when she was a child added to her self-doubt. Caleb's choice didn't help things."

"I heard a little about that. What more can you tell me?" He leaned forward. There was always more to the story.

"The entire town thought Caleb would marry Margaret. He escorted her to a few things, and I think he even thought he would eventually marry her since she knew ranching. Anyone with half an eye can see Margaret would be a hardworking wife. Then I came along, and things changed. I always regretted the way Margaret was hurt. Since then she has rejected any man's attempt to escort her anywhere. Not that many have tried since she's gotten so prickly." Lucy frowned. "Here comes Caleb. I'd better shut up." She laughed and winked at Josiah.

Caleb came toward them with a young man, a girl of about nine, and a little boy about three. "I don't think you've met the rest of the family. This is Jed and Eileen, Lucy's sister and brother. And the little guy is William, our son."

Josiah shook Jed's hand and teased Eileen a few minutes,

then went back to the refreshment table. By the time he got back to Margaret with punch, she was surrounded by men.

One was coaxing her to dance, and Josiah heard another asking her if he could get her some refreshments. The wave of jealousy that swept over him caught him off guard. He'd better watch his heart. He shouldered his way past the men and handed her the punch.

"Sorry, men, the lady is taken," he told them. Was that relief on Margaret's face? He smiled at her, and she smiled back. Elation raced through him. Why had he thought it fun to make her angry? Her smile warmed him like the first hot day of summer.

The men dispersed with a few grumbles. "Sorry if I was overbearing," he told her.

"You're not a bit sorry," she said. "You men get like a bull defending his territory."

"Guilty," he said. "Maybe I'm staking my claim to you." He nearly bit his tongue, but the words were out. What claim did he have on her? She would never look twice at him.

Her eyes widened, and she looked as though she wanted to say something, but then her white teeth clamped against her lip, and she looked away. Her stiff manner came back, and Josiah sighed. He'd messed it up again. This relationship stuff was hard to fathom. One step forward and two steps back. He was much more comfortable with his horse or the cattle.

He glanced around the crowd. His hackles rose when he saw a familiar figure. What was Richard doing here? If the townspeople got wind of what was going on, his job would be even harder.

"I'll be right back," he told Margaret. He put his drink on the floor next to her and hurried toward where he'd last seen Richard.

But though Josiah looked everywhere, Richard had disappeared. Maybe there was no harm done if he'd left. But if Richard put this job in jeopardy, Josiah would take it out of his hide. There was too much riding on the next few weeks. No one could be permitted to get in the way. His throat tight, he stepped outside and looked around.

❧

Margaret clutched the glass of punch in her hand. The coolness of the glass kept her rooted in reality. *Stake his claim, indeed.* Those other men weren't interested in her, only in her father's ranch. And the only claim Josiah was going to stake was on the bank's money. She had to make sure he failed in that attempt. Still, she wanted to weep, which wasn't like her. Not at all. But then, she hadn't been behaving in a characteristic way ever since Josiah had arrived. She had a sinking feeling that she was heading for major trouble. The sooner Josiah was exposed and out of her life, the better.

Where could he have gone in such a hurry? She stood and set her empty glass down among others on top of a barrel. Maybe she could overhear something if she found out where he went. She tried to be nonchalant as she strolled around the barn. But there was no sign of his tall figure. Heading toward the back door, she stepped out into the dark night that enveloped the yard.

She heard a murmur of voices from over by the feed trough. Stepping cautiously, she inched her way toward the voices. Just as she was nearly close enough to hear, she stepped in something. From the way it squished up over her ankle, she had the sinking feeling she knew just what it was. Then the unpleasant odor reached her nostrils, and she knew for certain it was a fresh cowpat. She sucked in her breath and gingerly tried to wipe it off on the grass.

She stumbled into the horse trough, and a pail clattered to the ground. The murmur of voices stopped, and she heard Josiah's familiar deep voice.

"Get out of here before someone sees you. I'll be in touch so we can make our final plans."

Another voice, different from the one she'd heard outside her room yesterday, answered. "Smart of you to come and sniff out the lay of the land here." Moments later the moon illuminated Josiah's white shirt as he came toward her.

"Margaret, what are you doing out here in the dark?" When he saw her trying to scrape her shoe, he grinned. "Need some help?"

She wanted to shout her questions at him, but she forced herself to smile at him instead. "I think I'll go to the house and get cleaned up. Tell Lucy, would you please?" She needed to get away from him before she said something she shouldn't.

"I'll come with you." He took her arm.

She wanted to shake his fingers off her arm. He was a bank robber, and the only reason he was working at the Triple T was to scout out the job he'd come here to do. It had nothing to do with her or any attraction he might feel. If there even *was* any attraction on his part. Maybe he was just a good actor. A man in his position would have to know how to lie and cover up the truth pretty well. Josiah was an obvious master at it.

He guided her across the yard to Lucy's front porch. "I'll send Lucy in to help you," he said. He hurried back across the yard toward the barn.

Margaret should have felt relieved at his absence, but she was furious with herself and her own gullibility. In spite of what she knew about him, she had begun to believe that he really did feel something for her. But that conversation she'd overheard had made it clear he had only one purpose in coming here tonight. She had made a good cover for him to meet with his cohorts.

That was the way it had been all her life. She was never loved for who she was, only for what she could provide. Tears burned the backs of her eyelids, but she fiercely willed them away. Josiah Cutler would rue the day he ever met her. She would expose his black heart and nefarious scheme. Then life would get back to normal, and all these odd feelings that had plagued her lately would be gone. She would take over running the ranch, and life would be good again.

By the time Lucy got to her, Margaret had already managed to get cleaned up. Lucy made suitable noises of commiseration. "I think I'll just go home," Margaret told her. "Could you loan Josiah a horse? I'll take the buggy and go home by myself."

"Oh, don't do that, Margaret! I'll fetch him and let him drive you. It's not safe to go alone."

"I've been doing it all my life." Alone was what she did best.

"Not at night," Lucy said firmly. She stopped and put a

hand to her stomach. "Oh, dear."

"What is it?"

"I–I think my water just broke." Panic raced over her face. "It's too soon! The baby isn't expected for more than a month."

Margaret looked down and saw a puddle of liquid at Lucy's feet. "Stay calm. You get to bed and I'll fetch Caleb and have Jed go for the doctor."

"The doctor is here," Lucy said faintly. She clutched Margaret's hand. "I'm scared," she whispered. "I thought I was ready for this, but now I'm not sure. What if the baby dies?"

"You'll both be fine," Margaret said firmly, though her heart fluttered at how fragile Lucy looked tonight. And this was very early for the baby. She prayed silently and ran for the door. "I'll be right back with the doctor and Caleb."

She collided with Josiah on the front porch. A wave of relief so intense passed through her that she shuddered. He put his hands on her shoulders to steady her, and his touch did just that: A sense of calmness quieted her turmoil.

"What's wrong?" he asked, alarm tinging his words.

"It's Lucy," she babbled. "The baby is coming."

He pulled away. "I'll fetch Caleb."

"And the doctor," she called after him. "He's at the dance, too." She rushed back inside to Lucy.

A confused expression on her face, Lucy sat woodenly in a chair. "I should know what to do, but I'm just befuddled."

"Let's get you undressed and into your nightgown." Margaret helped Lucy disrobe, then found her nightgown in the bureau. Lucy was trembling when Margaret dropped the nightgown over her head.

"I'm so scared, Margaret," she whispered. "I'm not strong and brave like you."

Strong and brave. That's how everyone saw her. What would they think if they knew it was all a facade? People thought of her as mannish because of her size, so she had obliged them by becoming even more that way. No one seemed to appreciate her feminine qualities, so why bother cultivating them? It was ironic. Lucy wanted to be more like her, and she wanted to be like Lucy.

"You're stronger than you think," Margaret said.

A white-faced Caleb burst into the room, followed by Dr. Benson. Caleb knelt and embraced his wife. "I'm here, Lucy. How are you feeling?"

"I–I'm not sure," Lucy stammered.

Caleb helped her to the bed, with Margaret trailing behind. The doctor shooed them all out of the room so he could examine Lucy.

Josiah was pacing across the parlor floor with William in his arms when Margaret stepped into the parlor. Jed was sitting in the rocker with his head in his hands. Eileen sat on the floor beside him. He sprang to his feet when he saw Margaret and Caleb.

"She's fine," Margaret said soothingly. Jed's stiff shoulders relaxed, and he sat back down.

"Will it be a long time?" he asked.

"Probably. Babies take their time," Margaret told him. She wanted to go to Josiah and feel his strong arms around her. She needed comfort and reassurance, too, but he wasn't the appropriate one to turn to for consolation. It was so hard to remember that he was not who he seemed to be. He looked solid and strong standing there with little William in his arms. His strong, craggy face looked like the face of someone who could be trusted. Unfortunately, looks were deceiving. He was a criminal. Margaret sighed and looked away.

Josiah put William on the floor, and the tot scampered across the room to his father. Caleb scooped him up. "You should be getting to bed, little one," he said.

"I'm going to have a baby brother," William announced.

"Maybe a brother but maybe a sister," Caleb said. "You'll like either one. Maybe the baby will be here when you get up in the morning. Like Margaret said, babies take a long time. Your new brother or sister might not make an appearance until tomorrow." He motioned to Jed. "Jed and Eileen will tuck you in and read you a story."

Jed took William from Caleb and carried him from the room. He was still protesting at being put to bed, but he didn't cry. Margaret wished the little one could have stayed. It would have given her something to do with herself.

The doctor came through the door wiping his hands on a cloth. "She's doing fine, but it's going to be awhile," he said. "Might as well get comfortable."

"What about the baby?" Caleb asked.

"Too soon to know. Pray we've just miscalculated the date," the doctor said. "Otherwise, we may lose it."

A lump formed in Margaret's throat. Josiah took her hand, and she looked up in surprise.

"Let's pray together," he whispered.

Pray with an outlaw. The thought seemed ridiculous, but as she bowed her head, Margaret found it wasn't ridiculous.

four

Through the long night, Josiah found himself watching Margaret and marveling at her calm efficiency as she saw to the needs of everyone in the Stanton household. She fetched boiling water and clean cloths for the doctor, disappeared into Lucy's room occasionally to offer comfort and encouragement to the laboring mother, soothed Caleb's frazzled nerves, and helped Caleb's father, Luther, usher the dance guests away from the party. This was yet another side to the intriguing Margaret O'Brien. And it made him want to know her all the more.

Josiah was dozing on the sofa when a noise awakened him. He blinked sleepily in the lightening gloom of early dawn and wondered what that sound was. It almost sounded like a kitten mewing. Then the sound strengthened, and he realized he was hearing the first cries of the newborn baby. He bolted upright, then jumped to his feet.

His hands gripped together, Caleb was standing at the door. An eager smile vied for worry on his face. "Where's the doctor?"

"Sounds like a healthy little one," Josiah said soothingly.

"Yes, but I don't hear Lucy." Caleb paced across the floor, then turned with determination. "I'm going in there."

Before he could reach the doorway, Margaret stepped into the parlor. She was carrying a tiny bundle. "You want to see your daughter, Caleb?"

"A–a daughter?" Dawning wonder broke over the new father's face. He approached Margaret and the baby with a tentative stride. "How's Lucy?"

"She's tired but fine. You can see her in a few minutes," Margaret said.

Josiah decided he'd waited through the long night with the rest, and he deserved a peek, too. He crowded behind Caleb and peered into the blanket at a tiny, wizened face topped by a tuft of red hair. "She has red hair," Josiah blurted.

"Just like her uncle Jed," Caleb murmured. "What's the doctor say about her?"

"Our prayers were answered. It was a simple miscalculation. He thinks she'll be fine."

"Thank You, God," Caleb whispered.

"Here, you hold her." Margaret gently handed the baby to her daddy.

Joy spread over Caleb's face. "She looks like Lucy," he breathed. "But she's so little. I might hurt her. I don't remember William being so small."

"She's tougher than she looks, just like all newborns," Margaret said. "Just think how tough those new calves are and you'll be fine." She gently put the baby in Caleb's arms.

Josiah watched with great interest. He'd never been this close to a newborn baby, and the thrill of new life was amazing. Margaret's face glowed, and so did Caleb's.

The baby was sucking on her fist and making small mewling sounds. Josiah glanced down at Margaret and saw the tender look on her face as she gazed at Caleb with his new daughter. The expression on her face tightened Josiah's stomach. She'd loved Caleb once and wanted to marry him. Did she still love him? Did she wish this child were hers and Caleb's? A lump formed in Josiah's throat. Would he ever hold a child of his own? It didn't seem likely, considering his line of work. But he couldn't imagine a greater joy than holding a little girl who looked like Margaret.

Josiah scowled and turned away. "I'll see to the stock, Caleb. You spend some time with your new daughter." He strode from the room. Let Margaret moon over Caleb. Josiah had more important things to do than watch.

The hard work in the stockyard cleared his thoughts. So what if she still yearned after Caleb? The man was married, and she could see that. Besides, Josiah had to keep his mind on this job at hand. Not until it was over could he think about anything else. But what then? Maybe it was time to change his profession. Maybe he should put his dangerous past behind him. Margaret would be worth the sacrifice.

By the time he went back to the house, enticing aromas were emanating from the kitchen, and his mouth watered. Until he smelled breakfast, he hadn't realized how hungry he was. He glanced into the parlor and found the new baby safely ensconced in a cradle, while Luther, Jed, and Eileen gazed at her raptly. Caleb was nowhere to be seen, and Josiah assumed he was with Lucy.

Josiah followed his nose to the kitchen and found Margaret bustling about in an oversized apron.

She jumped at his appearance. "Goodness, you startled me." Her face was pale and strained with exhaustion, and she waved a wooden spoon in one hand as though she might conk him with it for daring to frighten her.

Josiah grinned. "Is that your weapon of choice?"

She flushed and put her arm down. "Are you hungry?"

"Famished."

"Dig in. The kids and Caleb have already eaten."

Josiah sat at the table and watched her as she dished him up some potatoes, eggs, and bacon. When she set the plate in front of him, he caught her by the wrist and pulled her down onto his lap.

The look of astonishment on her face made him burst into laughter. Josiah wrapped his arms around her and kissed her. She smelled of sunshine, bacon, and baby. Who would have thought that combination could be so appealing?

Her arms crept around his neck. Then she suddenly pushed at his chest and clambered to her feet. "Would you stop doing that?" she whispered.

"Why? You know I care about you, Margaret. I think we would make a great team, just like Caleb and Lucy." He hadn't intended on declaring his intentions quite this soon. The distraction from the job before him would be too great, but he seemed unable to help himself when Margaret was near him. He had more and more a sense that she was the one God had planned for him.

"Don't say that!" She whirled and stalked to the dry sink. Pouring water from the pitcher into the dishpan, she began to scrub the pots.

He stood and stepped up behind her. "Why not? It's the truth. You'll make a wonderful mother to our children. You're strong, beautiful, and brave. What more could a man ask for?"

She spun around and shoved at his chest. "Stop mocking

me! Did someone put you up to this? Is Pa paying you or something?" Her eyes sparkled with tears.

Josiah's jaw dropped open. "Paying me? Is that what you think of me? What kind of man do you think I am, Margaret?"

"I think you're a bank robber!" she blurted. Her eyes grew round, and she put a hand to her mouth.

"I see," he said slowly. His thoughts raced. A bank robber. She was closer to the truth than she should be. He'd better back away until this job was over. The thought of putting her in danger was more than he could bear. He dropped a mask over his face and stepped back. "In that case, I reckon there's no more to say. Are you going to turn me into the sheriff?"

Margaret's face grew pinched. "Are you admitting it?"

"I'm admitting nothing. But I warn you to stay out of my affairs." He'd better be tough with her for her own good. Ben and Golda would chew her up and spit her out like a discarded pea pod if they got near her. Josiah couldn't risk that. Better to frighten her into keeping her mouth shut.

"And if I don't?"

"My partners might not take too kindly to interference. You wouldn't want anything to happen to your pa."

She put a hand to her throat. "You're despicable," she whispered.

"So I've been told," he said. Weariness descended, and he turned toward the door. "I'll borrow a horse from the barn and head on back to the Triple T. Give Lucy and Caleb my congratulations." He didn't wait for an answer. There was nothing more to say.

❧

Margaret was trembling when the door shut behind Josiah. He'd practically admitted he was a bank robber and was here for some nefarious purpose. But what could it be? Why would he pick the Triple T to hole up? Henrietta's bank had already been robbed. What was keeping him from moving on?

She had to do something. She couldn't go to the sheriff. Josiah had threatened her pa, and Margaret couldn't run the risk of causing harm to her father. Besides, she didn't know if she could bring herself to turn Josiah in. In spite of what she knew to be true about him, she had to be honest—her heart was more entangled than it should be. She squared her shoulders. She couldn't let that stop her from doing her duty. Josiah's words might be sweet, but he was not the man he seemed, and she would do well to remember that. If she could discover what the plan was and then foil it, maybe she could rid her heart of this pre-occupation with Josiah.

Once things were in hand at the Stanton household, she hitched up the buggy and drove home. Weariness settled on her like a heavy blanket. Maybe it would be better if Josiah had slipped away while she was gone. She wasn't strong enough or smart enough to discover his plan and stop it. But her innate sense of right and wrong reared its head, and she knew she had to do what she could. She wished she could confide in someone.

All she wanted to do was to crawl in bed when she got home. Helping Lucy all night had been tiring, but her problem with Josiah was even more exhausting. She climbed out of the buggy and walked into the house with dragging steps.

Her pa was sitting in the parlor with his Sunday suit on. "Everyone all right at the Stantons'? The ranch hands told me about Lucy. I wasn't sure if you'd be home in time for church," he said.

Church. She looked down at herself. There was no way she could go looking like this. But in spite of her exhaustion, she needed to go. Maybe sitting in the quiet atmosphere of worship would help her know what to do about Josiah. "Let me get cleaned up first," she said.

"Take your time. It's not time to leave yet, and I'm still waiting on Josiah. He's going with us this morning."

What a hypocrite! Robbing banks, then deluding innocent townspeople into thinking he was a fine, upstanding citizen they could trust. The thought made her want to gag. She squared her shoulders. If there was a way to stop him, she had to find it. The entire town was depending on her, if they only knew it.

She rushed to her room, and Maria helped her quickly bathe, change her gown, and braid her hair. By the time she got back to the parlor, her initial fatigue had dropped away, and she was filled with determination to be a thorn in Josiah's side and stop him from harming her valley and those she loved. He would rue the day he'd ever tried to deceive an O'Brien.

She stopped in the doorway when she heard his deep voice speaking to her father. Holding her head high, she waltzed into the room. "I'm ready." She speared him with her glance, just so he realized her utter contempt for him.

Unfortunately, his spirits seemed unbothered by her censure.

Her father went toward the door. "I'll get the buggy."

Josiah rose lazily to his feet, and his gaze swept her figure. "I like your hair down better," he said softly.

Heat rushed to her cheeks, and she scowled at him. "Then I shall be sure to keep it in its braid," she retorted.

His soft laughter followed her out the door as she stalked outside after her pa. The man was truly insufferable. He admitted he was a criminal, yet he had the gall to still flirt with her. She wanted to strangle him. The sooner he was gone from this ranch and her life, the better.

Squashed between Josiah and her pa, Margaret thought the trip to town would never end. Josiah's nearness was a torture, one she was determined to be rid of as soon as possible. She ignored the bereft feeling she experienced at the thought of never seeing him again.

Church was buzzing with the news of the Stantons' new arrival. Margaret recounted the events of the previous night while her father and Josiah found a pew. When she made her way to their side, she found her father on the inside, while Josiah had saved a spot for her on the aisle. She slid into the seat beside him and tried to ignore his presence. Easier said than done. He cleared his throat and opened his Bible to the passage Reverend Mitchell announced.

Margaret silently railed at him for being such a hypocrite. She turned her own Bible to John 13. The pastor began to preach about how Jesus loved Peter even though He knew ahead of time that Peter would deny Him three times.

"God loves us in the same way," Reverend Mitchell said. "Not because of what we do, but because of who He is. We can't earn God's favor by working for it. We don't earn it by our beauty or our possessions, for God is the One who gives those things anyway. His love is not dependent on anything. He loved us when we were unlovable, just as He did Peter."

Reverend Mitchell's words arrested Margaret's attention. Out of fear, she worked hard to earn the love of others and dutifully did what she thought God wanted. She was always afraid of not living up to the standards she never really understood. Could God really love her if she did nothing— just because He chose to love her—because she was His child? It didn't seem possible. The longer Reverend Mitchell preached, the more agitated she became.

Had she ever given God everything she had, everything she was, everything she did? She didn't think so. And she didn't know if she even could. The one thing from which she gained a bit of pride and satisfaction was her standing in the community. If she wasn't an O'Brien, she wouldn't be worth anything. At least that's how she looked at it. That was probably wrong, wasn't it? But how did she go about laying aside the baggage she carried and clinging only to God? And did she even want to?

Lacing her fingers together, she tried to control her agitation. Finally, with a murmured apology, she stood and hurried from the church. She rushed down the steps and found her way to a picnic area behind the church. Taking a deep breath, she considered all the pastor had said. Unconditional love. It seemed a chimera to her, something that was so elusive it was unattainable. Yet how she longed for it! She was tired of struggling to earn it. Tired of wanting to be something she could never achieve, not for God or for anyone else.

A shadow fell across her arm, and she whirled. His hands thrust in his pockets, Josiah stood staring down at her. "Are you all right?" he asked.

"I suppose you were worried that I'd gone to find the sheriff," she scoffed. Why couldn't he leave her alone?

"Not at all. He's still in the church." Josiah took a step toward her. "Anything I can help you with?"

As if she would tell him anything. "No."

"Was it the pastor's sermon?"

Though a hypocrite like Josiah should be the last person with whom she discussed truth, she was too unsettled by what the pastor said to hide her feelings, and she blurted out the truth. "Unconditional love seems impossible."

"Impossible?" He smiled. "With God, there is nothing that's impossible."

"You're a fine one to talk about God," she said. What did he know anyway? She must be crazy to even discuss spiritual topics with him, a self-confessed thief.

"Even criminals can know God's love," he said gently. "If I didn't believe in God's forgiveness and great love for me, my life would have no meaning or purpose. It's what drives me forward and gives me hope."

Maybe he wanted to turn from his life of crime. Margaret's heart began to beat quickly, and she leaned forward. "You believe in unconditional love?"

He leaned forward and touched her cheek. "Why do you think you're so unlovable, Margaret?" he asked softly.

Tears flooded her eyes. They were supposed to be talking

about him, not her. "Look at me," she whispered. "I'm too tall and gangly; my hair is too red. There are lots of reasons men don't find me attractive."

"I see the most beautiful woman I've ever met," he said. "And God sees beyond the blazing glory of your red hair and the strong children you would raise up. He sees the fierce caring of your heart and the loyalty you give to those you love. He sees the tender heart inside that's crying out for love and approval. He gives it to you freely, Margaret. As I—" He broke off abruptly.

Was that really how God saw her? She wished she could believe that. It would be so wonderful to rest in that love, to feel safe there. And what else had Josiah been about to say? She swallowed hard. "I wish I could believe you."

"Don't believe me. Believe God. He tells you in the Bible how much He loves you. You don't have to take someone else's word for it."

Josiah was an enigma. How could a bank robber be standing here talking to her about God's love? It didn't make any sense.

"Who are you, really?" she whispered.

His hand dropped from her cheek, and he stepped back. "Just a man trying to do his best in this world," he said. "One who has things in the past he would change if he could."

"Is that why you're here? To change those things?" She held her breath waiting for his answer, her heart pounding in her chest as though it might burst.

"Stay out of this, Margaret. I can't tell you anymore. Let's just say I've got more in my past to haunt me than you can imagine. But God loves me in spite of it all, just as He loves you. When are you going to let Him take that chip from your shoulder? When will you let go of that guard you put around your heart to keep out everyone, including God?"

"I don't keep people out."

He laughed. "How many close friends do you have, Margaret? Lucy is it, isn't she? And it's because she forced her love and friendship past that wall."

Maybe he had a point, but she wasn't about to admit it to him. What did he know of the pain of constant rejection, the agony of never fitting in with other people? It was all very well to sit in judgment of her, but he'd never walked in her size eleven shoes when all the other women wore size five. He'd never had to listen to the titters of other girls as they giggled behind a door when Margaret sat alone along the wall at every dance she'd ever gone to because no man liked a woman to tower over him.

She was an eel in a pond full of goldfish. And it was God's fault. That was the crux of the matter, she suddenly realized. Why had He made her unlovable to the world? She wouldn't do that to a child of hers, so why had He done it to her?

Josiah studied her face. "Have you ever thanked God for giving you the advantages He has?"

"Advantages?"

"All those things I've already mentioned. You're tall and strong, loyal and brave, kind and loving. You stand out in a crowd and you're a leader. He wouldn't trust those qualities with just anyone. He must love you a great deal."

She blinked at the thought. Could the things she thought

were curses actually have contributed to her character? She would have to ponder those thoughts. She shook her head again at the way Josiah seemed to understand spiritual things. She didn't understand him, and she was beginning to think she never would.

He looked back toward the church. "Looks like the service is over. I reckon your pa will be looking for us." He offered her the support of his arm.

"How did you learn all this?" she blurted. "You're a criminal."

He smiled, and the sadness in his smile broke her heart. "Someday maybe I'll tell you," he said softly.

five

The next few days sped by as the ranch geared up for the spring roundup. Josiah saw to having the men distribute hay bales to the fields for the cattle, he checked the repair of the buildings, and he got things ready for the roundup. Branding would take about a week, and he wanted to get it done before any bad storms hit. So far, they'd been lucky, but the rolling thunderstorms were a way of life in Texas. The days had been uncharacteristically warm, and he paused astride his horse to wipe his bandana across his sweaty face.

Margaret had worked hard these past few days as well, but he'd managed to keep his distance, even though he wanted to be around her, to listen to her throaty laughter, to see the sun glisten on her red hair. She despised him, though. He needed to find out how much she knew about his operation, but he was almost afraid to probe too deeply for fear he would discover she knew more than was good for her. And that was stupid of him. Forewarned was forearmed.

It bothered him he might have to consider her an enemy when all he wanted to do was get closer to her. But his life wasn't quite ready for that. He had to get this job done first. He sighed. It wouldn't be over too soon for him. Willy was about ready to see him, and he had to be ready when the word came to move.

The air pressed down on him in a nearly unbearable cloak of heat and humidity. High clouds had begun to build in the southwest, and Josiah frowned. They could be in for a bad storm. The air had that quality to it. It would bear watching.

The stock milled restlessly, too, another sure sign of inclement weather. He dug his heels into his gelding's flanks and turned toward the job at hand. Cutting calves from their mothers, he herded them toward the corral where the other animals waited. Tomorrow they would start the branding, a job he didn't look forward to.

Margaret was sitting on the fence around the corral when he got his small band of calves safely into the yard. Dust streaked her face, and the humidity had caused her red hair to spring to life with curls that had escaped the braid. She looked like she had a curly halo around her face, and he grinned at the sight.

She scowled at him. "What are you laughing at?"

"I like your halo. It suits you."

Her frown deepened. "What halo?" She cautiously reached up and touched the top of her head. Grimacing at the way her curls stood out from her head, she sighed and put her hand down. "I give up."

"You done for the day?"

She nodded. "I was about to go in and get cleaned up for supper." Her face froze, and her mouth dropped open as she stared at something behind him.

Twisting in the saddle, he turned to see a heavy black thunderstorm bearing down on them. Then the thunder rolled toward them. The herd milled restlessly as lightning began to flash.

"We've got to stop a stampede!" Margaret shouted.

Josiah nodded. "You go east; I'll go west," he yelled. "Round up any hands you see to help."

"They'll know and be on their way." She jumped on her horse and galloped toward the cows.

Josiah watched her for a moment as she moved among the cattle, distracting them from the storm and herding them out from under the trees. She was a remarkable woman. There had not been a trace of fear on her face when the lightning started.

He shook himself from his reverie and began to move the cattle. A particularly vicious bolt of lightning struck a tree near the largest group of stock. Their eyes rolled in terror, and they began to grow more restless. Josiah could feel the imminent stampede beginning to build as they turned and started toward the west pasture.

Margaret! He turned in his saddle to look for her. She was right in the middle of the path and would be trampled. A cow near him bawled in terror as the thunder and lightning intensified, and then Josiah's worst fears materialized. Three cows near him started on a run. Soon others joined them, and the stampede began to spread.

He shouted for Margaret to get to safety, but it was impossible to make himself heard over the sound of the storm. Turning his horse's head, he raced toward Margaret. Just before he reached her, she realized her danger. Her face whitened as she saw the wave of cattle coming her way. She shouted something, and he thought it was his name.

Just as he reached her side, her gaze locked onto his. She held up her arms, and he jerked her onto the saddle behind him.

She pointed toward a hillside. "Hurry!"

The cattle would not be able to run over the boulders and would turn and run around them. But he was not at all sure they would reach the safety of the mass of stones. As the stampede grew nearer, the thunder of the cattle's hooves was louder than the thunder overhead.

Urging his horse forward, they made the final few yards; then he and Margaret tumbled from the horse. The horse pulled the reins from Josiah's grasp and galloped off, his eyes rolling wildly with terror.

Josiah grabbed Margaret's hand, and they ran for safety. The thunder of hooves drowned out all other sounds. Diving into the ravine behind the rocks, Josiah and Margaret tumbled headlong among the stones and cactus. He tried to protect her from the worst of the fall, but he heard her cry out once or twice. The dust of the melee washed over them as they huddled behind the boulders.

Just as he'd hoped, the cattle skirted the outcropping and ran past them. Then the dreadful roaring of cattle's hooves subsided as a cold rain began to pummel them. Josiah raised his head and stared down at Margaret. Her eyes were closed, and blood oozed from a cut on her forehead. He sat up and pressed his fingers to her throat. Her heart beat strongly beneath his fingertips, and he breathed a prayer of thanks. He didn't know what he would do if he lost her.

He ran gentle hands over her arms and legs. Nothing seemed to be broken. She began to stir as the cold rain hit her face.

Opening her eyes, she blinked. "Are we dead?" she whispered.

"I don't think so," he said softly. "I hurt too much to be dead."

Her eyes widened, and she sat up. "You're injured?" Her gaze wandered over him.

Her anxious voice did wonders for his ego. She cared more than she allowed herself to admit. "Just cuts and bruises," he said. "Do you hurt anywhere?"

"My face." She touched the cut on her face, then pulled her hand back and stared at the blood on her fingers. "Is it bad?"

"Just a small cut. We were lucky."

"I hate stampedes." Her green eyes were the only color in her face.

"I kind of like them." He got up and dusted off his pants. "You have to admit it's exhilarating to face one of them and live."

"Some people aren't as lucky as we were," she said. She sat up, then took his hand and allowed him to haul her to her feet. "My mother wasn't."

"Your mother died in a stampede?"

She nodded, and tears stood in her eyes. "When I was three. She was out helping with roundup just like today. Pa tried to reach her to get her out of the way, but he was too late. I don't think he's ever gotten over it."

Josiah's heart ached for the hurt little girl he saw in her eyes. "I'm sorry. No wonder you were scared."

She tossed her head, but the terror still lingered on her face. "Don't feel sorry for me. These kinds of things are supposed to make me stronger, right?" She brushed herself off. "We'd better get to the ranch house and see if everyone is all right."

He found his horse, now grazing calmly, and he helped her mount, then swung up behind her. Her head reached his chin, and he could smell the scent of whatever she used to wash her hair. She held herself rigid, and he could feel the way she leaned away from him. "Relax," he murmured. "I won't bite."

But she continued to lean forward with her eyes straight ahead. And he wondered again how he could ever get past that wall she'd built around her heart.

※

Margaret was still trembling when she slid off Josiah's horse in front of her home. Men and animals thronged the track in front of the house, and she looked frantically around for her pa. Only when she saw his tall, spare form did the tension ease from her shoulders. She ran to him and threw her arms around him. "Oh, Pa."

He patted her shoulders awkwardly, then pushed her away. "My goodness, Daughter, you're a grown woman. I expected more backbone than this. It was only a little stampede. We've seen worse."

Backbone. Margaret stiffened her spine and managed to bring her trembling under control. "I'm sorry, Pa," she said. "You know how I hate storms and stampedes."

"And it's about time you got over that fear," he admonished.

"It's not entirely groundless," she reminded him.

His lips tightened at her words. "But I'll not have you hiding just because your mother was in the wrong place at the wrong time," he said. "An O'Brien doesn't run from anything."

"Yes, Pa," she said. Her throat closed with unshed tears. Not one word of joy that she was all right, not one ounce of approval from her pa. She should be used to it by now, but she still craved a smile of commendation.

She sensed Josiah's gaze on her. There was probably pity in his eyes, but she didn't want to see it. Right now, her inadequacy was all she could bear. "I'll check on supper," she told her father. Rushing away, she told herself that she would *not* cry.

All through supper she felt jittery. She jumped at the least noise, and her pa had to ask her twice if she was going to check the horses before bed. The animals were as unsettled as she was.

She grabbed her cloak and went out to the barn. The soft scent of the hay wafted to her nose, and the sound of the horses' nickers soothed her frazzled nerves. She patted her mare's nose, then turned to go back to the house. Josiah was standing in the doorway, his head nearly grazing the top of the barn door opening.

"Are you all right?" he asked. "You're like a calf in a new pasture, never settling to one spot."

"I'm fine." In no mood for bantering, she started past him.

He caught her arm. "I believe you should respect your pa, Margaret, but don't take his words too much to heart. There's a lot of hurt tied up in him. And guilt."

"Guilt?"

"He wishes he had been here to save your mother."

"How do you know that? He's never said a word about it."

He stared at her for a long moment. "That's how I would feel if something ever happened to you," he said.

A lump formed in her throat, and she struggled not to cry. All she'd done was cry since this man came into her life. She was sick of it. He was a criminal, and she had to get rid of him somehow. A void as deep as the canyon behind the ravine formed at the thought of never seeing him again. But what other choice was there? She could never chuck all she believed to go off with a man like him.

"You could turn yourself in," she said impulsively. "Tell the sheriff all you know. Help him find and capture the rest of the robbers. You'd probably get off if you did that."

"I can't," he said.

She clutched his arm. "Sure you can. Put this life of crime behind you. You said yourself God loved you and would forgive all your sins. And the sheriff is a good man. You could trust him."

He gave a faint smile. "You don't trust me a bit, do you, Margaret? What kinds of crimes do you think I'm guilty of?"

She dropped her hand from his arm. "Bank robbery for sure. Murder?"

"I've had to kill, but I don't think I'd call it murder. It depends on how you look at it," he said.

She felt sick. Murder was murder, no matter how you looked at it. Turning from his sober face, she ran past him to her room. No sheriff in the world would forgive that. If he were caught, he would hang. She rubbed her fists against her eyes. If only there were some way out of this mess for all of them.

An idea bloomed in her head. He didn't want to betray his comrades, but what if she found them and turned them in to the sheriff? Then they wouldn't betray him to the sheriff to get back at him for turning on them. She sat on the edge of the bed and thought about it. Though she had no notion of where the gang could be holed up, she could follow Josiah for a few days and see what she could find out.

He wanted to change; she could see that. His face reflected regret and a longing to put his past behind him. It was up to her to help him. She refused to examine her motives too closely. The answers she might find there might be more than she could handle right now.

&

The next morning she was still full of resolve to save Josiah from himself. She didn't know why she hadn't thought of it sooner. He just needed a little help to extricate himself from his life of crime. She did her chores and lurked around to see what Josiah was up to, but he spent the entire day branding calves and working in the barn just like most every other day. The entire week went by without any deviation from his normal schedule.

On Thursday, word came of another bank robbery, this one in Clarendon. Was Josiah involved? Margaret hoped it wasn't so, but she hadn't been able to tail him every minute. He'd looked tired yesterday, so maybe he *had* been up all night running with his gang. She wished she could be sure. She resolved to watch him more closely.

By Saturday, Margaret was about ready to give up. When did he sneak away to do what he came here to do? After supper she played checkers with him in the parlor for awhile, then went to her bedroom. Maybe she needed to shadow him at night. She'd tried a couple of nights ago, but she had fallen asleep before she saw anything suspicious. Her bedroom window looked out on the bunkhouse, but so far that had been no advantage. There was so much work to be done on the ranch that she was exhausted by bedtime.

If Josiah were involved in the robberies, how did he find the energy? She had to admit he was no slacker during the workday. Tonight she was determined to find out. She put on some britches and sat in the chair by the window with the lamp unlit. The night dragged by and her lids grew heavy. She finally slept, then awoke with a start. The moon shone in through the curtains, and she peered outside to see what had disturbed her. Only the sound of crickets reached her ears. Maybe she should just go to bed. No one was stirring tonight.

Then a shadow flitted by her window, and she drew back, her throat tight. Josiah's unmistakably tall figure joined another man at a dark corner of the barn. Their whispers didn't reach her open window, though. She had to hear what they were saying.

She tiptoed down the hall and let herself noiselessly out the kitchen door. Sneaking around the edge of the house, she sidled up to the bunkhouse until she was close enough to overhear. She prayed that he wasn't up to anything criminal. Against all odds, the more she got to know him, the less convinced she was that he was a thief.

"We're ready to move in tomorrow," the man's voice said. It was the same man she'd heard through her window once before. "You ready to act?"

"I reckon."

"You don't sound convinced. We've come too far to back out now. You getting cold feet?"

"I just don't want anyone hurt, least of all Willy." Josiah's voice was low.

"If everyone does what they're told, no one will get hurt. I know you want your baby brother out of the way, but this job is more important than what you want."

"And if they don't do what they're told?"

"Then they suffer the consequences. Don't tell me you're

getting soft after all these years. I want to make them pay, and you'd better not get in the way. I've gone out on a limb for you all I'm going to."

"I know, Richard, and I appreciate it. Not many friends would do what you've done for me. I won't let you down."

"You'd better not," the man Josiah called Richard growled. He clapped Josiah on the back.

"What time do I meet you tomorrow?"

"Midnight. I'll be at the cottonwood tree at the road that leads to the river."

"I'll be there," Josiah said.

So will I, Margaret vowed. She would save Josiah from himself, and save his little brother Willy, too, if she could. She tiptoed back to the house and went to her room. She had to carefully plan what she should do. The sheriff could help her, but the thought of betraying Josiah made her wince. Maybe she was wrong about what was going on, but what did that man Richard mean about making them pay? That didn't really sound like robbery. It sounded worse.

She prayed Josiah wasn't planning on murdering someone. This was such a hopeless muddle. He didn't seem like the kind of man who could do the things he seemed to be doing. If only she could be sure. Tomorrow would reveal it all if she had the courage to act. She resolved to find that courage somewhere. Tomorrow she would do what had to be done even if it hurt her.

six

The minutes ticked by. Moonlight glimmered through the trees, and in the distance a coyote yipped. Margaret wrapped her coat tighter around her body and pressed farther into the shadows of her hiding place. Where was he? Her ears strained to hear soft footfalls, but so far the only disturbance in the area had been the frogs.

Her breath fogged the air. This morning the temperature had finally taken a plunge and ushered in an almost winter coolness. Margaret longed for the warm temperatures of a few days ago. But at least the cold had quieted the sound of the crickets. She would be able to hear better.

A noise came through the trees. Someone cleared his throat; then she heard a rustle in the leaves. She cautiously peered around the trunk and saw the familiar set of Josiah's shoulders as he rode his horse into the clearing. Sucking in her breath, she barely moved. Moments later, another rider joined Josiah. They talked for a moment, but she was too far away to hear the conversation; then they both turned their horses' heads and left the clearing.

She was going to lose them. Margaret bounded to her feet and made her way to where she'd tethered her horse. She mounted and began to follow Josiah and the other man. Careful to stay well back, she nearly lost them at the turnoff to Miller's Canyon. At the last minute, she realized they'd taken the turn. So that's where the crooks were holed up.

She shivered, more from excitement than from the cold. It felt good to be doing something instead of just waiting fearfully to see what Josiah was planning. Tightening her jaw, she squinted through the gloom.

A figure leapt from behind a rock, and her horse reared. Caught off balance, Margaret struggled to stay seated in the saddle; then a hand caught the reins and jerked her horse's head down. The man's eyes glittered in the moonlight behind the mask he wore. Terror held her motionless, and then her shocked inertia faded, and she placed the pointed toe of her boot squarely in his chin. Leaning down, she jerked the reins out of his hand.

With a muttered oath, he fell onto his backside. Margaret didn't wait to see if he was hurt. She dug her heels into the horse's flank and raced away over tumbled rocks, sage, and cactus. The wind caught and tugged at her hair, and her breath came fast in her chest. She knew he would be right behind her—with his cohorts. Bending low over her horse's neck, she urged him to go faster.

She galloped over a hill and into a small valley. Margaret could see a series of campfires dotting the area. She pulled on the reins and slowed her horse to a walk. She listened but could hear no sounds of pursuit. Maybe she'd lost him. A nearby stand of trees looked safe. She dismounted and led her horse into the dark recesses of the grove and tethered him to a limb. Taking her rifle, she stepped into the clearing again and crept toward the flickering firelight.

Raucous laughter spilled from the men clustered around

the fire. She searched their faces but saw no sign of Josiah. Maybe these weren't the bank robbers at all. Her gaze traveled from face to face. Who else would be hidden in this valley? They were much too rough looking to be mere cowboys. They all wore six-shooters slung low on their hips, and the reek from their whiskey bottles made her wrinkle her nose. Cowboys would already be asleep after an arduous day of work. These men showed no signs of any inclination for sleep as they played poker and drank straight from their bottles.

"Well, well, what do we have here?"

Margaret spun around at the harsh growl behind her. A burly man of about forty had a gun pointed at her. His expression was cold as his gaze swept over her; then his eyes widened as he realized she was a woman. A leer tugged at his mouth.

"A woman! Hey, fellers, see what I just caught." He grabbed her roughly by the arm and dragged her toward the clustered men.

The other men turned at the man's shout and several got to their feet. When the man had dragged Margaret close enough to the fire for them to notice her femininity, several more stood as well.

"A woman clear out here?" A young man of about twenty-five stepped closer and peered into her face. "Hey, she's the O'Brien gal."

For some reason the young man looked familiar to Margaret, yet she knew she had never met him. He didn't look as rough as his companions, so she used eye contact to plead with him. *Help me,* she beseeched silently.

A shutter came down over his curious gaze, and he stepped back. No help there, she realized. She glanced around at the other men. They all wore expressions of eager anticipation, and she realized her arrival had provided them a break from boredom and routine. What would they do with her? Dread congealed in her stomach, and she struggled to break free from the iron grip on her arm.

But no matter how she struggled, the man's grip remained tight and painful. He dragged her closer to the nearest campfire, then shoved her to the ground. With hard hands, he bound her wrists together in front of her.

"Now you just explain what you're doing skulking around our camp in the middle of the night," he demanded. He crossed sinewy arms across his chest and glared down at her.

Margaret tried to swallow, but her throat was too dry. Who were these men? And where was Josiah? "Could I have some water?"

The man jerked his head at the young man who looked so familiar, and he handed her a tin cup filled with water. She took it in both bound hands and drank greedily. Handing it back to him, she tried to catch his gaze again, but he looked at the ground.

"Now answer my question," the first man said.

"I was looking for a friend," she said.

"A friend. At nearly one o'clock in the morning. Does your pa know you're out here?"

If she admitted no one knew where she was, she was at their mercy. If she said her pa knew she was here, he would know she was lying. "No," she said slowly.

"At least you're telling the truth. For now. Who is this

'friend' you're looking for? And why here? You're a far piece from home."

Before she had to fabricate an answer, she heard a shout to her left.

"Hey, Munster, we got company."

The man interrogating her swung around at the interruption. "Willy, go see what's going on."

Willy. That was the name Margaret had heard Josiah mention, his baby brother. The young man who had seemed so familiar nodded and jogged toward the disturbance. He must be Willy. No wonder he looked familiar. Now that she knew he was Josiah's brother, she could see the similarity in facial structure and eyes. She'd obviously stumbled onto the right group, but any hope she had of rescuing Josiah was gone. Why had she even thought she could go up against a bunch of bank robbers? And who would rescue *her?*

A few minutes later she sucked in her breath as Willy led a group of men back to the campfire. As a tall figure came into view of the flickering light from the fire, she recognized Josiah. He strode toward the group with his head held high. His confident stride faltered when he got near enough to see Margaret. A widening of his eyes was the only indication he gave that he knew her.

Margaret bit back a sob of relief. Just to know someone knew she was here was a great comfort. But the smoldering anger in Josiah's eyes told her he was not pleased at her meddling.

"What's she doing here?"

"We thought maybe you could provide the answer to that," Munster said smoothly. "She tells us she's been looking for a friend. Maybe you're that friend and have led her right to our camp."

Josiah laughed. "We're acquainted. What are you going to do with her?"

"I haven't decided. We could hold her for ransom. Her old man is one of the wealthiest cattle barons in the Red River Valley."

Josiah still didn't look at her. "Let me talk to her before you decide anything."

Ransom. Margaret couldn't hold back the gasp of dismay. Pa would tan her hide if he had to pay to get her out of this mess. Josiah's betrayal rippled through her almost like a physical pain. Some judge of character she was. She'd almost let herself believe Josiah cared about her in a special way. He was just using her. She glared at Josiah, but he didn't look at her, and the effort was wasted.

Munster sniffed. "I suppose," he said grudgingly. "You always were the smarts of the outfit, Cutler. You've been gone so long, I was beginning to think you'd turned legal." Munster picked his teeth with a piece of straw.

Josiah laughed. "You must have been eating locoweed. I want my share of that haul you just took."

"Hey, you had no part in that operation. That money's ours!"

"And how are you going to get out of here? You're boxed up tighter than a calf on branding day. You need me to figure out how to get you out of here alive."

Munster chewed on the straw. "You got a point. Okay, we'll cut you a share if you can get us out. You got a plan?"

Josiah smiled. "Don't I always?"

Margaret's heart grew sicker as the conversation continued. It had been mere wishful thinking on her part that Josiah wanted out of his criminal past. He was deeply enmeshed in this way of life. His tender words had been just trickery, but she wished she knew what his motive had been for breaking her heart. She hadn't asked to be pursued, yet he'd done just that. She should have known better than to let down her guard. When would she learn that men didn't find her attractive? She bit her lip in the struggle not to scream at him.

Josiah jerked his head toward her. "Got anyplace where I can talk with her?"

Munster grinned. "There's an old shack through those trees there if you want some privacy. Here, take a lantern." He handed Josiah a battered kerosene lamp.

Josiah took it, then set it on the ground while he removed Margaret's bonds. He picked up the lantern again and took Margaret's arm.

She felt sick at the wink Munster gave Josiah. Why had she ever come up with this harebrained scheme? She must have been crazy. She followed Josiah toward the grove of trees to a ramshackle cabin with part of the roof missing. Josiah thrust her inside and stepped in behind her. Even in the dim glow of the lamplight, she could see the stiff set of his shoulders and the icy glare in his eyes.

He shut the door and seized her by the arms. "Margaret, what do you think you're doing here? You've made my job even harder."

Margaret glared at him. "I was trying to save you," she spat. "You seemed to want to put your past behind you. I can see I was mistaken."

"Do you ever think before you act?" He sighed.

Margaret watched him until his gaze met hers again. "Let me go," she said. "You can say I escaped. They won't do anything to you—you're their *leader*," she ended sarcastically.

Josiah's lips thinned. "Is that what you think? You still have no discernment, Margaret. I care for you, but you refuse to see it. I don't know why I bother." He took off his hat and ran a hand through his thick curls. "I don't know how I'm going to get us out of this mess."

She pushed away the initial joy his words of love had brought. It was just more of his deceit. "I thought you had that all planned," she taunted. "Ransom and all that."

He snorted. "You really think Munster will follow through with that plan? More likely he'll take the money your pa pays and still plan to kill you. Munster isn't known for mercy." He chewed on his lip. "You're going to have to marry me, Margaret."

"What?" Surely she hadn't heard him correctly.

"It's the only way I can keep you safe. If the men think you belong to me, they will leave you alone."

"But you're a thief! I can't marry you."

"Better the thief you do know than the one you don't," he said. "At least I won't hurt you."

Margaret couldn't breathe. She had to get out of here. She bolted for the door, but Josiah caught her by the arm.

"I'm sorry the idea is so distasteful," he said grimly.

But what had appalled her the most was that the idea was far from distasteful. The thought of being married to Josiah nearly made her knees buckle from the sweetness of that hope. There seemed no way to reconcile this tender man who looked at her with pleading eyes with the rough man outside who spoke so casually of robbing banks, death, and ransom. Which one was the real Josiah Cutler? And what did he really want of her?

"I won't lie to them," he said. "Will you agree to marry me, Margaret? I'll tell them you've said yes and that they must leave you alone."

"What about my father, my life on Triple T? Do you expect me to follow you around the countryside while you rob every bank in Texas?" She shuddered.

Josiah grew still. "Can't you trust me just a little bit, Margaret? Things aren't always what they seem. That's all I can tell you."

"Things aren't always what they seem." She studied his face, unsure what he meant. His firm jaw and dark eyes gave away nothing. She longed to trust him, but she'd been hurt before. It was hard to let go and believe when the evidence before her was so condemning. Maybe he really did want to find a way to get out of this way of life. If so, she must do all she could to help him accomplish that.

What a strange thief he was. He would rob a bank, but he wouldn't lie to his fellow bandits. He could expound on Scripture with the best of preachers, but he donned a mask and went against every Scripture he could quote. He was an enigma, but she couldn't help but want to trust him in spite of herself.

He must have seen the struggle going on in her heart, for he leaned forward and brushed his fingers against her cheek. "It will be all right, Margaret. I won't let you down.

I love you, and I think you love me back, even if you won't admit it yet."

She hardened her heart against his sweet words. What did a bandit know of love? And the thought of giving him that power over her made her tremble. Once, trust hadn't been such a hard thing for her, but life's knocks had made her wary. And she saw no way to resolve the conflict between the two sides of this man.

He grinned. "Cat got your tongue? Or does the thought of marriage to me fill you with such joy you can't speak?"

A smile tugged at the corner of her mouth, but she quickly squelched it. His charm was too easy to believe. She had to remember that. "Let's just say we're engaged."

"You want a way to back out; is that it?"

She nodded.

He sighed and ran a hand through his hair. "You're a stubborn woman, Margaret O'Brien." He attempted to embrace her, but when she resisted, he quickly released her. "Our time will come, Margaret. I'll be patient for now, but you'll see you can trust me." He turned from her and paced across the floor. "I have to be careful how I proceed," he muttered. "So much is riding on the next few days."

She didn't understand any of this. Why had she ever gotten involved with this mess? "What about your brother?"

His restless pacing stilled. "Willy? What about him?" His tone was casual, too casual.

"How does he figure in all this?"

"Willy is why I'm here," he said.

"What do you mean?"

"Nothing, forget it. It's safer that way." He picked up the

lantern and took her hand. "They'll be wondering what's taking so long. Come with me and try to act happy."

It wouldn't be a total act. Part of her thrilled at the thought that she could have a future with Josiah. That part ignored the truth all around her that spoke of Josiah's lack of concern for the law and other people. But the rational part of her head knew that only heartache lay in wait for her. It couldn't be otherwise. In spite of Josiah's calm assurance that he would work things out, Margaret saw no possible way to resolve the problem. Either the robbers would kill them both or the posse would.

Once she threw in her lot with Josiah, no one would believe she had no idea who he really was or what his plans were. She forced a smile to her lips. Her name would be worthless among the people whose opinion she valued.

She glanced up into the night sky as he led her back to the campfire. *What should I do, Lord?* God couldn't possibly be in favor of a match between her and a bank robber, in spite of Josiah's profession of Christianity. But how could Josiah seem so upright and knowledgeable about the Scriptures one minute, then talk of ransom and bank robbery the next?

Just thinking about it gave her a headache. All she wanted was to find some hole to crawl in to sleep. She'd pull a blanket over her head and forget all about this for a few blessed hours. "You'll have to take care of this, Lord. I don't know what to do," she muttered under her breath.

"Did you say something?" Josiah asked softly.

She shook her head. "I was talking to God."

"Good idea. We need all the help we can get."

The two sides of Josiah made her head spin. Nothing had gone as she expected.

"Smile, we're almost there," Josiah whispered.

Smiling was the last thing she felt like doing, but she tried.

"Can't you do better than that? You look like an orphaned calf. Try to look excited at the thought of being Mrs. Cutler."

Mrs. Cutler. The thought sent a bolt of electricity tingling along her nerves. *Margaret Cutler.* She tried it on for size and found it fit amazingly well. She could get used to that name. If she lived long enough. She lifted her head and smiled at him.

He blinked, and the light in his eyes brightened. "That's more like it." He took her arm, and they stepped into the light of the campfire. Some of the men had gone to bed, but Munster and Willy still sat on logs near the fire. The fire was still blazing high and shooting sparks into the cool air.

Munster got to his feet as they neared. "She don't look like you roughed her up too bad," he chortled. "You find out why she came out here?"

"Looking for me," Josiah said.

The smugness in his voice made Margaret want to kick him, but instead she smiled sweetly and said nothing.

Munster narrowed his eyes. "I figured that much. *Why* is the question."

"She loves me," Josiah said. "You ever heard the word before, Munster? Even a reprobate like you must realize there're some fates a man can't run from. I'm going to marry this gal."

"Marry? You?" Munster burst into guffaws. His laughter trailed away when Josiah just stood there with a pleasant smile on his face. "What about the ransom?"

"We don't need a ransom. We'll make plenty on this next haul."

"You sure you ain't blackmailing her into a wedding? Maybe that's the ransom you're wanting. That way you get control of the ranch, too. Smart move." Munster nodded approvingly.

Margaret's chest tightened. She hadn't thought of that. Maybe that's what all his talk of love was about. His love of money and her pa's ranch. It made perfect sense.

seven

The next morning Josiah directed a glance in Margaret's direction. He made sure his expression betrayed none of his worry. They were both lucky her confident air had allayed any suspicions Munster and his gang might have had. A good night's sleep had given her more backbone and gumption.

The men had clamored for breakfast, and she'd finally agreed to fix some flapjacks. He watched her as she worked over the cooking fire. Even under duress she had kept her cool. A glow warmed his belly as he watched her deftly flip the flapjacks. He'd never met a braver woman.

His grin faded. Or one more stubborn. She was convinced she knew what he was all about, and nothing swayed her opinion. Still, that stubbornness could be turned to good use. Once she loved a man, she would stand and fight at his side.

What had possessed Margaret to follow him out here? When he saw her in the hands of these outlaws, he'd wanted to throttle her. That impulse had quickly been followed by a rush of pleasure that she cared enough about him to follow him. For all her protests, Josiah knew she felt something for him. He just had to help her discover what it was. She hadn't answered him when he told her he loved her, but he'd seen the struggle in her face. Once she understood why he was with this gang, maybe she would be able to face her feelings. All he could do was hope and pray that would be the case.

Her face glowed from the heat of the fire. The night had brought colder temperatures, and even this morning frost still limned the grass. Willy had brought her a blanket to pull around her shoulders. Her long red braid hung over one shoulder, and she looked a little bedraggled and distraught.

"I want out of here." She bent over the skillet with her back toward him. "I want to get on my horse and get home. Pa will be worried. Surely they'll let me go now that they think I'm going to marry you."

Josiah pressed his fingers against the hand she had on his arm. "You don't understand all that's going on here, Margaret. Please, just stay quiet and let me do what I have to do."

Bafflement darkened her eyes, and she sighed. "I don't have much choice."

He went toward the group of men sitting around the campfire. This operation was going to be tricky. Munster was no dummy. If he smelled a rat, he'd dump both their bodies in a ravine.

Josiah hunkered down beside Willy and picked up a stick. He poked the fire, and sparks flew into the air, leaving a tang of wood smoke and burning leaves. He could almost feel Margaret's gaze burning a hole in his back, but he forced himself to focus on the job at hand.

"Let's talk about the heist at the Henrietta bank. What do you think about using explosives, Cutler?" Munster asked.

The sharp look in his eyes reminded Josiah of a ferret. Munster was wily and dangerous, like a rabid fox. The knowledge sharpened Josiah's attention. "Might be all right if you use the right kind. We wouldn't want to get blown up along with the vault door."

Munster nodded. "When you joined us a year ago, you said you were an expert with nitroglycerin. I think we might be able to get our hands on some. You game to try it?"

"I'd rather not use orphan elixir," Josiah said, referring to the mining synonym for nitroglycerin. "Dynamite would be better, provided it's not old. I can use nitro if you insist, but it takes longer to get the right amount set. Dynamite would be quicker and easier. But the noise will bring the whole town running. You sure you want that?"

Munster nodded. "Guess you know what you're talking about."

"What was this—a test?"

Munster grinned. "You got it, Boy. I wanted to know if you were the expert you claimed to be. Guess you'll do." Picking up a stick, he drew lines in the dirt. "I figure we hit the bank next week. The last time was just a trial run to test the bank security. The back door is here." He poked the stick in the dirt. "A big deposit is expected on Wednesday, and we'll hit the bank on Thursday before they can ship it out again. The security will be beefed up, but they won't be expecting us to hit it again so soon. Pretty crafty, huh?" He gave a self-satisfied smirk.

Cutler nodded. It was pretty smart. No one ever said Munster was stupid. "How you figuring on getting past the guards?"

Munster's grin widened. "That's where you and your girlfriend come in. She's known in the community and so are you. You escort her in to make a withdrawal about closing time when the place is almost empty. You pull your gun and tie up the guards and the tellers. We'll be waiting around back. When you open the back door for us, we get the manager to open the vault and make a little larger withdrawal than they were expecting." He gave a hearty laugh.

His raucous laugher grated on Josiah's ears. "Good plan," he said. "But what if the manager won't cooperate?"

"Then we blow the door with dynamite. I've got plenty of power to handle the yokels in town."

"These few men?" Josiah gave a sweeping gesture with his hand.

"Oh, no, these are just the start. Kid Loco and his gang are throwing in with us."

Josiah bit back his dismay. Kid Loco was a notorious gunfighter who shot first and asked questions later. He hated Josiah, and the coming encounter would not be pleasant.

Munster grinned again. "I know you two have a history. The Kid has already been warned to leave you be."

The Kid never listened to advice. If he'd been told to leave Josiah alone, that would be enough to make him try to pick a fight. "If you think he'll listen, I reckon you don't know him as well as you think you do," Josiah said. This could ruin the entire plan. A year of hard work was about to pay off mightily, and he would have to carefully think about how to get around the Kid.

Munster narrowed his eyes. "He'll do whatever I tell him if he wants his share."

"He may take yours along with his. He's a loose cannon."

"Yeah, well he says the same thing about you. You must have some really bad blood between you. Bet it's over a woman."

Munster's guess would be right. Josiah's jaw tightened at the thought of Kid Loco and what he was capable of. Josiah didn't want him anywhere near Margaret. But they were in the thick of this now, and Josiah didn't see any easy way out. Not without ruining his plans.

A buckboard clattered around the curve, and several of the men sprang to their feet, brandishing their guns. The driver, a young woman in her midtwenties drove recklessly, her golden hair flying behind her. Josiah recognized her when she got out of the buckboard, and his heart sank. Margaret was not going to like this one bit. He gave an uneasy glance back to where she still stirred the stew.

"It's just Golda," Munster said. "Put those peashooters away before you hurt someone."

The men put away their guns and sat back down as Golda sauntered toward them. Her golden hair rippled down her back in the sunlight, and her lithe body swayed as though to an inner tune, a tune that proclaimed her the most beautiful woman in the world. She walked and acted as though every man should turn and look. And Josiah had to admit she wouldn't be far wrong about that. For sheer beauty, few women could compete. Unfortunately, she was as corrupt as her brother, Munster.

Eyes as blue as the sky fastened on Josiah, and she gave a slow smile. "Why, it's our runaway come home," she cooed. "I've been wondering when you'd show your face again." She gave a becoming pout. "Though I should slap you for leaving without saying good-bye."

She came closer, and her overpowering perfume wafted toward Josiah. He took a step back and wondered how he was going to explain this to Margaret.

❧

Margaret watched a ravishing blond woman get out of a buckboard and walk toward the group of men around the campfire. The woman's pristine appearance made Margaret feel like a drudge. She knew her own hair hung in bedraggled wisps around her face from the heat. Dirt and soot marred her shirt. She brushed at her shirt ineffectively and tried to pat her hair into place. This woman was the type who would take one look at Margaret and turn up her nose.

The woman sauntered up to Josiah and put her hand on his arm. With her head thrown back, she smiled into Josiah's face. A shaft of sunlight illuminated her beauty even more, and Margaret's heart sank to her dusty boots. She gave a sniff. What did she care? Let the woman have him. He was a bank robber and no great catch anyway. But Margaret's heart gave a painful throb at the thought that he might prefer the woman to her. Why wouldn't he? The woman would turn heads anywhere she went.

The woman's throaty laughter floated on the spring air, and Margaret tossed down the ladle. He'd said they were engaged, and an engaged man didn't allow some other woman to touch his cheek the way that hussy was doing. Margaret straightened her shoulders and marched toward the group. It was about time she made her position known.

The woman's head swiveled at her approach. Her eyes

narrowed as she took in Margaret's appearance. "Who's this?" Her voice was coarser than her appearance.

Margaret didn't wait for anyone else to introduce her. She stepped forward and took Josiah's unencumbered arm. "I'm Josiah's fiancée, Margaret O'Brien."

The woman's eyes widened, and her hand fell away from Josiah's other arm. "Fiancée?" Her blue eyes flashed, and she glared at Josiah. "What's this nonsense?"

Munster laughed. "Miss O'Brien, this is my sister, Golda. I'd say you've put her nose out of joint. She had pegged Cutler here as her personal property."

Personal property. Margaret had a notion that Josiah would never be anyone's personal property. He was too much of a man to be owned by any woman, even a beautiful one like Golda.

Golda bared her teeth at her brother, then flew at Munster and slapped his face. His brows drew together, and he drew back his hand. He hit her across the face, and she fell to the ground. Staring up at her brother, the beautiful face twisted into an ugly mask of petulance and anger.

Before anyone could help her to her feet, she jumped up and flew at her brother again. "I hate you!" she screamed. Her nails raked his face; then she grabbed a handful of hair and gave it a vicious tug.

He held her at arm's length and laughed in her face, which seemed only to inflame her. "Not woman enough to keep him, are you?"

She spat in his face, and he shoved her away.

She attacked him again, and he grabbed her by the shoulders. "Behave yourself, Golda," Munster snarled. He shook his sister, and the fight seemed to finally leave her. Her shoulders slumped, and she pulled out of her brother's grip.

Tears shimmered in her eyes, and Margaret almost gasped at how beautiful she looked when she showed her vulnerability. Petite and dainty, she made Margaret feel like a bumbling bull in a sheep pen. She tightened her grip on Josiah's arm.

Golda turned her blue-eyed gaze on Josiah. "How could you do this to me?" she whispered.

"Oh, knock it off, Golda." Munster's tone was impatient. "Cutler never made you no promises. Just because you got shut out by another filly is no reason to carry on like a madwoman."

Golda's full lips trembled, and Margaret almost felt sorry for her. In spite of her beauty, she was a bit childlike in her willfulness. It was as though she'd had her favorite doll taken by a neighbor child. Margaret slanted a glance into Josiah's face. His gaze was on her, not on Golda, and she took heart at that.

There seemed to be a bit of worry in his glance, and she wondered if he really cared whether she was hurt over Golda's appearance. He needn't worry. Margaret knew better than to believe the lies men told her.

But she couldn't bear to look in his eyes and find him comparing her to this golden-haired beauty. Forcing her gaze upward, she stared into his eyes. There seemed to be only approval in his gaze. She tore her gaze from his and glanced back at Golda. The young woman was examining Margaret in great detail.

"Why on earth would you choose her over me, Josiah?"

Contempt curled her lip. "She isn't even feminine. Why, look at the size of her feet and hands. And redheads freckle in the sun. You need a woman to grace your home with style and elegance, not one who is more like a man than a woman. You want softness, not someone like this."

"You don't know me well enough to know what I want," Josiah said. "I don't want to hurt you, Golda, but this is really none of your business."

Golda sniffed and flounced away. Margaret was disappointed that he didn't tell Golda why he had chosen her. She would like to know the answer to that question herself. He could pick any woman he wanted. His looks would be sure to have the women flocking around him. Maybe other women were better judges of character than she was. She'd fallen for a bank robber.

Her face grew hot at the thought, and she pushed it away. She hadn't fallen for him. This was just an arrangement to keep her safe. There could be nothing between them once this ordeal was over. An engagement could be broken. He would likely break it himself.

The men settled back around the fire. "That stew about ready?" Munster asked. "We're starved."

"It's ready." Margaret turned to go back to her pot.

"I'll help you," Josiah said.

Munster guffawed. "She's got you roped and tied already, Cutler."

Josiah didn't answer; he just slipped his hand under Margaret's elbow and escorted her back across the hard ground. "I'm sorry," he said in a low voice.

"For what? For dallying with a beautiful woman?"

"I never dallied with her. She just had it set in her head that she wanted to marry me."

"I find that hard to believe. Most women would need some kind of encouragement to display the emotion that Golda did."

"She's not like most women. Golda is like a child who sees a toy and decides it belongs to her regardless of reality. I just happened to be that bauble this time. She'll get over it."

"How callous! You break that young woman's heart, then say she'll get over it." Margaret wondered why she was goading Josiah like this. She knew he was telling her the truth. Golda was exactly as he described.

"Brokenhearted?" He huffed and then shook his head. "She'll have her sights set on some other sap by tomorrow morning."

"Does that make it right that you let her fall for you?"

"She only loves herself." He gripped Margaret's arm and pulled her toward him. "Don't you know yet that you're the only woman I want? You're more woman than ten women like Golda. When are you going to let go of that chip on your shoulder? So what if you're taller than most women? You've also got more heart and guts. I don't want some lifeless doll who plays parlor games and invites people to tea. I want a real woman, and you're that woman, Margaret."

Her breath caught in her throat as his lips found hers. She clung to him for a long moment, then pulled away with a sob. "I don't know what to believe! But I have a ranch to run. You're a distraction I can't afford."

He didn't let her loose. "I'm a distraction you can't

avoid," he murmured against her hair. "Can't you just trust me a little? I'll get us out of this, and we'll put the past behind us."

"How?" she whispered. "You'll never be able to put the past behind you. The law will be looking for you until you're caught."

He gave her a little shake and released her. "I'll make things work out. You'll see. Just try to put your doubts aside until this is over."

That was asking the impossible. She could think only of her doubts. And this fiasco with Golda hadn't helped much. Margaret knew very little about Josiah. Maybe he really was a man who liked to break women's hearts, and she was just his latest project. She narrowed her eyes at him. Maybe he just wanted to get his hands on the Triple T ranch. The easiest way would be to marry the only heir. But why would he want the ranch when he planned to make his money robbing other people? Oh, it made her head hurt to try to figure it all out.

She just wanted to go back to bed and sleep a few more hours. The short night of four hours' sleep had left her with a fuzzy head. Maybe with a fresh day she could figure it out. She turned her back on him and ladled the stew onto tin plates. Josiah carried them to the men spaced around the camp. The aroma of burned coffee mingled with that of the stew, and Margaret realized she was hungry herself. She hadn't eaten all day yesterday. Her stomach had been too on edge from nerves as she waited to follow Josiah.

What must Pa think? He surely had men out looking for her by now. Two of the men were good trackers. Maybe they would be able to lead Pa to this camp. She didn't know whether to pray for deliverance or hope they couldn't find her. She had to figure out a way to help Josiah out of this mess. He truly didn't seem to want to follow a larcenous life anymore. But if she left him, she had no doubt he'd quickly fall back into his old ways. It was obvious he was a trusted member of the gang.

Margaret shook her head, unable to make sense of her conflicting thoughts. She cleaned the empty pot, using sand to scrub the baked-on parts until it was spotless. Josiah had disappeared, no doubt to finish plotting the robbery. At least she had a few hours away from his distracting presence.

She should be in church right now. Pa was doubtless looking for her instead of being in attendance himself. But she could worship God right here, she realized. She left the camp behind and went down a track to a meadow along the banks of the Red River, just beyond the sound of the men laughing and playing cards.

Sitting on a rock, she listened to the gurgling water and silently prayed for wisdom, strength, and help.

"Want some company?"

She turned at the sound of Josiah's voice. He probably had the plans all laid out. The thought made her wince, but unfortunately it was probably the truth. She'd overheard the men talking about explosives and other plots that made her shudder.

Josiah grinned at her unwavering stare. "You act like I'm a stranger."

"You are. The longer we're here, the stranger you seem." She turned her back to him and stared back out over the water.

She heard him move through the brush, and then he settled beside her on the rock. "I bet your pa is looking for you," he said.

"I'm sure he is. He can't run the ranch by himself."

"You think that's the only reason he's searching for you?" Josiah's voice was gentle.

Did she think that? She considered it, then shook her head. "I'm sure he loves me. In his own way."

"And what way would that be?"

"As a substitute for the son he wishes he'd had." Margaret picked up a rock and tossed it into the stream. Birds scattered from the trees at the sound.

Josiah slipped his arm around her, and she stiffened. "I think he's proud of you for who you are, Margaret. I know I would be if I had a daughter like you."

She turned and gazed into his warm brown eyes. Why did he make her feel so safe, so accepted? More so than in any other person's presence, except maybe for Lucy. It made no sense for her to be drawn to someone like him.

The smile he gave her warmed her heart, and she relaxed ever so slightly, allowing herself to lean against him. "Why do you talk like this to me?" she whispered. "I don't want to be hurt."

"I wouldn't hurt you, Margaret." His gaze never wavered from hers. He leaned forward and pressed his lips to hers.

Margaret closed her eyes and breathed in the male scent of him mingled with the soap from his morning shave. She reached up and touched his cheek. He pulled her closer; she tore her mouth from his but didn't jerk out of his embrace. Instead, she laid her head on his shoulder. She couldn't think when he was this close.

They both jumped when they heard Munster calling for Josiah.

"I'd better go," he said reluctantly. "While you're out here, ask God what to do. He'll show you." He pressed a kiss against the top of her head and released her.

With a sore heart, she watched him walk away. God didn't seem to be answering her question about Josiah. Could that be an answer in itself? She rubbed her head and went back to the camp.

❧

The day dragged. Margaret prepared meals and endured angry glances from Golda. The best Margaret could do was ignore the other woman and try to stay out of the way of the men.

As soon as it was dark, Margaret decided to go to bed. She shook her bedding out to make sure no critters had crawled in, then spread it out again and slipped inside. She found it hard to fall asleep in spite of her exhaustion. The men laughed and played cards far into the night, and the clink of whiskey bottles and the sound of their harsh laughter woke her every time her eyelids drooped. It seemed a long time since she'd gone to bed, when she began to be aware that the men's voices had changed. They no longer merely played cards but had begun to discuss the upcoming heist. The breeze carried their words to her ears.

The Henrietta bank—the bank her father used—was the next target. She nearly jumped from her bedroll at this new revelation. Her father had just deposited the money from the spring sale. She had to find a way to get out of here and warn him. Otherwise, her family would lose all they owned to these misfits. Her nerves seemed strung as tight as a barbwire fence.

Then an idea slowly took root. Maybe Golda would help her. She wanted Josiah, so she could have him if Margaret were gone. The thought of leaving Josiah in that woman's clutches appalled her, but her pa came first. Pa and the ranch—those two things were more important than the way she felt about Josiah. He had made his bed, and he would have to lie in it.

He was planning on taking money from her and her father. What kind of man could even contemplate that? And he was completely involved. She heard his voice in the discussion as well. Her father would be so disappointed in him. Pa really cared about Josiah. He'd said he wished he had a son like Josiah.

She gulped as she thought about her pa's reaction. Josiah was missing as well. Would Pa think they had eloped? She felt sick. He might not even be looking for her if he thought she had run off to marry Josiah. It was very likely that was exactly what he did think. It made sense with both Josiah and Margaret gone. She sucked in a deep breath. It was up to her to get herself out of this mess. Her plan to escape with Golda's help took on a new urgency.

According to the conversation Margaret had overheard, she only had a few days to get away and get help. Tomorrow she would have to get Golda alone and come up with a story the woman would believe. "Help me, Lord," Margaret whispered. She would need His strength to do what she had to do. Turning her back on her feelings for Josiah would be the hardest thing she'd ever done. She settled back on her bedroll, but sleep was a long time coming.

eight

Margaret stretched out the aching muscles in her back. If she hadn't known better, she would have sworn she was lying on lumps of coal all night. Her eyes felt leaden from lack of sleep, and it wasn't only because of the hard ground. Her heart ached at what she knew she had to do today, and moping around about it wouldn't change the facts.

After their late night, the men still snored in their blankets. The camp was silent except for their occasional snorts and the huffing of the horses in the makeshift corral. It would be a perfect time to seek out Golda. Margaret rose silently and tiptoed out of the camp in the direction of the Red River. From here she could hear the sound of the water rushing over rocks and tree roots. She wished she could bathe, but there was no privacy for that.

Crouching by the river, she splashed water on her face and arms and washed away the worst of the dust. Her hair was another matter. She had no comb or brush, nothing to bring her hair to some semblance of order. Using her fingers, she worked the knots out until her hair was as smooth as she could make it. It lay down her back in a heavy curtain, and she began to part it into sections to braid it again.

"Don't."

She whirled at Josiah's deep voice and almost tumbled into the river. He caught her arm and steadied her.

"I thought you were all sleeping," she whispered.

"The rest of the men are. I thought you'd be here." His eyes caressed her face.

She felt herself flush and stepped away. Running her fingers through her hair again, she began to braid it.

"I wish you'd leave it down. It's so beautiful. I've never seen hair like that. It's the color of red maple leaves in the autumn." He reached out and wound a strand around a finger.

The touch of his hand in her hair made her mouth go dry. She hurriedly tugged the lock of hair away from him and briskly braided it in with the rest. As far as she was concerned, he belonged to Golda now. "It's too messy to leave loose. I must look a sight."

"A beautiful one," he said.

She whirled and put her fists on her hips. "I wish you'd stop staying things like that. I know they aren't true. I've figured out your game."

"What game?" His voice grew cold, and a muscle twitched in his cheek.

"This pretense of paying court to me, of wanting to marry me. You're after the ranch, aren't you? Admit it." With all her heart, Margaret wished he could deny it. She wanted someone to love her for herself, not for what she possessed. Josiah talked of unconditional love, but she didn't think it existed.

"You think I care about the ranch?" He took off his hat and wiped his brow. "You sure have a great opinion of me, don't you?" He turned and stalked away.

He hadn't denied it. Her eyes burned, and she swallowed the lump in her throat. The plan, that's what she had to concentrate on. She had to save Pa's ranch.

She watched Josiah as he left the clearing, but then he turned and walked back toward her. "What about you, Margaret? You talk of being a believer, but you can't seem to trust anyone, not even God. You cling to your wealth as your security and carry the baggage of being unworthy even though God loves you and has forgiven you. You should have listened a little closer to that sermon in church last week."

He opened his mouth as though to say more, then shook his head and turned away again. His tall form disappeared among the trees as he headed farther out from camp.

She gulped and raised her hand to stop him, then let it drop. Was he right? With horror, she realized she did cling to her status as a wealthy ranch owner for her identity. And she trusted very few people. Her eyes burned. How did she let go of all the baggage she carried?

"I don't want to be like that, Lord," she whispered. "Help me to trust You more. Guide me today and help me be strong."

She sat beside the river until a gentle peace enveloped her. In her heart she knew she could trust God. He had this situation under control. . .but, she told herself, she had to be willing to do what was necessary. Even if it broke her heart.

Full of resolve, she made herself as neat as she could without a comb or clean clothes, then walked back to the camp. The men still snored beside the smoldering coals, their breath pluming in the cold morning air. Margaret hurried toward the tent where Golda had disappeared the night before.

She scratched at the tent opening. "Miss Munster? Can I talk to you?"

Only silence greeted her at first. Finally, she heard, "Give me a minute, will ya?" Margaret glanced around to make sure no one was watching while she waited for Golda.

Golda thrust open the tent opening. Her hair fanned over her shoulders and down her back like molten gold. "What do you want? I don't think we have anything to say to one another." She sneered, and her hostile blue eyes raked over Margaret. "You ready to admit defeat? Josiah will take one look at you this morning and run the other way."

Margaret winced. That was pretty much what he'd done. "I'd like to talk to you. In private."

Golda rolled her eyes but stepped back to allow Margaret entry. Margaret blinked as her eyes adjusted to the darkened interior of the tent. As her vision focused, she saw clothing and possessions strewn around the tent as though a fitful child had taken everything from her closet and heaped it on the floor. There was barely room to stand without stepping on a lovely dress or two.

"Let's get this over with. I need my beauty sleep."

"You're already the most beautiful woman I've ever seen," Margaret blurted out.

Golda raised an eyebrow, but a pleased smile spread over her face. Then her smile faded. "I know what you're trying to do. I'm not stupid. You won't get on my good side that easily. I want you out of here."

"And that's what I want, too. I need your help, though."

Golda's angry flush faded, and her blue eyes were speculative. "You want to leave Josiah? Why?"

"This is the busy time of year at the ranch. My pa needs me, and I really need to get home."

"What about Josiah? I think there's more to it than that."

Looking into Golda's shrewd eyes, Margaret knew she had to make this convincing. "I don't think he really loves me. My ranch is worth a lot of money, you know." She gestured toward Golda. "How could he really care about someone like me when he could have you?" She wished she could believe differently.

Golda nodded and preened a bit. "You're a smart lady, Miss O'Brien. I like a rival who knows when she's licked."

"Then you'll help me get away?"

"I'll think about it."

Margaret stared at her. "What's to think about? You want Josiah, and you can have him with me gone."

Golda shrugged her slim shoulders. "I need to make sure my brother doesn't have other uses for you. Ben Munster is not a man to cross."

Looking into Golda's darkened eyes, Margaret had little doubt Golda's desires were stronger than Ben Munster's plans. Margaret shifted uneasily. Something wasn't quite right, but she couldn't put her finger on it. "He has no plans for me. I'm not even supposed to be here. I was following Josiah and just stumbled on the camp."

"So you say. I'll check around. We'll talk more tomorrow."

"Tomorrow? I need to go today." Margaret caught at Golda's sleeve.

The other woman pulled away with a scowl. "This silk wrapper cost the earth, and you're crushing it!"

Margaret released the sleeve. "Please, it's got to be right

away." Otherwise she would lose her resolve. The more time she spent with Josiah, the more her emotions became entangled.

"Well, it won't be today," Golda said crossly. "I said I'd check it out. Now get out of here before Ben sees you, or Josiah will be stuck with you for sure." She pushed Margaret out the doorway, then yanked the opening closed.

Margaret stood staring at the closed tent flap. Her heart beat in her chest as though it wanted to get out with the same desperation as she longed to escape the camp. She had to find some other way. She couldn't wait on Golda. The other woman had probably gone back to bed, and it might be days before she decided whether or not to help.

She turned and bumped into a broad chest. Strong hands reached out and gripped her shoulders. She knew those hands. Staring into Josiah's face, she felt her frantic desire to leave ebb away. She loved him. The shock of that realization nearly brought her to her knees. This wasn't attraction or some other kind of mild feeling. This was love, pure and simple. That was why she was so desperate to leave. She hadn't wanted to face the fact that she was totally and completely in love with a bank robber.

Who would have thought she would have so little sense? That she—who prided herself on her common sense and straightforward approach to life—would lose her heart to a man like Josiah Cutler? He'd asked her to trust him; he'd said that not everything was all it appeared. But the evidence kept piling up against him. How could she trust him when he was so deeply embroiled with these criminals? She stared up at him, and his gaze bored into hers.

"I was just looking for you," he said. "I'm sorry I rushed away. I think it's time we had a talk. I keep telling you to trust me, but I don't give you any reason to do that. God showed me how wrong that was."

God again. How could a bank robber talk about God the way he did? As though He were a best friend Josiah consulted all the time. It made no sense to her. His relationship with God made her envious.

A man on horseback rode into camp. Josiah glanced over his shoulder, then grabbed Margaret's arm. "Come with me." He steered her toward the woods at the other end of the camp.

Margaret's pulse quickened. Maybe she would finally understand why they were here—why Josiah was friends with these men. They had almost reached the edge of the woods when Munster's voice reached them.

"Hey, Cutler, come 'ere. Our plans just got moved up."

Josiah grew very still. Margaret could feel the coiled tension in his arm. He released her and stepped away. "Be right there," he called. He bent his head and whispered in her ear, "Don't wander far. Things may call for quick action. Wait for me by the river. I'll try to be as quick as I can."

Margaret nodded numbly. There would never be time for them to sort out all this mess.

❧

Josiah kept his face impassive as he strode toward Munster. The gang leader's red face spoke of his anger and agitation. "What's up?" he asked Munster.

"I've just found out the money is going to be transferred out tomorrow. We have to get it today at closing time. Can you and the lady friend be ready?"

"Sure." Josiah's stomach clenched. He had to get Margaret out of danger. This job wasn't as important to him as she was. But how did he whisk her out of harm's way with every member of the gang watching every move they made? There had to be a way. He had to get Willy as well. The tasks seemed overwhelming with the time frame even shorter.

"Your brother's on lookout. Go get him, and we'll ride within the hour."

Josiah nodded. Maybe he'd be able to talk to Willy alone. There hadn't been any opportunity to do that since he'd arrived. Richard had kept in the background as well, and only a nod from him had confirmed to Josiah that all the plans were still on target.

Margaret's appearance had changed everything. He clambered over rocks and boulders as he made his way to the top of the lookout hill. A rifle across his knees, Willy sat with his back to the camp. His hat was pulled low to shield his face from the sun, but in spite of his tough stance, Josiah saw the little boy he'd always loved.

"Munster sent me to get you," he told his brother.

At the sound of Josiah's voice, Willy grabbed his rifle and spun around. "Oh, it's you," he said. Relief lightened his freckled, sunburned face.

"The job has been moved up. We ride today."

Willy wet his lips with his tongue, and his youthful face looked suddenly old and worn. "Munster sure we can handle it?"

"You having second thoughts?"

"Nah, I can handle it."

His brother's swaggering bravado touched Josiah's heart. All of nineteen, Willy's desperate desire to make a name for himself—even if it was a bad one—had brought him here. Josiah touched Willy on the shoulder. "You got time to come to the river with me? Margaret is waiting there, and I need to talk to both of you."

"My relief is coming now." Willy nodded toward Sheppard, a surly man of about fifty, who was climbing the steep hill toward them.

"Great. I'll meet you there." Josiah went back down the hill toward the river. His heart sped up at the thought of the coming revelations he had to make to Margaret and Willy. He prayed they would understand.

❧

Margaret sat on a rock and enjoyed the warm sunshine on her arms. The cool morning had quickly given way to a hot spring day. Dark clouds gathered in the southwest, their tops reaching toward the heavens in dark masses. The coming storm would blow this warmth away, so she'd better enjoy it while she could. A movement caught her eye, and she saw Golda coming toward her along the path from camp. She kept looking furtively back over her shoulder.

"I thought I'd find you here," she said, huffing from the exertion of the walk. "You ready to go?"

"Now?" Margaret's heart plummeted. Josiah wanted to talk to her, to explain things. He was on his way here right now.

Golda frowned. "It has to be right now while Ben is occupied with the coming job. I have horses waiting by

Thunder Creek." She scowled. "You'd better not change your mind. I want you out of here."

Margaret was not at all sure she wanted to go now. Maybe there was some way to work this out with Josiah. She wanted to trust him, to believe in him. But this opportunity would not come again. She either went now or stayed and threw her lot in with the gang.

Golda didn't wait for an answer. She grabbed Margaret's hand and tugged her to her feet. "Come *now*. Ben will be looking for us any minute. There's no time to waste."

Margaret allowed Golda to drag her toward the path. She really didn't have much choice. Pa had to be warned, and it was up to her to do it. There would be time to hear Josiah's explanations later.

She and Golda made their way along the path to a small tributary that fed into the river. Two horses munched on grass beneath the tree where they were tethered. One of them was Margaret's own mare, Rolly, and Margaret smiled, glad that she wouldn't be leaving her equine friend behind.

She and Golda mounted their horses; then Golda led the way along a path sprinkled with wildflowers. They came to a crossroad, and Golda turned her gelding's head to the fork that went to the right. Margaret wasn't familiar with the area, but the path didn't go in the direction of home. She pulled Rolly's head up short and stopped in the middle of the path.

"This isn't the right way," she told Golda.

The other woman grinned, but the smile didn't reach her hard blue eyes. "Oh, it's the right path, all right. You'll see. Come along."

Her stomach churning, Margaret followed. After about half an hour, the path had not changed direction, and she stopped again. "Thanks for your help. I think I can take it from here." Maybe the woman had no sense of direction. Margaret knew all she had to do was go south, then a little east, and she would be able to find her way to the Triple T.

Golda laughed, and the sound was full of mockery. She whistled, and three riders came from behind an outcropping of rocks. Margaret was surrounded before she realized what was happening. One man grabbed her reins, and the other two men flanked her mare on each side.

"What's going on?" Margaret cried. Tension rippled through her body.

"You said your ranch was worth a lot of money. It must be if Josiah was willing to marry *you*," Golda sneered. "You didn't think I would let you waltz out of camp without making sure I got a piece of that, did you? If Josiah wanted you with the ranch, he'll want me with a large chunk of cash from it." She fished in her saddlebag. "You're going to write a note to your pa and tell him that you're being held for ransom by Josiah Cutler. If he doesn't pay fifty thousand dollars in two days, he'll never see you again."

"I won't do it!" Margaret tried to wrench the reins from the henchman's grasp, but he growled at her and swatted her across the face. She fell from the saddle to the ground, her face burning where he'd struck her. She raised a hand to her throbbing cheek.

"You'll do what you're told, or we'll kill you here and now," the man told her.

Margaret rubbed her cheek. "Why blame Josiah?"

"I don't want there to be any chance that he can go running back to the ranch. He shows his face at the ranch after this, your pa would shoot him."

"Not if I tell him the real story." As soon as the words were out of her mouth, she realized the truth. Once they had the money, she was expendable. Her heart squeezed in her chest, and her mouth went dry. She should have stayed with Josiah. At least he professed to love her and had tried to take care of her. Now she was in the clutches of a madwoman.

nine

Josiah hurried toward the river. The storm clouds still continued to gather overhead, and flocks of birds circled above him, but he barely noticed; he was so intent on seeing Margaret. Once the truth was out, he could relax. Just looking forward to that moment eased the tension from his shoulders.

As he approached the rock where he had expected to find her, he stopped and looked around. There was no sign of her, but maybe she had gotten tired of waiting. He had taken longer than he'd expected. Munster would be looking for them both, and there was no time to waste. He ran back toward camp, slowing to a walk just before entering the clearing where the camp was located. He didn't dare let anyone see his agitation. He skirted the edge of the clearing but saw no sign of Margaret. Maybe she was waiting in a different spot at the river.

He plunged back into the trees and hurried back to the Red River. But fifteen minutes later, he had to admit defeat. Margaret was missing. He found Willy waiting by the big rock.

"Where you been?" his brother asked.

"Looking for Margaret." Josiah's stomach churned, but he was unable to put his finger on why he was so uneasy. Surely she was fine.

"I saw her with Golda heading away from camp. Kid Loco and two other men were right behind them."

Josiah's unease mushroomed to full-fledged panic. Golda was pure evil, even more so than her brother. Whatever she was up to, it couldn't be good. And Kid Loco was every bit as bad.

"Show me!" Josiah hauled Willy to his feet and shoved him toward the camp. "I'll grab the horses and meet you at the base of Lookout Hill. Don't tell anyone where we're going."

"I reckon I don't know nothing to tell," Willy said.

Josiah didn't, either, but he felt sick inside to think that Margaret was in jeopardy because of him. He had to find them. He slipped into the remuda of horses and found his gelding and Willy's mare. The horses were all saddled in preparation for the ride to the bank. Josiah knew Munster would be after them the minute he discovered the horses were gone. The problems were multiplying faster than a pet rabbit, and he didn't know what to do about it.

He led the horses to the meeting place where Willy waited, and they both mounted. "Show me where you saw them," Josiah said.

Willy led the way down the rocky path, and Josiah concentrated on finding the trail left by Golda's little band. He finally found it and saw where they veered off at the track away from Henrietta. So they weren't taking Margaret home. His last hopes that Golda wasn't up to something sinister ebbed away.

"You going to tell me what this is all about?" Willy asked.

"Not now. We have to focus on finding Margaret."

"You really love her, don't you?" his brother asked.

"Sure do. I didn't know I could feel this way about a woman." Josiah didn't want to talk about it. A terrible fear and foreboding gripped him that his obsession with his own plans was going to lead to Margaret's death. He couldn't live with that. Hardening his jaw, he vowed he would not let anything happen to her. He prayed silently as they hurried along the trail.

"Munster is going to be on our trail like a duck on a June bug," Willy said after a few moments. "The rest of the gang is all ready to go rob the bank. We're going to miss out on all the fun."

"Munster won't go without us," Josiah said. "Me and Margaret are key players in his little drama." Only after he said the words did he realize how dry and critical his words were. Willy caught his tone, for his head came up sharply and he stared at Josiah.

"You don't like Munster much, do you?" Willy asked. "You were part of his gang long before I was. Why did you leave?"

"It's complicated," Josiah admitted.

"Why did you come back, then?" Willy turned a hard gaze on Josiah.

"Because of you," Josiah told him. "When we find Margaret, we'll have a long talk, and I'll tell you everything. We've got a lot to talk about, a lot you don't know."

Willy scowled. "I want to hear it now."

Before Josiah could respond, the trail turned toward a small butte. "Wait here," Josiah told his brother. He dismounted and handed his reins to Willy. "I'll check it out.

Maybe they're holed up there."

Crouching behind rocks and scrubby bushes, Josiah crept forward. Soon the sound of voices drifted to his ears. He paused and listened. Golda's voice. He couldn't make out the words, but the mockery in her tone was hard to miss. He retraced his steps to where his brother waited.

"They're just ahead," he told Willy. "Leave the horses here and take your rifle." He grabbed his own Winchester from the saddle and led the way back to where Golda held Margaret captive.

Lying on their bellies, Willy and Josiah peered from behind a rock at the camp where Golda and her henchmen had holed up. A series of caves sprinkled the rocks behind the group. Josiah scanned the area for Margaret and finally spotted her lying near the mouth of one of the caves. Her eyes were closed in her white face, and for one heart-stopping moment, he feared he was too late. Then she opened her eyes and sat up. When he saw her holding her head, he realized part of the red wasn't her hair but blood.

A cold rage settled in his bones, and he nearly rushed into the camp with his guns blazing, but an inner voice counseled caution. Willy nudged him, and he saw the lookout Golda and her gang had posted. The man was about thirty feet from their hideaway, and he hadn't spotted them yet. Josiah motioned for Willy to circle around the other way so they could rush the lookout from both sides.

Willy crept along the rocks. When his brother was in place, Josiah crawled closer. Picking up a rock, he aimed it at the man's head. The rock zinged through the air with precision and hit the lookout in the forehead. He went down without a whimper. Josiah scrabbled to the man's prone form and took his gun; then Josiah tied him up and gagged him with a bandana. That should keep him quiet. One down and two more men to go.

He and Willy slithered down the slope toward the camp. One of the men was arguing with Golda. He recognized the men as Kid Loco and Marty Nelson, who was one of Kid Loco's best friends. As Josiah got nearer, he was finally able to hear what they were saying.

Kid Loco's hard voice carried well on the rising wind from the approaching storm. "I say we kill her now and get it over with. We can seal her in one of these caves, and no one will be the wiser. We're going to kill her anyway."

"We may need her. Until her pa delivers that money, she's collateral," Golda told him.

"Who says you make the decisions around here?" Kid Loco sneered. "What's to keep me from killing her right now?"

"You don't want to do that, Kid." Golda's voice was heavy with menace. "I don't like people to cross me."

Kid Loco held up a hand. "I was just joshing you, Golda. We're partners. I don't double-cross partners."

"You'd better not." Golda's voice turned silky, but there was still a trace of warning in her tone.

Josiah had heard that expression in her voice before, and he knew Kid Loco had better beware. She was a black widow spider, and she couldn't be trusted. If she didn't do it herself, she would have her brother see that he paid for any slur on her.

"Marty, you take the ransom note into town. Get directions to the ranch and get it delivered. I'll stay here and watch over the prisoner," Kid Loco said.

"She don't look like she'll give you much trouble." Marty picked at his teeth with a piece of straw, then took the paper Golda held out to him and sauntered to his horse. "I'll be back in a few hours. You staying here?"

"Yeah, the caves should give us some shelter from the storm that's brewing," Kid Loco said.

Marty rode off, and Josiah let out the breath he'd been holding. Another down. The odds were much better now, but Kid Loco was still no man to fool with. His reputation with the gun had reached as far as California. The notches on his belt numbered twenty-two the last time Josiah had heard. Still, if they could get the draw on him before he knew they were there, they had a chance.

He motioned for Willy to follow him. They crept still closer.

"You reckon Cutler is looking for her yet?" Kid Loco asked.

"He'll find me," Margaret said, raising her head.

Warmth spread through Josiah at the certainty in her tone. There was actually faith and trust in her voice. Maybe he was finally getting through to her. He crept a bit closer.

Golda gave an unladylike snort. "Why would he bother finding you? You're certainly no beauty. He's probably on his way to rob the bank right now. He has more important things on his mind than searching for you."

Josiah clenched his fists. He didn't understand why other people didn't see Margaret's beauty. She was lovely beyond description. His gaze wandered to her, and he longed to get her to safety. Margaret rose and brushed the dust from her skirt. Josiah wished she would stay back in the relative safety of the cave, but she walked slowly forward until she faced Golda.

"You're not going to get away with this, Golda. God is in control."

Golda burst into gales of laughter. "Oh, she's religious, Kid." She spat the words as if they left a bad taste in her mouth.

A rush of joy at Margaret's words rose in Josiah's chest. Maybe she was learning to walk closer to the Lord through this experience. The next step was for her to accept His unconditional love. Maybe then she could accept Josiah's own love for her. His heart throbbed with hope.

"Laugh all you want," Margaret said. "But I won't let you hurt my father." She walked toward the horses.

"Where do you think you're going?"

"Home. And if you intend to stop me, you'll have to kill me now. I won't let you rob us." Margaret's voice was strong with determination.

"That can be arranged," Kid Loco growled. He drew his gun.

"Oh, please stop showing off," Golda said with an impatient wave of her hand. "Margaret knows she's not going anywhere. Tie her up, Kid."

But Margaret darted to the horse and threw herself atop its back before Kid Loco could react. He took aim at her back, and Josiah made his move. His rifle came up almost of its own volition. He fired, and the bullet slammed into Kid Loco's wrist. The gunfighter dropped his gun with a yowl. The surprise on his face was worth everything Josiah had endured this day. If he'd had time, Josiah would have laughed at the snarl Kid gave when he recognized him.

"Cover me!" Josiah told Willy. He leaped forward into the clearing. Margaret was astride the horse and heading down the path away from him.

"Margaret, wait!" Josiah ran forward and kicked the gun away from Kid Loco. Willy ran to help him and stood guard over the gunfighter.

Kid looked up at Josiah and drew back his teeth in a snarl. "You're a dead man, Cutler."

"Nice to see you, too, Kid." Josiah turned, then stepped back as Golda screamed and rushed at him.

Golda flew at him and raked her nails over his face. "What's wrong with me?" she panted. Her face was wild with insane jealousy, and she went at his eyes with her nails. "You choose that red-haired Amazon over a real woman?"

Josiah caught her hands and stopped her from inflicting any more damage, though he could feel the blood already beginning to trickle down his face. Grabbing the rope that had been intended for Margaret, he tied Golda's hands together, then pushed her down beside Kid Loco. Then he tied Kid Loco as well.

Margaret must have heard his shout, for she came cantering back toward them. "Josiah!" She waved and dismounted. He caught her as she ran into his arms. With her in his embrace, all the world seemed right again. He buried his face in her hair. Never again would he let her be put in this kind of danger. If anything had happened to her, he wouldn't have been able to live with himself.

She patted his face. "You came," she murmured. "I knew you would."

"Sorry I was late," he whispered against her hair. He held her close and breathed in the scent of her hair. She fit against his heart as if she were made just for him. As far as he was concerned, God had done just that.

❧

Margaret had thought she was dreaming when she heard Josiah's voice. Nestled against his chest, she knew how much she loved him. Yet it all seemed so hopeless. How did she choose between her love for him and her love for Pa and the ranch? As much as she loved Josiah, she couldn't see how she could ever turn a blind eye to his bank robbing ways. How could she live with never knowing when he would be killed or caught and sent to prison?

But she wouldn't think about that now. Now the only reality she wanted was the sense of his strong arms around her and the sound of his heart against her ear. She branded into her memory the sensation of being cradled against his chest. It might be all she had to remember when this episode in her life was over.

"Very touching." A harsh voice broke into their reunion.

Margaret jerked around to find herself and Josiah staring down the barrel of a gun. Munster was at the other end of it, and behind him clustered the rest of the gang. Josiah's arms tightened around her, and she reveled in his protection.

"Would someone mind explaining what's going on?" Munster growled.

Golda jumped to her feet. "What does it look like?" she cried. "They planned to hold me for ransom to get all of the bank money instead of just their fair share."

Margaret drew away. "That's a lie!" she cried. She touched her head. "Look at me; I'm bleeding. Your sister has already sent a ransom demand to my father. She and her men were going to kill me."

Munster scowled at her. "You think I'd believe you over my own sister?" He jerked his head at one of the men. "Untie her and Kid Loco."

The man hurried to obey, and Margaret's stomach plummeted at the thoughtful glance Munster turned on Josiah and her. What would he do with them? They were heavily outnumbered.

Golda rubbed her wrists. Kid Loco retrieved his gun and stalked toward Josiah with his eyes narrowed. "He's mine," he snarled.

Munster held up his hand. "This can all wait. We've got a bank to rob, or the bulk of that money will be gone tomorrow." He shoved Margaret toward the horse.

Josiah started toward him with his fists clenched, but Kid Loco slammed the butt of his gun in Josiah's stomach. Josiah doubled over and gasped.

Margaret jerked her arm out of Munster's grasp and went to Josiah. "Don't fight them now," she whispered. "We'll figure out a way to get out of this."

"I still need you both," Munster said. "You're going to get me in that bank. After that, we'll let Kid Loco use you for target practice. No one messes with the Munster family. You're both going to wish you'd never been born."

He made them mount their horses, and they turned toward Henrietta. As they rode along, Margaret glanced at Josiah.

"Why does the Kid hate you so much?" she whispered.

"It's a long story," Josiah said.

"It's a long ride."

He sighed. "It's not something I'm proud of," he admitted. "The gang had just robbed a bank in Houston, and we were holed up in a cabin outside Fort Worth. The Kid was in town, and he was flirting with my cousin Sarah. Sarah had no idea who or what he was, but I knew. I thought I shouldn't get involved, though, so I didn't say anything. One of his cronies took a liking to her, too, and there was a gunfight. A stray bullet killed her. She was only nineteen."

He fell silent, and Margaret could feel his pain.

"That was before I began to trust God, and I went looking for Kid Loco and the other man. I killed the other man in a fair gunfight, but the Kid has never forgiven me. He intends to get revenge someday."

Josiah had killed a man. Margaret swallowed hard. The knowledge hurt even though he'd admitted as much once. What else had he done? Bank robbery, killings—yet he spoke of God. Glancing at him from the corner of her eye, she realized that God *had* forgiven him. It shone out of everything Josiah did and said. Then what was he doing back with these crooks again? He'd left them for a time. How could he go back to that life of crime?

She didn't understand, but she desperately wanted to. If only there were some way to allow herself to love him.

ten

This was all his fault. Josiah flexed his muscles against the ropes that bound him, but all he succeeded in doing was to rub even more skin from his raw wrists. Rivulets of perspiration trickled down his face. The heat and humidity had built through the day, and the towering clouds had not yet brought the relief of a rainstorm. So many people were counting on him, and he'd let them all down. He glanced around the shack where they were confined. About three feet away, Margaret wrestled with the ropes on her wrists as well. Her green eyes stared out of her white face, and she bit her lip as she fought against her bonds.

Munster had confined them here while he checked out the town. He wanted to make sure there weren't too many people around before they made their move. Guards were posted just outside the open door.

The desperation on her face renewed Josiah's urgency to free himself. Gritting his teeth, he ignored the pain and struggled to wrest his wrists from the ropes. There—they gave just a bit. The guards didn't seem to be looking, so he inched closer to Margaret.

She stopped her struggling and stared up into his face. "I'm scared, Josiah. What's going to happen?"

Her fear strengthened his resolve. "We've got to get free. I'm going to scoot around when the guards aren't looking.

See if you can untie me." He wiggled around until his hands touched hers.

Her hands moved up to his wrists. "You're bleeding," she gasped.

He heard the concern in her voice, and guilt wracked him. What had he gotten her into? Before he came along, she had lived a safe and happy life with her father. Because of him, she was in deadly danger. "I'm sorry," he whispered. "I never meant to put you in jeopardy. I promised to protect you, and I've failed."

She turned her head, and the whisper of her breath touched his neck. An ache of love built in his chest. He'd never be able to express that love if he didn't get them out of this mess somehow.

"I'm not," she said softly.

His thoughts blurred as he tried to sort out what she meant. She wasn't in danger or she wasn't sorry?

"I'm not sorry I spent this time with you. I want the chance to get to know you better," she said. "We'll get out of here. Will Willy help us?"

"I think so. If I could just talk to him in private, make him understand what I'm doing here."

"What *are* you doing here?" Her fingers continued to fumble with the knots, but so far they remained as tight as before.

"That's what I was going to tell you." He lowered his voice even further. If Munster found out the truth, he would string them up at the first tree he found. "I'm a Texas Ranger now, not a bank robber. A ranger who helped me after I was shot in a robbery led me to Christ. He convinced me that if God could forgive Paul in the Bible, He could forgive me. I turned my back on crime and joined the Rangers with Richard's help. He was the short, blond-haired man who was part of the gang when we were first brought here. He infiltrated the gang, too, and we were both sent to apprehend them. I'm not sure what's happened to him.

"The Rangers wanted to move in and arrest the gang two months ago, but I persuaded them to let me get Willy out before he actually broke the law. So far, all he'd done was to join them. After the bank robbery, I won't have any choice but to arrest my own brother. I can't let that happen." The thought of his brother behind bars made his voice tremble, and he cleared his throat.

"A ranger," Margaret breathed. Her nails dug into Josiah's arm.

He gasped a bit. "What's wrong?"

"You're a ranger." She exhaled softly. "That's almost worse than being a bank robber, at least as far as Pa's concerned." She drew a ragged breath. "Pa would never sanction me hooking up with you." Her fingers plucked desperately at the rope, and the bonds began to loosen.

"What are you talking about? I'm the law. You sound like I just crawled out from under a rock." One wrist broke loose, and he furtively slipped his other out of the ropes, then flexed his fingers.

"A Texas Ranger killed my uncle." Her voice was hoarse with suppressed emotion. "Pa would tan my hide if I got involved with a ranger. He hates them worse than scorpions, and that's saying something."

"I don't want to marry your pa; I want to marry you." He

drew an exasperated breath.

She shook her head. "It's out of the question now."

Margaret sounded near tears, and he quickly untied her. "We'll talk about this when we get out of here," he whispered. He had to stay focused on the problem at hand. He'd handle her pa when the time came.

Movement at the door of the shack made him freeze. Willy poked his head inside the cave.

His brother carried a tin cup and two plates of beans. "I brought you some supper," he said. He set the plates on the dirt floor. "I'll have to untie you so you can eat, but don't try anything. I'd have to shoot you, and I don't want to do that." His voice quavered, and he blinked rapidly.

"You wouldn't shoot me, and you know it, Willy," Josiah said. He couldn't let Willy see they were loose. Not yet.

"I would if I had to." Willy's words were almost too low for Josiah to hear.

Josiah knew better. "Let's get out of here, Will. Pa needs you back on the ranch. He asked me to bring you home."

Willy sucked in his breath, and his gaze darted to Josiah's. "Pa said that?" he breathed.

The hope in his voice almost broke Josiah's heart. It held all the emotion of Willy's lonely growing-up years as the nearly forgotten son. "Yes, he did," Josiah told his brother. "And there's more, Willy." He wished his brother were young enough to take in his arms. This news would be hard for him to take. It was still hard for Josiah to grasp. "Pa's dying. He wants you home to make his peace with you."

Josiah heard Margaret gasp at the same time as Willy's

face crumpled. He visibly struggled to maintain his composure, swallowing hard and shaking his head. Tears began to stream down Willy's face, and he buried his face in his hands. "Not Pa," he choked.

Josiah hated to hurt him. For years Willy had lived in his older brother's shadow. Even when Josiah had been robbing banks, his pa had never realized what his adored oldest son had become. Pa had always thought Josiah was perfect. Willy had tried to get Pa's attention, but their father had lavished everything he had on Josiah, and there was nothing left for Willy.

Josiah wanted to put his arms around his brother, but he didn't know if Willy would allow it. He glanced at Margaret; she was staring at Willy with tears in her eyes. She rose and went to Willy and put her arms around him. He buried his face against her shoulder.

"There, there," she said soothingly as she patted his back.

Willy's sobs tore at Josiah's insides. Josiah clenched his fists at his side and wished there was some way to take the pain for his brother.

Willy's sobs finally subsided, and he raised his head. His glance dropped to Josiah's hands. "You're untied," he said. "Munster will have a fit."

"Let's get out of here, Willy," Josiah said. "You don't belong with this gang. I realize you were trying to hurt Pa, but put away childish thoughts like that. Now is the time for us to hang together as a family."

Willy stared at him for a long moment, then nodded. "Okay, Josiah. I don't know how we'll manage it but okay. Munster will be back any minute. We'd better hurry with whatever we do." He wiped his eyes with his sleeve. "I'll try to keep anyone from coming in here."

"We'll need a diversion to get past all of them," Margaret said. "I'll provide one."

"I reckon that won't happen. You stay put right where you are," Josiah said. "I've put you in enough danger already."

"You don't have any say in it, Mr. *Ranger,*" she said.

Willy gasped. "Ranger? What's this?"

Margaret dropped her gaze and turned away to let Josiah explain.

He sighed. "I'm a Texas Ranger, Willy, sent to bring in the gang. I want you out of the way before you do something that's against the law, and I have to bring you in, too."

"A ranger," Willy breathed. "You always said you wanted to be a lawman when we were kids. Does Pa know?"

Josiah nodded. "I went home six months ago and confessed everything. He knows it all, my bad past and the good God has done in my life."

"God?" Willy's eyes went wide. "You never had time for religion before, Josiah. Pa neither. What did he say about that?"

"When a man's dying, his perspective can change. Pa is a believer now, too. That's why he sent me after you. He wants you to forgive him."

Willy's eyes welled with tears again. "He said that?"

Josiah nodded. "That and more." He put his hand on Willy's shoulder. "But there will be time later for explanations. We have to get out of here."

Willy slowly backed up. He shook his head. "But I can't let you arrest my friends."

"They're not your friends, Willy. Real friends wouldn't want to kill your only brother," Josiah pointed out. "They're just using you. Any willing gunman would do for them."

"That's not true," Willy said hotly. "They care about me."

"Hey, Willy, you hand-feeding them?" a voice called from out by the cooking fire. "Get out here and clean up this mess."

"See what I mean?" Josiah whispered urgently. "You're just a servant to them. Think about Pa, Willy, about what it would do to him if you went to prison or were hung."

Willy blinked rapidly, then uttered an inarticulate cry and rushed from the shack. Margaret went to Josiah and buried her face against his chest. "We're in trouble, aren't we?"

"I don't think he'll betray us." Josiah cradled her closer. The scent of her hair and the feel of her in his arms soothed him. He kissed the top of her head. If he could only keep her close and protect her all the days of their lives. But first he had to get them out of here.

"We'll wait fifteen minutes, then we'll act. With or without Willy." Josiah's eyes burned at the thought of leaving his brother behind. But he had a responsibility to Margaret and to his job. He had no choice.

She nodded and lifted her head. He bent and pressed his lips to hers. Her soft kiss gave him courage and hope. God would get them out of this. "Right is on our side," he whispered. "Things may look dark now, but God has it all under control."

She smiled tremulously. "No wonder all the talk of God didn't fit. You're a knight on a quest, not an evil man. No wonder you kept my head spinning."

"Here I thought I kept your head spinning with my kisses," he teased.

Her face turned scarlet, and she started to draw back, but he clutched her closer. "You make my head spin, so it's only fair if I do the same to you," he whispered.

She nestled against his chest again, and he rested his chin on top of her head. At least she wasn't fighting him right now. He should enjoy this while it lasted. "This is not getting us out of here," he said reluctantly.

"No," she agreed. She drew back and looked into his eyes. "This is hopeless; you know that, don't you? Pa would never let me marry you now."

"We'll worry about that when the time comes."

"Are you trying to back out now?" she asked, her lips curving in a smile.

A dimple played at the corner of that delectable mouth of hers, and it just made him want to kiss her again. "You couldn't get rid of me with a horsewhip," he said with a grin. He had to think, and he couldn't do that with her so near. He released her reluctantly.

"We need to come up with a diversion. Got any ideas?" he asked. He stepped away from her and peered through the gloom. The wind was beginning to pick up again as the towering clouds moved closer. They were going to get wet for sure.

A dust devil, kicking up a cloud of sand, raced through the camp, pausing once to whirl around the place where the horses were tethered. The animals snorted and wheeled in terror to escape the sting of the wind-driven sand. The men shouted and cursed as they raced to grab the horses before they could stampede.

"This is our chance," Josiah whispered. "Thank You, God!" He grabbed Margaret's hand and dashed into the blowing sand. Crouching behind a rock, he watched to make sure the men were occupied, then made a run for the cover of a thicket of brush. Thorns tore at his flesh, and he knew Margaret was battling the same thing when he heard her soft gasp. They dove into the thicket and lay breathless on the ground as the men fought to control the horses.

"How do we get any mounts now?" Margaret brushed the bits of thorns and twigs from her skirt.

"We may have to use the old shank's mare and hoof it on our own two feet," Josiah said. "Let's go." They wriggled their way through the brush to the other side.

"What about Willy?" she asked.

"I'm here."

They both whirled at Willy's voice.

"I'm going with you," Willy said. "I can't let Pa die thinking I'm a criminal." He swallowed hard, and Josiah saw the glimmer of tears in his eyes.

"I'm proud of you, Boy," Josiah said.

"I'm not a boy any longer, Josiah. Not anymore."

Josiah nodded and clapped Willy on the shoulder. "You're right. You're a man, Willy. One Pa and I are both going to enjoy getting to know. Let's go."

Josiah led them down a path toward Jacksboro. He knew a contingent of more Rangers waited for word from him at Fort Richardson. If they could get there, they would be safe.

Margaret looked around anxiously as they walked the

path. After several minutes, she stopped short in the path. "This isn't the way to Henrietta."

"We're not going to Henrietta. We're going to get the rest of my men at the fort."

She shook her head. "I'm going to Henrietta. We have to warn the sheriff before those men get my pa's money."

"My men will handle the robbers."

"Not if they get to the bank first. Henrietta is closer. I'm going there." She wheeled and hurried toward the fork in the trail.

Josiah grabbed her arm. "No, it's not safe, Margaret. We need help."

When he saw the determination in those green eyes she turned toward him, he knew it was useless to argue. And it was up to him to see that she didn't die trying. "All right, we'll go to Henrietta. But you're to do exactly as I tell you. Our future kids are counting on us to survive."

&

Our kids. The way Josiah said those words—as if it were a foregone conclusion that they would marry and have children—brought a tide of emotion roiling in Margaret's stomach. She'd never thought to marry, let alone have children. Not since Caleb married Lucy, anyway. Margaret trudged along the path at the fastest clip she could manage and tried not to think about what Josiah had said. It was impossible, of course.

Pa was irrational when it came to the Texas Rangers. Everyone else she knew held the Rangers in the highest regard, but not Pa. To hear him talk, the Rangers were only a step removed from the devil himself. And changing Pa's mind was like lassoing a twister—the effort alone could get you killed.

Still, Margaret wished that Josiah's words could come true. In her mind's eye, she saw little boys with Josiah's dark eyes and the dimple in his chin. Maybe a little girl or two with her red hair. But no, she wouldn't wish this mess of a mop on any child of hers. Better to have Josiah's dark curls. She smiled at the thought of dark ringlets on a cherubic face.

"What's so funny?" Josiah asked. His face shone with perspiration, and his breath came fast from the exertion of jogging toward town.

Heat swept over her face. Wouldn't he just love to know she was thinking about children? He would smile that self-assured grin of his as if he knew it was going to happen. Well, it wasn't going to happen. There was no way Pa would ever allow it. She would have to run off to do that, and she couldn't hurt her pa like that. Besides, the expanses of grass and valley were a part of the sinew and bone of her very being. Surely Josiah wouldn't ask her to give that up.

She wiped the smile from her face. "Nothing," she said.

His gaze swept over her face, but he didn't argue with her. The grin that so infuriated her tugged at his mouth, but there was no way he could know what she'd been thinking. At least she prayed that was so. Surely she wasn't that transparent.

They paused under a juniper tree. Josiah sank to the ground and lay there with his hands laced behind his head. "Storm's almost here," he said. Willy leaned his back against a rock and closed his eyes.

The wind had steadily built for the past hour, and the roiling clouds had turned to a blackish green that foreshadowed a bad storm. Margaret prayed they would reach Henrietta before the storm hit. She bent over and caught her breath. Every muscle ached, and a blister on her foot felt as though it had broken open. If only she could have a good cry. There were all kinds of pent-up emotions just begging to be let out.

Josiah patted the ground beside him. "Sit and rest. Tell me more about why your father hates Texas Rangers."

She didn't want to talk about it. Margaret glanced at the sky. "We really should be moving along. That storm is imminent."

"We all need a rest. Five minutes won't kill us."

Margaret sat beside him on the lush green carpet of grass and wildflowers. She plucked a bluebell and buried her nose in the flower.

"Quit lollygagging, and tell me what barriers I'm going to have to overcome with your father. I think he'll listen to reason. He likes me."

"That's when he thought you were a cowboy," she pointed out. "When he hears you're a ranger, he'll order you off the property with his gun."

"It can't be that bad."

"It's worse," she told him. "You'll be lucky if he doesn't shoot you."

Josiah grinned. "I can handle your pa. Just tell me why he hates Rangers."

Margaret sighed. "My uncle Charles was out rounding up cattle for the fall trail drive three years ago. He had a fire going and was branding the few strays we'd missed marking in the spring. A ranger came through looking for cattle thieves. He took one look at Charlie's branding operation and jumped to the conclusion that my uncle was a cattle thief. When the ranger tried to arrest him, Charlie drew his gun, and the ranger shot him."

"Sounds like it was as much Charlie's fault as the ranger's. Why didn't Charlie explain who he was?"

"He was always a bit of a hothead. No one knows for sure why he pulled the gun, but when it was all over, Charlie was dead, and Pa vowed vengeance on all Texas Rangers. He wrote letters and tried to get the man in trouble, but nothing was ever done." Margaret shivered at the remembrance of those dark days.

"I'll see what I can find out," Josiah promised.

"It won't change anything. Pa would rather see me dead than married to a Texas Ranger." Sadly, Margaret was sure that was true. Only two things were important to her father—the ranch and family honor.

"We'll see." Josiah stood and held out a hand to her. "We'd better get on the way again."

Margaret gave him her hand, and he tugged her to her feet. He pulled her into his arms. "Don't give up on us, Love," he whispered. "We'll find a way around your pa."

Margaret prayed he was right. Little by little, she realized she was trusting God to work things out according to His will. That knowledge brought her comfort she'd never expected.

eleven

A sense of urgency pushed Margaret on though her feet throbbed and weariness slowed her steps. At this rate it would take two days to reach Henrietta. She paused and wiped the perspiration from her brow. "You have any idea where we are?"

Josiah grinned, his white teeth gleaming in his dirt-streaked face. "You're the native; I'm just a transplant. Nothing looks familiar?"

She shook her head. "I'm lost. This is probably Stanton land, though. If I could get my bearings, we might be better off to make for Caleb's ranch house and borrow horses."

He nodded toward a lone cottonwood. "Think you could climb that tree, Willy?"

"Sure." His brother took off at a trot.

"I'll have to do it," Margaret said. "I know the area, and neither one of you do." She followed Willy and Josiah to the tree. She hadn't climbed trees in years, but surely it wasn't something a person forgot. She'd practically lived in the oak outside her bedroom window when she was growing up.

From that oak tree she had dreamed her girlish dreams of her hero riding over the hills to sweep her away to some enchanted existence far from the red dirt of northern Texas. She would dress in stylish clothes that minimized her size, and when she came back to visit, the other girls would stare with envy. They would all want to be her friends instead of giggling behind her back.

Instead, she had learned to love the land as the husband she would never have. And the men of the area had given her their respect. The reminder of how many other ranchers were depending on her strengthened her resolve as she stared up through the branches. She had to get to town in time to save the money everyone had worked for all year.

"Give me a leg up," she told Josiah. He laced his fingers together and offered them to her. She put her foot in his big hands, and he lifted her as she reached up to grasp the lowest branch. The rough bark bit into her hands, but she gripped it firmly anyway. It was a good thing she was wearing britches.

She swung her leg over the branch and scooted firmly onto it, then stood and began to climb higher. Through the leafy canopy, she could see miles in all directions. Staring at the landscape, she searched for a familiar landmark. There. That formation of three rocks. In an instant, Margaret knew where she was. On the other side of that formation was a track that would lead to the Stanton homestead.

"Got it!" she crowed. "I'd know this land anywhere." She scrambled down the tree limbs. Pausing at the last branch, she gauged the distance to the ground, then jumped. Instead of landing smoothly on the grass, her ankle twisted and she fell. Pain seized her ankle and refused to let go.

Josiah whipped around at her muffled groan. Concern shone from his dark brown eyes, and he knelt beside her. "You should have let me help you," he said.

Burning pain radiated around her ankle and left her gasping for breath. She groaned softly. "You'll have to go on without me. Just beyond the rock formation is a track that will take you to Caleb and Lucy. You'll be there in half an hour or less."

"I'm not leaving you here." Josiah's warm fingers probed the tender flesh of her ankle and she winced.

"You have to. I'll be fine." Bracing herself against the pain, she shook her head. "I'm sorry."

"You've been amazing." Josiah's voice vibrated with emotion.

Margaret searched his gaze through a haze of agony. Her ankle felt like it was being squeezed flat. "Hurry," she panted.

Josiah folded her into his arms. Cradled close to his chest, she felt safe and protected. "I'll pray," she whispered. "Go now."

His heart beat steadily under her ear, a comforting sound of constancy and steadfastness. Josiah was someone she could trust—she felt that in her bones. But there was always that niggling doubt in the back of her mind that he would grow weary of her lack of feminine wiles and fripperies. That he would look around at the type of woman he could have had and realize he'd been cheated. She couldn't bear for him to regret wanting her. She sucked in a breath. She was done with worrying about it. It was time to trust God with that, too.

Josiah's gentle fingers brushed the curls back from her face. "I'm not leaving you," he said again. He pressed his lips against her forehead. "We'll go on together or not at all. I'll help you."

"I could go for help," Willy said.

Josiah pressed his lips together. "I'd rather we stayed together," he said.

"Don't you trust me?" Willy's voice was hurt.

Margaret drew back a bit from Josiah's grasp. "Let him go," she said quietly. "I'm not going to be able to walk that far, even with help."

"I'll carry you."

"You're not carrying me two miles!" The thought made Margaret pull even farther away. Her weight alone would be proof to Josiah that she was no slip of a girl.

"You can trust me," Willy broke in. "I won't run off or go back to the gang. I'm through with that."

"I trust you," Josiah said. "I'm more worried about the gang catching up to you."

"I can take care of myself," Willy said.

"I reckon I don't have a choice," Josiah said. "But be alert. Munster and Golda won't give up easily. Get back here as quick as you can."

"Don't fuss like Ma. I'll be fine." Willy tightened the gun holster around his hips, then strode off in the direction of the Stanton ranch.

Margaret sighed. "I feel so helpless. There should be something I can do."

Josiah sat down beside her and slipped his arm around her shoulders. "You can sit here and tell me what a wonderful husband I'm going to be. We can decide how many kids we want and make some plans for what we want to do."

"The ranch won't be mine if we marry," she said. "I told

you how Pa feels about Texas Rangers."

Josiah shrugged. "He'll change his mind. God has brought us this far. He won't desert us now."

She knew her pa. He was irrational when it came to Rangers. She'd better not get her hopes up. This might all fade like a mirage once they were back to the Triple T. She pulled away from Josiah.

"What's wrong?" He tried to draw her back against his chest, but she resisted. "What did I say?"

"Nothing." She leaned away from him and wrapped her arms around herself. Perilously near tears, she felt cold inside in spite of the heat and humidity that still shimmered in the air.

Josiah leaned forward and tipped her chin up. She refused to meet his gaze and tried to turn away her head, but his hard fingers refused to allow it. "You've gone all prickly again. Sometimes talking to you is like walking through a field of cowpatties. I'm afraid of putting a foot in the wrong place."

Her lips twitched at his words, but she clamped down on the bubble of laughter rising in her.

"Tell me what's wrong."

"I told you nothing is wrong." She jerked her head away from his fingers. "I just want to get out of this mess and get life back to normal. Pa's probably worried sick, and Munster and his gang are probably riding to Henrietta right now."

"You were smiling until we mentioned your pa. You're really worried about what he'll say, aren't you?"

"The Bible says to honor your father and mother. I know you wouldn't want me to go against what God says."

"We won't. I have faith in God's provision in this situation. Think of all the ways He's been faithful in these past weeks, Margaret. He'll be faithful in this, too. We belong together. Can't you feel that in your bones? And if that's true, we know God will work it out."

"I don't know what I feel." But even as she said the words, she knew he was right. God had performed miracle after miracle for them. A glimmer of hope began to beat in her chest.

"You know. In your heart you know." He pulled away and folded his arms across his chest.

She felt even colder and wished she could take back her words. "I'm sorry," she said softly. "You're right. I'm just afraid, so I'm trying to be practical."

"You're not being practical; you're being pigheaded. You refuse to see how God has brought us together and how His hand has guided us through. He will help us soothe your pa and see our way to the future."

"I'll try," she whispered, laying her head on his shoulder.

She could feel the tension ease out of him, and he embraced her. A sound reached their ears.

"Someone's coming," he whispered.

Her heart hammering, she held her breath as he stood and peered through the brush that hid them. "It's Willy and Caleb."

She closed her eyes at the relief in his voice. Trying to get to her feet, she winced at the pain in her ankle.

He must have heard her soft inhalation, for he turned and came toward her. "Let me help you." He swept her up into his arms.

Margaret gasped and clasped her arms around his neck. "Put me down! I'm too heavy for you to be toting around like a feed sack."

"You don't weigh anything," he scoffed. Striding to meet Caleb and Willy, he carried her as he would a child.

She felt light and free in his arms. Staring into his face, she watched to see signs of overexertion, but he carried her easily. His muscles bulged beneath his shirt, and she couldn't help the thrill of admiration at his strength and compassion. He was the kind of man who would make a woman feel safe and protected. She was glad she was that woman.

&

Josiah wanted to keep walking with Margaret in his arms. Just walk into the sunset all the way home to El Paso. He would teach her that she was beloved by both him and God. Her hands clasped him at the back of his neck, and she felt warm and pliable against his chest. They belonged together, and he would do all in his power to show her that fact.

Caleb waved. "The cavalry is here." The horse led behind him jerked his head and snorted at Josiah's appearance.

Josiah grinned and stopped in front of him. "I don't see any blue coat."

"My blue shirt will have to do." Caleb stared at Margaret and his smile faded. "What have you gotten yourself into now, Margaret? You've got Lucy in a tizzy, and the baby is screaming her head off. It was all I could do to keep Lucy from coming with me. I had to remind her that her first priority was our baby."

Josiah frowned. Why did everyone make remarks that made Margaret feel even more inadequate and foolish?

One look at her set face, and he knew Caleb's words had hurt her. He tightened his arms around her, then reluctantly put her down. Focus—that's what he needed. There would be time enough to sort this out when the Munster gang was behind bars.

Margaret's face was pale, but she bit her lip and leaned against him for support as she smiled at Caleb. "You know I hate boredom, Caleb." She limped toward the horse Caleb had brought for her.

She never let anyone know she was hurt. Holding her head high, she trod through life with determination and grit. Josiah was fortunate she revealed her inner hurt and feelings to him. With God's help, he would make sure he never betrayed that trust.

Josiah put his arm around her waist to help her. When she came alongside the horse, he lifted her into the saddle and she grabbed the reins.

"Let's get to town. There's no time to waste. We have no way of knowing whether or not Munster is hitting the bank even now. We have to stop them."

"I promised Lucy we'd stop by the house so she could take a look at your ankle. It was the only way I could get her to stay behind," Caleb said.

"There's no time!"

"We have to make time. I promised her. We'll be going right past there, and we'll just stop for five minutes." Caleb tossed the reins of the other horse to Josiah, then turned and started back the way they'd come.

Josiah mounted up and fell into place behind Willy. His brother had been quiet, and Josiah wanted to talk to him, to reassure him that they would work things out. Margaret led the way and kept them at a fast clip. Her tense shoulders gave Josiah a sense of urgency as well. The gang planned to hit the bank at five. That was only two hours away. Margaret would never forgive herself if she failed and the robbery took place.

By the time the Stanton ranch came into view, Margaret was swaying in the saddle. When they stopped in front of the house, Josiah quickly dismounted and rushed to help her down. She practically fell into his arms.

"I'm sorry," she gasped. "I'm not usually such a weakling."

"You've been through a lot." He lifted her into his arms and carried her to the house.

Lucy met them at the door. "Lay her on the sofa," she said urgently. Her blue eyes were dark with worry.

At least there was someone who cared about Margaret. Holding her protectively, Josiah carried her to the sofa and gently laid her down. "You're going to be fine," he soothed. "I know you're worried, but I'll head on into town and take care of things there. You let Lucy take care of you. I'll get back as quick as I can."

Her green eyes darkened, and she shook her head. "I'm going with you. Don't leave without me."

"You're not going anywhere." Lucy pushed Josiah out of the way. "Look at you—you can barely hold your head up. There's no way you're getting back on that horse."

"You've got the baby to worry about. I'm fine. I'll check in with the doctor when this is all over." Margaret attempted to rise, then fell back against the sofa.

Before Josiah could insist she stay put, shots rang out.

Willy burst through the door.

"We've got trouble!" he cried. "Munster and the gang have the house surrounded. They barely missed me."

He held out his hat, and Josiah saw a bullet had punched a hole clean through the crown. "You got any extra rifles?" he asked Caleb.

Caleb was already rushing to the gun cabinet. He handed two rifles to Josiah and two to Willy before taking another two for himself. Grabbing a bag of bullets, he ran toward the window. Just as he reached it, the glass shattered and bullets rained through the opening.

Caleb dropped to the floor. "Stay down!" he cried.

"Give me a rifle," Margaret muttered. She struggled up from the sofa and limped to the gun cabinet.

"Get down! We'll take care of this!" Josiah rushed toward her as a bullet whizzed through the air and narrowly missed her.

"Thank God that didn't hit you," he whispered. He embraced her, and she leaned against his chest.

"We can't let them win," she whispered.

"They won't. Let Lucy look at your ankle. I'll handle Munster and the gang." He led her back to the sofa.

"I'll take care of her. Go!" Lucy pushed away his hands.

He relinquished his position by Margaret's side, though he didn't want to. But he knew Caleb and Willy needed his help. He crawled on his belly to a window and broke it with the butt of his gun. Poking his rifle through the hole, he began to fire.

All around them the bullets flew as the gang moved closer. Josiah, Caleb, and Willy were hopelessly outnumbered, and

Josiah began to pray for God to intervene. He couldn't bear the thought of Margaret back in Golda's clutches. Golda was out there somewhere; he was sure of that.

As he mindlessly fired, then reloaded and fired again, he gradually became aware that the air had taken on an even more oppressive feel. The sky was a strange greenish tint. Then a rumble rattled through the parlor. His ears popped, and he saw debris begin to fly.

"It's a twister!" Willy screamed.

Even as his brother shouted, Josiah saw the tail of the storm begin to descend almost directly over the barn. Other tails began to spin and dance away from the main one, then converged and split again. Sharp bits of sand bit into his face as the tornado sucked the air from the house. Windows blew out, and he heard men outside begin to shout and curse.

The storm whirled around them, and the main tail began to approach the house. "Get to the cellar!" Caleb screamed. "Lucy, get the baby and I'll get Eileen. Josiah, grab little William."

Josiah turned and struggled through air that had suddenly turned as heavy as molasses. He fought to get to Margaret and William. If he were going to die, Josiah wanted to be looking into Margaret's face.

Then the storm bore down on them in all its fury.

twelve

Margaret had feared tornadoes all her life. All too often she had seen the black demon drop from the sky to ravage a home, a town, a friend. Now a twisting snake full of fury with the sting of death in its tail was right on top of her. She lurched to her feet as the debris began to fly. Strangely, she found her terror fading as she concentrated on making sure everyone she loved was safe.

Josiah grabbed her hand, and she barely felt the pain of her twisted ankle—though in the back of her mind she knew she would pay later—as they hurried toward the kitchen as fast as her swollen ankle would allow. Pressure built in her ears as the storm loomed closer.

At the door to the kitchen, Josiah scooped up William without breaking his stride. "I've got William," he called to Caleb as they rushed on.

Caleb hollered for Jed as he escorted Eileen, Lucy, and the baby to safety. Willy put a hand against Margaret's back and urged her to go faster.

"He's in the barn!" Lucy screamed.

Margaret's stomach churned. The tornado was directly over the barn. She could see boards flying across the yard as the twister ravaged the outbuildings. Josiah dropped Margaret's hand. Time seemed to stand still, though she knew it was only seconds that he stared into her eyes.

"I'm going for the boy," he said. "I love you, Margaret." He passed William over to her, then bent and pressed his lips to Margaret's for one brief moment. Then he was gone.

She blinked. *Dear God, keep him safe.* Her throat was so tight she could not have spoken if she'd tried. Eileen's face was white with terror, and Margaret smiled encouragingly as they rushed toward the cellar.

She seemed to run in slow motion. Time had run out. The serpent had found them and was preparing to gobble them up. The roof lifted above her head. Her ears popped. Margaret screamed and dove toward the heavy wooden kitchen table, tucking William's head against her shoulder. She heard Caleb shout; then Eileen, Lucy, and the baby were huddled under the table with them. Willy dove under the table as well.

"Caleb!" Lucy screamed.

Lucy fought to go to her husband, but Margaret grabbed her arm. "No, Lucy, you have to keep the baby safe."

Lucy sobbed and buried her face against the newborn. Clutching William tightly, Margaret strained to see through the swirling dust and debris, but there was no sign of Caleb. And Josiah was out in this as well. Crushing fear for the men bore down on her, and she choked as she fought to keep from wailing with Lucy. The storm would be over soon, and they would find their men. Margaret clung to that hope.

"Please, God," she whispered. In that moment she knew that all the things she'd thought so important didn't matter at all. The ranch, what people thought of her. They were dross that God was using the storm to burn away. Facing eternity, she saw the things that were really important—trust in God and a love that loved her even when she was unlovable. There were two who had that love for her. God and Josiah.

"Save us all, Lord," she prayed. "Bring Josiah, Caleb, and Jed through this safely. Put Your hands of protection around them. You're stronger than any storm."

"Oh, yes, please help them, Lord," Lucy echoed. Her sobs could barely be heard above the screaming of the wind.

The storm seemed endless, a maelstrom that time didn't touch. Crouching beneath the table with her heart beating in her ears and the shriek of the wind raging through the house, Margaret prayed with an intensity she'd never felt. And in that fury, she gradually became aware that God was with them. It was as though He held them in a safe little bubble, a world the tornado couldn't touch.

She glanced over at Lucy's wide eyes.

"You feel it, too," Lucy whispered.

Margaret nodded. Awe kept her tongue-tied.

Then as suddenly as the storm had started, it was over. The wind faltered, then died. The swirling sand came to rest again on the earth. The bubble around them burst, and the world felt familiar again. The rain started then. With the roof gone, there was no escape from the cold, stinging chill as the last of the wind blew the rain under the table onto them.

Eileen gave a hitching sob. "Is it gone?" she asked piteously.

Margaret pulled her onto her lap with William, then rocked both children a bit. "Yes, Sweetheart, it's all over," she told the little girl. Margaret crawled from beneath the table to find that it was the only thing left in the kitchen.

Her feet rested on a bare wooden floor. The dry sink was gone, as were the chairs, the ice chest, the canned goods, and all the utensils. The storm had picked up everything. Everything but the table and the people. A miracle straight from God's hand.

Lucy stood next to her and shook out bits of debris from the baby blanket. Miraculously, the baby wasn't crying. She had her thumb corked in her mouth and stared with blue-eyed wonder at her mother. Her tiny face grimaced as the cold rain hit it.

Margaret set William on the floor, but the little boy clung to her skirts with tight fists. "I want Jed," he wailed. "And where's Papa?"

Margaret patted him on the head. "I'll go find them," she promised. "You keep him with you," she told Lucy. She didn't want the little boy to come until she knew what had happened to the men. Caleb had been in the kitchen just minutes ago. She limped to the parlor. The rain pelted down and left the floor slick. It ran in rivulets down her face and soaked her clothing.

The parlor was empty except for a heap of debris against the one remaining wall. Then part of the debris moved, and she heard a groan. A hand reached out from the flotsam, and Caleb's face appeared. He was covered in mud, but he was alive.

"Lucy, it's Caleb!" She ran toward him, but Lucy reached her husband first. She thrust the baby into Margaret's arms, then knelt beside her husband. Tossing the debris to one side, she finished uncovering him. A huge bruise covered half his forehead, and there was a lump on his head.

Lucy gave a cry and she fell onto his chest. "Oh, Caleb, you're alive!" As she sobbed, Caleb's arms circled her, and he patted her back.

"Don't take on so, Luce. We'll rebuild everything."

"I'm just so happy you're all right!"

"I don't know about all right, but I'm alive." He grinned and tried to sit up. Grimacing, he put a hand to his chest. "Feels like I might have a busted rib or two. Where're Jed and Josiah?"

"I was just going to look for them," Margaret said. She handed the baby back to her mother.

"I'll go with you." Caleb started to get up, then fell back with a groan. "Give me a minute."

"You stay here. The danger is past. Willy will come with me." Her mouth dry with dread, Margaret limped to the edge of what used to be the house and stepped down into the yard. "You check out the side yard," she told Willy. He nodded, and she saw the fear and misery in his face. He moved to the side yard, and she limped toward the barn.

The rain tapered off to a light mist, and she was thankful for that. Light-headed from all she'd been through, she staggered, then clutched the nearby well pump for support. Spots danced in her vision, but she blinked fiercely. She had to find Josiah.

Her vision cleared, and she started toward the barn. Puddles had formed, and she stepped around them as she hobbled along. The tornado had torn away chunks of the yard. Where there had once been roses and lilac bushes, there were now gaping, muddy holes. The winds had scoured the bark from the giant oak tree that had stood in the yard. Most of its branches were ripped away as well. With dread, Margaret turned her attention toward what was left of the barn.

It had no roof, and two of the sides were gone. The door hung haphazardly to one side, attached only by one hinge. Her heart in her mouth, Margaret approached the barn. "Josiah? Jed?" she called.

Only the creak of the door answered her. Hope was beginning to fade. There was no guarantee Josiah had even made it to the barn. He might have been exposed to the full fury of the tornado. She blinked back the tears that had begun to burn her eyes. No, she wouldn't believe that. Still calling his name, she entered the barn.

Like the house, most of the insides had been lifted away. Only a few stray wisps of straw lay scattered over the floor. Several pieces of straw in the barn door had been embedded in the wood by the force of the wind.

The floor creaked, and she whirled. "Josiah?" The words died in her mouth.

"You're just who we've been looking for." Ben Munster grabbed her arm.

Before Margaret could react, she heard a screech. She jerked her head toward the sound and flinched back at the sight of Golda Munster. Her immaculate blond hair now in wet strings around her face, she rushed toward Margaret with her hands curved into claws. "I'll kill you!" she screamed. "This is all your fault."

Ben stepped into her path, and with a casual backhand motion, he felled his sister with one blow. "There's time for killing her later. If we hurry, we can still get that money before it is sent on." He grabbed Margaret again as she turned to flee.

His calloused fingers bit into the tender flesh of her forearm, and she winced. Margaret jerked her arm out of his grasp, then backed away from him. "I'm not going anywhere with you."

"Yes, you are," Golda said, slowly getting up. Her mouth twisted in a sneer. "Unless you want a world of hurt to come down on your friends. And with a new baby, that wouldn't be nice at all." She pointed toward the house. "Ben has a gun trained on that pretty blond lady right now. You come along without a fight and no one will be hurt."

The spunk went out of Margaret. With the walls of the house gone, the Stantons had no protection, and Caleb was too hurt to defend them. But she wasn't going anywhere until she knew what had happened to Josiah. "Where's Josiah?" she demanded. "Do you have him, too?"

"He's dead." Golda smiled as she said the words.

Margaret closed her eyes against the cruel satisfaction she saw in the other woman's eyes. "You don't know that," she whispered.

Golda's smile deepened as she held out a bloody shirt. "Recognize this?"

Margaret recognized it all right. It was the shirt Josiah had been wearing. Blood soaked it with crimson betrayal. No one could bleed that much and live. Her knees went weak, and she would have fallen except for Golda's cruel grip on her arm.

"None of that," Golda said. She propelled Margaret toward the back of the barn. Several of the gang waited with a buggy outside the barn. Margaret moved through a fog of pain. She wanted to cry and scream a denial to the wind, but all she could do was numbly obey. Josiah couldn't be dead. She clung to hope, but it was fading like the morning mist.

Riding to town through the mud-soaked track, she was barely aware of the throb in her ankle. The pain in her heart far overshadowed it. They stopped just outside Henrietta. Golda rooted around inside her valise. Drawing out a comb, she handed it to Margaret.

"Here, make yourself presentable. There's not much we can do about your attire. You're far too large for any of my clothing." Golda's gaze raked Margaret's figure, and she gave a disdainful sniff.

Even Golda's contempt failed to hurt any longer. Margaret had left that baggage far behind while the tornado shrieked its fury. Nothing could penetrate the misery that choked all other emotions from Margaret's heart. What did it matter if her father lost his money, if he even lost the ranch because of it? It didn't matter that the sky would be blue again or that the birds would sing. The world was a darker place without Josiah. He made her laugh, and he made her believe in herself.

Why, Lord? The question kept pounding itself over and over in her brain. Why would God take Josiah? He had so much to give to those who met him. A sparkling sense of humor, caring and compassion, a real faith that showed itself in everything he said and did. All these traits made Josiah a special person, one whom God could use mightily. It made no sense to take him now.

She slowly loosened her braid and ran her fingers through her tangled hair. Working the comb down the tangles lock by lock, she combed it until it was smooth, then neatly braided it again. They'd stopped beside a stream, so she splashed water on her face and arms to remove the worst of the dirt.

"That's good enough. The bank will be closing in fifteen minutes," Ben said. He pulled her roughly to her feet and pushed her toward her horse. "You and Golda are going to go into the bank. You get the tellers and the manager locked up; then open the back door for the rest of us. Don't try anything. Golda won't hesitate to shoot you."

Margaret knew Golda would relish it. In fact it would be a miracle if Margaret even survived the next few minutes. Golda would look for any excuse to harm her. She hadn't taken kindly to Margaret's escape from her snare.

She mounted again and followed Golda to the bank. They stopped in front, and Margaret looked around. Strange that there weren't more people out. Maybe the storm had driven them inside. Rain had left the debris-littered streets a muddy quagmire.

Golda got out of the buggy. "Remember what Ben said," she warned. "Don't give me an excuse to shoot you."

"I didn't think you needed an excuse," Margaret said.

"I don't. So don't try my patience." Golda shoved her in the small of the back. "Smile and act like nothing is wrong. If we get enough money, maybe I'll let you live."

Margaret knew better than to believe her. Death was in every line of Golda's face. Margaret approached the bank door with a sense of dread beginning to penetrate her grief.

She tried to smile, but her lips trembled and tears felt close. How could she smile when her heart was breaking? Right now she felt like she would never smile again.

She pushed open the door and limped inside.

Orville Meyer pushed his spectacles up on his nose. His thinning hair lay in a carefully contrived placement, and his mouth dropped open. "Miss Margaret, the whole county is looking for you!"

Margaret had always liked Orville. He had a caring way about him, and she wished she could tell him to run. She nodded to him. "Good afternoon, Mr. Meyer. I've come to withdraw some funds for my pa."

He frowned. "What are you talking about, Miss Margaret? Where you been? Your pa's worried half to death."

"This is getting us nowhere." Golda drew the gun from her valise. "I want all of you to back up slowly. Mr. Meyer, you open the safe."

"The safe?" Orville blinked slowly and shook his head. "Not again!"

"You heard me, Mister." Golda motioned with the gun, and the tellers backed away. "Margaret, open the back door."

"You're in this with her? My, my," Orville said with a worried frown.

"It was her idea," Golda sneered.

Margaret wanted to tell him the truth, but she knew Golda would shoot her if she opened her mouth. She had to find a way to stop her.

"Quit dawdling and go open the door!" Golda shouted at Margaret. "And while she's gone, you get that safe open."

"My, my." Orville hurried to the safe and knelt in front of

it. He licked his fingers and applied them to the tumblers.

Margaret limped toward the back room. She would be out of Golda's sight when she stepped into the back room, but the other woman would come looking for her if she didn't hear the back door open immediately. Her gaze darted around the room as she stepped inside. What could she use for a weapon? And she had to make sure no one else got hurt.

The back room held empty cash sacks, coin rolls, and other small items. Nothing that was any defense against the gun in Golda's hand.

"What's taking so long?" Golda shouted. "Don't make me come back there!"

What if she waited until Golda came to check on her? She could hide behind the door and jump her when she stepped into the room. It was a lame plan, but it was the only one Margaret had. Then she spied a large feed sack. Maybe she could pull that over Golda's head when she came through the door.

Margaret snatched it up, then slid behind the door. She watched through the crack in the doorway.

Golda shouted at her again as she backed slowly toward the back room. "I'm warning you, Margaret. Get that door open and get back in here now!" She kept the gun trained on the bank employees. She got to the back room door and braced her back against the door that Margaret hid behind. Her gaze darted between the men in the bank and the dingy back room.

"You can't hide from me," she snarled. She took another step into the room and finally she was clear of the door.

With a silent prayer for help, Margaret lunged out from behind the door and brought the feed sack down over Golda's head.

The other woman screeched and clawed at the rough burlap that covered her face. The hand holding the gun waved wildly in the air, and she tried to crack Margaret over the head with it before Margaret wrestled the gun away. Although Margaret was bigger and stronger, Golda fought like a caged cougar, and it was all Margaret could do to subdue her.

Orville ran to help her. Grabbing a rope from the back room wall, he quickly trussed up Golda, then snatched the sack off of her head. "Great work, Miss Margaret," he panted. "I knew you wouldn't have any part of stealing from your pa."

Now that it was over, Margaret was unutterably weary. The strength ran out of her legs, and she sagged against the door. All she wanted to do was find a quiet spot to grieve and remember Josiah.

Golda spat in her face. "You're dead," she snarled. "When my brother catches up to you, you'll wish you'd never been born."

"He can't hurt me more than I already hurt," Margaret said.

The other woman smiled. "Too bad Josiah didn't suffer more. He was already pretty far gone by the time we found him. His last words were of you. Does that make you feel better?"

Margaret clenched her fists so tightly that her nails bit into the palms of her hands. The pain was more than she could bear. He died not knowing she loved him. She wished she could live the last twenty-four hours again. In fact, she wished she could live the last few weeks again. But that wasn't possible. She would have to live with the regrets the rest of her life.

She swallowed hard and squared her shoulders. She was Paddy O'Brien's daughter, and she'd been raised to take whatever life dished out. The fact that it had turned out badly was not unusual. She'd grown to expect it all her life.

"I have a plan," she told Orville. Now it was time to show those men they'd picked the wrong woman to mess with. She would finish the job Josiah had come here to do.

thirteen

Golda drummed her fingers angrily against the top of a desk in the bank manager's office. "Ben is too smart to fall for your little tricks," she said.

Margaret saw through her bravado. Golda's face was a sickly color beneath the plenteous rouge she wore, and her blue eyes were haunted. Margaret found it in her heart to pity the woman. Maybe Golda had never known any other way of life, but in prison she would realize the things she'd done had consequences.

Margaret looked at Golda. She seemed to have everything it would take to be a success in the world. Beauty, brains, guts. But she'd used it all for the wrong purposes. As she stared at Golda, Margaret realized that it wasn't looks or any other physical attribute that mattered. God had given her His love, and she'd despised it by longing for more. Right then and there she resolved to thank God every day for what He *had* given her instead of focusing on what she thought were shortcomings.

She took a deep breath. How free she felt to know that God saw her as special. She would strive to always remember and thank Him for the way He'd made her. First the baggage of caring too much for her worldly possessions had dropped away, and now the sense of blaming God for how He had created her was gone, too. She would go on from here, grieving over Josiah but rejoicing in the fact that God was with her. And she would see Josiah again. He couldn't come to her, but she could go to him someday. She would never stop loving him, not for a moment.

She tied Golda's hands behind her back, then left her with one of the tellers. Taking Golda's gun, Margaret went to the back room and tiptoed toward the door. She pressed her ear against the door and tried to determine whether Ben and the rest of the gang had run or if they just thought things were taking longer than expected.

At first there was only silence; then she heard low voices and some shuffling movements. Good. They still lingered by the door. But not for long. She had to move quickly.

She motioned to Orville. "Can you open the vault and transfer the money somewhere else?" She seized a fistful of money bags from the desk. "I'll stuff these, and you can put them in the safe in place of the real money." Looking around, she spied a pile of newspapers by the door. "We can use newspaper," she said.

Orville began to grin. "That just might work. We've got a temporary safe in my office where I can lock the money." He hurried from the room.

Margaret began to stuff the bags with newspaper. There was a slight tap on the back door.

"Golda, you in there?" The whispered hiss belonged to Ben.

Margaret jumped, and her heart galloped in her chest. They would have to make their move soon, or Ben would get suspicious and escape. She couldn't allow that. He had to pay for Josiah's death. She swallowed and turned her thoughts from Josiah. Grief would only distract her from her mission.

A few minutes later, she had the bags stuffed. Carrying them quickly to the vault, she helped Orville load them inside the small room. She felt claustrophobic in the windowless vault and breathed a sigh of relief when she finally escaped to the sunshine-filled main room.

"I think we're ready," she said. "Is the sheriff around?"

Orville nodded. "I saw him and his men take up their positions in the hotel across the street. I think there were Texas Rangers with him."

She nearly gasped at the pain of his words. Reinforcements were here but too late for Josiah. The sting of tears nearly broke her concentration, but she fiercely willed herself to go on, to finish Josiah's job.

"I'll let Ben inside now." Her palms were sweaty, and she felt light-headed. Ben would kill her if he got wind of the trap. He wouldn't go peacefully to jail. She took a deep breath and walked to the back room. Was he gone? She and Golda had been inside twenty minutes, far longer than Ben had anticipated.

She rushed to the door and fumbled with the lock. Throwing open the door, she peeked out. There was no one around. Her heart in her mouth, she stepped outside. "Ben?" she whispered.

He stepped from the shadows and grabbed her arm. "You pullin' a double cross?"

She gasped and jerked away. "The safe is open. Golda had a little change of plan. She couldn't wait to see how much was there. You'd better hurry. She took a bunch of sacks out through the front. I think she got more than her share."

Ben scowled. "She wouldn't dare." He drew his gun and rushed inside. The rest of the gang followed him.

Praying it would work, Margaret followed him.

Ben ran through the storeroom and into the vault room. He saw the open vault and rushed inside. The other men crowded in behind him, and they all snatched up money bags.

"She's robbed us!" Ben shouted. "There should be more than this."

He started toward the vault exit, but Orville stepped from behind his hiding place and slammed the vault door shut.

Margaret sagged against the counter. Giddy with relief, she closed her eyes. Not a shot fired, and the thieves were all safely locked up.

The front door burst open, and six men rushed into the room. The Rangers were here. Then Margaret's eyes widened, and she gasped at a tall figure limping through the door behind the others. Josiah? She closed her eyes, then opened them again. Her mouth went dry, and her heart thumped painfully in her chest with the almost overwhelming hope. "Josiah," she whispered. Tears blurred her vision as she thanked God for the miracle she saw before her.

Josiah stared around the room. "Where is he?" he growled.

A tide of warmth rushed over Margaret. She could see the love he had for her in his tightly clenched fists and the fierce tone in his voice. Josiah would never let anyone hurt her as long as he lived. The knowledge made her feel cherished in a way she'd never known. She wanted to rush to him, but there were too many other men in the way. This love she bore for him was too new and precious to be displayed in front of others.

The sheriff came through the door of the bank with his pistol drawn. He skidded to a halt and looked around. "Where are the bandits?"

Margaret gestured to the bank vault. "Waiting to be taken into custody," she said.

"We'll take charge of them," a man said.

Margaret recognized the voice as the man Josiah had talked with several times. The other ranger, Richard.

Margaret remained frozen in place as Josiah explained who he was and what he was doing in the area. She longed to run to him and throw her arms around him, but shyness held her in place. Now that she knew how she really felt about him, she found herself looking at him with new eyes.

His face was a bit pale, and his shoulder was bleeding, but he was alive. Alive! Joy bubbled in Margaret's heart like a freshwater spring. It was all she could do to stay where she was.

"You've done good work here, Son," the sheriff said. "But it looks like you could use Doc's services. Margaret, you'd better help your young man down the street before he falls over."

Only then did Margaret's stiff muscles obey. She moved to Josiah's side and slipped her hand around his arm. "It's this way," she whispered.

⁂

Josiah fought the disappointment that raged inside. He'd hoped that Margaret would show some sign that she'd worried about him, that she cared. She had just looked at him with wide green eyes and practically ignored him.

He knew she loved him, so why did speaking the words seem so hard for her? Hearing the words was important to him. How did he break through that wall she had around her? It seemed an impossible task. If the events of the last few days hadn't done it, he didn't know what would. Maybe nothing.

Margaret limped beside him with her cold fingers on his arm. He wasn't sure if she was helping him or if he was helping her. They were both pretty war torn and road weary. At least they were both going to live.

They walked around the corner of the bank and headed down the main street. Margaret stumbled, and he slipped an arm around her waist. She stopped and stared up at him. Were those tears in her eyes?

"I thought you were dead," she whispered. "And Jed—is he all right?"

"He's fine. I was searching for you and found him under a wheelbarrow in the barn. Scared and a little scratched up but all right." Josiah examined her face. There was something going on in that beautiful head, but he couldn't quite decipher the expression in her eyes.

"What happened to you? Golda told me you were dead. She showed me a bloodstained shirt."

"The wind blew me through the air, and I landed by the end of the porch. I crawled under it before the tornado could carry me off completely. A branch stabbed me in the shoulder, and I bled like a dead rooster. I reckon I passed out. When I came to, the storm was over and Caleb was hollering for me and Jed. I crawled out from under the porch and tossed the shirt in the weeds. I found one of

Caleb's in a tree and borrowed it. Then I went looking for you. When I couldn't find you, I figured Ben had to have taken you."

"Thank God," she said. "I–I thought you'd died without. . ." She stopped and buried her face in her hands.

Sobs shook her, and the sound of her crying broke his heart. He pulled her into his arms. Her arms came up and wrapped around his neck in a tight grip that was almost painful. "What's wrong? I'm fine. A little beat up, but it would take more than a tornado to make me leave you."

She only wailed more and burrowed harder against his chest. "Hey, this shirt may not take any more watering," he said gently. "Don't take on so."

"I thought you died without knowing I loved you," came the muffled reply against his chest.

A budding joy exploded in his chest. She'd finally said the words. He gripped her shoulders and pulled her back from his chest so he could look in her face. Though her eyes were red and swollen from her weeping, he'd never seen a more beautiful sight than Margaret's face shining with love.

"You love me," he whispered. "It's about time you admitted it. I knew the truth weeks ago. It was sure hard waiting for you to realize it."

Her lips trembled. "Don't ever leave me," she said. She reached up and touched his face.

"A mad bull couldn't drag me away," he said. "No more objections to marrying me?"

She shook her head so violently that her braid whipped around and smacked him in the face. "Pa isn't going to like it, though."

"I'll explain it to him," Josiah said. He still couldn't believe his luck. No, it wasn't luck. This love was God's gracious gift, and Josiah would thank Him for it the rest of his life.

He bent and kissed her. She kissed him back, and for the first time, Josiah could feel her whole heart in that kiss. "Let's go talk to your pa," he whispered when he could breathe again.

"What about your wounds?" she asked with a worried frown.

"What wounds? Your kiss cured me." He grinned at her, and she blushed.

"Pa is going to be mad," she muttered.

"Let's get it over with," he told her. He went to hire a horse and buggy while she rested her ankle on a boardwalk bench. Though he felt as though he were walking on a cloud, he couldn't help a niggling sense of worry. What if her pa's disapproval made her question her decision? The disappointment now would be more than Josiah could bear.

He drove the buggy to where she waited, then helped her up onto the seat. Feeling almost proprietary as he rode out of town with Margaret beside him, he was determined not to let anyone stand in their way now. They belonged together. Surely her pa would be able to see that.

As they started out of town, they passed the church. Josiah looked down at Margaret. "Maybe we should ask the preacher to help us talk to your pa," he suggested.

Relief lit her face. "Pa really respects Pastor Williams. Maybe that would help."

Josiah nodded and stopped the buggy. He went inside

the church, and the pastor agreed to join them at the ranch as soon as he could get away. Josiah went back outside and climbed up beside Margaret. At least they had reinforcements.

As they rode up to the Triple T, the house seemed almost deserted. Dusk had settled over the ranch, and a group of cowboys were singing softly around the campfire. Josiah stopped the buggy and climbed down. He lifted Margaret to the ground, and they both started for the house. The front door was flung open, and her father stood in the doorway. He swayed as though drunk, though Josiah knew the man was a teetotaler.

Paddy O'Brien's bleary eyes surveyed them. "Margaret?" He took a handkerchief out of his pocket and rubbed at his red eyes. "I thought cougars had gotten you." His gaze fastened on Josiah. "You been with him the whole time?" His tone became accusing. "You come slinking back here after running off with a man? Your mama would roll over in her grave."

"Pa, Josiah saved your money at the bank. We were kidnapped by robbers." Margaret's words were fast and clipped as though she knew she didn't have long to spill the whole story. She talked for what seemed like hours but could have only been minutes. A lot had happened in the three days they'd been gone.

Paddy blinked, and his heavy brows came together in a frown. "How would a ranch foreman stop a bunch of bank robbers?"

He might as well get it out in the open. "I'm not a real cowboy, Paddy. I'm a Texas Ranger."

Paddy's owlish stare narrowed, and his mouth thinned. "A ranger," he spat. "I should have known!" He leaned back inside the doorway of the house and grabbed a rifle. "You git, Mr. Ranger. There's no Texas Ranger welcome on my property."

"I'm resigning as a ranger, effective tomorrow," Josiah said. He couldn't believe the change in Paddy. Margaret was right—her father was irrational about the subject of Texas Rangers.

"You'll still stink of them," Paddy said. He aimed the gun at Josiah's stomach.

Margaret stepped in front of him. "I'm going to marry Josiah, Pa," she said.

Her pa's eyes widened. "Never!" he spat. "You'll not see one acre of ground if you marry him."

"I love him, Pa," Margaret said. "I discovered something important these past few days. My security is in God, not this ranch. And He loves me—the gangly, red-haired me— just as I am."

Her declaration brought a lump to Josiah's throat. "We'd like to have your blessing, Paddy," Josiah said. "I know you want Margaret to be happy."

Paddy gasped, and his face reddened. "Don't do this to us," he said in a low voice to Josiah. "I want Margaret to marry another rancher."

"Who?" Josiah said. "I'll love her for the rest of my life, Paddy. We'll give you those grandchildren to dandle on your knee. Strong kids like you and Margaret."

Paddy's gaze wavered, then fell before Josiah's. "A ranger," he muttered. "You don't know what you're asking."

"I'm asking you to think of your daughter and put your prejudices aside. Isn't her happiness all that matters?"

Paddy's eyes watered. "I want her to be happy," he muttered. "But what about the ranch?"

"You haven't had any complaints about my foreman ability so far, have you?" Josiah felt a glimmer of hope. He knew Margaret couldn't enjoy a wedding without her pa's blessing.

Paddy shook his head.

"Be happy for me, Pa," Margaret said. Her voice was choked with emotion.

Paddy waved his hands in the air. "I give up," he said. "Marry him, but don't come crying to me when he shows his true colors."

Margaret threw her arms around her father's neck. "I know his true colors, Pa. He's pure white and true blue, my knight in shining armor."

Paddy patted her awkwardly. "I knew I never should have let you read all those books," he grumbled. "Knights and damsels in distress were all you talked about when you were thirteen. You're a grown woman now, Margaret. It's time you put foolish dreams behind you."

"I have, Pa," Margaret said, gazing into Josiah's eyes. "I can see the difference between pure gold and the dross that burns away." She pulled away from her father and went to Josiah.

Nearly busting with joy and love, Josiah put his arm around her. "I hope you don't make me wait too long," he said.

Margaret looked over his shoulder. "Here come the

Stantons with Willy and Pastor Williams. Would this evening be soon enough? We've got a preacher and witnesses."

Josiah froze. "Do you mean it?" Hope choking his throat, he stared into her eyes and saw the answer shining there.

≈

Things moved so quickly, Margaret felt as though she couldn't catch her breath. Lucy heard the news, and the two women rushed into the house to prepare for the wedding. Maria took them to the attic to look for something suitable to wear.

"Your *madre* wore this to marry your *papá*." Maria reverently lifted a white dress, softly yellowed with age, from the trunk under the eaves. "She would be proud to have you wear it."

Margaret ran her fingers over the soft fabric. "It seems like a dream somehow," she said. If it were a dream, she didn't ever want to waken from it.

Maria carried the dress downstairs and pressed it while Margaret bathed and washed her hair. It felt good to be clean again.

When her hair was dry, Margaret held up her arms as Maria slipped the dress over Margaret's head and fastened the tiny pearl buttons down the back.

"As I said, it fits perfectly." Maria sighed.

"Leave your hair down," Lucy said when Margaret started to braid it again. Lucy combed it, then pulled the top back in a ribbon. "You look beautiful."

And somehow Margaret *felt* beautiful for the first time in her life. God had made her for Josiah, and they were a perfect match. She stood with her head held high and walked to the door.

Josiah met her outside the door. His jaw dropped. "How lovely you are," he whispered. He held both her hands in his and gazed into her eyes.

The strains of "Red River Valley" drifted through the night as the ranch hands sang. "Come and sit by my side if you love me. Do not hasten to bid me adieu. Just remember the Red River Valley, and the girl who has loved you so true." The words of the song echoed on the wind.

"That song seems somehow appropriate, doesn't it?" Josiah asked softly. "I never thought to find a woman like you, Margaret. We'll build this ranch into an empire we can give to our children. But even more important, we'll pass on the most important things. Faith in God, hope for the future, and unconditional love." He turned and led her toward the door and the waiting friends and family. "Come and sit by my side if you love me," he sang under his breath.

"Just remember the Red River Valley," she sang back to him. "And the girl who has loved you so true." With her hand clasped tightly in Josiah's, Margaret knew she had found a love that time would never fade.

A Letter To Our Readers

Dear Reader:

In order that we might better contribute to your reading enjoyment, we would appreciate your taking a few minutes to respond to the following questions. We welcome your comments and read each form and letter we receive. When completed, please return to the following:

Fiction Editor
Heartsong Presents
PO Box 719
Uhrichsville, Ohio 44683

1. Did you enjoy reading *Red River Bride* by Colleen Coble?
   ❏ Very much! I would like to see more books by this author!
   ❏ Moderately. I would have enjoyed it more if

   _____

   _____

   _____

2. Are you a member of **Heartsong Presents**? ❏ Yes ❏ No
   If no, where did you purchase this book? _____

   _____

3. How would you rate, on a scale from 1 (poor) to 5 (superior), the cover design? _____

4. On a scale from 1 (poor) to 10 (superior), please rate the following elements.

   _____ Heroine   _____ Plot
   _____ Hero   _____ Inspirational theme
   _____ Setting   _____ Secondary characters

6. How has this book inspired your life?_____
_____
_____

7. What settings would you like to see covered in future
   Heartsong Presents books? _____
   _____
   _____

8. What are some inspirational themes you would like to see
   treated in future books? _____
   _____
   _____

9. Would you be interested in reading other **Heartsong
   Presents** titles? ❏ Yes ❏ No

10. Please check your age range:
    ❏ Under 18   ❏ 18-24
    ❏ 25-34   ❏ 35-45
    ❏ 46-55   ❏ Over 55

Name _____
Occupation _____
Address _____
City_____ State_____ Zip_____
E-mail _____

Ohio

The first decade of the nineteenth century is full of promise and adventure for the infant state of Ohio. But for the three Carson sisters, it is filled with trepidation as they struggle with the loss of their parents in the battle for statehood.

What will be Kate, Annabelle, and Claire's legacy of faith and love for following generations?

Historical, paperback, 512 pages, 5 ³/₁₆" x 8"

Heart♥ong

Any 12
Heartsong
Presents titles
for only
$30.00*

HISTORICAL ROMANCE IS CHEAPER BY THE DOZEN!

Buy any assortment of twelve *Heartsong Presents* titles and save 25% off of the already discounted price of $3.25 each!

*plus $2.00 shipping and handling per order and sales tax where applicable.

HEARTSONG PRESENTS TITLES AVAILABLE NOW:

(If ordering from this page, please remember to include it with the order form.)

MONEY TA

MONEY TALKS

■■■

CORPORATE PACS AND POLITICAL INFLUENCE

■■■

Dan Clawson
Alan Neustadtl
Denise Scott

BasicBooks
A Division of HarperCollinsPublishers

Designed by Joan Greenfield

95 96 CC/RRD 9 8 7 6 5 4 3 2

Library of Congress Cataloging-in-Publication Data

Clawson, Dan.
Money talks: corporate PACs and political influence / Dan
Clawson, Alan Neustadtl, Denise Scott.
    p. cm.
Includes bibliographical references and index.
ISBN 0–465–02680–X (cloth)
ISBN 0–465–04752–1 (paper)
1. Business and politics—United States.   2. Corporations—United
States—Political activity.   3. Political action committees—United
States.   4. Campaign funds—United States.   I. Neustadtl, Alan,
1957– .   II. Scott, Denise, 1955– .   III. Title.
JF467.C53   1992
322′.03′0973—dc20   91-59019
                                                            CIP

To Laura Clawson

CONTENTS

•••

***

▪ 1 ▪

MONEY CHANGES EVERYTHING

▪ 2 ▪

RAISING MONEY AND RUNNING THE PAC

■ 3 ■

GIFTS: NETWORKS OF OBLIGATION

■ 4 ■

ACCESS: "I CAN GET TO WAXMAN FOR $250"

■ 5 ■

IDEOLOGY: DEFENDING FREE ENTERPRISE

LIST OF FIGURES AND TABLES

■■■

FIGURES

TABLES

ACKNOWLEDGMENTS

■■■

The corporate executives quoted in this book generously shared with us their time, wit, and insights. We appreciate their willingness to talk honestly. We don't acknowledge these executives by name only because we promised them confidentiality. They were charming, shrewd, and perceptive about politics, but they are key participants in a system we strongly oppose. We regret that they probably won't be happy with what we have to say, even when—perhaps especially when—we use their own words to make our case.

The study of campaign finance has dominated our professional lives for a decade, and in that time we have incurred many debts. We confine these acknowledgments to those most directly involved with this book.

When we first decided to interview corporate executives, Mike Useem, then at Boston University and now at the University of Pennsylvania, took us in hand and gave us step-by-step instructions on techniques and possible pitfalls. When the book manuscript was complete, he gently persuaded us that parts of our draft needed major revisions.

Bill Domhoff of the University of California at Santa Cruz is committed to producing clear, engaging work that both makes a scholarly contribution and can be read with enjoyment by nonspecialists. Bill's work is a model for us; his enthusiasm, support, and ideas have assisted and inspired us.

Of the many people who read the manuscript, three provided especially insightful comments and contributions. Ray Jones, a doctoral student at the University of Massachusetts at Amherst and a

ACKNOWLEDGMENTS

prisoner incarcerated at the Massachusetts Correctional Institution at Lancaster, sharpened our theoretical analysis, challenged our preconceptions, and did more than any other individual to help us think analytically about our writing. For years we have traded ideas and shared work with Mark Mizruchi, now at the University of Michigan, and once again his reactions and suggestions were crucial. Extensive and penetrating comments by Jerry Himmelstein of Amherst College shaped the character of our chapter on ideology.

Many others gave us their time, energy, and insights by reading part or all of our work, identifying its strengths and weaknesses, and often suggesting solutions. We acknowledge their gift and hope to repay the obligation: Mary Ann Clawson, Patrick Clawson, Ken Dolbeare, Ken Fones-Wolf, Naomi Gerstel, Ed Herman, David Jaffee, Stephen McMahon, Sandi Morgen, Bill Newman, John O'Connor, Joe Peschek, Harland Prechel, John Schall, Michael Schwartz, Glenn Scott, students in Dan Clawson's political sociology seminar, Tie-ting Su, and Robert Zussman.

The labor and support of others made this project possible. Karen Mason and Thora Dumont of the Social and Demographic Research Institute at the University of Massachusetts did a terrific job transcribing the interviews. Three grants from the National Science Foundation made this research possible: Grants SES-8512021 and SES-8721982 were to Dan and Alan; grant SES-9001440 was to Denise for her dissertation. A Kellogg National Fellowship (for Dan) got the project started.

Generous support also was provided by the University of Maryland. The Graduate Research Board and College Designated Research Initiative Fund (headed by Dean Murray E. Polakoff) both provided substantial financial assistance. William Falk, chair of the sociology department, provided release time from teaching responsibilities for Alan. Finally, the computer science center at Maryland provided resources for the quantitative portions of this book. None of the organizations that provided support is responsible for, or endorses, the views we express here.

University of Massachusetts library personnel guided and assisted us in tracking down key facts and references. We especially want to thank reference librarians Jill Ausel, Marjorie Karlson, Paula Mark, Barbara Morgan, Jeffrey Tenenbaum, and Ann Wood; government documents librarians Leonard Adams and William Thompson; and Stephen Shraison in microforms.

A number of people were critical to the publication process itself.

Fred Fierst and the National Writers Union helped us understand book contracts. Sam Bowles introduced us to Basic Books, where at key junctures Martin Kessler's interventions guided us and made this a better book. Akiko Takano and Michael Mueller helped turn a manuscript into a book. Rosemary Winfield sharpened and clarified our prose; every page bears her imprint.

We wish to extend special thanks to several people:

Dan: In recent years two governors and many legislators have worked to destroy public higher education in Massachusetts, repeatedly slashing the budget of the University of Massachusetts at Amherst. In these difficult times Naomi Gerstel, as friend and colleague, has made life at UMass far pleasanter and more rewarding.

The task of our "new left" generation is at best unfinished. Laura Clawson, to whom I dedicate this book, is part of a new generation. I am proud of Laura always, but never more so than when she fights for justice and equality, for peace and freedom—as increasingly she does. I hope she and her generation will continue the struggle to build a better world.

Mary Ann and Laura Clawson accommodated their schedules to the book's demands while providing emotional, material, and intellectual support. I owe Mary Ann more than I can say for, among other things, contributing to this book, introducing me to half the good books I've read, and always sharing ideas and insights.

Alan: I have many intellectual and emotional debts associated with this book. I wish to thank the large number of people, friends, family, and students, who have tolerated my often large absence from their lives due to work. In this regard, Betty Levine made the largest sacrifice, and I will always appreciate her support. Finally, many in the sociology department have kept me laughing, especially Sharon Morey, Jay Teachman, Bear and Ruby, and Jerry Hage.

Denise: I am grateful to the many graduate students at the University of Massachusetts who shared the ups and downs associated with the book and with graduate student life in general. Special thanks to Jennifer Eichstedt (now at the University of California, Santa Cruz), Patricia Hanrahan, Kathy Johnson, Jeff Kuenzi, and Gretchen Stiers, whose friendships have been important to my intellectual and personal life. Most of all I am indebted to my family; to Cecile, Jeffrey, and Theresa Benoit for their moral and material support; and to Glenn

Scott for his understanding and encouragement, as well as for the countless occasions when he took over the day-to-day chores of living so that I could devote full attention to my academic work. Without their contributions, participation in this project might not have been possible.

Insofar as possible the facts and figures in *Money Talks* are current as of January 1992. Statistics are for 1988, the last presidential election year; as of January 1992 the Federal Election Commission had not released its summary computer tape with information on the 1990 election.

Chapter 1

■■■

MONEY CHANGES
EVERYTHING

■■■

In the past twenty years political action committees, or PACs, have transformed campaign finance. The chair of the PAC at one of the twenty-five largest manufacturing companies in the United States explained to us why his corporation has a PAC:

> The PAC gives you access. It makes you a player. These congressmen, in particular, are constantly fundraising. Their elections are very expensive and getting increasingly expensive each year. So they have an ongoing need for funds.
>
> It profits us in a sense to be able to provide some funds because in the provision of it you get to know people, you help them out. There's no real quid pro quo. There is nobody whose vote you can count on, not with the kind of money we are talking about here. But the PAC gives you access, puts you in the game.
>
> You know, some congressman has got X number of ergs of energy, and here's a person or a company who wants to come see him and give him a thousand dollars, and here's another one who wants to just stop by and say hello. And he only has time to see one. Which one? So the PAC's an attention getter.

Most analyses of campaign finance focus on the candidates who receive the money, not on the people and political action committees that give it. PACs are entities that collect money from many contributors, pool it, and then make donations to candidates. Donors may give to a PAC because they are in basic agreement with its aims, but once they have donated they lose direct control over their money, trusting the PAC to decide which candidates should receive contributions.

Corporate PACs have unusual power that has been largely unexamined. In this book we begin the process of giving corporate PACs, and business-government relations in general, the scrutiny they deserve. By far the most important source for our analysis is a set of in-depth interviews we conducted with corporate executives who direct and control their corporations' political activity. The insight these interviews provide into the way corporate executives think, the goals they pursue, and the methods they use to achieve those goals is far more revealing than most analyses made by outside critics. We think most readers will be troubled, as we are, by the world view and activities of corporate PAC directors. In the final chapter we use the analysis developed in the book to show why many proposed reforms would be ineffective and to outline a proposal that, if it were adopted, would, we believe, be effective.

Why Does the Air Stink?

Everybody wants clean air. Who could oppose it? "I spent seven years of my life trying to stop the Clean Air Act," explained the PAC director for a major corporation that is a heavy-duty polluter. Nonetheless, he was perfectly willing to use his corporation's PAC to contribute to members of Congress* who voted for the act:

> How a person votes on the final piece of legislation often is not representative of what they have done. Somebody will do a lot of things during the process. How many guys voted against the Clean Air Act? But during the process some of them were very sympathetic to some of our concerns.

In the world of Congress and political action committees things are not always what they seem. Members of Congress want to vote for clean air, but they also want to receive campaign contributions from corporate PACs and pass a law that business accepts as "reasonable." The compromise solution to this dilemma is to gut the bill by crafting dozens of loopholes inserted in private meetings or in subcommittee hearings that don't receive much (if any) attention in the press. Then the public vote on the final bill can be nearly unanimous: members of

---

*Both to simplify language and to make it gender neutral, we generally use *members* to refer to members of the U.S. Senate or U.S. House of Representatives. Many corporate officials also use the term *members,* although others refer to *senators* and *congressmen.* In quotations we have preserved the usage employed by the person we have interviewed.

Congress can assure their constituents that they voted for the final bill and their corporate PAC contributors that they helped weaken the bill in private. We can use the Clean Air Act of 1990 to introduce and explain this process.

The public strongly supports clean air and is unimpressed when corporate officials and apologists trot out their normal arguments: "corporations are already doing all they reasonably can to improve environmental quality"; "we need to balance the costs against the benefits"; "people will lose their jobs if we make controls any stricter." The original Clean Air Act was passed in 1970, revised in 1977, and not revised again until 1990. Although the initial goal of its supporters was to have us breathing clean air by 1975, the deadline for compliance has been repeatedly extended—and the 1990 legislation provides a new set of deadlines to be reached sometime far in the future.

Because corporations control the production process unless the government specifically intervenes, any delay in government action leaves corporations free to do as they choose. Not only have laws been slow to come, but corporations have fought to delay or subvert implementation. The 1970 law ordered the Environmental Protection Agency (EPA) to regulate the hundreds of poisonous chemicals that are emitted by corporations, but as William Greider notes, "in twenty years of stalling, dodging, and fighting off court orders, the EPA has managed to issue regulatory standards for a total of seven toxics."[1]

Corporations have done exceptionally well politically, given the problem they face: the interests of business often are diametrically opposed to those of the public. Clean air laws and amendments have been few and far between, enforcement is ineffective, and the penalties for infractions are minimal. On the one hand, corporations have had to pay billions; on the other hand, the costs to date are a small fraction of what would be needed to clean up the environment.

This corporate struggle for the right to pollute takes place on many fronts. One front is public relations: the Chemical Manufacturers Association took out a two-page Earth Day ad in the *Washington Post* to demonstrate its concern for the environment; coincidentally many of the corporate signers are also on the EPA's list of high-risk producers.[2] Another front is research: expert studies delay action while more information is gathered. The federally funded National Acid Precipitation Assessment Program (NAPAP) took ten years and $600 million to figure out whether acid rain was a problem. Both business and the Reagan administration argued that no action should be taken until the study was completed.[3] The study was discredited when its summary of findings minimized the impact of acid rain—even though this did not accurately represent the expert research in the report. But the key site of struggle has been Congress, where for years corporations have succeeded in defeating environmental legislation. In 1987 utility companies were offered a compromise bill on acid rain, but they "were very adamant that they had beat the thing since 1981 and they could always beat it," according to Representative Edward Madigan (R-Ill.).[4] Throughout the 1980s the utilities defeated all efforts at change, but their intransigence probably hurt them when revisions finally were made.

The stage was set for a revision of the Clean Air Act when George Bush was elected as "the environmental president" and George Mitchell, a strong supporter of environmentalism, became the Senate majority leader. But what sort of clean air bill would it be? "What we wanted," said Richard Ayres, head of the environmentalists' Clean Air Coalition, "is a health-based standard—one-in-1-million cancer risk." Such a standard would require corporations to clean up their plants until the cancer risk from their operations was reduced to one in a million. "The Senate bill still has the requirement," Ayres said, "but there are forty pages of extensions and exceptions and qualifications and loopholes that largely render the health standard a nullity."[5] Greider reports, for example, that "according to the EPA, there are now twenty-six coke ovens that pose a cancer risk greater than 1 in 1000 and six where the risk is greater than 1 in 100. Yet the new clean-air bill will give the steel industry another thirty years to deal with the problem."[6]

This change from what the bill was supposed to do to what it did do came about through what corporate executives like to call the "access" process. The main aim of most corporate political action committee contributions is to help corporate executives attain "access" to key members of Congress and their staffs. Corporate executives (and corporate PAC money) work to persuade the member of Congress to accept a carefully predesigned loophole that sounds innocent but effectively undercuts the stated intention of the bill. Representative Dingell (D-Mich.), chair of the House Committee on Energy and Commerce, is a strong industry supporter; one of the people we interviewed called him "the point man for the Business Roundtable on clean air." Representative Waxman (D-Calif.), chair of the Subcommittee on Health and the Environment, is an environmentalist. Observers of the Clean Air Act legislative process expected a confrontation and contested votes on the floor of the Congress.

The problem for corporations was that, as one Republican staff aide said, "If any bill has the blessing of Waxman and the environmental groups, unless it is totally in outer space, who's going to vote against it?"[7] But corporations successfully minimized public votes. Somehow Waxman was persuaded to make behind-the-scenes compromises with Dingell so members didn't have to publicly side with business against the environment during an election year.[8] Often the access process leads to loopholes that protect a single corporation, but for "clean" air most special deals targeted entire industries, not specific companies. The initial bill, for example, required cars to be able to use strictly specified cleaner fuels. But the auto industry wanted the rules loosened, and Congress eventually modified the bill by incorporating a variant of a formula suggested by the head of General Motors' fuels and lubricants department.

Nor did corporations stop fighting after they gutted the bill through amendments. Business pressed the EPA for favorable regulations to implement the law: "The cost of this legislation could vary dramatically, depending on how EPA interprets it," said William D. Fay, vice president of the National Coal Association, who headed the hilariously misnamed Clean Air Working Group, an industry coalition that fought to weaken the legislation.[9] An EPA aide working on acid rain regulations reported, "We're having a hard time getting our work done because of the number of phone calls we're getting" from corporations and their lawyers.

Corporations trying to convince federal regulators to adopt the "right" regulations don't rely exclusively on the cogency of their arguments. They often exert pressure on a member of Congress to intervene for them at the EPA or other agency. Senators and representatives regularly intervene on behalf of constituents and contributors by doing everything from straightening out a social security problem to asking a regulatory agency to explain why it is pressuring a company. This process—like campaign finance—usually follows accepted etiquette. In addressing a regulatory agency the senator does not say, "Lay off my campaign contributors, or I'll cut your budget." One standard phrasing for letters asks regulators to resolve the problem "as quickly as possible within applicable rules and regulations."[10] No matter how mild and careful the inquiry, the agency receiving the request is certain to give it extra attention; only after careful consideration will they refuse to make any accommodation.

The power disparity between business and environmentalists is enormous during the legislative process but even larger thereafter.

When the Clean Air Act passed, corporations and industry groups offered positions, typically with large pay increases, to congressional staff members who wrote the law. The former congressional staff members who work for corporations know how to evade the law and can persuasively claim to EPA that they know what Congress intended. Environmental organizations pay substantially less than Congress and can't afford large staffs. They are rarely able to become involved in the details of the administrative process or influence implementation and enforcement.[11]

Having pushed Congress for a law, and the Environmental Protection Agency for regulations, allowing as much pollution as possible, business then went to the Quayle Council for rules allowing even more pollution. Vice President J. Danforth Quayle's Council, technically the Council on Competitiveness, was created by President Bush specifically to help reduce regulations on business. Quayle told the *Boston Globe* "that his council has an 'open door' to business groups and that he has a bias against regulations."[12] The Council reviews, and can override, all federal regulations, including those by the EPA setting the limits at which a chemical is subject to regulation. The council also recommended that corporations be allowed to increase their polluting emissions if a state did not object within seven days of the proposed increase. Corporations thus have multiple opportunities to win. If they lose in Congress, they can win at the regulatory agency; if they lose there, they can try again at the Quayle Council. If they lose there, they can try to reduce the money available to enforce regulations, tie up the issue in the courts, or accept a minimal fine.

The operation of the Quayle Council probably would have received little publicity, but reporters discovered that the executive director of the Council, Allan Hubbard, had a clear conflict of interest. Hubbard chaired the biweekly White House meetings on the Clean Air Act. He owns half of World Wide Chemical, received an average of more than a million dollars a year in profits from it while directing the Council, and continues to attend quarterly stockholder meetings. According to the *Boston Globe*, "Records on file with the Indianapolis Air Pollution Control Board show that World Wide Chemical emitted 17,000 to 19,000 pounds of chemicals into the air last year."[13] The company "does not have the permit required to release the emissions," "is putting out nearly four times the allowable emissions without a permit, and could be subject to a $2,500-a-day penalty," according to David Jordan, director of the Indianapolis Air Pollution Board.[14]

In business-government relations attention focuses on scandal. It is outrageous that Hubbard will personally benefit by eliminating regulations that his own company is violating, but the key issue here is not this obvious conflict of interest. The real issue is the *system* of business-government relations, and especially of campaign finance, that offers business so many opportunities to craft loopholes, undermine regulations, and subvert enforcement. Still worse, many of these actions take place outside of public scrutiny. If the Quayle Council were headed by a Boy Scout we'd still object to giving business yet another way to use backroom deals to increase our risk of getting cancer. In *Money Talks* we try to analyze not just the exceptional cases, but the day-to-day reality of corporate-government relations.

THE CANDIDATES' PERSPECTIVE

Most of *Money Talks* focuses on the world as corporate PAC directors see it—how they establish political action committees, raise money for them, choose candidates, give them contributions, and gain access so they can win loopholes. But we begin by establishing the dependence of candidates on fundraising in general and PACs in particular. The candidates' constant need for money gives PACs leverage.

Money has always been a critically important factor in campaigns, but the shift to expensive technology has made it the dominant factor.[15] Today money is the key to victory and substitutes for everything else—instead of door-to-door canvassers, a good television spot; instead of a committee of respected long-time party workers who know the local area, a paid political consultant and media expert. To be a viable political candidate, one must possess—or be able to raise—huge sums. Nor is this a one-time requirement; each reelection campaign requires new infusions of cash.

The quest for money is never ending. Challengers must have money to be viable contenders; incumbents can seldom predict when they might face a tight race. In 1988 the average winning candidate for the House of Representatives spent $388,000; for the Senate, $3,745,000.[16] Although the Congress, especially the Senate, has many millionaires, few candidates have fortunes large enough to finance repeated campaigns out of their own pockets. It would take the entire congressional salary for 3.1 years for a member of the House, or 29.9 years for a senator, to pay for a single reelection campaign. Most members are therefore in no position to say, "Asking people for money is just too big a hassle. Forget it. I'll pay for it myself." They must raise the money from others, and the pressure to do so never lets up. To pay for an average winning campaign, representatives need to raise $3,700 and senators $12,000 during *every week* of their term of office.

Increasingly incumbents use money to win elections before voters get involved. Senator Rudy Boschwitz (R-Minn.) spent $6 million getting reelected in 1984 and had raised $1.5 million of it by the beginning of the year, effectively discouraging the most promising Democratic challengers. After the election he wrote and personally typed a secret evaluation of his campaign strategy:

> "Nobody in politics (except me!) likes to raise money, so I thought the best way of discouraging the toughest opponents from running was to have a few dollars in the sock. *I believe it worked. . . . From all forms of fund-raising I raised $6 million plus and got 3 or 4 (maybe even 5) stories and cartoons* that irked me," he said. "In retrospect, I'm glad I had the money."[17]

Fundraising isn't popular with the public, but candidates keep emphasizing it because it works: the champion money raiser wins almost regardless of the merits. *Almost* is an important qualifier here, as Boschwitz would be the first to attest: in his 1990 race he outspent his opponent by about five to one and lost nonetheless.[18]

Since candidates aren't allowed to directly buy and sell votes and influence, in order to raise money they must persuade people to give it to them. As *National Journal,* probably the most authoritative source on the Washington scene, reports:

> There is widespread agreement that the congressional money chase has become an unending marathon, as wearying to participants as it is disturbing to spectators. . . . Members of Congress, especially in the Senate, complain that they are consumed by the demands of raising money. "During hearings of Senate committees, you can watch senators go to phone booths in the committee rooms to dial for dollars," an aide to a Democratic Senator said.
>
> But many Members say that they feel they have no choice. . . . "In both the executive and legislative branches of government, public officials are consumed with the unending pursuit of money to run election campaigns, to fund party organizations, to help colleagues raise campaign funds," [Senator George] Mitchell [D-Maine and majority leader] said at a May 3 news conference.[19]

It is not only that senators leave committee hearings for the more crucial task of calling people to beg for money. They also chase all over the country because reelection is more dependent on meetings with rich people two thousand miles from home than it is on meetings with their own constituents:

> When then-Rep. Thomas A. Daschle, D-S.D., was running for the Senate in 1986, he journeyed to Los Angeles almost as regularly as he visited Sioux Falls, the biggest city in his home state. In the two years before the election, he said recently, he flew to California more than 20 times to meet with prospective contributors. . . . Senators frequently complain that they spend too much time jetting around on their transcontinental money chase. But when faced with the alternative—not being able to buy as much television advertising as they may want—most take to the airways as often as they can on week-ends or during recesses.[20]

This process is sometimes carried to an extreme: Representative John Murtha (D-Pa.) was criticized because at one point he had raised nearly $200,000, of which only $1,000 came from his district.

Do members of Congress incur any obligations in seeking and accepting these campaign contributions? Bob Dole, Republican leader in the Senate and George Bush's main rival for the 1988 Republican presidential nomination, was quoted by the *Wall Street Journal* as saying, "When the Political Action Committees give money, they expect something in return other than good government."[21] One unusually outspoken business donor, Charles Keating, made the same point: "One question among the many raised in recent weeks had to do with whether my financial support in any way influenced several political figures to take up my cause. I want to say in the most forceful way I can, I certainly hope so."[22]

Candidates tend to go where the money is. Suppose a member holds a $10-per-person fundraising dinner—a barbecue in the park on Memorial Day or Labor Day. Even if 500 people attend, the gross take will be only $5,000, and the net will be considerably less, no matter how cheap the hot dogs and hamburgers. And that takes no account of the problems of notifying and persuading 500 people to attend. Members therefore increasingly prefer to raise money at "big ticket" events.[23] Selling ten tickets for a $1,000-per-person fundraiser brings in more than twice as much as the 500-person barbecue in the park.

THE CURRENT LAW

The law, however, regulates fundraising and limits the amount that any one individual or organization may (legally) contribute. According to current law:

1. A *candidate* may donate an unlimited amount of personal funds to his or her *own* campaign. The Supreme Court has ruled this is protected as free speech.
2. Individuals may not contribute more than $1,000 per candidate per election, nor more than $25,000 in total in a given two-year election cycle.
3. Political action committees may contribute up to $5,000 per candidate per election. Since most candidates face primaries, an individual may contribute $2,000 and a PAC $10,000 to the candidate during a two-year election cycle. PACs may give to an unlimited number of candidates and hence may give an unlimited amount of money.
4. Individuals may contribute up to $5,000 per year to a political action committee.
5. Candidates must disclose the full amount they have received, the donor and identifying information for any individual contribution of $200 or more, the name of the PAC and donation amount for any PAC contribution however small, and all disbursements. PACs must disclose any donation they make to a candidate, no matter how small. They must also disclose the total amount received by the PAC and the names and positions of all contributors who give the PAC more than $200 in a year.
6. Sponsoring organizations, including corporations and unions, may pay all the expenses of creating and operating a PAC. Thus a corporation may pay the cost of the rent, telephones, postage, supplies, and air travel for all PAC activities; the salaries of full-time corporate employees who work exclusively on the PAC; and the salaries of all managers who listen to a presentation about the PAC. However, the PAC money itself—the money used to contribute to candidates—must come from voluntary donations by individual contributors. The corporation may not legally take a portion of its profits and put it directly into the PAC.
7. Corporations may establish and control the PAC and solicit stockholders and/or managerial employees for contributions to the PAC. It is technically possible for corporations to solicit hourly (or

nonmanagerial) employees and for unions to solicit managers, but these practices are so much more tightly regulated and restricted that in practice cross-solicitation is rare.

8. The Federal Election Commission (FEC) is to monitor candidates and contributors and enforce these rules.[24]

These are the key rules governing fundraising, but the history of campaign finance is that as time goes on, loopholes develop—and some of them are large enough to drive a truck through. What is generally regarded as the most important current loophole is that there are no reporting requirements or limits for contributions given to political parties as opposed to candidates. Such money is ostensibly to be used to promote party building and get-out-the-vote drives; in 1988 literally hundreds of individuals gave $100,000 or more in unreported "soft money" donations.[25] Many of these loopholes are neither accidents nor oversights. Three Democrats and three Republicans serve as federal election commissioners, and commissioners are notorious party loyalists. Because it requires a majority to investigate a suspected violation, the FEC not only fails to punish violations, it fails to investigate them.

CORPORATE PACs

The Federal Election Commission categorizes PACs as corporate, labor, trade-health-membership, and nonconnected. Nonconnected PACs are unaffiliated with any other organization: they are formed exclusively for the purpose of raising and contributing money. Most subsist by direct-mail fundraising targeted at people with a commitment to a single issue (abortion or the environment) or philosophical position (liberalism or conservatism). Other PACs are affiliated with an already existing organization, and that organization—whether a corporation, union, trade, or membership association—pays the expenses associated with operating the PAC and decides what will happen to the money the PAC collects.

Candidates increasingly rely on PACs because they can easily solicit a large number of PACs, each of which is relatively likely to make a major contribution. "From 1976–88, PAC donations rose from 22 per cent to 40 per cent of House campaign receipts, and from 15 per cent to 22 per cent of Senate receipts."[26] Almost half of all House members (205 of the 435) "received at least 50 per cent of their campaign contributions from PACs."[27] The reliance on PACs is greater in the House than in the Senate: PACs give more to Senate candidates, but Senate races are more expensive than House races, so a larger fraction of total Senate-race receipts comes from individual contributions.[28]

Although other sorts of PACs deserve study, we believe the most important part of this story concerns corporate PACs, the subject of this book. We focus on corporate PACs for three interrelated reasons. First, they are the largest concentrated source of campaign money and the fastest growing. In 1988 corporate PACs contributed more than $50 million, all trade-membership-health PACs combined less than $40 million, labor PACs less than $35 million, and nonconnected PACs less than $20 million. Moreover, these figures understate the importance of corporate decisions about money because industry trade associations are controlled by corporations and follow their lead.[29] In addition, corporate executives have high incomes and make many individual contributions; a handful of labor leaders may attempt to do the same on a reduced scale, but rank-and-file workers are unlikely to do so. Second, corporations have disproportionate power in U.S. society, magnifying the importance of the money they contribute. Finally, corporate PACs have enormous untapped fundraising potential. They are in a position to coerce their donors in a way no other kind of PAC can and, if the need arose, could dramatically increase the amount of money they raise (see chapter 2).

Corporate PACs follow two very different strategies, pragmatic and ideological. Chapters 4 and 5 discuss these in detail, but we outline them here, since they are the major alternative approaches to corporate political action.

Pragmatic donations are given specifically to advance the short-run interests of the donor, primarily to enable the corporation to gain a chance to meet with the member and argue its case. Because the aim of these donations is to gain "access" to powerful members of Congress, the money is given without regard to whether or not the member needs it and with little consideration of the member's political stance on large issues. The corporation's only concern is that the member will be willing and able to help them out—and as we show in chapter 4, virtually all members, regardless of party, are willing to cooperate in this access process. Perhaps the most memorable characterization of this strategy was by Jay Gould, nineteenth-century robber baron and owner of the Erie Railroad: "In a Republican district I was a Republican; in a Democratic district, a Democrat; in a doubtful district I was doubtful; but I was always for Erie."[30]

Ideological donations, on the other hand, are made to influence the political composition of the Congress. From this perspective, contributions should meet two conditions: (1) they should be directed to politically congenial "pro-free enterprise" candidates who face opponents unsympathetic to business (in practice, these are always conservatives);[31] and (2) they should be targeted at competitive races where money can potentially influence the election outcome. The member's willingness to do the company favors doesn't matter, and even a conservative "free enterprise" philosophy wouldn't be sufficient: if the two opponents' views were the same, then the election couldn't influence the ideological composition of Congress. Most incumbents are reelected: in some years as many as 98 percent of all House members running are reelected. Precisely because incumbents will probably be reelected even without PAC support, ideological corporations usually give to nonincumbents, either challengers or candidates for open seats.

Virtually all corporations use some combination of pragmatic and ideological strategies. The simplest method of classifying PACs is by the proportion of money they gave to incumbents: the higher this proportion, the more pragmatic the corporation.[32] As figure 1.1 indicates, corporations recently have clustered at the pragmatic end of the spectrum. In 1988 about a third (36 percent) of the largest corporate PACs gave more than 90 percent of their money to incumbents, and another third (34 percent) gave 80 to 90 percent to incumbents. Although roughly a third gave less than 80 percent to incumbents, only eight corporate PACs gave less than 50 percent of their money to incumbents (that is, more than 50 percent to nonincumbents). Examples of such PACs are Cooper Industries PAC (CIPAC), Flowers PAC, and Political Action Coors Employees (PACE). The pragmatic emphasis of recent years is a change from 1980, when a large number of corporations followed an ideological approach.

Our Research

We began studying the system of congressional campaign finance, and especially the role of corporate political action committees, in 1982, when corporations were much more ideological. Our early research attempted to explain the conservative successes of 1980 and 1981 through quantitative analyses of corporate PAC contributions; eventually we used quantitative methods to analyze contributions to all elections held from 1976 to 1988—over 150,000 donations by corporate

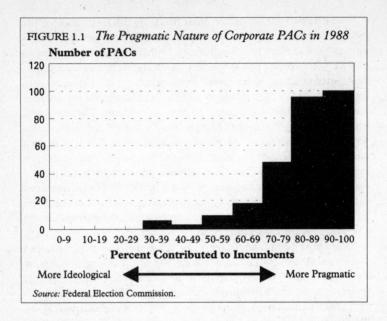

FIGURE 1.1   *The Pragmatic Nature of Corporate PACs in 1988*

Number of PACs

Percent Contributed to Incumbents

More Ideological ◄──────► More Pragmatic

Source: Federal Election Commission.

PACs.[33] However, the limitations of purely quantitative analysis led us to undertake a series of in-depth interviews with corporate PAC directors. These interviews are the foundation for our analysis, but combining interviews and quantitative analysis produces an account that is richer than either could be on its own. Thus our interview sample was drawn more systematically than it would have been without previous quantitative research, and the quantitative analysis helped guide many of our interview probes. We can compare what each corporation says with what Federal Election Commission records indicate it actually did.

Our quantitative analyses concentrate on Democrats and Republicans in general-election contests for congressional seats. We focus on the 309 corporate PACs that made the largest contributions in the period from 1975 to 1988.[34] As might be expected, these are almost exclusively very large corporations: on average in 1984 they had $6.7 billion in sales and 48,000 employees. However, not all large corporations have PACs: such well-known giants as IBM, Procter & Gamble, and ITT do not. Moreover, not all firms with large PACs have huge sales, so our sample includes about twenty-five "small" firms with 1984 revenues of less than $500 million.[35]

Politically these 309 corporate PACs are diverse. To qualify for the sample, the PAC had to have been one of the largest for at least one of the elections from 1976 on, and this is reflected in their average 1988 donations of $128,294. But this average conceals a considerable range—from the largest, AT&T, with donations of $1,287,862 in the 1987–88 election cycle, to twenty-seven companies with total donations of less than $20,000 during the 1988 election.[36] On average, in 1988 these PACs gave 52.7 percent of their money to Republicans and 47.3 percent to Democrats.[37] They gave 83.6 percent of their money to incumbents, 10.2 percent to candidates for open seats, and 6.2 percent to challengers.

The PAC officials we interviewed were selected from this set of the 309 largest corporate PACs and were representative of the larger sample in terms of both economic and political characteristics. Thus ten of our thirty-eight interviews were at corporations with sales over $10 billion and ten were at "small" corporations with sales of less than $3 billion.[38] Interviewed corporations gave 54 percent of their money to Republicans, compared to 53 percent for the larger sample. They gave 83 percent to incumbents, compared to 84 percent for the larger sample (see figure 1.2).[39]

A third source of original data supplements our quantitative analyses of the 309 largest corporate PACs and our 38 in-depth interviews. In November and December of 1986 we mailed surveys to a random sample of ninety-four directors of large corporate PACs, achieving a response rate of 58 percent.[40] For the most part, we use this to place our interview comments in context: if a PAC director tells us a story of being pressured by a candidate, how typical is this? How many other PAC directors report similar experiences? Finally, our original data also are supplemented by books, articles, and newspaper accounts about campaign finance.

THE INTERVIEWS

Most corporate PAC officials initially were reluctant to be interviewed but ultimately agreed.[41] We requested permission to tape record interviews, which was granted in thirty of thirty-eight cases (79 percent of the cases). Most interviews were a little over an hour long, and transcribed they produced hundreds of pages of material. At the beginning of each interview we presented the PAC director with a set of graphs and charts that analyzed their PAC's contribution patterns and compared it to the other large PACs we studied in our quantitative

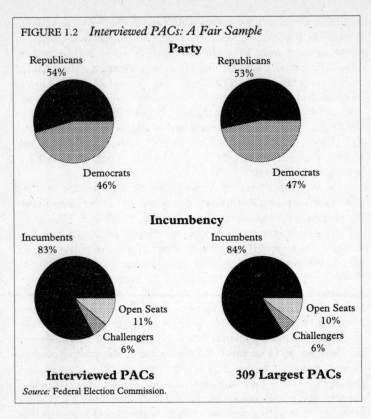

FIGURE 1.2   *Interviewed PACs: A Fair Sample*

Party

Republicans 54%

Republicans 53%

Democrats 46%

Democrats 47%

Incumbency

Incumbents 83%

Incumbents 84%

Open Seats 11%

Open Seats 10%

Challengers 6%

Challengers 6%

Interviewed PACs   **309 Largest PACs**

Source: Federal Election Commission.

analysis. This virtually eliminated the PAC directors' use of vague public relations generalities and provided an entry point for a number of probes about their PAC's orientations and priorities.

All those we interviewed were promised total confidentiality, both for themselves and their companies, and we have done our best to provide it.[42] Identifying information has therefore been deleted from quotations. In a limited number of instances we have changed a quote slightly to protect an informant's anonymity—for example, by changing the industry mentioned, the size of the PAC, or the specific incident being described. Every effort has been made to make relatively minimal changes and make them in ways that do not affect the meaning of the material.[43] On occasion we have also altered quotes to make them read better, taking out some of the false starts, repetitions, and "Ummm, you knows" that characterize speech, even speech that sounds fluent and literate. We want to emphasize, however, that except for omission of identifying information and editing for readability, all quotations are presented exactly as we recorded them.[44] Guarantees of confidentiality do not apply to the FEC records of actual corporate contributions or to news stories, and we use this material whenever appropriate, sometimes identifying specific corporations by name. We also include references to identifiable members of Congress when we can do so without compromising our informants' confidentiality.

The research reported here differs from journalistic accounts in two ways. First, our research is more scientifically grounded, both in its attempts to interview a representative sample and in the ability to relate these interviews to systematic quantitative data. Second, and equally important, is our promise of confidentiality to the people we interviewed. The most common question corporate executives asked during initial contacts and at the beginning of the interview itself concerned confidentiality. People were willing to talk either with or without confidentiality but told us that they would be more open with a promise of confidentiality. The main question was some version of, "Am I going to be seeing this on '60 Minutes' or reading it on the front page of the *Washington Post?*"[45] Informant confidentiality is appropriate in this study because our focus is not on specific instances of abuse but rather on the normal operation of the campaign finance system. The corporate executives we interviewed made some revealing statements and impressed us by the extent of their candor. They undoubtedly maintained their guard despite the promise of confidentiality, only rarely revealed specifics, and most assuredly showed us only the proverbial tip of the iceberg. But even that much is extremely revealing.

Overview and Background

Money Talks uses corporate PAC executives' own words to explain how corporate PACs work—what they try to do and how. We provide background, a framework, and our own views and analysis, which are critical of business and the current campaign finance system. Understanding how the system operates is the necessary basis for evaluating proposed reforms, and in the final chapter we develop a reform proposal that, if enacted, could seriously reduce the impact of special-interest money on Congress.

Chapter 2 examines how corporations raise money for their PAC and organize the PAC for internal decision making. We argue that corporate PACs differ from other PACs in two ways: (1) as employees, managers can be—and are—coerced to contribute; and (2) corporate PACs are not democratically controlled by their contributors (even in theory).

Chapter 3 analyzes the PAC contribution itself—how it should be understood, the criteria the corporation uses in deciding who receives it, and what corporations give in addition to PAC donations. We argue that PAC contributions are best understood as gifts, not bribes. They create a generalized sense of obligation and an expectation that "if I scratch your back you scratch mine." We also look at the way PACs present money to candidates: what really goes on at a fundraiser?

In chapter 4 we investigate the "access" process. These are the donations observers find most troubling. A corporation uses the member of Congress's sense of indebtedness for past contributions to help it gain access to the member. In committee hearings and private meetings the corporation then persuades the member to make "minor" changes in a bill, which exempt a particular company or industry from some specific provision.

Even some corporations are troubled by this "access" approach, and chapter 5 considers the alternative: donations to close races intended to change the ideological composition of the Congress. In the late 1980s and early 1990s only a small number of corporations used this as their primary strategy, but most corporations make some such donations. In the 1980 election a large group of corporations pursued an ideological strategy. We argue this was one of the reasons for the conservative successes of that period and examine why many of these corporations changed to access-oriented behavior.

In chapter 6 we investigate the degree of political unity among corporations. Do competing firms or industries oppose each other in Washington, such that one business's political donations oppose and cancel out those of the next corporation or industry? More generally, how much power does business have in U.S. society, and how does its political power relate to its economic activity?

The book concludes with an examination of campaign finance reform. The PAC directors we interviewed are not very worried about reform: they don't expect meaningful changes in campaign funding laws, and they assume that if "reforms" are enacted, they will be easily evaded. We use the analysis developed throughout the book to briefly indicate why most reform proposals would be ineffective. We then offer a program that we believe would lead to meaningful and enduring reform. It won't be easy to enact such a reform, but we hope that if people understand how the current system operates, and what would be needed to clean up the system, they will demand significant change.

Three interrelated points, each developed in its own section below, are further explored in most chapters in this book. First, power is exercised in many loose and subtle ways, not simply through the visible use of force and threats. Power may in fact be most effective, and most limiting, when it structures the conditions for action—even though in these circumstances it may be hard to recognize. Thus PAC contributions can and do exercise enormous influence through creating a sense of obligation, even if there is no explicit agreement to perform a specific service in return for a donation. Second, business is different from, and more powerful than, other groups in the society. As a result, corporations and their PACs are frequently treated differently than others would be. Other groups could not match business power simply by raising equivalent amounts of PAC money. Third, this does not mean that business always wins, or that it wins automatically. If it did, corporate PACs would be unnecessary. Business must engage in a constant struggle to maintain its dominance. This is a class struggle just as surely as are strikes and mass mobilizations, even though it is rarely thought of in these terms.

WHAT IS POWER?

Our analysis is based on an understanding of power that differs from that usually articulated by both business and politicians. The corporate PAC directors we interviewed insisted that they have no power:

> If you were to ask me what kind of access and influence do we have, being roughly the 150th largest PAC, I would have to tell you that on the basis of our money we have zero. . . . If you look at the level of our contributions, we know we're not going to buy anybody's vote, we're not going to rent anybody, or whatever the cliches have been over the years. We know that.

The executives who expressed these views[46] used the word *power* in roughly the same sense that it is usually used within political science, which is also the way the term was defined by Max Weber, the classical sociological theorist. Power, according to this common conception, is the ability to make someone do something against his or her will. If that is what power means, then corporations rarely have power in relation to members of Congress. As one corporate senior vice president said to us, "You certainly aren't going to be able to buy anybody for $500 or $1,000 or $10,000. It's a joke." In this regard we agree with the corporate officials we interviewed: a PAC is not in a position to say to a member of Congress, "Either you vote for this bill, or we will defeat your bid for reelection." Rarely do they even say, "Vote for this bill, or you won't get any money from us." (These points are discussed in more detail in chapter 4.) Therefore, if power is the ability to make someone do something against his or her will, then PAC donations rarely give corporations power over members of Congress.

This definition of power as the ability to make someone do something against his or her will is what Steven Lukes[47] calls a *one-dimensional view of power*. A *two-dimensional view* recognizes the existence of nondecisions: a potential issue never gets articulated or, if articulated by someone somewhere, never receives serious consideration. In 1989 and 1990 one of the major political battles, and a focus of great effort by corporate PACs, was the Clean Air Act. Yet twenty or thirty years earlier, before the rise of the environmental movement, pollution was a nonissue: it simply didn't get considered, although its effects were, in retrospect, of great importance. In one Sherlock Holmes story the key clue is that the dog didn't bark.[48] A two-dimensional view of power makes the same point: in some situations no one notices power is being exercised—because there is no overt conflict.

Even this model of power is too restrictive, however, because it still focuses on discrete decisions and nondecisions. Tom Wartenberg calls these *interventional models of power* and notes that in such models "the primary locus of power . . . is a specific social interaction between two social agents." Such models do not recognize "the idea that the most fundamental use of power in society is its use in structuring the basic manner in which social agents interact with one another."[49] Wartenberg argues instead for a *field theory of power* that analyzes social power as similar to a magnetic field. A magnetic field alters the motion of objects susceptible to magnetism. Similarly, the mere presence of a powerful social agent alters social space for others and causes them to orient to the powerful agent.[50] One of the executives we interviewed took it for granted that "if we go see the congressman who represents [a city where the company has a major plant], where 10,000 of our employees are also his constituents, we don't need a PAC to go see him." The corporation is so important in that area that the member has to orient himself or herself in relation to the corporation and its concerns. In a different sense, the mere act of accepting a campaign contribution changes the way a member relates to a PAC, creating a sense of obligation and need to reciprocate. The PAC contribution has altered the member's social space, his or her awareness of the company and wish to help it, even if no explicit commitments have been made.

BUSINESS IS DIFFERENT

Power therefore is not just the ability to force people to do something against their will; it is most effective (and least recognized) when it shapes the field of action. Moreover, business's vast resources, influence on the economy, and general legitimacy place it on a different footing from other so-called special interests. Business donors are often treated differently from other campaign contributors. When a member of Congress accepts a $1,000 donation from a corporate PAC, goes to a committee hearing, and proposes "minor" changes in a bill's wording, those changes are often accepted without discussion or examination. The changes "clarify" the language of the bill, perhaps legalizing higher levels of pollution for a specific pollutant or exempting the company from some tax. The media do not report on this change, and no one speaks against it. On the other hand, if a PAC were formed by Drug Lords for Cocaine Legalization, no member of Congress would take its money. If a member introduced a "minor" amendment to make it easier to sell crack without bothersome police interference, the proposed change would attract massive attention, the campaign contribution would be labeled a scandal, the member's political career would be ruined, and the wording change would not be incorporated into the bill. This is an extreme example, but approximately the same holds true for many groups: equal rights for gays and lesbians could never be a minor and unnoticed addition to a bill with a different purpose.

Even groups with great social legitimacy encounter more opposition and controversy than business faces for proposals that are virtually without public support. Contrast the largely unopposed commitment of more than $500 billion for the bailout of savings and loan associations with the sharp debate, close votes, and defeats for the rights of men and women to take *unpaid* parental leaves. Although the classic phrase for something noncontroversial that everyone must support is to call it a "motherhood" issue, and it would cost little to guarantee every woman the right to an unpaid parental leave, nonetheless this measure generated intense scrutiny and controversy, ultimately going down to defeat. Few people are prepared to publicly defend pollution or tax evasion, but business is routinely able to win pollution exemptions and tax loopholes. Although cumulatively these provisions may trouble people, individually most are allowed to pass without scrutiny. *No* analysis of corporate political activity makes sense unless it begins with a recognition that the PAC is a vital element of corporate power, but it does not operate by itself. The PAC donation is always backed by the wider range of business power and influence.

Corporations are different from other special-interest groups not only because business has far more resources, but also because of this acceptance and legitimacy. When people feel that "the system" is screwing them, they tend to blame politicians, the government, the media—but rarely business. Although much of the public is outraged at the way money influences elections and public policy, the issue is almost always posed in terms of what politicians do or don't do. This pervasive double standard largely exempts business from criticism. We, on the other hand, believe it is vital to scrutinize business as well.

Many people who are outraged that members of Congress recently raised their pay to $125,100 are apparently unconcerned about corporate executives' pay. One study calculated that CEOs at the largest U.S. companies are paid an average of $2.8 million a year, 150 times more than the average U.S. worker[51] and 22 times as much as members of Congress.[52] More anger is directed at Congress for delaying new environmental laws than at the companies who fight every step of the way to stall and subvert the legislation. When members of Congress do favors for large campaign contributors, the anger is directed at the senators who went along, not at the business owner who paid the money (and usually initiated the pressure). The focus is on the member's receipt of thousands of dollars, not on the business's receipt of millions (or hundreds of millions) in tax breaks or special treatment. It is widely held that "politics is dirty," but companies' getting away with murder—quite literally—generates little public comment and condemnation. This disparity is evidence of business's success in shaping public perceptions. Lee Atwater, George Bush's campaign manager for the 1988 presidential election, saw this as a key to Republican success:

> In the 1980 campaign, we were able to make the establishment, insofar as it is bad, the government. In other words, big government was the enemy, not big business. If the people think the problem is that taxes are too high, and the government interferes too much, then we are doing our job. But, if they get to the point where they say that the real problem is that rich

people aren't paying taxes . . . then the Democrats are going to be in good shape.[53]

We might also note that in our focus on PACs we usually discuss business intervention at the level of Congress, but most of our analysis and criticisms apply with at least as much force to the operations of the executive bureaucracy and regulatory agencies.

We argue corporations are so different, and so dominant that they exercise a special kind of power, what Antonio Gramsci[54] called *hegemony*. Hegemony can be regarded as the ultimate example of a field of power that structures what people and groups do. It is sometimes referred to as a world view—a way of thinking about the world that influences every action and makes it difficult to even consider alternatives. But in Gramsci's analysis it is much more than this; it is a culture and set of institutions that structure life patterns and coerce a particular way of life. Susan Harding[55] gives the example of relations between whites and blacks in the South prior to the 1960s. Black inferiority and subservience were not simply ideas articulated by white racists; they were incorporated into a set of social practices—segregated schools, rest rooms, swimming pools, restaurants; the black obligation to call white men *Mister,* the prohibition on referring to black men as *Mister,* the use of the term *boy* for black males of any age and social status; the white right to go to the front of any line or to take the seat of any African-American; and so on. Most blacks recognized the injustice and absurdity of these rules, but this did not allow them to escape, much less defy, them. White hegemony could not be overthrown simply by recognizing its existence or articulating an ideal of equality; black people had to create a movement that transformed themselves, the South, and the country as a whole.

Hegemony is most successful and most powerful if it is unrecognized. White hegemony in the South was strong but never unrecognized and rarely uncontested. White Southerners would have denied they exercised power and probably done so quite sincerely: "Why our nigras are perfectly happy; that's the way they want to be treated." But many black Southerners vigorously disputed this when talking to each other.[56] In some sense gender relations in the 1950s embodied a hegemony even more powerful than that of race relations. Betty Friedan titled the first chapter of *The Feminine Mystique*[57] "The Problem That Has No Name" because women literally did not have a name for and did not recognize the existence of their oppression. Women as well as men denied the existence of inequality

or oppression and denied the systematic exercise of power to maintain unequal relations.

We argue that today business has enormous power and exercises
effective hegemony, even though (perhaps because) this is largely
undiscussed and unrecognized. *Politically* business power today is
similar to white treatment of blacks in 1959: business may sincerely
deny its power, but many of the groups it exercises power over recognize it, feel dominated, resent this, and fight the power as best they can.
Economically business power is more similar to gender relations in
1959: virtually no one sees this power as problematic. If the issue is
brought to people's attention, many still don't see a problem: "Well, so
what? How else could it be? Maybe we don't like it, but that's just the
way things are." (This point is further discussed in chapter 6.)

Hegemony is never absolute. African-Americans and women both
were (and are) forced to live in disadvantaged conditions but simultaneously have fought for dignity and respect. Key individuals always violated conventions and tested limits. A hegemonic power is
usually opposed by a counterhegemony. Thus, although children in
our society are taught to compete with each other to earn the praise
of authority figures, it is also the case that "teacher's pets" are likely
to face ostracism by their peers. We hope this book makes a small
contribution to weakening business hegemony and to developing
a counterhegemony.

THE LIMITS TO BUSINESS POWER

We have argued that power is more than winning an open conflict,
and business is different from other groups because of its pervasive
influence on our society—the way it shapes the social space for all
other actors. These two arguments, however, are joined with a third:
a recognition of, in fact an insistence on, the limits to business power.
We stress the power of business, but business does not feel powerful.
As one executive said to us,

> I really wish that our PAC in particular, and our lobbyists, had the
> influence that is generally perceived by the general population. If you see
> it written in the press, and you talk to people, they tell you about all that
> influence that you've got, and frankly I think that's far overplayed, as far
> as the influence goes. Certainly you can get access to a candidate, and
> certainly you can get your position known; but as far as influencing that
> decision, the only way you influence it is by the providing of information.

Executives believe that corporations are constantly under attack, primarily because government simply doesn't understand that business is crucial to everything society does but can easily be crippled by well-intentioned but unrealistic government policies. A widespread view among the people we interviewed is that "far and away the vast majority of things that we do are literally to protect ourselves from public policy that is poorly crafted and nonresponsive to the needs and realities and circumstances of our company." These misguided policies, they feel, can come from many sources—labor unions, environmentalists, the pressure of unrealistic public-interest groups, the government's constant need for money, or the weight of its oppressive bureaucracy. Simply maintaining equilibrium requires a pervasive effort: if attention slips for even a minute, an onerous regulation will be imposed or a precious resource taken away. To some extent such a view is an obvious consequence of the position of the people we interviewed: if business could be sure of always winning, the government relations unit (and thus their jobs) would be unnecessary; if it is easy to win, they deserve little credit for their victories and much blame for defeats. But evidently the corporation agrees with them, since it devotes significant resources to political action of many kinds, including the awareness and involvement of top officials. Chief executive officers and members of the board of directors repeatedly express similar views.

Both of these views—the business view of vulnerability and our insistence on their power—are correct. A university analogy illustrates the contradictory reality. After six years of teaching, an assistant professor comes up for tenure; if awarded tenure, he or she is supposed to be guaranteed a job for life[58] and promoted to associate professor, but if denied tenure, the assistant professor is fired. Even in highly selective schools, 74 percent of all people who come up for tenure receive it.[59] To an outside observer this might imply that untenured faculty don't have much to worry about and should relax. But the junior faculty under the gun are much more aware of the other side of it: there is better than a one in four chance they will be fired (under circumstances that would make it difficult to ever again receive as good a job), even though they have been doing a fine job and no one has complained about their performance.[60] More important, these high success percentages are possible only because individuals with weak cases are pressured to leave before coming up for tenure, and the junior faculty who stay spend six years with their nose to the grindstone neglecting their families and personal lives in order to publish, publish,

publish. Anyone who failed to do so, who tried to simply work a forty-hour week, would be virtually certain to be denied tenure.[61] The "success" rates therefore ignore both that the weakest cases get dropped before they come to the test and that virtually every success is the result of years of hard work.

Business political successes are comparable. Like the rest of us, business executives can usually think of other things they'd like to have but know they can't get at this time or that they could win but wouldn't consider worth the price that would have to be paid. More important, the odds may be very much in their favor, their opponents may be hobbled with one hand tied behind their back, but it is still a contest requiring pervasive effort. Perhaps once upon a time business could simply make its wishes known and receive what it wanted; today corporations must form PACs, lobby actively, make their case to the public, run advocacy ads, and engage in a multitude of behaviors that they wish were unnecessary. From the outside we are impressed with the high success rates over a wide range of issues and with the lack of a credible challenge to the general authority of business. From the inside they are impressed with the serious consequences of occasional losses and with the continuing effort needed to maintain their privileged position.

Business power does not rest *only* on PAC donations, but the PAC is a crucial aspect of business power. A football analogy can be made: business's vast resources and its influence on the economy may be equivalent to a powerful offensive line that is able to clear out the opposition and create a huge opening, but someone then has to take the ball and run through that opening. The PAC and the government relations operation are, in this analogy, like a football running back. When they carry the ball they have to move quickly, dodge attempts to tackle them, and if necessary fight off an opponent and keep going. The analogy breaks down, however, because it implies a contest between two evenly matched opponents. Most of the time the situation approximates a contest between an NFL team and high school opponents. The opponents just don't have the same muscle. Often they are simply intimidated or have learned through past experience the best thing to do is get out of the way. Occasionally, however, the outclassed opponents will have so much courage and determination that they will be at least able to score, if not to win.

Chapter 2

■■■

RAISING MONEY AND RUNNING THE PAC

■■■

The "special interest" label is often applied equally to all kinds of political action committees. Corporate PACs, however, differ from others in two key ways: (1) corporate employees, unlike union members, can be coerced to contribute, and their promotions and career advancement may depend on PAC contributions; and (2) contributors to corporate PACs cannot control PAC policy by voting for the organization's political agenda or leadership. Congress did not intend either of these characteristics. Moreover, virtually no one identifies these differences between corporate and all other PACs as a significant public policy issue.

This chapter analyzes the history and consequences of the unique status of corporate PACs. We begin with a brief history, including an account of how corporate PACs won a set of rules that treat them differently from other PACs. The key event was a ruling by the Federal Election Commission, the SUN-PAC decision, that normally receives only cursory attention in histories of campaign finance. Yet without this decision corporate PACs as we know them could not exist, and corporations would have far more difficulty raising enough money to be politically effective. More generally, it is surprising how little attention of any kind has been directed at the internal structure and operations of corporate PACs.

Establishing the Rules

A BRIEF HISTORY OF CAMPAIGN FINANCE

Wealth has influenced American elections from colonial days:

> When [George Washington] ran for the Virginia House of Burgesses
> from Fairfax County in 1757, he provided his friends with the "custom-
> ary means of winning votes": namely 28 gallons of rum, 50 gallons of rum
> punch, 34 gallons of wine, 46 gallons of beer, and 2 gallons of cider royal.
> Even in those days this was considered a large campaign expenditure,
> because there were only 391 voters in his district, for an average outlay
> of more than a quart and a half per person.[1]

In the 1890s Mark Hanna raised $6 million to $7 million for William
McKinley's campaign against William Jennings Bryan, assessing each
company an amount based on its size and "stake in the general prosperity." Thus banks were assessed one-quarter of 1 percent of their
capital, "Standard Oil about a quarter of a million dollars, and the large
insurance companies slightly less."[2] In response the 1907 Tillman Act
prohibited direct contributions by corporations, a prohibition extended to unions in 1943.

Political action committees were started by CIO labor unions in
the 1930s as a way for workers, few of whom could make substantial
donations as individuals, to pool their money and let the union use it
for maximum advantage. Labor PACs quickly became important and
have remained so ever since. Corporate PACs were of dubious legality
and virtually nonexistent until 1971, when the first of a series of campaign finance laws was passed.

The pre-1971 campaign finance laws had more exceptions and
loopholes than they did rules or enforcement. Although Herbert Alexander made a valiant effort to study and report on the financing of
elections from the 1950s on, learning much from the study of even
these partial disclosures,[3] it was easy for contributors and candidates
to evade both donation limits and reporting requirements. Thus
W. Clement Stone gave $2.1 million to Nixon's campaign, Richard
Mellon Scaife gave $1 million, and John Mulcahy gave nearly $600,-
000.[4] During the 1970s the campaign finance laws were repeatedly
changed (in 1971, 1974, 1976, and 1979), partly in response to public
outcry and partly to address court rulings about previous laws. Probably the single most important factor leading to reform was the Water-

gate burglary and coverup and the associated revelations of the Nixon era. For example, Nixon campaign workers pressured corporations to evade the reporting requirements of the 1971 law by making contributions prior to April 7, 1972, when new reporting rules took effect. Many corporations gave $100,000 each in illegal contributions, but prior to the new law it was easy to avoid detection. When the donations were uncovered during Watergate-related investigations, revelations of the way these "contributions" were extorted from corporate slush funds further spurred reform efforts.[5]

Because effective reporting requirements were introduced only in the 1970s, it is difficult to assess how much real change there has been in the level of campaign contributions by businesses and their executives. Before 1971 probably the most common form of corporate contribution was "bundling." As one of our PAC directors explained, "In the old days if someone was running for Congress and he had a fundraiser, you had to go around individually and say to each one of your directors and vice presidents, 'Can I have $100? Can I get $100 from you? Can I get $100 from you?' getting the money together." The executives might never have heard of the candidate but would contribute in an amount suggested by the government relations officer, who would collect checks from the requisite number of corporate employees, put them in one bundle, and present them to the candidate. Even if the donations were reported, no information identified individual donors, so there was no easy way for outsiders to uncover the corporate connection—although the candidate knew. This system was ad hoc, so corporate employees had to have money available when it was needed and needed to be asked each time the corporation wanted to make a contribution. Employees tended to resent being asked, so in most companies only high-level employees were solicited. It was illegal to reimburse the corporate officials who made these "voluntary" "individual" donations, but corporations regularly did so through fake expenses, one-time bonuses, or additions to base pay.[6] Corporations also contributed money to campaigns in other ways—by providing materials and supplies (including free use of company cars and planes), assigning corporate executives to work for the campaign while on the company payroll, and simply delivering used bills in plain envelopes.

SUN-PAC: THE HIDDEN FACE OF POWER

For corporate PACs the key piece of legal history is not an act of Congress but a 1975 decision by the Federal Election Commission that legalized corporate PACs in their current form. The 1975 SUN-PAC decision is easily the most important in the FEC's history and the basis for the rise of corporate PACs. However, most analyses of campaign regulations focus primarily on the legislation, while giving the SUN-PAC ruling scant attention.

The 1971 law that began the modern campaign finance reform process continued the previously existing ban on corporate and union contributions to political campaigns. Three exceptions were made:

1. Communications by a corporation to its *stockholders* and their families or by a labor organization to its *members* and their families on any subject.
2. Non-partisan registration and get-out-the-vote campaigns by a corporation aimed at its *stockholders* and their families, or by a labor organization aimed at its *members* and their families.
3. Solicitation of contributions to a separate segregated fund to be utilized for political purposes by a corporation or labor organization.[7]

The clear intent of the act was to establish equality between corporations and unions by requiring that union members and corporate stockholders obey the same rules. Because the organization has a special relationship to those individuals who (at least in theory) democratically control the organization, it may also use its own revenues (member dues for unions or profits for corporations) to communicate with them about political issues or to urge them to vote.

No one disputed that the 1971 law's first two provisions applied to corporate stockholders and union members, and the Federal Election Commission legal staff held that the third exception was also intended to apply to corporate stockholders and union members[8]—that "separate segregated funds"[9] (PACs) could be established and their administrative costs paid as long as union PACs restricted themselves to soliciting from union members and corporate PACs restricted themselves to soliciting from stockholders. Sun Oil Corporation, however, asked for an FEC ruling permitting it to solicit donations from absolutely anyone, arguing that the third clause contained no explicit restriction. By this interpretation the act effectively ended most legal restrictions on corporate political activity, and the first two exceptions were without purpose. If corporations and unions were allowed to use their money to solicit donations from anyone, they would have license to engage in any and all kinds of political advertising without restriction. The corporation could pay for an unlimited number of ads promoting a candidate or political position—simply by adding a short message to the effect that "if you agree with us, please send us a contribution."

The FEC staff argued that Congress intended to permit corporations to solicit contributions from their stockholders and unions from their members. Two of the FEC commissioners quoted instance after instance of testimony from the congressional authors of the bill to show the intent of those who wrote the language. The 1971 bill was referred to as "the Hansen Amendment" after its author, Representative Orval Hansen (R-Ida.), who made the following comments on its purpose:

> At the present time there is broad agreement as to the essence of the proper balance in regulating corporate and union political activity required by sound policy and the Constitution. It consists of a strong prohibition on the use of corporate and union treasury funds to reach the general public in support of, or opposition·to, Federal candidates and a limited permission to corporations and unions, allowing them to communicate freely with members and stockholders to register and vote, and to make political contributions and expenditures financed by voluntary donations which have been kept in a separate segregated fund. This amendment writes that balance into clear and unequivocal statutory language. . . .
>
> If an organization, whether it be the NAM, the AMA or the AFL-CIO, believes that certain candidates pose a threat to its well-being or the well-being of its members or stockholders, it should be able to get its views to those members or stockholders. As fiduciaries for their members and stockholders the officers of these institutions have a duty to share their informed insights on all issues affecting their institution with their constituents. Both union members and stockholders have the right to expect this expert guidance.
>
> This reasoning, of course, applies as well to solicitations for contributions to voluntary political funds.

The two FEC commissioners pointed out that these and other quotes from congressional debates unequivocally established that Congress intended to allow corporate PACs to solicit from stockholders. They also argued that the congressional debate provided *no* evidence that Congress intended to permit corporations to solicit employees.

Despite congressional intent against them, corporations did not give up; they simply moved the battle to another front. Sun Oil modified its request and asked for an FEC ruling allowing it to solicit from employees as well as stockholders, but indicated it did not intend to solicit from the general public. At this point the corporate position received a major assist from President Ford's Department of Justice. Richard Thornburgh, at the time Assistant Attorney General and later Attorney General in the Bush administration, informed the Federal Election Commission that the Criminal Division he headed would not prosecute corporations that used their funds to solicit employees as well as stockholders. His bland statement that the Justice Department would not uphold the law was buried by the *New York Times,* literally on the obituary page.[10] When the Federal Election Commission considered the issue, a majority (four of six commissioners) reached the same somewhat peculiar decision. The statements of those who authored the law clearly indicated that corporations should be restricted to soliciting stockholders; the entire context of the bill and provision made this the reasonable interpretation. The literal language of the particular sub-section could be interpreted as imposing no restrictions on either corporate or union solicitations. The majority of the commissioners ignored both the intent of the authors of the bill and its literal language. They simply created an entirely new set of rules. The Commission majority legalized corporate solicitation of employees as well as stockholders, but refused to permit corporate funds to be used to solicit the general public. The Commission then recommended guidelines "to minimize the appearance or perception of coercion."

The decisive vote on the 1975 SUN-PAC decision was cast by Neil Staebler, the one Democrat who sided with business and the Republicans. Staebler was a long-time business Democrat: he became a partner in his father's firm at age ten, was treasurer of a family-owned oil company from age twenty-one, and also participated in real estate and land development ventures. He served a single term as an at-large member of Congress from Michigan in 1963 and 1964 and received the Democratic nomination for governor, losing to Republican George Romney in a year when Democrat Lyndon Johnson carried the state by nearly a million votes, a record margin. Staebler was a controversial figure in the Michigan Democratic party, consistently opposed by the United Auto Workers because of his lack of support for labor issues. Thus the key vote in support of corporations was cast by someone who was himself a business owner and executive.[11]

The FEC decision was not the final word. Congress always retains the option of passing new legislation to override court or regulatory agency decisions. In response to labor leaders and others' strong opposition to the FEC's SUN-PAC decision, in 1976 Congress passed amendments that imposed additional restrictions on corporations' ability to raise funds from employees. But the SUN-PAC decision gave corporations the upper hand. Had labor supporters attempted to restore the status quo ante, in order to prevail pro-corporate senators needed not a majority, but only enough strength to mount a filibuster or sustain a veto by President Ford. Corporate opponents were therefore constrained to "be reasonable," that is, accept the general outlines of the fait accompli introduced by the corporate-Justice-FEC axis and press for only minor changes.

A further obstacle to winning new congressional legislation to reaffirm the original intent of the campaign finance laws was the position taken by much of the mass media, which presented corporate solicitation of employees as "restoring balance." The 1975 SUN-PAC ruling was applauded by the _New York Times_ in an editorial titled "Election Fund Equality" that claimed "the Federal Election Commission has now put corporations on virtually the same basis as labor unions. . . . By this decision, corporations would for the first time be given approximate equality with labor unions." The _Times_ would have preferred that both unions and corporations be banned from any form of political contribution, but "in the absence of an across-the-board prohibition of group activity based on economic self-interest, this seems the fairest solution." The _Washington Post_ said the decision would allow corporations to "counterbalance" unions; the _Wall Street Journal_ headlined an article "Equal Treatment"; and _Newsweek_ said the decision would allow corporations to "match" unions.[12]

The SUN-PAC decision was vital to the creation of corporate PACs as presently constituted. Virtually all FEC votes end in a three-to-three tie, with the three Democratic commissioners voting one way and the three Republicans the other. Most of the important "actions" by the FEC are _failures_ to reach any decision and thus allow the continuation of various loopholes and abuses. SUN-PAC is the most important decision made by the FEC in its entire history. The commission not only reached a decision but reached a decision that went well beyond enforcing the intent of existing legislation by making new policy—effectively rewriting the law. The consequences were immediate and dramatic. The initial act authorizing corporate PACs was passed in 1971. Over three years later, at the end of 1974, only eighty-nine corporate PACs had registered with the FEC. The SUN-PAC ruling came in late 1975, and by the end of 1976 the number of corporate PACs had more than quadrupled to 433, a number that continued to increase rapidly for several years thereafter.[13]

Raising Money

Because of the Federal Election Commission's SUN-PAC decision allowing corporate political action committees to solicit employees as well as stockholders, corporate PACs differ from other PACs in two significant ways: (1) corporate PACs are not democratically operated by their contributors, an issue discussed later in this chapter; and (2) corporations can in practice coerce both actual and potential PAC contributors. The next section focuses on how corporations persuade managers to contribute to the PAC.

Before a PAC can spend money it must raise it. The corporation can pay all the costs of operating the PAC but cannot use its funds for direct contributions to candidates. That is, the corporation can spend $500,000 of its own money in order to raise $100,000 in "voluntary" contributions from managers, but only these voluntary employee contributions may be donated to congressional candidates.

CAMPAIGNS TO RAISE MONEY

Our interviews indicate that most corporations promote their PAC through periodic campaigns to drum up support. The level of PAC participation, and the total raised for the PAC, depends on the success of the campaign and how long it has been since the last campaign. One corporation more than tripled the size of its PAC through a model campaign:

> I went to the chairman and the president and said, "Look, if we are going to get this thing done, you've got to support it." They said, "Fine." *"You* have got to start. You've got to talk to each of your division heads. I want the division heads to talk to all their senior managers. And I want all the senior managers to talk to all their groups and keep the groups no bigger than thirty."
>
> We've got eligible maybe 5,800 employees around the country, and we have probably talked to 80 percent of them in groups of thirty or less. . . . And then we set goals of how much: if you make less than $25,000, it was a quarter of a percent of your salary. And $25,000 to $50,000, was a half, and $50,000 and up, we suggested you contribute 1 percent of your salary.

This campaign contained all the key elements for success—commitment from the top, managers at each level talking to their immediate subordinates, small-group presentations, suggested donation levels, aggressive follow-through, and highly competent PAC staff. Other successful campaigns had the same general character:

> In the past we had a big, company, *total* commitment from the top down. The company founder and CEO was just absolutely a 110 percenter on the PAC, so the solicitation process was one of him talking to his subordinates, and his subordinates talking to their subordinates, saying, "Bob wants this." And the result was we had a pretty damn high percentage of participation, more than most PACs.

Campaigns that lacked one or more of these crucial elements were less successful in building participation. One corporation had someone who worked full-time on "marketing the PAC" but met with managers in groups of 100 to 150. This increased participation, but only a small proportion of managers ever contributed to the PAC. Another corporation sent out letters inviting, but not requiring, attendance: only 5 to 10 percent of those solicited came to meetings. The PAC staff made a presentation, but none of the employees' immediate superiors did so, and only 10 to 20 percent of those who came to the meetings ever enrolled in the PAC.

Some corporate PACs with aggressive campaigns offer a reward for participation, usually a token that differentiates contributors from noncontributors. Probably few would hang a plaque on an office wall, but a coffee mug with the PAC logo and slogan might be used. A yearly luncheon for PAC contributors with the company president has no monetary value but might be particularly rewarding to aspiring managers and certainly sets off participants from nonparticipants.

Occasionally the rewards are more substantial. A few corporations place contributors' names into a drawing for prizes. One always offers a trip to Washington and various activities there, a prize that reinforces the connection between the PAC and government. Another corporation ran a sweepstakes for all employees, whether or not they contributed to the PAC, but many people felt reluctant to participate in the sweepstakes without contributing to the PAC. At each location ten sweepstakes participants won savings bonds, and the national grand prize winner collected a trip to Hawaii. The costs of the sweepstakes may have been greater than the money employees contributed to the PAC, but the corporation could legally pay for sweepstakes prizes although it could not legally put money directly into the PAC.[14]

The most effective long-term PAC money-raising device is payroll deduction, the predominant and preferred method at virtually every corporation. Payroll deduction makes it easy and painless to contribute. Once employees sign up, they never again need to remember to contribute. Moreover, at many corporations the pledge is not for a fixed dollar amount but for a percentage of salary, so PAC receipts increase with pay raises. The person no longer needs to make an active commitment to the PAC; rather he or she must make an active decision to withdraw.

Level of participation in the PAC campaign is the most important determinant of amount of money generated, but a second significant factor is the length of time since the last campaign. At one extreme, a company had not conducted a PAC solicitation campaign for six years:

> That's the last time we ever solicited for the PAC, We have a little packet; when a new employee signs on, if they are an eligible PAC employee, they get a packet. That's one thing we are really overdue on, is to go back and resolicit, but we just have not done it.

Others also reported that "membership has eroded" and "we're going to try to put on a full court press next year." Another reported that "every time a guy gets transferred the thing falls off; when a guy transfers in here he doesn't tell us."

COERCION TO CONTRIBUTE

The ability to solicit employees as well as stockholders means that corporations are able to coerce contributors in a way no other kind of PAC can. Noncorporate PACs clearly receive only voluntary contributions because the PAC has no way to coerce potential donors. By law no one may be rewarded or penalized for a campaign contribution to either a candidate or a PAC. PACs formed solely to collect money and distribute it to candidates, with no connection to any other organization, have no possible way to violate this injunction. The situation is almost as clear for a trade or membership organization; belonging to the Sierra Club certainly doesn't coerce you to contribute to its political action committee, and roughly the same logic applies to the Pharmaceutical Manufacturers Association. Labor unions might seem the most similar to corporations, and they do sometimes negotiate with an employer to make it possible for union members to voluntarily withhold part of their wages for the union's PAC. This is similar to payroll deductions for corporate PAC contributions, and as with corporations, the individual union member must specifically sign up for the deduction.[15] The difference, however, is that a union has virtually no power to reward or penalize members for their contribution decisions.

If corporate PACs solicited only stockholders, as was intended by Congress, then corporate PACs would be in the same position as other PACs—able to plead for contributions, able to make contributing painless and barely noticeable, but unable to exert any meaningful pressure on contributors. Corporations could ask stockholders to designate that a percentage of their dividends be withheld automatically and given to the PAC. But under the rules as modified by the FEC's SUN-PAC decision, a corporation is able to solicit professional and managerial employees, a group subject to various forms of corporate control and pressure.[16] The corporation determines managers' pay, hours, job assignments, working conditions, reimbursement for expenses, and potential for upward mobility within the organization.

Studies of managers indicate the difficulties of objectively evaluating managerial performance, so companies generally use loose indicators of whether the person is a "team" player. In these circumstances coercion need not be blatant or crude. No employer need say, "If you don't give to the PAC, you'll never get another raise as long as I'm your boss." All an executive needs to say is, "This is important to the company, and I hope you can support me on this." Since evaluating managerial employees inevitably involves exercising subjective judgments, and since every personnel decision is based on various qualitative factors, managers generally strive to remain in upper management's good graces.[17] A refusal to contribute to the PAC would simply be part of a constellation of factors influencing the boss's evaluation, with even the boss unable to specify how much weight should be attributed to what factor. Under these conditions, a young middle-level executive with ambition could reasonably conclude that $200 a year to the PAC is a good investment in career promotion.

The only company we interviewed that admitted it had used an employee's refusal to participate in the PAC as a factor in penalizing the employee presented the case in exactly these terms:

We were never one bit nor are we reluctant in saying, "Hey, this is an important part of our business. We can't do without you. We really appreciate your assistance. Here's a guideline for contributions based on your income level." But the honest-to-God's truth of the matter is, I can tell you sincerely I don't think it's played any significant role anywhere in decisions about somebody's pay or bonus or any of those things. We genuinely did not take that approach—not for one single person in this company. Well, for fear that when I go to heaven one day God will remind me of that, with the exception of one or two people, and those were really for reasons where the PAC was one part of a whole series of problems with that person. People with just shitty attitudes in general including shitty attitudes about the PAC.

This company used less pressure than many others.[18] Probably few companies punish people specifically for refusing to contribute to the PAC. But a refusal to contribute to the PAC (or, at higher levels, making minimal contributions) undoubtedly becomes a factor in evaluating a person's attitude and management potential. Note the person quoted above says only that a person's attitude toward the PAC did not play any "significant" role in personnel decisions—not that it was never mentioned in discussions.

Employees can be pressured in ways not directly intended by top management. One PAC officer explained, "We have a United Way drive, a blood drive, a savings bond drive, all those kinds of things. Some departments take those things very seriously, and they are anxious to have 90 percent participation." A few managers treated PAC solicitation in the same way, and do the things necessary to achieve 90 percent participation. Some people who contributed to this corporation's PAC called the PAC officer to say, "I just want you to know that I really got my arm twisted." This PAC officer genuinely did not want contributions in such circumstances and returned their checks, but we have no way of knowing how many people who felt their arms had been twisted did not have the nerve to call and complain.

Only one of the corporate PACs we interviewed is structured to guarantee complete confidentiality to contributors. At this corporation, all transactions are done through the mail, employees are not directly solicited in person by another employee, no group meeting is held, no visible indicators of PAC participation are displayed, and no one in the company knows the names of contributors. This is a model operation, but the drawback is obvious: such a procedure is likely to raise far less money than more coercive methods. A significant number of additional corporations provide substantial confidentiality, but a nervous employee would have grounds for concern. A majority of corporations pressure employees without actively coercing them, and in a minority of cases the coercion is noticeable.

The PACs with the highest participation rates created conditions where many employees undoubtedly felt pressured—and correctly so, despite all the assurances of their PAC officials. The chair of the PAC committee at the corporation with the highest participation rate said, "There is no pressure," four separate times, but the process he describes belies this characterization. Every year he and the company's lobbyist go to each work unit and hold an employee meeting: "We talk about the PAC and what it means to the company and what it means to them as individuals, and we solicit their membership; if they are members we solicit an increase in their gift." Then the employees' boss is asked "to get up and say why they are members and why they think it's important for an employee to be a member." The upper-level manager clearly has no confidentiality, which in itself sends a strong message to others. In fact, a number of coercive elements converge in this solicitation: the meeting is public, employees are asked to commit themselves right then and there in the public meeting, the boss recommends that subordinates contribute, and the impression conveyed is probably that the boss will be evaluated on the basis of his or her employees' participation rate. This PAC committee chair insists there is no pressure but admits employees feel differently:

> And yet regardless of how many times you say that, there's always going to be some employees who feel that you got them into that meeting to put pressure on. But if they feel pressure, it's self-imposed from the standpoint of the solicitation. Because there will be several of us, including myself, who will get up and say, "We want you to be a member and here's why."

Even the chair's explanation of what he means by "no pressure" is enough to cause concern: "But as far as a manager or anybody getting up and telling you that if you don't participate we're going to fire you . . . there's no pressure." Perhaps no one says that employees will be fired for failing to contribute, but it seems likely that they will be told their boss is disappointed and their contribution or noncontribution will be remembered.

Most PACs fall somewhere in between these two extremes. Their companies undertake active campaigns only once every few years, campaigns generally involve compulsory small-group meetings during work time, and employees are solicited by someone who has been designated by the boss to undertake the task and thus potentially to report on results. Several PAC officers reported checking up on contributors:

I couldn't tell you how many of them are contributing at the suggested level [as a percentage of salary]. I look at the vice presidents, I look at the officers to get kind of a judge to see where they are. And to see where I'm letting down. The officers will contribute if you just go ask them. And I can spot check that. I can see where I am not coming through when we acquire new companies.

This kind of checking does not need to happen frequently to convince employees that it could happen to them next. One person we interviewed insisted that at her company top managers "absolutely don't" know who contributes to the PAC, but she also said, "I think that PAC members think that management knows."

The fact that many managers feel at least some coercion to contribute does not mean that all managers experience such pressure. Aside from those corporations that are scrupulously careful not to pressure anyone, at most corporations there is relatively little pressure on lower-level managers. The overall participation rates reflect this: most eligible employees do *not* contribute. In the corporations we interviewed, the lowest participation rate was under 4 percent of eligible employees; the highest was 92 percent. Regulated industries that make a major effort had the highest participation rates—generally half or more of their eligible employees. In our mail survey of PAC directors a majority of PACs had participation rates between 11 and 40 percent, with 30.2 percent in the 11 to 20 percent range and 24.5 percent in the 21 to 40 percent range. Only 5.7 percent received donations from fewer than 10 percent. At the upper end, 3.8 percent of PACs reported 100 percent participation rates, 9.4 percent reported rates between 81 and 99 percent, 9.4 percent reported rates of 61 to 80 percent, and 17.0 percent reported rates of 41 to 60 percent.[19] In such a situation lower- and even middle-level managers who refuse to participate are not alone, and the corporation is unlikely to focus much attention on any one person.

Many companies with modest participation rates, however, indicated virtually total participation by upper management. Even the corporation with the lowest participation rate, under 4 percent of eligible employees, reported that "the senior officers of the company are all members of the PAC, and for the most part a majority of upper-level management is." Many corporations did not even solicit all of the eligible employees, preferring to limit themselves to the higher levels, or had begun by doing so. Others solicit widely but make more effort and achieve greater success with the higher ranks; soliciting middle-level managers is almost an afterthought:

> We have forty-three officers or division officers in the Chairman's Club, and they give three-quarters to one-half of 1 percent of their base salary on a continuing basis. So every time they get a raise their contribution goes up. This goes on in perpetuity unless they say no. The Corporate Future Club is for middle managers, and we have ninety of those, and they give a minimum of $200 a year. And the rest of the people—we have about 700 people who give, 711 to be exact this year—give $1 or $2 a pay period, and we're talking about two-week pay periods.
>
> So 71 percent of our money is raised from 130 people. Those people aren't going to get out of it unless they change the law because I'm convinced those people realize what the PAC means. These are the people who take the interest. I still want to have the lower guy, but I don't push him as much. We send out newsletters, and the chairman writes a letter saying we think it's good government to do, but nobody's hassled and those are modest contributions.

High participation rates by top managers have at least two alternative explanations (which are not necessarily contradictory): (1) top executives are integrated into the corporate culture and likely to identify with the company, share its values, and trust its leaders; and (2) top managers are also visible and subject to coercion. In many companies, anyone in—or aspiring to—the upper levels of the corporation might well feel that refusing to contribute to the PAC would be held against him or her. Thus managers' hopes for advancement lead them to increase their PAC contributions, which furthers the corporation's political agenda.

UNTAPPED POTENTIAL

The potential for coercion is much greater than is now being exercised. Corporations put relatively mild pressure on employees compared to what they could do because most corporations already have as much money as they need. The company that admitted penalizing employees for their attitude to the PAC also reported the following:

> We have a pretty good level of participation. And moreover we've got enough. Once you get, for us, for what we want to do—if we get over

$100,000 a year in contributions, then we're really looking for ways to spend money.

Several other PACs reported, "We don't want to be much larger" and "We choose not to be bigger than we are." Other PACs wanted to be a little larger but not much. Only one person interviewed expressed a concern that her company was not able to raise enough money, and in our opinion this was the PAC with the least company commitment and the least sense of how to proceed. If this PAC simply undertook the kind of program that was standard at other companies, it could have significantly increased contributions.

The importance of this point cannot be stressed enough: business *chooses* to limit its campaign contributions and has the potential to enormously increase the amount it raises and distributes. With the possible exception of a few regulated utilities, no corporation we talked to has approached the limits of the amounts it could raise within the existing rules. The one corporation that reported making a major effort to increase its donations tripled the size of its PAC in a period of three years to become one of the largest corporate PACs—and it still had only a 27 percent participation rate. Virtually no corporation uses the kind of coercion that is available to them, and many put relatively little effort into raising PAC money.

How is this to be interpreted? A corporate spokesperson could reasonably argue that it is evidence of corporate responsibility and fair play and that most corporations are committed to obeying both the letter and spirit of campaign finance laws. We make an alternative argument: (1) current practices give corporations enough money to achieve a satisfactory if not ideal level of political influence; (2) more coercive fundraising techniques might be resented and resisted by the company's managers; and (3) business is already the largest source of PAC money, and additional contributions might create a public back-lash. Therefore, *as long as business political dominance is not seriously challenged,* corporations have no major incentive to raise additional PAC contributions.

Corporations could enormously increase the amount their PACs collect from managerial and professional employees. Corporations with PACs could raise far more from their contributors, and those without PACs could form them.[20] Even a small corporation, one with 200 managerial employees, that enrolled half of them in the PAC, contributing an average of $10 a week deducted from their pay, would raise $52,000 a year, or $104,000 per two-year election cycle.

Were corporations ever seriously challenged politically, the PAC mechanism now in place would make it relatively simple to dramatically increase business campaign contributions. A quick calculation indicates how much could be raised if all corporations raised PAC money as aggressively and successfully as today's best fundraisers.

In 1987–1988 Seagram's raised $8.71 in PAC money for every employee.[21] Ten percent of our manufacturing corporations had PACs that raised that much or more; 90 percent, less. Had every corporation in the *Fortune* 500 industrials raised this much per employee, those 500 corporations would have raised $111 million for PAC contributions. The service company at the ninetieth percentile, Morgan Stanley, raised $21.09 per employee. If the *Fortune* 500 service companies had each raised this much, they would have generated $232 million. Thus just these one thousand companies would have contributed $343 million, more than six times the total actually contributed by all corporations ($56 million). The *Fortune* 500 service and industrial companies together employ 24 million people, but there are 100 million workers in the private-sector labor force.

This hypothetical analysis of how much corporate PACs could raise if they tried can be counterposed to another hypothetical case: what might have happened if corporations had been held to the law as passed by Congress and allowed to solicit PAC funds from stockholders but not from employees? Without the FEC ruling allowing solicitation of employees, corporate PACs would be vastly less significant as a political force. We ourselves fell victim to business's success in removing the SUN-PAC decision from the public agenda. Because earlier researchers had not identified the issue of soliciting employees as opposed to stockholders, we at first erred in our research and failed to systematically investigate this question. It was not included on our survey, and we did not specifically ask about it in our interviews. As far as we know, no figures exist on the proportion of corporate PAC money that comes from stockholders as opposed to employees. Most of the corporate executives we asked indicated that none of their PAC money comes from stockholders, and no PAC reported that a significant fraction of its money comes from stockholders who are not also employees. If corporate PACs could solicit only stockholders, they would be chronically underfunded, short of the money needed to make gifts to politicians and build networks of obligation.

Running the PAC

The corporate PAC's major internal task is to raise money. But other aspects of internal structure and operations are also important. Corporations want to ensure that the PAC is oriented around the corporation's goals and interests and not those of either the contributors or the PAC officer. Moreover, the corporation also wants, if possible, to mobilize its managers as a political force—not so much from a concern that managers will actively oppose the corporation (although this is possible on issues such as environmentalism) but from a concern that they will be apathetic. Political power can be undermined by apathy as well as direct opposition; part of a successful hegemony is being sure that the people in your camp actively promote your position. Although most corporations we interviewed were primarily concerned with fund raising, several insisted that "it's as important to us that our employees be involved, write their congressmen, as it is that they give $100 or $200 for our PAC."

THE PAC'S INTERNAL STRUCTURE

The key means of ensuring that the PAC serves the corporation's purposes is the fact that by its nature, structure, and theory the PAC is *not* democratic. Noncorporate-affiliated PACs, such as those operated by labor unions or trade associations, are sponsored by organizations with an elected leadership that is responsible for the character and direction of the PAC. At least in theory opposition to the PAC's contributions could become an issue in the organization's next election campaign, and the membership could vote out its elected leaders.[22] If corporate PACs solicited contributions only from stockholders, as the law originally intended, they also would be democratically controlled, with those solicited by the PAC able to change the character of the PAC leadership.[23] It is often difficult for a democratic movement to replace an entrenched leadership, as the recent history of either the Teamsters[24] or Sears[25] shows, but the possibility is ever present, and at least in theory it is conceded that union members and corporate stockholders have the right (and responsibility) to control the organization.

The basic decisions about the PAC are usually made by a PAC officer, who typically is appointed by a top executive. Some PAC officers have been high-level aides to members of Congress or executive branch lobbyists. Others work their way up through corporate government relations departments, and still others work in government relations for only part of a career primarily spent in other areas of company management.[26]

In most corporations PAC officers, and government relations personnel more generally, have a great deal of influence in choosing candidates who receive donations. The PAC officer draws up a list of candidates and suggested donations. PAC officers, however, do not operate independently. Virtually all the companies we interviewed have a PAC committee that reviews and approves the PAC officer's suggested contributions. In our mail survey of corporate PAC directors, conducted in November 1986, 91 percent of respondents reported their corporation had a PAC committee. At least one high-ranking executive usually serves as a member of the PAC committee. In our survey, 11 percent reported that the chief executive officer is regularly involved in PAC decisions, 31 percent that an executive or senior vice president is, and 44 percent that a vice president is. Only 15 percent of responding corporations do not routinely include a vice president in PAC decision making.[27]

The PAC committee usually includes a representative from each of the corporation's major units. In the most common selection procedure a top executive, usually the CEO but sometimes an executive vice president or senior vice president, appoints the chair of the PAC committee, who consults with the heads of divisions in selecting other members. The most powerful PAC officers also chair the PAC committee, but more typically the committee chair significantly outranks the PAC officer. Units where the impact of government is clear and important develop more interest in the PAC and a tendency to involve higher-ranking employees. Existing literature on the political consciousness of corporate officials stresses the owners and top executives,[28] but PAC committees are used by corporations to extend political awareness and involvement to lower levels as well.

The PAC committee helps the PAC serve its corporate purpose by guaranteeing that the PAC and the government relations unit are aware of, and accountable to, the needs of the entire corporation. The PAC committee prevents corporate government relations officials from simply adopting a Washington insiders' perspective by constantly reminding them of the views and needs of a cross section of corporate units and departments. Because PAC officers must present and justify recommendations to half a dozen managers, each representing an operating division, they become sensitive to the viewpoint of line managers. The PAC also provides a set of contacts for government relations personnel to use when they solicit technical and political assistance from other parts of the corporation, which can be vital to the success of the access process (see chapter 4), both in identifying problems and in crafting solutions. Finally, committee discussions help to build political awareness and consensus within the corporation.

The vast majority of PAC officers' suggestions are accepted, but the PAC committee must approve all donations. If a PAC officer proposes 100 donations, of which ninety are accepted routinely, ten are vigorously debated, and only three rejected, then the committee has approved 97 percent of the PAC officer's recommendations. Nonetheless, the three rejected and ten disputed are likely to be long remembered and influence future suggestions. The discussion and occasional rejection of recommendations is part of the process by which the government relations staff comes to better understand the company's operating divisions and their concerns. At the same time, the operating units learn what is politically possible and how issues should be presented for maximum political effectiveness.

The PAC committee operates within a framework that guarantees it will adopt the basic corporate viewpoint: the committees are appointed, the corporate hierarchy selects individuals who are expected to take the corporate purpose as their own, and managers know that they will be evaluated on their performance on the committee. At the same time, however, the PAC committee creates at least the illusion of managerial participation and democracy. The PAC committee may be appointed, not elected, but it is democratic in the sense that committee members do vote on donations, even if they must operate within a framework determined by top officers. Because committee members are expected to defend their decisions, an attack on the PAC's contributions is a criticism of committee members, not just of a distant government relations officer. Because every major subdivision has a representative on the PAC committee, managers can meet someone in the course of routine business or socializing and say, "Joe, you're friends with Bill. Ask him why the hell the PAC gave a thousand bucks to that SOB in the state next door." Finally, the rotation of managers on and off the PAC committee creates a pool of at least minimally politically knowledgeable company employees.

Although the PAC officer and the PAC committee decide which candidates will receive donations, they do so within a framework established by the CEO and/or the board of directors. PAC officers recognize they are expected to serve the corporation's purposes. One PAC officer who was a senior vice president explained the limits to his power:

> All policy comes out of this company's corporate headquarters, and no matter what government liaison organizations within companies think they are doing, they are not making policy. They are there to carry out policy. It's the hardest thing for any government relations guy to admit, but he is sometimes called in to say, "This can't be done" or "If we are going to accomplish anything, this is what we can get done," but it still isn't making policy. Policy is made by the top of the company, and it filters down. They tell you what they want, and you do it.

No PAC officer disputed this, and none was in any doubt about it.

At the same time, however, most top managers allow PAC officers and PAC committees considerable discretion and do not attempt to micromanage the details of PAC decisions:

> We don't get a call from the forty-second floor saying, "These five senators and these ten representatives." That doesn't happen. . . . I can't recall an instance when we have just been told, "You have to do this or that." In fact, they really don't look over our shoulders that close as to what we are doing. I think there is a certain amount of confidence in our ability.

The structure ensures that subordinates will carry out policy that is made at the top. Top executives don't want to spend time deciding which incumbents should receive contributions to facilitate future access. The chair of one PAC committee, an executive vice president and member of his company's board of directors, explained:

> My role is really one to provide philosophical guidance as to whether the PAC is on the right track—if it's doing the kind of things that are consistent with our corporate culture, with our norms, with our mores, with what we feel strongly about in terms of both the board and the management as a philosophical direction of the company. So it's to provide that philosophical leadership, if you will, but it's not to get involved in the day-to-day implementation.

PAC officers and PAC committees then make the day-to-day government relations decisions—decisions that rarely are challenged, one PAC officer explained, "because we give them [top executives] what they need."

INCREASING MANAGERS' POLITICAL PARTICIPATION

Corporate PACs increase managerial awareness of politics. As one PAC officer reported, "We have found if you have some sort of organization where employees can put their money in, and then go out and help educate the employees about where their money is going, they become a lot more politically astute." The corporation heightens and shapes managers' political awareness by publishing PAC newsletters, inviting members of Congress to speak at company facilities, and requiring managers to attend meetings about the PAC. Most corporations send contributors information about PAC activities, although some provide very little. One ideological PAC, for example, does not list the political party of the candidates to whom it contributes because a high proportion of its contributions go to Republicans and the company doesn't want Democratic managers to realize this.

Contributors are usually allowed to suggest donations to specific candidates. The typical experience is that "it's rare that we get a suggestion, but when we do, it's rare that the request isn't honored." A corporation that emphasized its efforts to get suggestions from PAC contributors was especially unhappy about the results:

> I don't know whether it's because they don't care, whether they just have a great deal of trust in what we do, or whether they feel because of what we do, we know more about it. In any case, we go out of our way to get suggestions. Every time a communication goes out—a couple times a year from our chairman, once or twice a year from me, once or twice a year from [my assistant]—we always say in there some way, "Look, we solicit your support. Tell us the information you want to know. Tell us if you want us to do something. Tell us who you would like to have us support. I guarantee that if you make a suggestion, it will get the same review as anything I suggest." But I think the participation is abysmal. Our problem is not we got too many leaders. Our problem is how do you wake them up. I wouldn't want that attributed to me.

Many PAC officers felt that managers' interest in the PAC is linked to the degree to which it affects them directly:

> I think that the people that are out in the field who have to deal with the things that government gives you in business are probably more likely to give. That's why we have so many chemical employees that give. Because they have to put up with all this environmental stuff all the time. And they

feel like, "Hey, if there's ever anything that we can do to change some of this, give it a go."

Sometimes managers become concerned with government relations because they can see a direct connection to their own pay:

> You feel sorry for some of these guys who are poor little district managers out in the plants who are going to get screwed because [a proposed law] says, "You have to upgrade your asbestos control to this level." And he's budgeted for a lower level for this year, and he knows he is going to take a $500,000 hit. And he's crying because his bonus for the year or his merit award is down the tubes. And you can't tell him, "It's not a major issue for us, it's only a half million bucks."

A handful of corporations have aggressive campaigns to involve their managers in politics. Once a year they send perhaps a hundred managers to Washington to attend a seminar on the political process and to meet with their member of Congress and/or appropriate staff. The PAC officer at one such company reported that:

> At the time we began this, I would say 80 percent of the [company] employees who were there in the various plant locations would no more go up and speak to a congressman or senator than fly to the moon. They somehow felt that a senator or congressman just put on his pants differently than they did. But we didn't leave it up to them; we scheduled appointments. This program is a wonderful, wonderful device in getting people keenly interested in participating and giving them knowledge of the issues.

The contrast between this program and what most corporations do indicates how limited political activity and mobilization usually are. Corporate managers have higher voting participation rates and more active political involvement than the general population, but these levels are still fairly low. For example, studies indicate that only 73 percent of managerial employees in this country bother to vote in elections; 88 percent of *workers* vote in Sweden.[29] Here, as with raising money, corporations have only scratched the surface of their ability to increase managers' political mobilization.

DEMOCRACY IN ACTION?

The internal functioning of corporate PACs indicates how they relate to and evaluate democracy. Most aspects of the political system are beyond the direct control of corporations, but they *can* determine how their PACs operate and make decisions. As a result, in all but a handful of corporate PACs democratic control is not even a theoretical possibility. The PAC raises its money from employees, but employees do not and cannot vote on the leadership or policies of either the PAC or the corporation. The PAC officer who runs the PAC is appointed; no corporation elects its PAC officer—any more than employees elect any other corporate official. Although PACs do sometimes change political directions, this happens because the corporation is acquired, or a new CEO takes office, not because contributors are dissatisfied.[30]

Not only the PAC officer is appointed: virtually all PAC committees are appointed, not elected. The chair of one of the handful with elections explained:

> We have a steering committee that's elected by the members. We send out ballots for the steering committee. It's a Russian election,[31] admittedly: there is a slate of nominees and there is an opportunity for people to write in, but as a practical matter it's almost impossible for a write-in to win.

The only corporation that reported that it does have some contested elections concurred that, in general: "It is an elected-appointive—it's kind of a pseudo-election, I guess, is what it amounts to."

Because ideological PACs stress general principles of support for democracy and the "free" enterprise system, it would be logical to assume they would be exceptions to the undemocratic organization of corporate PACs. Not at all. At one corporation that prided itself on its support of the "free enterprise system," the chair of the PAC matter-of-factly noted, "If our [company] chairman said, 'We are going to have a certain kind of PAC,' then we'd have an option of resigning or doing it the way he wanted." At another ideological PAC, where all members of the PAC committee are among the top ten corporate officers, PAC committee deliberations are

> never heated because it's not a very democratic system. The thoughts that you have and the thought processes coming out of those individuals are pretty much congruent and consistent with the others. They are all senior management. It would be different, I think, if you had a plant manager here or employee relations people or a salesperson from California or whatever on that committee.

The undemocratic character of corporate PACs is consistent with the principles guiding the corporation as a whole. Corporations are not run on democratic principles, and employees don't vote on the leadership and policies of the corporation. In fact, many corporate executives are dubious about democracy in general. Leonard Silk and David Vogel attended a set of meetings organized by the Conference Board for top executives and concluded that

> while critics of business worry about the atrophy of American democracy, the concern in the nation's boardrooms is precisely the opposite. For an executive, democracy in America is working all too well—*that is the problem.*[32]

Similarly, a report to the Trilateral Commission, a group organized by David Rockefeller and composed primarily of top executives, although also including opinion leaders from academia and a sprinkling of labor leaders, argued that "an excess of democracy means a deficit of governability."[33]

CONGRESS APPROVES

Are members of Congress and the Federal Election Commission aware of, and concerned about, the fact that corporate PACs can coerce employees, that those who control the corporation control what is done with the "voluntary" contributions made by managers? Yes and no.

No, they aren't concerned about the consequences of the SUN-PAC decision for U.S.-owned corporations. No significant group in Congress is trying to make corporate PACs behave like other PACs. This gives corporations an extraordinary advantage in fundraising: corporations would raise far less money if corporate PACs were restricted to soliciting from stockholders, as the law originally intended before the FEC's SUN-PAC decision.

Nor is Congress concerned that corporations do not reflect the views and preferences of managers who contribute to the PAC—that the corporation shapes the managers' views, mobilizes them, and directs them to serve corporate purposes. If a member of Congress receives a delegation of constituents who understand the law and speak against it, the meeting has an effect, even if the member recognizes that these managers have heard only the company's side and are making the lobbying trip on full pay at company expense.[34] These uncontested features of corporate PACs are both evidence of, and further reinforcements to, business hegemony.

Although Congress is untroubled by the extraordinary advantages of *U.S.-owned* corporations, it worries about *foreign-owned* corporations. To Congress the problem is not the lack of democracy; the problem is that U.S., not foreign, capitalists should be dominating U.S. managers. Several members have proposed that U.S. subsidiaries of foreign-owned corporations should be prohibited from forming or operating PACs. At present, a PAC may be formed by a foreign-owned subsidiary, "provided that its principal place of business is in the United States, that its PAC is administered by American citizens and that only American citizens contribute to the PAC."[35] Senator Lloyd Bentsen wrote a letter to his Senate colleagues in May of 1990 proposing legislation to restrict foreign-controlled corporate PACs, arguing that the FEC had permitted

"foreign companies to buy into our political process by acquiring U.S. subsidiaries." This, he said, "creates inevitable pressures on employees to use their PAC muscle in ways acceptable to the corporate masters in London or Frankfurt or Tokyo." The senator's letter said his bill "would safeguard U.S. employees from cross-pressures or potential conflicts of interest and would limit what has been a rapidly growing source of foreign influence on domestic American politics."[36]

Members of Congress have no wish to restrict the owners of U.S. corporations in order to prevent them from controlling the actions of their employees. On the contrary, Representative Marcy Kaptur (D-Ohio), cosponsor of similar legislation in the House, said, "Our elections should be controlled by U.S. interests, not foreign interests that may conflict with our own on a world-wide basis."[37]

Most corporations frankly admit that the PAC serves the corporation's interest, and managers are not at all reluctant to talk about it:

The thing that the committee has to keep in mind is this: what we do is not a manifestation of our own personal political preferences. It is a manifestation of what we collectively think is good for [the company]. I've got Bill Gallagher, who is our corporate treasurer: he's to the right of Attila the Hun. So when we have to give money to a liberal, it's very hard for him. But the purpose of the PAC is *not* to pander to his particular political leanings.

The next chapter examines what the purpose of the PAC is.

Chapter 3

###

GIFTS: NETWORKS OF OBLIGATION

###

PAC contributions are generally viewed in one of two ways: as bribes or as a way of using money to "vote" for candidates whose positions the PAC supports. Too often reform advocates have seen campaign contributions as a form of legalized bribery, a view encapsulated in Will Rogers's famous remark that we have "the best Congress money can buy" (also the title of Philip Stern's 1988 book). This narrow definition of the issue is likely to undercut meaningful reform. First, most corporate campaign contributions are given to people who already are sympathetic to the company's position. And most attempts to show that members of Congress switch sides in response to donations have found only weak effects. Second, the bribe metaphor concentrates attention on those instances with the most direct linkage between the contribution and the member's action. Although these cases may involve the most spectacular abuses, we argue that they are incidental to the *system* of campaign finance. Even were all such abuses eliminated, the fundamental character of the system would remain the same: disproportionate influence by those with money and power.

The primary alternative perspective argues that PAC contributions are like votes. A contribution is simply another way of expressing support, says one executive:

> What business PACs ought to be is a device by which business managers with similar political views can act together in support of those political views. Most businessmen don't have very much time to devote to understanding candidates and politics. They have a great interest in it; they don't have much time for it. The congressman from Nevada votes for the

legislation that affects you in Massachusetts and Michigan just as much as the congressmen from Massachusetts and Michigan: that's a reality. Therefore, you have an interest in all of them. You don't have time to research it. Business PACs are a very convenient and effective device by which business managers with similar interests can voluntarily band together to support those political interests and values.

This view argues that PAC contributions are disinterested and perhaps even noble means of participating in the democratic process. The executive who offered this view ran an ideological PAC; he felt this was the way a corporate PAC "ought to be. And if it were, that'd be a damn good thing." However, in his opinion most corporate PACs are engaged in a form of bribery. This chapter, and the book as a whole, develops a third perspective. In our view most PAC contributions should be analyzed as gifts that are intended to create a feeling of obligation.

Understanding Gifts

Candidates can't legally offer to exchange money for favorable policy decisions, and PACs (or others with money) can't legally require a candidate to take a certain position in exchange for money. The money that changes hands is a *gift*—theoretically freely given without the expectation of an equivalent being returned.[1]

Modern capitalist society is based on the market and market exchanges. In cash transactions some people are nice, some mean, most treat each other like nonpersons; but personal relations usually don't affect the transaction.[2] The market is so pervasive that its language, forms, and modes of thought dominate many aspects of life: virtually all social phenomena, even congressional votes, are for sale. Can't find a date in other ways? Pay a dating service to arrange a proper match. Need someone to listen, sympathize, and lend you support? Pay a therapist. Do you treasure the great outdoors—blue skies, sparkling streams, untouched forests? Some economist has calculated how much they are "worth" and recommended appropriate public policy based on these imputed values.[3]

The recognized and accepted alternative to the market is relations based purely on selfless love or friendship—above all the family. Friendships and families are not organized on market principles and, according to the myth, involve no rules, limits, or calculations. The family is said to be a unit where each member is valued beyond price, all work together for the common good with no consideration of who is doing more or less, and each is prepared to support the others "for better, for worse, for richer, for poorer, in sickness and in health, until death do us part." To a lesser degree the same is said to characterize friendships.

These two kinds of social relations—market exchange and self-lessness—are the primary models available in our society. Although people recognize that most relations fall somewhere in between these two extremes, our culture pushes people to think in terms of one of these models. This is true for the corporate PAC officials we interviewed as well; their comments revealed that they often had difficulty escaping the bounds imposed by these categories. They do not have a language or framework in which to understand or explain their own activity. Thus during an interview an individual frequently would alternate points of view—at times arguing that contributions bought them absolutely nothing and thus had no impact on the decision-making process and at times arguing that the PAC was a vital means of gaining access to members of Congress. It would be easy to see this vacillation as a public relations strategy and an attempt to deceive, but we think the confusion is real and that participants as well as ordinary voters lack a way to understand the meaning and effect of donations.

Spurred by the women's movement, social scientists have attempted to overcome this dualistic thinking. Arlie Hochschild pointed out that many market relations are based on *The Managed Heart:*[4] the flight attendant is required to smile and be friendly, the bill collector to be stern and unforgiving. Even the automated and depersonalized fast-food industry emphasizes its friendly service. Nor are family relations untouched by the market: a host of studies have shown that families involve economic relations and unequal power.[5]

Similarly, we want to question the dualism prevalent in many popular views of rules. Actions are often conceived either as enforced by state power in a legal bureaucratic system or else as unregulated. In fact, *social* regulatory processes often are more powerful and effective than *legal* enforcement. The most successful and pervasive rules may be precisely those that are not recognized as rules. People who violate unarticulated rules—who talk to themselves out loud in public, turn their backs to people when talking to them, or stand facing the back of the elevator—may be labeled as "crazy."[6] One study of "Middletown" residents argued that such social rules influence conduct even if people do not think of them as rules and resent having them identified as such.

Regarding one of these rules, Caplow argues that "few of the written laws that agents of the state attempt to enforce with endless paperwork and threats of violence are so well obeyed as this unwritten rule that is promulgated by no identifiable authority and backed by no evident threat."[7] Similarly, PAC officials frequently insist that their gifts are not necessarily reciprocated, that they do not expect them to be, and that PAC contributions have little or no impact on a member's behavior. Such self-serving claims may be knowingly deceptive, but PAC officials, like "Middletown" residents, may not recognize the rules they obey and may resent having them articulated.

While we generally shy away from thinking about gifts systematically and analytically, gifts, whether in the United States or Samoa, follow *rules* that regulate what is and is not socially appropriate. The general principles regulating gift giving have been analyzed for "primitive" societies where gifts are the fundamental organizing principle of social exchange. The classic work is Marcel Mauss's *The Gift: Forms and Functions of Exchange in Archaic Societies,* originally published in French in 1925. Mauss had no knowledge of corporate PACs, but his analysis often reads as if it were developed specifically for them. Mauss opens with a quote from the Scandinavian *Havamal:*

> "That friendship lasts longest . . . in which friends both give and receive gifts. A man ought to be a friend to his friend and repay gift with gift. . . . If you have a friend in whom you have sure confidence and wish to make use of him, you ought to exchange ideas and gifts with him and go to see him often. . . . A gift always looks for recompense."[8]

He begins his own text by noting that "in Scandinavian and many other civilizations contracts are fulfilled and exchanges of goods are made by means of gifts."[9] Mauss says such gifts are supposedly "voluntary, disinterested and spontaneous" but in fact are "obligatory and interested."

In the campaign finance system, the process of giving and receiving money is fundamental to the creation of the social world shared by members of Congress and corporate government relations officials. Caplow finds that Christmas gifts should be wrapped and typically are opened at public occasions. Similarly, corporate PAC officials don't just drop their checks in the mail; they insist on delivering them personally and using this delivery to create a personal connection. Caplow has noted that "ritualized gift giving, in any society, is a method of dealing with important but insecure relationships, whereby gifts are offered to persons or collectivities whose goodwill is needed but cannot be taken for granted."[10] In campaign finance, tremendous uncertainty, for both members and businesses, leads both sides to feel vulnerable and to seek some way to give themselves an advantage. A company's very existence may depend on government action (or inaction). A member's political survival at the next election may depend on having enough money to buy extra television ads. A gift, either of political influence (by a member) or of cash (by a PAC), goes at least part way to reduce the uncertainty about how the other will respond.

In markets each exchange involves its own reciprocal: I give you $11.98, and you give me the latest album by the Housemartins. We each accept this as a fair and even trade and have no expectation that one of us will later do something additional to complete this exchange.[11] I may regard the Housemartins' album as a pearl beyond price or may find it terribly disappointing, but unless the record is damaged, this exchange is finished and we need never see each other again. A gift, however, creates a more enduring relationship. From the moment I receive your gift until the time I am able to reciprocate it, we are bound to each other; me by the (implicit but very real) obligation to provide you with an object or service, you by the (unstated but nonetheless real) expectation of receiving an equivalent.[12] Thus gifts create denser and more enduring social relationships than market exchanges.

Gifts are governed by what Alvin Gouldner[13] calls "the norm of reciprocity": if I do something for you, you are expected to reciprocate. You probably do not respond to my gift with an exact equivalent; to do so reduces the breadth and impact of the social relationship, and creates the sense of a forced and measured response, rather than the illusion of one given freely and without calculation. If I unexpectedly need someone to watch my children and ask my neighbor to do so for me, the appropriate response when I pick up my kids is simply to thank my neighbor, perhaps adding, "Let me know if I can help you out sometime." To hand them an IOU reading "Good for fifty-eight minutes of child care at an emergency time of your choosing" would be insulting, implying that they helped me only in hopes of a return, I will compensate them exactly, and thus this is a market exchange creating no bonds or claims to a future relationship. Nonetheless, over time gift exchanges usually are roughly in balance; when they are not, both sides probably are aware of this fact.

Relationships that are not in balance are likely to reflect a recognized difference in power and status. Thus employers regularly give their domestics old clothing and discarded objects. Judith Rollins[14] reports the reactions of a domestic to this practice:

> This woman was always giving me her old size five-and-a-half shoes. I wear an eight! But my mother always said, and she did domestic work for years, she said, "No matter what they give you, you take it." . . . But if it was something I didn't want, I'd thank her, walk out of there, go around that corner and the first trash can I got to, I'd throw it in.

The domestic is required to show effusive and eternal gratitude, even if the objects are worthless and totally unwanted. Almost universally, domestics express hostility to, and resentment for, a system that degrades them: They put up with this system because of the power differential in this relationship; were a domestic to offer an employer a gift of used clothing or equipment, it would be perceived as grossly insulting and probably lead to her being fired. Candidates for political office sometimes feel they are in a similar situation. "Hubert Humphrey described campaign fund-raising as 'the most disgusting, demeaning, disenchanting, debilitating experience of a politician's life.' And he died before it got bad."[15] People "maintain ascendancy by regulating the indebtedness of others to them. . . . William F. Whyte, for instance, notes that the leader takes care not to fall into debt to his followers but to insure, on the contrary, that the benefits he renders unto others are never fully repaid."[16] Corporate PACs want always to have contributed to a member of Congress before they ask him or her for a favor.

Mauss's categorization of the Maori system in New Zealand is particularly appropriate to corporate PAC contributions to members of Congress: "In this system . . . one gives away what is in reality a part of one's nature and substance, while to receive something is to receive a part of someone's spiritual essence."[17] Corporations and members of Congress each give a part of their nature and substance—money for corporations, favors for members. On the one hand this nature and substance of both members and corporations is public information, but at the same time "the presentation of a gift is an imposition of identity."[18] When members accept campaign contributions, they implicitly indicate they view the donor as legitimate and will in the future be willing to discuss issues. Members return campaign contributions on occasion, though rarely.[19]

Deciding on Contributions

REQUESTS AND MEMBER PRESSURE

Individuals give gifts to their friends, to those who invite them to special occasions, to those with whom they would like to be friends, and sometimes to those working for a worthy cause. Wedding gifts are almost never unsolicited; an invitation virtually demands a present, whereas an announcement makes a gift optional. Similarly, PACs rarely contribute except in response to requests: "We don't go out looking for people to give money to anymore. We are inundated with requests for money." This flood of invitations reduces the practical consequences of giving only in response to invitations:

> I think any PAC administrator will tell you that we are just besieged with requests—both in Washington and the whole industry—for funding. It's horrendous. Whether they have campaigns or not, opponents or not.

On the other hand, it is significant that PACs felt they should only respond to requests and indicated that in many cases a member did not receive a contribution simply because he or she did not ask for one.

Most of the media attention has focused on the ways PACs coerce members of Congress,[20] but the reverse is also true. Mauss notes that to refuse to accept a gift, and sometimes even to refuse to give one, is "the equivalent of a declaration of war; it is a refusal of friendship and intercourse."[21] In the great majority of cases the member's request for a contribution is low key, a simple invitation in the mail. At other times, however, the request resembles the Godfather's "I'll make 'em an offer they can't refuse." One common experience of pressure beyond the mail invitation, but a very long way from any kind of threat, is the mention of a fundraiser:

> You go into an audience with a member and his staff and somebody, usually a staff guy, is going to mention they have a fundraiser coming up. That's how it happens sometimes. Or if you're not a contributor, your people come to town, you'll get a young staff member, while if you're a contributor, particularly in the thousand up—oh, I don't know, strike that, even a contributor, 250, 500, or whatever—then you're going to get a more important staff member.

The congressional staff who mention a fundraiser are sending the PAC officer a gentle reminder that one good turn deserves another.

Member messages can be much stronger. One lobbyist told the *Wall Street Journal* that for Senator Alfonse D'Amato (R-N.Y.), "Nothing is enough. It's continuous pressure. If you don't contribute, they don't return your calls."[22] One corporate government relations officer we interviewed reported that in 1978 a member wanted to know if his corporation had a PAC before agreeing to schedule a meeting. (The corporation didn't but promptly formed one.) Others have gone even further:

> Heavy-handed is a precise way of describing the tactics employed by South Dakota's Republican Senator James Abdnor in hitting up Washington lobbyists and PAC managers to buy $1,500 tickets to a fundraising dinner at which President Reagan was to be the star attraction. Abdnor sent the invitation around by messenger, with a reply card giving the invitee three choices: to make a $5,000 PAC contribution; to buy one or more tickets; or to say "No, our PAC does not wish to support the Salute to Jim Abdnor featuring President Reagan." What angered many PAC managers was Abdnor's instruction to the messenger not to leave the invitee's office without a response of some kind.[23]

These PAC officers were at least given the chance to say no without any stated consequences. Although it is uncommon for members or congressional staffs to demand contributions as a quid pro quo for favors rendered, many PACs have experienced demands at least occasionally:

> We just last year contributed to Lloyd Bentsen [D-Tex. and chair of the Senate Finance Committee]. That was in the off year, I think: the year preceding the election. And that was out of necessity. We contacted his office for something and were pretty much told point blank that "you don't contribute to us; why should we even help you?" I know that to this day that makes one of our executives sick—that we contributed to Bentsen. Our executive was still gagging last fall because we had done that.

Another PAC officer reported that though John Kerry (D-Mass.) makes a public issue out of not accepting PAC contributions, his staff nonetheless called the corporation to say that $5,000 in personal contributions were expected from the company's executives.

No one really knows what happens if the PAC does not contribute, but if the member is aggressive and is someone the corporation has had or expects to have dealings with, its officers feel unwilling to risk the possible consequences. The corporation cannot anticipate its future problems or predict how long the member and staff will remember the refusal to contribute or what the member will (or won't) do if he or she does remember. But in a situation where this member's support or opposition could change the company's bottom line by millions or even billions, is it worth incurring displeasure to save a measly $1,000 in PAC money?

> It would be a natural thing for a member or their staff to say, "Gee, we're having a fundraiser, and I hope you can be there." Well, I would imagine that if you can't be there and you can't be there over time, that you probably would not be too welcome.

Members and their staffs are prepared to accept an occasional refusal, especially if there is a prior history: "Some cases your relations with a guy go back so far, he might get upset and call you a cheap bastard, but he would not end the relationship."

PACs told us many stories of members of Congress who pressured them to contribute. In the mail survey we conducted, five out of six (83.7 percent) PACs that responded reported that candidates pressured their PAC for a contribution at least occasionally, and one in five (18.8 percent) said this happened frequently. Asked to assess the amount of pressure candidates place on PACs in general, not just on their PAC, only one in twenty-five (3.6 percent) answered "none," almost a third (30.9 percent) said "a small amount," a majority (52.7 percent) answered "a moderate amount," and one in ten (10.9 percent) said "a great deal." Candidate pressure is not a rare event, but neither is it a major problem for most corporate PACs. It does, however, establish a framework for daily activity and is a factor that most PACs are conscious of much of the time. PAC officers feel that this pressure is increasing:

> In the past we have always gotten calls from the administrative assistants to congressmen. Now the congressmen are so hungry for money they are calling themselves. I had two congressmen call last week.

Although PAC officers are partly responsible for this, many of them are nonetheless unhappy when it happens:

> The other thing that makes me sad is when my phone rings and it's Senator So-and-So calling me on the phone to beg for money. And I say to myself, "Jesus Christ, the business of running this government is more important than you being on the phone all day calling PAC people!"

In addition to requests for contributions from members of Congress and their staffs, PACs also receive requests from officials of other corporations, and those are among the ones most likely to be honored. Networks of obligation thus are created between one corporation and another as well as between a corporation and a member—an important point discussed further in chapter 6 on business unity.

It is perfectly legal for members of Congress to pressure PACs, just as it is legal for PACs to proposition members. Recent rulings of the Reagan-Bush Supreme Court make it very difficult to convict anyone of bribery or extortion: "a public official, to be guilty of extortion under Federal law, must promise to do a specific favor in exchange for money or other compensation he received."[24] A member of Congress can aggressively ask for money and can even promise vague assistance, but as long as the request is for a gift, with no explicit promise of a specific quid pro quo, the Supreme Court sees no legal problem.

THE DECISION PROCESS

Pragmatic and ideological PACs make different kinds of contributions and use different decision-making criteria. The overwhelming majority of corporate contributions are pragmatic. They can be compared to a wedding gift given to a friend as part of a set of reciprocal exchanges, based on both friendship and obligation. A few PACs are primarily or exclusively ideological, and most give at least some such contributions. These are similar to charitable gifts: the donor's main aim is to help see to it that good works continue to be performed, although the donor also may appreciate being recognized as a patron.

No PAC contributes to all candidates, so each PAC must decide which requests to honor. The initial screening of candidates is done by the government relations office and referred to the PAC committee composed of middle- and upper-level managers from all divisions of the corporation. Requests that are denied by the government relations office are very unlikely to be considered thereafter:

> Seventy-five percent of the requests that come for contributions to federal candidates are processed through the Washington office and just get filed. They decide they don't want to recommend a contribution. So it just never shows up on the agenda.

In corporations where the PAC committee is taken seriously, the PAC officer or government relations representatives fill out forms about the candidates they recommend for contributions. Forms are kept to one or at most two pages so that committee members can glance through each and check the one or two factors that most concern them.[25] In a typical access PAC the government relations staff "gives us all the background and then gives us a little bit of a summary on what committees and subcommittees they're on and what things they have helped us on in the past." Ideological PACs provide basic information about the candidate but supplement that not with committee assignments but with "voting records, the recommendations of outside organizations, what the positions of the challenger are, how close the race is expected to be. I pick out key issues that are important to us and say here's how they voted on these issues—Clean Air Act, product liability, plant closing, and there's one other I did last year." Most companies with active PAC committees supplement these forms by buying each member of the committee a copy of one or another standard reference work such as the *Almanac of American Politics*. These invaluable guides contain about two pages of text and information about each member of Congress—their voting records, reputation, any issues they are identified with, whether they have been involved in scandal, their past opponents, whether they are expected to face a tough challenge, the character of the district, and so on. The *Almanac* is engagingly written, thoroughly researched, and often surprisingly hard hitting in its evaluation of each member's perceived intelligence, competence, and character. These sources make it possible for PAC committee members to make informed judgments and not simply rubberstamp decisions made by the government relations office.

PRAGMATIC CRITERIA

Pragmatic PACs evaluate as key factors the members' committee assignments, past relationship with the company, and willingness to help out. As a senior vice president at one utility company explained:

> When people help you get a tax abatement or someone goes out of their way to make certain that rights of way are more easily procured or certain bureaucratic obstacles are removed, you tend to want them to be there if you ever need to come back again. So you will make those contributions in that situation.

Most of these decisions are fairly simple and nonproblematic:

> If we have a member in Congress that's on the energy committee or has helped us with acid rain or environmental issues, we don't question that a whole lot because that's kind of what we're about.

On the other hand, some access-oriented PACs give even to members who have opposed their positions, trying to create a sense of indebtedness even among adversaries:

> We have operated our education program on the basis of not only getting to the people we know are sympathetic to our activities and what we think our needs might be, but also to help win over some of the folks who are presumed to be on the other side. And if you don't do anything with them, if you just leave them alone, they are bound to be on the other side. So we have helped some people who actually were negative on our issues. If you back off and leave it to the opposition, then for sure we'll lose their support. You might not be able to get that person's vote, but you might be able to neutralize them to the point that they would understand that there is another side to that issue and might be willing to walk away from the issue rather than go in and do something that you may not like.

Much academic literature argues that members of Congress frequently do favors for companies not because they have received corporate PAC contributions but because the company and its employees are the member's constituents. Constituency relationship is said to be more important than campaign contributions in explaining which companies get access to and support from which members. PAC directors often agreed with the logic of this academic argument and argued that if the company had a large plant in a member's district, they didn't need a PAC to see the member. Nonetheless, PACs *do* contribute to such members. Corporations reinforce the constituency relationship with a PAC contribution. In our mail survey of corporate PACs, 60 percent indicated that having company operations in a member's district makes "a great deal" of difference in their decision, and a further 25 percent indicated it makes "a moderate amount" of difference. Time after time PACs took it for granted that they would contribute to races in the districts where they have employees or investments. It is therefore mistaken to contrast PAC contributions and constituency relationship.

Why would a company give donations if it already had a constituency relationship with a member? Wouldn't constituency by itself be enough to gain the company access? One of our PAC directors explained the practical fallacy in the academic argument:

First, you have to remember if you have a plant with 500 people, 450 are labor or union or nonmanagement. And so if you look around on that basis, in theory the member normally is not going to vote with you because normally the guy in the plant is not concerned with the same issues that our chairman of the board is.

Secondly, I find it's not unusual for a member of the House, or particularly a senator, to not be conversant with the fact that you are in his state or district—until you get to one of the staffers, and you remind him you are X, Y, and Z. "Oh yes, now I remember you." I think we also have a tendency to think the first thing they do when they wake up is think, "How is [our corporation] doing?" And that's not the first thing they do in the morning. They may never do that during the day. I think that most of the people that I talk to, constituency relationship is clearly one of the criteria.

Pragmatic PACs are also influenced by two rather apolitical considerations—general competence and compatibility:

I think it is much more important to be able to get in and see even an opposition member that will work and pay attention to what you say, and when they realize their natural inclination is not what is correct, they've got your input, than it is to have some yo-yo out there who is with you all the time but doesn't understand. Because they are ineffective in influencing their colleagues. And you can't get a whole body that is going to do what you want to do. So the idea is that the smarter they are and the more access you have to them, the more useful they are in the process.

Some PAC officers also stressed that there were certain candidates with whom they just "hit it off" and found it easy to deal with. One woman PAC officer had met a woman candidate for an open seat at a "meet and greet" sponsored by the Republican party and had enjoyed talking to her. Even though the company targeted the bulk of its money to incumbents, the PAC made a donation to this candidate, who went on to win, and the relationship has continued.[26]

IDEOLOGICAL CONTRIBUTIONS

Ideological PACs, or access PACs making one of their limited number of ideological contributions, have a somewhat harder time of it. Giving to challengers generally means that the PAC cannot be guided by past giving but must research the candidates anew each year. Moreover, ideological contributions are targeted to close races, and it is generally difficult to predict in advance which races they will be. Some contributions are given as seed money to help a challenger become viable; those decisions can be made ahead of time, but many decisions need to be compressed into the last few months of a campaign. Access-oriented contributions, on the other hand, can be made almost equally well at any time, since the issue is not the election but the member's power and willingness to help.

Most ideological PACs rely in significant part on the recommendations of BIPAC (the Business-Industry Political Action Committee), the Chamber of Commerce, and in a perverse way on the ADA (Americans for Democratic Action) and the AFL-CIO's COPE (Committee on Political Education). This simplifies their decision making.

> We use the Americans for Democratic Action, and we use its mirror image, the ACA [Americans for Constitutional Action]. You can take a look at those five numbers, and you know what he is. He can sit and make speeches to you all day, but you look at those five numbers. If the ADA says he's liberal, and the ACA says he's liberal, and the AFL-CIO/COPE says that he is pro-labor, and the U.S. Chamber of Commerce says he's the most anti-business son-of-a-bitch you ever saw, and BIPAC says he doesn't have an ounce of fiscal responsibility, you got a fix on him. It doesn't matter what he tells you.

BIPAC analyses are particularly useful because they also make an effort to seek out promising "free enterprise" challengers:

> BIPAC analyses are good; they're hunting for the same kind of candidates as we are; therefore, they tend to be very relevant to us. . . . They're very active in this, and they've got some first-rate people doing the analysis. We don't always agree with them, but we always find their analyses relevant.

Academic studies often use ratings as predictors of corporate PAC contributions. The results are generally disappointing, and our interviews make it clear why this is so: most corporate PACs are pragmatic and access oriented. Therefore they are concerned with a candidate's position on a specific company issue rather than with their broad general philosophy. As one access PAC officer said:

> Some people use ratings, which I hate because they are the grossest generalizations that you could ever imagine. Those people that may be on

the Chamber of Commerce good government scale or whatever they say, know nothing about our business, don't care about our business, and in fact if they are from the northeast, would vote to screw our business. It has nothing to do with reality. I haven't looked at a rating. . . . I have people throw those at me all the time. Generally I can come back and say, "So what? Since when did they vote yes on natural gas decontrol?" Or "I know he is a screaming liberal but he helped us go get our coal permit. Helped us get that land out there to mine because he knew the situation that was involved. If he hadn't been paying attention, we wouldn't have been able to get it."

Three other factors are more problematic for ideological than for pragmatic PACs—political party, social issues, and preexisting friendships between executives and candidates.

POLITICAL PARTY. What surprised us the most about PAC decision making is the small, virtually nonexistent, influence of political party. Although party loyalty has declined in the last thirty years, most voters still see political party as one of the key considerations, but corporate PACs see the political world very differently. Virtually all corporate PACs ignore political party. Without a single exception access-oriented PACs insisted that it is irrelevant whether a candidate is a Democrat or a Republican; party affiliation simply isn't a consideration for them. Some ideological PACs consider political party significant, and some do not. Most ideological PACs would prefer to be strictly bipartisan but given their orientation find it difficult to do so:

> The direction of our political views is for fiscal responsibility, and it tends to be for conservative candidates; it tends to be in favor of Republican candidates. We try very hard to be bipartisan, but given the current makeup of the parties and the ground rules we have, we have some ground rules that make it hard to find Democrats. The guidelines are that you've got to have a competitive race for us to make a contribution to you. You've got to need the money in terms of the sources available to your opponent. In addition to that, you've got to be meritorious in terms of public policy values that are reflected by our PAC.
>
> Most of the Democrats that are attractive to us are extremely well-funded and win overwhelmingly and do not have serious competition. . . .
>
> We work hardest trying to find Democrats that we can support and that our members want to support. The trouble is, if you've got a PAC of American manufacturing managers in the U.S. in the late 1980s, and you only give to contested races, you are unlikely to have a Democrat

running against a Republican and more attractive to a business manager. There are some Democrats who meet that criteria, but golly, they're safe. They've been in there a long time. They got a lead pipe cinch. We don't give to Republicans like them either.

There's nothing that has frustrated me as much. . . . The one thing that I think we've failed at is having a sufficient partisan balance, and I don't know how to do it. I've tried like hell, but it seems to me that the partisan bias is a reflection of the realities of American politics today. And I can't do anything about that. We could change our criteria; we could say, "By God, we're going to support at least one-third Democrats, whether they need it or not."

Some ideological PACs are so concerned about remaining bipartisan that they give to Democrats who don't really fit their criteria:

Well, someone says, "How come you only contribute to Republicans?" Well, we are only contributing to pro-business candidates. It just so happens that the pro-business candidates are Republicans—nine times out of ten. In the last election I searched out probusiness Democrats. I came up with some, and I came up with some that we had missed in years past. And we made a point to contribute to them this time around if they needed the money, sometimes lesser contributions even when they didn't necessarily need the money—like Congressmen [Richard] Ray [D-Ga.] and Ralph Hall [D-Tex.] we contributed to. There were some that we had missed somewhere along the line. I just made it a point to make those contributions. This time I think we made much more of an effort to reach out to try to support Democratic candidates when we thought that we could do it. There were some that were border line, and some that if we went strictly by ideology we would not have contributed to, but we chose to make a small contribution.

A few ideological PACs expressed a clear preference for Republicans. As one said, "We are obviously a more Republican PAC than a Democratic PAC":

We have contributed heavily to Republican senatorial candidates, and that's been primarily a strategy on our part to help maintain a Republican majority in the Senate. . . . When one party controls Congress for so long, you don't have the balance that I feel is good for the free enterprise system. So if you look at our contributions, we have specifically targeted Republican challengers and incumbents to help maintain or help increase the Republican majority to give balance in the Congress.

One or two companies that expressed a preference for Republicans nonetheless gave most of their money to Democrats. As one of the latter explained to us:

> You've got to be pragmatic about it as well. As I've said, we support very heavily Republicans in the Senate but in the House the Democrats are in the leadership. They control the committees; all of your legislation that you are vitally concerned about has to go through them, so obviously you'll find many of our contributions are to Democrats in the House. . . .
>
> [Our CEO] was invited up earlier this year to speak to a Republican leadership group. I forget what they call it; they've got a lot of these little caucuses in the House. Bob Michel [R-Ill. and Republican leader in the House] was there, and there must have been twenty Republican candidates. Because they all know he's a Republican, strongly Republican, one of the questions they raised to him was, "Why are so many of your contributions to Democrats? Why aren't we getting more of them?" And he had to say, "Well, just pragmatically you aren't running the Congress." He said, "We do give to challengers and to others that we would like to support, but by and large many of our contributions on the House side are to those in the leadership positions and they are Democrats."

These are problems that access-oriented PACs need never face.

SOCIAL ISSUES. Issues such as abortion, school prayer, and censorship seem to have the same potential that political party affiliation has to cause problems for ideological PACs. In practice, however, the PACs we spoke with insisted that they do not consider social issues. Even the most ideological PAC we spoke with said, "We don't have a position on pro-choice or pro-life" or other social issues. Many corporations take a strong stand in favor of "free enterprise," but social issues were important only by their absence. As one ideological PAC officer noted, "If you looked at people's voting records on abortion, you'd probably make half the people that contribute to the PAC mad one way or the other."

FRIENDSHIPS. Ideological PACs do have trouble, however, with preexisting friendships between candidates and executives. For pragmatic PACs this is a pure benefit. Since their aim is to gain access to and support from a member of Congress, such a friendship is ideal. It hardly matters what the candidate's politics are; the corporation can only benefit from having a friend in Congress:

I think we have to make a more personal decision based on our experience with the individuals. That's one of the things we are looking for. We tell our people that if you know somebody that's running for office that you think deserves to be supported by the [company] PAC, tell us about it. Because there is nothing better than having a personal contact, next door neighbor, or some close association.

Many corporations made at least a few contributions this way: the candidate had gone to school with a top executive, was a fraternity brother, was an ex–company employee, or was in some other way an acquaintance. For an ideological corporation, however, this contribution could pose problems if the candidate had a moderate or liberal voting record and the company normally supported only "free enterprise" die-hards:

> From my perspective it is somewhat of an embarrassment with our PAC, but it's only one candidate. We contribute to him every year, and he doesn't have a pro-business voting record. He just happens to be a *frat brother* of the number-three person in the company. Fortunately we only have one of those. But we were able at least to cut his contribution back to $500 this year instead of $1,000. That's the one where the other executives are giving the one grief. There is a lot of kidding back and forth about "Are we going to support that communist again?" But no one's going to say, "Why don't you just contribute to him yourself, instead of having the PAC do it?" We don't do that. We just honor that request. It's the only one we have.

CONTROVERSY: WHY AND HOW OFTEN?

At many corporations PAC committee contribution decisions are made peacefully, and controversy is almost nonexistent. Issues are settled "pretty much by consensus; we don't have many heated exchanges at all." Sometimes this is because "everybody pretty much agrees on the general orientation of the PAC," as one ideological PAC reported. In other cases controversy is rare because the high-level executives on the PAC committee have other duties they see as more pressing:

> Sometimes I get a question: "Why did you give to him?" Recently one of my vice chairs asked me why I gave to more Democrats than Republicans. But I've never had a serious complaint or an issue that wasn't easily resolved. Most of these people are so busy themselves that they couldn't care less about the PAC.

A few PACs, however, experience a great deal of controversy. The most common and heated disagreements are in pragmatic PACs operated by diversified corporations whose divisions have differing interests. One highly diversified corporation, asked if they ever had any differences of opinion about who to support, replied:

> Oh, absolutely. I could think of numerous examples where one of our business sectors wants to support candidate A and the other says, "Golly, he's not really one of our very good friends. We ought to support his opponent. He's not supportive at all. Stay out of that race." So we do have a lot of disagreements. We have our PAC executive committee comprised of a representative from each of our business sectors plus the corporate staff, so those business sectors have ample opportunity and ample voice to get involved in our decision-making process.

Several corporations reported some version of the same experience, where the division of opinion inside the corporation was extreme:

> There may be candidates who have taken a high profile on an issue. . . . Some guy is all for wilderness: that's death for our exploration division; they wouldn't give him a dime. But maybe that same guy is on Ways and Means, and he's been very helpful for taxes.

Some of these corporations report that committee meetings often become quite heated: "It gets pretty exciting sometimes. When the pitch reaches a certain level, we have to table the issue till the next meeting." The hope is that by then tempers will have cooled down, committee members will have more information, or something will help resolve the issue. A few cases get set aside and resolved some other way after people have cooled down:

> On rare occasions we come to loggerheads: 90 percent of the time we reach consensus; 10 percent of the time we can't. But 90 percent of that time we will come to the point of voting for the record, and the disagreeing party goes on record as being opposed, but we contribute on the basis of the vote. In extraordinarily few circumstances since I've been here has the conflict been so great that it cannot be resolved. The two parties were so fiercely in disagreement that the other board members wouldn't even vote, that they've said the issue has to go out of this room and be resolved in some other way. That's happened maybe twice.

At the great majority of corporations relatively few donations are challenged or even questioned, but some ideological complaints are made about pragmatic donations. These objections are generally infrequent and muted, with little or no open conflict. Such concerns may be raised by members of the PAC committee, by ordinary managers, or by top executives. Typically they take the form of someone wanting to know, "Why are we giving to such a liberal Democrat?"

Most ideological controversies stay quite mild and differ in tone from pragmatic controversies between corporate divisions with differing interests. Typically,

> One person will say, "I cannot vote for that individual." And the other one might say, "Well, I can understand how you might feel, but here's some good things." And the other one will say, "I don't care. I cannot vote for that person. I do not believe that they stand for what this PAC stands for."

Another common response is, "One person will say, 'Well okay, but I want to be recorded as voting no.' " Contributors who question PAC decisions can usually be persuaded to go along:

> Occasionally somebody raises a question, but usually they can be satisfied. We don't ever give to somebody without some reason. Generally the people who ask are satisfied.

Some complaints are more vigorously presented:

> We have members of the PAC who believe firmly and strongly that we should never give to somebody that doesn't have a voting record that is exactly consistent with theirs. And when we give those people money or make contributions to them, they get very upset. And they call. Or they make their views known at the PAC meeting if they are on the steering committee.

Dissenters weren't always satisfied with the responses they received, or the PAC officer didn't consider it worth the effort to persuade them:

> We have had a couple of people drop out of the PAC because they didn't like the fact that we were giving to, for example, a Democrat on the Energy and Commerce Committee who represents [an area near headquarters and] who isn't necessarily all that good a friend of business. We were trying to establish a relationship with him because of his committee spot. The PAC member that wanted to drop out, he had some problems

with a couple of other contributions, and he was very, very conservative. I told him that it would probably be best if he did drop out because I didn't think he was going to be able to learn to live with contributions that we were making.

Top officers' concerns are much like those of other managers. Most of the time, in most corporations, they have no complaints: "I've been chairman of this PAC for three years, and I have yet to have an officer call and quiz me about a contribution"; "I took over the PAC in 1986 and I have never had one senior manager ever say, 'Why did you do that?'" On the other hand, such queries are by no means unknown:

> INTERVIEWER: Do they ever call you up and say, "I have problems with the PAC having contributed to So and So"?
>
> PAC DIRECTOR: Yes. And you try to explain why you did it. Usually—in fact, always—they say "Okay." They never say, "Don't do it" or "Get the money back."
>
> INTERVIEWER: Do you ever come out of a conversation feeling you are in trouble?
>
> PAC DIRECTOR: No. They are kind of rational guys—if you have a rational explanation. He didn't get to the top of this company because he was emotionally involved—except for the business, of course. So they tend to take your explanations as long as they are rational. But they get emotional once in a while. They are like citizens. They are fans. They read the newspapers, and they see the guy holding a demonstration outside. But I say, "Yes, the guy's holding a demonstration. That's what he has to do to get elected. You can't take that personally. What we have to deal with is how did he respond on an issue or how did he help us ameliorate the problem that he is addressing in another way?"

There was a clear sense that a substantial number of complaints could be expected if the PAC donated to a well-known liberal who represented an area near a main center of corporate employment. "Liberal" in this context could mean someone who, on the national scale, is regarded as a moderate—either a Democrat or a Republican. However, when the PAC officer explained the reasoning, people were usually satisfied:

> Jim Wright and Jim Mattox too—their own personal philosophy, the way they act, in particular as it relates to social issues, is liberal. My employees

read the newspaper, and they see the stance that they take on those issues does not fit their philosophy of government, so they have a tendency to say, "Well, because Jim Mattox or Jim Wright supported that issue, I don't want to give him the dollars. And so, if you guys want to do that I'm just going to get out of the PAC."

But generally if an employee says that they're unhappy with what we have done, if we have an opportunity to talk to them before they get so bent out of shape, we can explain why the contribution was given. Generally it satisfies them. If you can maintain a level of communication with your membership, and they understand that this PAC is not involved with the social issues, that it's involved strictly with industry issues, then they will be satisfied.

Virtually all these ideological disputes involve conservatives objecting to donations to liberals. The reverse is almost but not quite hypothetical: one corporation could not actually remember a specific controversy but knew liberal sentiments were a consideration:

> We also have liberal Democrats who are unhappy. I don't know what would happen if somebody ever suggested we give money to Jesse Helms. I'm not sure we have ever given money to Helms. I don't think we have ever been asked.

The character and frequency of these internal disputes is counterintuitive: controversy is frequent and heated when PAC committees argue about which of two incumbents should get a pragmatic access donation, but it is rare, mild, and usually polite when people have ideological objections to giving to candidates they consider too liberal. Pragmatic donations can generate heated controversies for at least two reasons: (1) both sides in a pragmatic controversy are defending the interests of the corporation as they understand them; and (2) PAC committee members are primarily accountable to the head of their division, and aggressively standing up for their division's interests will help, not hurt, their career. This kind of dispute is sanctioned by the corporation: PAC committee members primarily or exclusively concerned with the interests of their particular part of the company are likely to be rewarded, not penalized, by their superiors.[27] Therefore, in diversified corporations with pragmatic PACs, such disputes are frequent and people are prepared to hold their ground.

In an ideological controversy, however, particularly if the PAC is primarily pragmatic, objections to a candidate can be seen as putting personal values above the best interests of the corporation. Therefore, such disputes are tentative and understated—even though committee members are likely to care much more deeply about ideological disputes than they do about pragmatic arguments between divisions. The most important factor shaping disputes is not individual feelings and preferences, but rather what the corporation encourages or discourages.

Creating a Sense of Indebtedness

GIVING MORE THAN A CAMPAIGN CONTRIBUTION

Virtually all corporations use political action committee contributions as a mechanism to establish a connection with a member of Congress (or non-incumbent candidate). Corporations generally see PAC donations as legitimate and appropriate. These donations must be reported to the Federal Election Commission, and the FEC makes it easy for academic researchers, reporters, or other candidates to see exactly what PACs and candidates have done. But corporations can form connections with candidates in a variety of other ways, some of which have many of the characteristics of a bribe but are, or until recently were, legal.

REVERSE ACCESS. *Access* as a code word in campaign finance usually means the company's ability to get in to talk to the member of Congress. But sometimes the company can aid the member gain access to constituents:

> We also invite the member of Congress to come to our facility. And they love to come. They get there in the morning before [work gets going and makes access difficult]. We usually give them a chance to make a speech and usually arrange coffee and donuts or something. Any member that visits with us remembers us. We'll do that during election time; if the challenger wants to visit us, we'll give him the same opportunity.

A member may get more benefit from a visit to a major company facility than from a PAC contribution of $500 or $1,000. Companies sometimes provide a member free publicity through their PAC newsletter, with a picture of the member and text explaining what he or she has done for the company and why the PAC considers this candidate to be worth supporting.

Companies sometimes help a member do a favor for a constituent. Constituents occasionally call or write their member of Congress for help dealing with the gas, electric, or telephone company. Someone on the member's staff calls the company's government relations unit, and that person straightens out the problem or at least explains it. The customer is guaranteed careful attention, and it's reasonable to suspect they are more likely than the average customer to get the rules bent in their favor.

TAX-EXEMPT ORGANIZATIONS. Members of Congress can form tax-exempt organizations that can accept donations of unlimited size and never disclose the names of donors. Donations to such organizations are themselves tax-exempt charitable contributions, and corporations may contribute directly without having to use PACs. Such organizations are supposed to be nonpartisan and used only for educational and research activities, but in practice they are difficult to monitor. Moreover, Congress recently *loosened* the restrictions on members' using such organizations. A study by *National Journal* found that "51 Senators and 146 House Members were founders, officers, or directors of tax-exempt organizations."[28] Charles Keating used this mechanism to funnel $850,000 to Senator Alan Cranston.

SPEAKING FEES. A common but dubious way for a business to go beyond a PAC donation is to pay a member of Congress to give a speech. Trade associations frequently use this method to increase the impact of an intimate fundraiser. In addition to collecting $500 campaign contributions from twenty-five to thirty corporate PACs, the member receives a speaking fee, a maximum of $2,000. Until 1990 members could keep $26,850 a year of this money as personal income with no restrictions whatsoever (that is, use it to pay for groceries or a fur coat). These appearance fees had many of the characteristics of a bribe: someone paid money to get a public official to do something they would not otherwise do, specifically to provide information or engage in dialogue about official matters under their jurisdiction. The same action by an employee of the executive branch would be a felony.[29]

Beginning in 1991 members of Congress were prohibited from accepting honoraria to augment their personal income. In exchange for accepting the ban on using speaking fees as personal income, Congress gave itself a $28,500 pay raise.[30] Both the pre- and post-1990 rules, however, had separate provisions for speaking fees that were donated to charity. Before 1990 there were virtually no rules, about either the maximum fee per speech or the total amount the member could earn. Since 1990 the maximum fee per speech has been $2,000. The member no longer may be personally enriched by such fees but certainly can earn political credit by donating the fees to charities in the home district. For example, Dan Rostenkowski (D-Ill.), chair of the House Ways and Means Committee, topped the 1989 honoraria list. Under the rules prevailing at the time, he kept the legal maximum of $26,850 for himself,[31] keeping the first $2,000 per speech he received for January and February speeches. But he collected a total of $285,000, most of it at $7,500 an appearance (the fee for twenty-five of his forty-four charity appearances, with an additional five appearances where he kept $2,000 for himself and gave $5,500 to charity), with the balance of $258,500 donated to charity. Virtually all of Rostenkowski's 1989 speaking fees came from business. He was paid for one union appearance and one presentation to a state housing group, but all the rest of the money came from corporations or industry groups.[32]

FREE TRIPS. Members of Congress also may receive free trips, and business is the only group with the resources to make much use of this provision. According to Public Citizen, a watchdog group founded by Ralph Nader, senators reported taking 669 expense-paid trips in 1987, 452 in 1988, and 506 in 1989. Beginning in 1990 "tough" new rules apply: trips can't be longer than four days for domestic trips or seven days for trips outside the United States, although the amount the group spends to provide this trip is still unlimited, as is the number of trips a member may accept. Thus Senator Alan Dixon (D-Ill.) owns a condominium in West Palm Beach Florida; in February and March he accepted five free trips to and from Florida, all paid for by business.[33]

A business can combine a free trip with a speaking honorarium:

In November 1986, the American Council of Highway Advertisers held its 50th annual meeting on Barbados, one of the more distant Caribbean islands (round-trip coach airfare from Washington, D.C.: $777). Among members of Congress who found several free days in their schedule to accept the council's invitation: Senator Larry Pressler of South Dakota (and Mrs. Pressler), who spent four days on the island, courtesy of the council, and picked up a $2,000 honorarium. Among the House members who made the journey: Representative Wayne Dowdy of Mississippi (and Mrs. Dowdy), who stayed three days and received $1,000, and Pennsylvania Democrat Robert Borski, who got a $1,000 honorarium.[34]

Companies can get even more access to a member of Congress by seeing that the free trip is in a luxurious company plane. Many companies use their executive jets to fly members where they want to go, although one PAC officer explained that his company refused to do so:

> Our company has a tradition in politics of very, very careful adherence not just to the letter but the spirit and beyond the spirit of election laws—to the extent that we as a matter of policy refuse to fly any member of Congress or staff in our corporate aircraft anywhere, even if they reimburse us. We feel it is bad for them and bad for us. Not worth it. You may or may not be able to imagine the pressure that is placed on people flying in corporate airplanes. The temptation is tremendous. Get a member in the air for two hours—feed him, drinks, take him someplace. So if we won't do that, we're damn sure not going to do a lot of other things people may or may not want us to do.

PERSONAL GIFTS. One final way a PAC can attract a member's attention is by accompanying the campaign contribution with a personal gift. Lobbyists can spend unlimited amounts to wine and dine members of Congress, and neither the lobbyist nor the member needs to disclose these meals and beverages. Corporate lobbyists also take members and staffers to basketball or football games. Gifts worth $75 or less are also permissible and don't need to be reported: $75 is not a lot of money but can pay for considerably more than a coffee mug or a pad of paper. A few of the corporations we interviewed mentioned token gifts they prepare for members that provided something useful but also reminded the member of the corporation. However, gifts aren't always this benign. In the fall of 1990 ABC television broadcast secretly filmed footage of nine House members on a junket in Barbados. In this case the taxpayers, not corporations, paid for the trip, but some lobbyists came along to provide the extras—meals, drinks, and some of those undisclosed (and therefore unpoliced) under-$75 contributions: "In a memorable scene, a cigar-chomping lobbyist pulled out a wad of cash and peeled off bills to pay for jet-ski rides for two members."[35]

Campaign contributions themselves can effectively enrich members. There are virtually no controls on the way campaign money is used. "For instance, Representative C. W. Bill Young, Republican of Florida, bought a light blue $30,000 Lincoln Continental with campaign funds. Carroll Hubbard Jr., Democrat of Kentucky, decorated his office with a $3,000 portrait of his father. Stephen Neal, Democrat of North Carolina, took $57,173 in campaign funds for rent and improvements on his home, which conveniently doubles as his permanent campaign headquarters."[36] If members took office before January 1980 and retire by 1993, there are no limits to what they may do with leftover campaign cash. Thus Dan Rostenkowski, chair of the House Ways and Means Committee, could decide to retire and keep the more than $1 million in his campaign fund. When Joe Minish (D-N.J.) was defeated for reelection in 1984, he pocketed $200,000 in campaign cash.[37] In fact most members use their campaign funds for defensible expenditures, and most of those elected before 1980, who could keep the excess cash in their campaign treasuries when they retire, have indicated that they do not intend to do so.

PAC CONTRIBUTIONS BUILD NETWORKS

The public is understandably upset by many of these campaign contribution practices, which have been a primary focus of reform efforts. If businesses pay members of Congress to make speeches and answer questions about public policy issues, and members use these fees as unrestricted personal income, then members who are short of cash will be tempted to take probusiness positions that result in paid invitations to speak. If members and their families can take vacations paid for by industry groups, then members who don't want to lose these free vacations will be reluctant to vote against the industry's position. And lobbyists peeling bills off rolls of cash raises the specter of outright bribes. It is easy to believe that these forms of business contributions create a feeling of indebtedness and obligation by the member to the corporation, and it is equally easy to see why these practices are most likely to be the focus of ethics inquiries and rule reforms.

Most of these dubious contributions come from corporations, either directly or through intermediaries such as lobbyists and trade associations, but these are not the primary ways corporations try to influence member behavior. By far the most common form of corporate political action is the PAC contribution—more than 25,000 of them every two-year election cycle. These should therefore be the primary focus of analysis. PAC contributions also make the public uncomfortable, but they are seen as much more defensible. Corporations can—and do—point out that the money comes from "voluntary" contributions by corporate employees, donations are made openly, records of all such donations are available for public scrutiny, it is illegal to ask for a direct quid pro quo, and most corporations do not do so. The PAC contribution, corporate officials and sympathizers imply, is a disinterested part of the democratic process—a way for employees to exercise their rights as citizens.

This public defense captures an important reality: the corporation wants to build personal networks with members of Congress to create a sense of obligation and indebtedness by members to the corporation, without engaging in distasteful practices with the potential to threaten its corporate image. The challenge is to create a sense of connection and obligation even if the corporation is "only" giving a PAC contribution. Corporations think carefully about how to present their PAC money. Although their primary aim is to build networks and obligations for use at some future time when the company faces a problem, the process of presenting the money is usually also part of the next step in the process—using this sense of obligation to gain access to the member of Congress (or other key players) in order to advance the corporation's interests.

JUST DROP IT IN THE MAIL? If campaign contributions were made solely to aid the democratic process and promote the best candidate, with no ulterior motive, then it would not matter how the money was delivered. If members of Congress were never influenced by the money they received, then it would make no difference whether or not they were aware of the contribution. The very same people who insisted their PAC money gave them absolutely no power or influence also insisted that it was extremely important that donations be given in person. As one said, "When push comes to shove, I'm the one that they expect to get the job done, so I want to be the one that the member knows is the guy who has delivered."

When we asked PAC officers how their corporation delivered the contribution, virtually all of them insisted that "you don't just write out a check and drop it in the mail." In fact, "the very last thing that we do is put a check in the mail. That, in my opinion, is the worst thing to do."

BACK-HOME FUNDRAISERS. Washington fundraisers cost much more than those held in the home district. Today the minimum entry price for a Washington fundraiser is likely to be $500, and it is unlikely that even a handful of the member's constituents will attend. Tickets to fundraisers in the home district are more likely to cost $15 to $100, and virtually everybody there is a constituent.

One advantage of attending a fundraiser in the member's district is that "you can get a whole table for a back-home fundraiser for what you would have to pay for one ticket at a Washington fundraiser." As a result, "we get much more bang for the buck with minimal PAC dollars if you have the money presented out in the field." Some of these are picnics like the Muskegon, Michigan, "Fry for Guy" held by Guy Van Der Jagt, one-time chair of the Republican Congressional Campaign Committee. A company can pay for all of its local managers to attend such an event, have a good time, meet other local influentials, and be introduced to the member of Congress. The event can be fun for employees; one corporation reported that it passed out tickets and "a bunch of people went, took their kids, and really liked it." A back-home fundraiser emphasizes to the member that many constituents are employees of the corporation and that he or she depends on the corporation not only for money but also for votes. Because the corporation is responsible for employees' jobs, salaries, and benefits, harming the corporation is likely to hurt the employees and influence not only their votes, but also the votes of their friends and relatives.

On the other hand, such an event also has many limitations. In the first place, it is only possible if the company has employees in the member's district, and most companies have operations in a limited number of districts. Unless the corporation is prepared to confine its PAC contributions to the ten or twenty districts where it has a significant number of employees, this home-district contribution pattern is insufficient. The members who serve on the committees most crucial to the corporation may well represent districts where the company has no employees. Moreover, although these fundraisers create a sense of dependence on and connection to the company, they do relatively little to aid the lobbying process, since at a large affair no one individual makes much impression on the member and the company's lobbyist is unlikely to attend a function outside Washington.

PERSONAL VISIT. Many of the PAC officers said they disliked fundraisers, and it's easy to see why: PAC officers put in a nine to five work day and then have to go to one, two, or even three fundraisers before they can head home. Moreover, at a large fundraiser there's not likely to be much contact with the member of Congress, nor is the corporation likely to be favorably remembered: "To tell you the truth, even when I was in Washington, I rarely went to fundraisers. Why in the hell should you give somebody a thousand dollars in the presence of a hundred other guys giving him a thousand dollars?" Corporations that had the clout tried to avoid the fundraiser and get time one-to-one with the member: "If it's a big fundraiser, what we may do is go earlier and deliver the check to his office[38] and sit and talk with him." Of course, this defeats some of the purposes of the fundraiser: the member wants to get everybody together at once in order to reduce the time he or she spends dealing with campaign contributions and also to show the world how much support he or she has.

WASHINGTON FUNDRAISERS. Despite these reservations and the frequently expressed preferences for delivering money in the home district, Washington fundraisers are the most common way of making a contribution. There are so many of them that a newsletter, *Political Activity Calendar,* has been started just to list them all. Here are the listings for June 27, 1990:[39]

> Rep. Tony P. Hall, D-Ohio, National Democratic Club, 8:30 A.M., $500
> Rep. Nancy Pelosi, D-Calif., National Democratic Club, 5:30 P.M., $500
> Rep. Michael Biliraikis, R-Fla., American Trucking Associations Inc., 6–8 P.M., $500
> Rep. Larry E. Craig, R-Idaho, Washington Court, 6–8 P.M., $1,000
> Sen J. J. Exon, D-Neb., Washington Court, 6–8 P.M., $1,000
> Rep. Robert J. Mrazek, D-N.Y., 301 Constitution Ave. N.E., 6–8 P.M., $500
> Rep. Thomas E. Petri, R-Wis., Anton's, 6–8 P.M., $300

Increasingly, the functional equivalent of a Washington fundraiser will be held in other cities around the country—that is, a Minnesota member of Congress will hold a $500-per-person fundraiser in Houston.

Fundraisers provide advantages for donors as well as members. First, they offer a chance to see the member and speak with him or her. The very largest corporations may have little difficulty doing so whenever they want, but most corporations, even multibillion-dollar ones, don't always find it easy to talk to members or even their staffs:

> Everybody thinks we spend all our time up on the Hill and every time you pick up the phone, Senator X's staff calls you back right away and you go up and sit down and talk. Sometimes it takes you days to have phone calls returned. If it's a crisis and you say I'd really like to talk to him, that's

different. But I know people that I've called and they will call you back at 6:00 at night because they have just got done with a committee meeting or doing something in the Senate. By then you are gone. It's tough to catch these busy, busy people. So it's an opportunity to see them.

The access at the fundraiser can lead directly to a solution to the company's problem:

These guys are very hard to see; it's hard to get an appointment with these guys because they're so busy. But at a fundraiser you get a chance to shake a hand, to talk to somebody for a couple of minutes. I know one example perfectly—in fact, the issue we were talking about earlier. I just happened to mention to the member, I said, "Look, we've got a unit that probably knows more about this subject than anybody, and particularly this segment of the market—the small business market that you're concerned about; and we've got an enormous amount of data, and our guy's an expert in this area and would like to help." And this particular senator said, "Boy, I would be delighted to have a chance to talk with him further," and he grabbed his appointment secretary and said, "Please talk to Bill, get an appointment. I want to do this." But the fundraising event and the PAC enabled me to be there and to raise that question in a way that would have been a lot harder if I had to go through a formal appointment.

Some fundraisers, especially for important members of Congress, are huge, but probably the most common format is the cocktail party attended by forty or fifty people. Everyone meets the candidate, the candidate makes some remarks, and then he or she answers questions: "The ones I've been to, there's never been a case where the candidate was not asked to say something and where the candidate did not respond to questions." At a more focused fundraiser a small group is concerned about the same issues—typically a breakfast organized by an industry trade association. "The most opportune kind of fundraiser that we prefer to go to is an intimate breakfast or dinner with less than twenty-five or thirty people and you place your guy next to the person. . . . In fact, I don't care if you sit at the end of the table. The fact of the matter is there is some personal interchange, dialogue that goes on."

Second, the fundraiser is an opportunity to show support for and connection with a particular member and to let other people see you talking with the right people. Even PAC officials who avoid fundraisers may attend to show support: "Sometimes if it's a friend—somebody we are particularly close to—they might not only want the money but want the bodies there, want the physical support as well as the money."

Third, attending fundraisers offers an opportunity to see *other* members of Congress and their staffs, many of whom attend the fundraisers of friends and associates.

Fourth, the government relations staff from other corporations attend fundraisers and can provide useful information about issues, who is doing what, and who might be able to help with a problem. Many of the same people attend these affairs, and people sometimes see the same twelve other people three times in the same night, but each fundraiser has a slightly different cast of characters. As one PAC director said, "Issues develop where we need to work with these other lobbyists, and it's interesting to see who shows up." Fundraisers become one of the main ways that corporate personnel, lobbyists, congressional staff, and members of Congress meet and interact with each other, form friendships, and build networks that facilitate future cooperation.

Normally the fundraiser is attended by the one or two key government relations personnel from the company. For junior staff, attending the fundraiser is obviously an honor and an opportunity—but the corporation must be careful that it does not appear to slight the member. One PAC officer told about attending a fundraiser held in the company's headquarters city in honor of a major congressional leader who is widely regarded as on the way up. At her company the PAC officer was a relatively low-level employee and was not a voting member of the PAC committee that decided who received donations. However, her company was not very interested in government relations, so despite her junior status they sent her to this fundraiser. All the major figures in state politics were present, and other corporations were represented by top executives or CEOs: "It's great exposure for me. But I also feel kind of out of place. Protocol wise that's not the way it should be. You send the president or senior VP."

Sometimes the person attending the fundraiser or making the private visit in the name of the corporation is an independent lobbyist retained by the corporation. This happens when the lobbyist has a particular area of expertise or set of connections (the two are virtually inseparable in these circumstances) or when the corporation's government relations operation is too small to handle all issues. If the lobbyist is representing the corporation on a key issue, he or she is the person who should present the check, in the name of the corporation, to the member or staff: "It helps to focus the member's sight on where that funnel is, where they get these contributions."

Occasionally the corporation's CEO presents the check. This may reflect the importance of that member, but it may be largely an accident of scheduling: the CEO is in town for other reasons and available. One company for whom government actions are particularly important reported as follows:

Depends on who the person is. We don't use our CEO unless the person whom we're dealing with is heavy duty. What happens is that our chairman is one of our most effective lobbyists. We get him into the scene when he can be particularly useful, and that's usually with leadership people. Or particularly our home state delegations. He is involved in lobbying and sometimes also hands over the check. But a senator may stop by here [the home office], or he may be in Washington and go to a cocktail party. Usually if we don't have to then the chairman will not hand over the check. Somebody will go along with him, and he will give the check. We don't want to be unseemly about it. Our chairman is very much involved in our political efforts, which may include dispensing PAC money. That is fairly rare. His actual talking with members is becoming increasingly common.

When company survival depends on government action (or inaction), as in this case, the CEO is likely to be directly involved. This was reported to be most common in heavily regulated industries. In other companies the CEO generally seemed to be less involved, with individual exceptions based in part on the CEO's personal history and interests.

USING THE MAIL. Most companies put a premium on being sure a member of Congress knew they had contributed. They made every effort to present their gift in person in order to create more personal contact and increase the sense of obligation. But some companies did send checks through the mail. Who were they, and why did they do so?

Mail delivery appeared to be used in three situations: First, as an exceptional case for a company that normally delivered checks in person:

Occasionally when you get down to the end of a year, they need the money. You can't do it personally. But they are asking you, so you mail it to them. But in general it's all hand delivered in some form or fashion.

Second, companies with access oriented government relations programs that were, in our opinion (an opinion sometimes but not always shared by the company itself), weak operations. One company had been subjected to a major raid by a Boone Pickens type operator and had been forced to split itself in two and radically downsize. The government relations staff had been reduced from eight people to two. The PAC officer agreed that it was best to deliver the check in person:

> Sure, that's the best way to go. Sometimes it works out that way, but like I said, with fewer people doing this stuff, sometimes it's hard to orchestrate things the way we used to be able to.

The final situation in which checks are delivered through the mail is when the PAC is *not* oriented to access—when its concern is ideology, and it self-consciously renounces pragmatic considerations. Many ideological PACs deliver checks in person, but for others personal delivery does not seem to hold the same sort of priority. Thus one of the heavily ideological PACs reports that it totally separates the PAC from its lobbying activity. It does not approve of fundraisers; if one is held in their headquarters city for a candidate they support, they might attend, but this would be a "very rare exception." The normal delivery procedure is to mail the check (this happens about 70 percent of the time). If one of the company's divisions is working closely with a member, the check will be sent to the division to hand carry it, but on reflection the chair of the PAC committee said, "The check goes out to the divisions, but what they do with it when they get it, I don't know." The PAC officer for another ideological PAC indicated that when the company had a facility in the district, the check was delivered by people at the facility; in other cases she tried to make personal deliveries where convenient but often used the mail.

Conclusion

Political action committee gifts create the networks of obligation that corporations use when they want access to members of Congress to ask for favors. Despite the many donations PACs make, corporations make every effort to personalize them:

> Counting state legislatures, last year we were involved in 532 races. I can't make that many contributions personally. So we use the networks that we have—our corporate lobbyists, our people on retainer, and our employees. We try to make the contributions as personal as possible.

It can reasonably be asked whether members of Congress even remember who has contributed to them. In PAC officers' experience, by the time someone gets to Congress,

> . . . they have proven they are good enough at the game, that they've got a pretty good idea, and if they don't know, they can find out. They may only know two days a year, and that's when their political staff briefs them on what they are doing. But at some point in there, they are aware of it.

In fact, the member's memory is one crucial test of the success of the corporation's government relations office:

> If we are making a contribution to somebody who doesn't know it, we're screwing up. So that's one of the tests. That's one of our internal tests. If we are just sending money out to somebody and they are not aware of it, we've got no business giving them a contribution because they are not doing any good.

In the access process—the subject of the next chapter—the corporation finds out how much "good" its contributions are doing.

Chapter 4

■■■

ACCESS: "I CAN GET TO WAXMAN FOR $250"

■■■

The access process is key to most corporate government relations operations. Raising money, running the political action committee, and giving gifts are only means to an end, and the end is to gain "access" to members of Congress. This chapter challenges four myths or misconceptions about corporate political activity in the access process: that what matters is persuading members of Congress to vote a certain way on crucial laws; that corporations exert influence through an explicit exchange of PAC money for congressional votes; that Democrats and Republicans, or liberals and conservatives, differ fundamentally on the issue of special benefits for corporations and industries; and that this process operates automatically with no significant effort by corporations and in any case has minimal consequences.

Myth One: Key Votes Are the Issue

Many critics of PACs and campaign finance seem to feel that a corporate PAC officer walks into a member's office and says, "Senator, I want you to vote against the Clean Air Act. Here's $5,000 to do so." This view, in this crude form, is simply wrong. The (liberal) critics who hold this view seem to reason as follows: (1) we know that PAC money gives corporations power in relation to Congress; (2) power is the ability to make someone do something against their will; (3) therefore campaign money must force members to switch their votes on key issues. We come to the same conclusion about the outcome—corporate power in relation to Congress—but differ from conventional critics on both the understanding of power and the nature of the process through which campaign money exercises its influence.

The debate over campaign finance is frequently posed as, "Did special interests buy the member's vote on a key issue?" Media accounts as well as most academic analyses in practice adopt this approach.[1] With the question framed in this way, we have to agree with the corporate political action committee directors we interviewed, who answered, "No, they didn't." But they believed it followed that they have no power and maybe not even any influence, and we certainly don't agree with that. If power means the ability to *force* a member of Congress to vote a certain way on a major bill, corporate PACs rarely have power. However, corporations and their PACs have a great deal of power if power means the ability to exercise a field of influence that shapes the behavior of other social actors. In fact, corporations have effective hegemony: some alternatives are never seriously considered, and others seem natural and inevitable; some alternatives generate enormous controversy and costs, and others are minor and involve noncontroversial favors. Members of Congress meet regularly with some people, share trust, discuss the issues honestly off the record, and become friends, while other people have a hard time getting in the door much less getting any help. Members don't have to be forced; most of them are eager to do favors for corporations and do so without the public's knowledge. If citizens did understand what was happening their outrage might put an end to the behavior, but even if the favors are brought to light the media will probably present them as at least arguably good public policy.

HIGH-VISIBILITY ISSUES

Corporate PAC officers could stress two key facts: First, on important highly visible issues they cannot determine the way a member of Congress votes; second, even for low-visibility issues the entire process is loose and uncertain. The more visible an issue, the less likely that a member's vote will be determined by campaign contributions. If the whole world is watching, a member from an environmentally conscious district can't vote against the Clean Air Act (discussed in chapter 1) because it is simply too popular. An April 1990 poll by Louis Harris and Associates reported that when asked, "Should Congress make the 1970 Clean Air Act stricter than it is now, keep it about the same, or make it less strict?" 73 percent of respondents answered, "Make it stricter"; 23 percent, "Keep it about the same"; and only 2 percent, "Make it less strict" (with 2 percent not sure).[2] Few members could risk openly voting against such sentiments. To oppose the bill they'd have to have a very good reason—perhaps that it would cost their district several hundred jobs, perhaps that the bill was fatally flawed, but never, never, never that they had been promised $5,000, $10,000, or $50,000 for doing so.

The PAC officers we interviewed understood this point, although they weren't always careful to distinguish between high- and low-visibility issues. (As we discuss below, we believe low-visibility issues are an entirely different story.) Virtually all access-oriented PACs went out of their way at some point in the interview to make it clear that they do not and could not buy a member's vote on any significant issue. No corporate official felt otherwise; moreover, these opinions seemed genuine and not merely for public consumption. They pointed out that the maximum legal donation by a PAC is $5,000 per candidate per election. Given that in 1988 the cost of an average winning House campaign was $388,000 and for the Senate $3,745,000,[3] no individual company can provide the financial margin of victory in any but the closest of races. A member of Congress would be a fool to trade 5 percent of the district's votes for the maximum donation an individual PAC can make ($5,000) or even for ten times that amount. Most PACs therefore feel they have little influence. Even the one person who conceded possible influence in some rare circumstances considered it unlikely:

> You certainly aren't going to be able to buy anybody for $500 or $1,000 or $10,000. It's a joke. Occasionally something will happen where everybody in one industry will be for one specific solution to a problem, and they may then also pour money to one guy. And he suddenly looks out and says, "I haven't got $7,000 coming in from this group, I've got $70,000." That might get his attention: "I've got to support what they want." But that's a rarity, and it doesn't happen too often. Most likely, after the election he's going to rationalize that it wasn't that important and they would have supported him anyway. I just don't think that PACs are that important.

This statement by a senior vice president at a large *Fortune* 500 company probably reflects one part of the reality: most of the time members' votes can't be bought; occasionally a group of corporations support the same position and combine resources to influence a member's vote even on a major contested issue. Even if that happens, the member's behavior is far from certain.

LOW-VISIBILITY ISSUES AND NONISSUES

This is true only if we limit our attention to highly visible, publicly contested issues. Most corporate PACs, and most government relations units, focus only a small fraction of their time, money, and energy on the final votes on such issues. So-called access-oriented PACs have a different purpose and style. Their aim is not to influence the member's public vote on the final piece of legislation, but rather to be sure that the bill's wording exempts their company from the bill's most costly or damaging provisions. If tax law is going to be changed, the aim of the company's government relations unit, and its associated PAC, is to be sure that the law has built-in loopholes that protect the company. The law may say that corporate tax rates are increased, and that's what the media and the public think, but section 739, subsection J, paragraph iii, contains a hard-to-decipher phrase. No ordinary mortal can figure out what it means or to whom it applies, but the consequence is that the company doesn't pay the taxes you'd think it would. For example, the 1986 Tax "Reform" Act contained a provision limited to a single company, identified as a "corporation incorporated on June 13, 1917, which has its principal place of business in Bartlesville, Oklahoma."[4] With that provision in the bill, Philips Petroleum didn't mind at all if Congress wanted to "reform" the tax laws.

Two characteristics of such provisions structure the way they are produced. First, by their very nature such provisions, targeted at one (or at most a few) corporations or industries, are unlikely to mobilize widespread business support. Other businesses may not want to oppose these provisions, but neither are they likely to make them a priority, though the broader the scope the broader the support. Business as a whole is somewhat uneasy about very narrow provisions, although most corporations and industry trade associations feel they must fight for their own. Peak business associations such as the Business Roundtable generally prefer a "clean" bill with clear provisions favoring business in general rather than a "Christmas tree" with thousands of special-interest provisions. Most corporations play the game, however, and part of playing the game is not to object to or publicize what other corporations are doing. But they don't feel good about what they do, and if general-interest business associations took a stand they would probably speak against, rather than in favor of, these provisions.

Second, however, these are low-visibility issues; in fact, most of them are not "issues" at all in that they are never examined or contested. The corporation's field of power both makes the member will-

ing to cooperate and gets the media and public to in practice accept
these loopholes as noncontroversial. Members don't usually have to
take a stand on these matters or be willing to face public scrutiny. If the
proposal does become contested, the member probably can back off
and drop the issue with few consequences, and the corporation probably can go down the hall and try again with another member.

WHAT A TYPICAL BILL IS LIKE

People usually think of a congressional bill as a relatively short and
simple statement specifying new tax rates or mandating cleaner air.
Japanese laws typically are brief: a single paragraph may authorize the
appropriate government department to formulate policies to clean up
air pollution.[5] In the United States, however, most important bills are
"Christmas trees" covered with dozens of special provisions, and Congress insists on writing many of the details of the regulations.

For example, the Tax "Reform" Act of 1986 as printed in the U.S.
Code *Statutes at Large* is 880 pages long. Much of it is incomprehensi-
ble, and intentionally so, even to a tax lawyer, unless he or she knows
the hidden references. That is, a provision is written to apply to one
and only one company, but in order to protect the guilty (both member
and corporation), the company is described without being publicly
named. The purpose of the description is to be sure that reading the
act won't be enough for someone to know what's going on. Outsiders
may know it's fishy, probably rotten—but they won't be able to tell
who is benefitting or by how much. Large sections of these 880 pages
are filled with passages like the following:[6]

(5) SPECIAL RULES FOR PROPERTY INCLUDED IN MASTER
PLANS OF INTEGRATED PROJECTS—The amendments made by
section 201 shall not apply to any property placed in service pursuant to
a master plan which is clearly identifiable as of March 1, 1986, for any
project described in any of the following subparagraphs of this paragraph:
   (A) A project is described in this subparagraph if—
      (i) the project involves production platforms for off-shore drilling,
      oil and gas pipeline to shore, process and storage facilities, and a
      marine terminal, and
      (ii) at least $900,000,000 of the costs of such project were incurred
      before September 26, 1985.
   (B) A project is described in this subparagraph if—
      (i) such project involves a fiber optic network of at least 20,000
      miles, and

(ii) before September 26, 1985, construction commenced pursuant to the master plan and at least $85,000,000 was spent on construction.

(C) A project is described in this subparagraph if—

(i) such project passes through at least 10 states and involves intercity communication links (including one or more repeater sites, terminals and junction stations for microwave transmissions, regenerators or fiber optics and other related equipment),

(ii) the lesser of $150,000,000 or 5 percent of the total project cost has been expended, incurred, or committed before March 2, 1986, by one or more taxpayers each of which is a member of the same affiliated group (as defined in section 1504[a]), and

(iii) such project consists of a comprehensive plan for meeting network capacity requirements as encompassed within either:

(I) a November 5, 1985, presentation made to and accepted by the Chairman of the Board and the president of the taxpayer, or

(II) the approvals by the Board of Directors of the parent company of the taxpayer on May 3, 1985, and September 22, 1985, and of the executive committee of said board on December 23, 1985.

(D) A project is described in this subparagraph if—

(i) such project is part of a flat rolled product modernization plan which was initially presented to the Board of Directors of the taxpayer on July 8, 1983,

(ii) such program will be carried out at 3 locations, and

(iii) such project will involve a total estimated minimum capital cost of at least $250,000,000.

This sort of material goes on for pages and pages. Even a careful reading of the act by an informed observer isn't enough to know what companies are referred to, and that is of course the point. A huge amount of detective work is necessary to figure out which companies are referred to or how much money the taxpayers are giving them. It would be much simpler to write the law to say:

(5) SPECIAL LOOPHOLES—The rest of you suckers have to pay the full taxes specified in the law, but the following corporations are exempt from most taxes:

(A) Octopus Oil

(B) Monopoly Phone Company

(C) Oligopoly Phone Company

(D) Super Steel, Inc.

However, someone reading this section might find it outrageous, and might know where to focus attention. As things now stand, the long descriptions sound as if they must in some way be general explanations of circumstances in which the taxes would not be appropriate. In fact their only purpose is to specify one and only one corporation without naming it and without making its loophole available for public scrutiny. Even if you know the provision is an outrage, there still isn't any way to know who is getting away with theft.[7]

Two Pulitzer prize–winning journalists, Donald L. Barlett and James B. Steele of the *Philadelphia Inquirer,* tackled the job of uncovering the loopholes in the 1986 Tax Reform Act, and in the process won themselves a second Pulitzer prize. Despite their reputations and the resources available to them for their search, they needed fifteen months to track down only a small fraction of the thousands of tax breaks buried in the law: "The congressional tax-writing committees and their staffs refused to provide any information, insisting that the identities of the beneficiaries of the preferential tax provisions had to be kept secret." Barlett and Steele wrote to the chairs of the relevant committees, but not one of their letters was answered. In fact, even members of Congress aren't allowed to know what they are voting for:

> In 1986, congressional leaders withheld even a partial list of tax preferences from House Members until after they voted in favor of the legislation.
>
> The process has become so byzantine that, at times, key lawmakers involved in writing tax bills profess their ignorance about breaks that they personally approved.[8]

Barlett and Steele were able to identify beneficiaries for many of the tax loopholes in the 1986 law, but hundreds more remain hidden. Even when Barlett and Steele found the beneficiary, they often were unable to determine which members of Congress deserved the "credit" for the loophole.

The search for beneficiaries of tax law loopholes is made still more difficult by the fact that tax provisions are not necessarily contained in tax laws. A persistent member of Congress, perhaps under the pressure and inducements of a needy or greedy business, can try again and again. If a measure is rejected by the tax committee, sometimes it can be slipped into a bill on an entirely different topic. For example, the Recreational Boating and Safety Act of 1980 also contained a provision, sought by forest products companies, granting them the investment tax credit for planting trees.[9]

THE BOTTOM LINE

When we asked corporate PAC officers to give us an example of what their office tries to do, about 90 percent described a tax loophole they had won. It reached the point where we started asking for an example of anything but taxes. The Tax Code has become the de facto U.S. industrial policy, a policy made in the most haphazard and particularistic process imaginable.[10] Although we didn't ask PAC officers to give us examples of their successes, virtually all of them did, presumably because it validated their worth and contribution to the company. We suspect that part of the reason they preferred examples of tax loopholes is that the benefits can be precisely quantified: "This provision saved our company X million dollars." Many government relations departments emphasize the bottom line: "That's one question I always ask people when they call up. What's the dollar impact on the business?" Or as another said, "We don't do things altruistically. We don't do things just because it's the right thing to do. There ought to be a bottom-line approach to it."

Many of the people we interviewed apparently feel their corporation is entitled to special-interest loopholes. One PAC director offered as proof of the extreme peculiarities of her corporation—its uncompromising ideological fervor and opposition to lobbying—the fact that it had *not* sought such provisions in the 1986 Tax "Reform" Act. The company operates one of the largest corporate PACs, had $20 million in investment tax credits, but made no effort to get a "transition rule" allowing it to keep these tax credits (necessary because the tax "reform" supposedly abolished such loopholes). The PAC director noted that "these transition rules that they write, every company gets them." Her assessment is basically correct: virtually any major corporation that wants a tax loophole can get one, but to prevail it must play the game, maintain one or more lobbyists, make contributions to incumbents, and establish access. The provisions are not automatic; companies have to work for them.

How much do these tax loopholes cost? Congress estimated the revenue loss through loopholes in the 1986 Tax "Reform" Act at $10.6 billion, but this number is taken seriously only by those who still believe in the tooth fairy. Consider Barlett and Steele's estimates for the losses incurred by just one loophole:

The cost of one break was originally placed by the Joint Committee at $300 million. After passage of the legislation, the figure was adjusted upward to $7 billion.

That worked out to a 2,233 percent miscalculation, a mistake so large as to defy comprehension. It would be roughly akin to a family who bought a house expecting to pay $400 a month on its mortgage but who discovered, belatedly, the payments would actually be $9,332 a month.[11]

Or consider the cost of the special tax provision to help the Long Island Power Authority buy and shut down the Shoreham nuclear power plant. This provision was buried in what Congress referred to as a deficit reduction measure. The Joint Committee on Taxation originally said the bailout would cost $1 million, then revised that just a tad to $241 million. The true cost is estimated at $3.5 to $4 billion.[12]

This kind of special-interest provision is put into all kinds of bills, not just the Tax Code. In many ways the tax give-aways are the least of it. With them all we lose are tens of billions of dollars, a basic sense of fairness, and our trust in and respect for the political system. With clean air, discussed in chapter 1, much more is at risk—all the same elements as the Tax Code, along with the cancer rate and the future of the earth. If a few million dollars are transferred to the Bechtel family (already on the *Forbes* list of the 400 richest Americans) as a subsidy for a luxury cruise ship, all we lose is money. But if industry is allowed to "save" a few hundred million by pumping poison into the air, we may never be able to clean it, and trying to do so will certainly cost a great deal more than the amount that the companies "saved" by picking our pockets. Like the PAC officials we interviewed, we tend to focus on the Tax Code because it is possible to at least attempt straightforward estimates of the bottom line, but this process operates everywhere, and its most serious aspect is not the immediate cash costs.

BUSINESS HEGEMONY

One of the best indications of the power of business is that not only are corporations able to win themselves billions of dollars through tax loopholes, but they are able to do so without much public exposure or blame. Hegemony is most effective when its operation is invisible. Companies not only receive what amount to large government hand-outs, but these are rarely discussed and exposed. The obscure language of the Tax Code subsections is an admission of guilt, a clear indication these provisions could not withstand public scrutiny. And yet Congress and virtually all of the media cooperate in handing over the money and keeping the public from knowing what is happening. It is outrageous that members of Congress routinely vote in favor of bills with secret provisions promising benefits the members themselves don't understand.

On those rare occasions when the media do identify and focus on a provision, the company and member can and do defend themselves, providing a thousand reasons why this is good policy, why this provision isn't really a loophole at all, why this is a way of improving the bill, of preserving the spirit of the bill without creating unfortunate consequences that were never intended for this particular case. Benefitting a company in the member's district is always an adequate reason to support a provision. A member who helps a respectable business to increase its profits is almost never vulnerable. If the business is near bankruptcy or is held to have immoral purposes, the member is potentially vulnerable, but even then the vote will rarely come to public notice. If the company is not in the member's district, and if the member has received a *lot* of money from the company, there is a potential for negative publicity—but rarely very much. Since most voters (correctly) assume that most members engage in such behavior, being caught rarely becomes a major issue.

The senators who have received the most publicity for providing special-interest assistance to a campaign contributor are the so-called Keating 5—five senators who received substantial donations from Charles Keating and pressured federal regulators on his behalf. The fact that these senators received public criticism is exceptional, but perhaps the exception that proves the rule. Charles Keating funneled large amounts of money to each of these senators, far beyond the maximum legal PAC contribution of $5,000: Senator Cranston received more than $850,000. The senators pressured regulators in a way that is unusual and questionable even by the relaxed standards of Washington. Keating openly bragged that his money bought him influence. Despite all this, the issue of campaign contributions and Senate influence emerged only *after* Keating's company had gone bankrupt, at a cost to the taxpayers of $2.5 billion. If Keating had been able to keep his company afloat, the campaign contributions would never have received much attention. Finally, despite all the publicity and the need for a scapegoat for the savings and loan crisis, of the five senators only Cranston was disciplined, and even he received only a mild rebuke. The senators involved had trouble seeing what they did wrong, since they, unlike most of the public, knew that they had done nothing very different from what most senators do much of the time.

One indicator of the success of business hegemony is the recent redefinition of the term *special interests.* Not only Ronald Reagan but a leading Democratic liberal (Gary Hart) and the media have used this term to refer to traditional Democratic constituencies—especially unions but also people on welfare, those who would like to breathe clean air and drink pure water, old people on limited incomes, child-care workers, and so on. As used in the contemporary United States, the term *special interest* conjures up an image of a powerful union "boss" (opposing the "public good" by attempting to protect workers against inflation or rising medical costs) or the "social welfare establishment" (trying to win not pay raises for themselves but adequate services for their clients). When they use the term *special interest,* neither the media nor the Democrats expose the kinds of loopholes and special provisions that corporations routinely receive. (Most Democrats can't expose these provisions because they are fully complicit in them; in this regard there is little or no difference between the parties. See myth three below.)

Myth Two: Money Is Explicitly Exchanged for Votes

ARE THESE LOOPHOLES AVAILABLE TO EVERYONE?

A reader imbued with the me-first spirit of Reaganism ought to be asking, "How can I get in on the action? How much would it cost me to get out of my taxes, and to whom should I give the money?" Even a cautious cost-benefit analysis shows that campaign contributions to members of Congress are one of the best "investments" available. Philip Stern offers the following calculation:

> Because of the tax loopholes enacted by Congress over the years, a single company (AT&T) was able to earn nearly $25 billion in profits from 1982 through 1985 without paying one penny of taxes—in fact, the government actually paid AT&T $635 million in tax rebates. The company's tax savings totaled more than $12 billion.
>
> AT&T has had a number of PACs. From 1979 through 1986, those PACs contributed nearly $1.4 million to congressional candidates, mainly incumbents. So an officer or director of AT&T might calculate that on the $12.1 billion tax savings alone, the nearly $1.4 million given by the company PAC netted a return of 867,145 percent.[13]

Not all companies are as successful in evading taxes as AT&T or General Electric or Sears Roebuck, but hundreds of companies received special exemptions under the 1986 Tax "Reform" Act. If the average company in our study were able to cut its taxes by $20 million a year,[14] based in significant part on average PAC contributions of less than $200,000 a year, their payoff would be $100 in tax savings for each dollar of PAC contributions, certainly a better investment than most.[15] Applying this ratio to individual taxpayers, people with $10,000 in annual taxes (a single person with a taxable income of $44,300 or a married couple filing jointly with an income of $50,100) ought to be able to completely eliminate their taxes through a campaign contribution of $100. If I (Dan) decide that I'd rather not pay taxes, could I just walk in and offer John Olver, my member of Congress, $100 to write a provision saying, "Anyone living on Munroe Street in Northampton, who was born on August 18, 1948, doesn't have to pay taxes"?

No one will be surprised to hear that working stiffs can't do this. Part of the reason is simply economies of scale: members would need to process two thousand loopholes for individual taxpayers to equal one corporate loophole.[16] But of course that isn't the primary reason: loopholes for corporations are regarded as only slightly sleazy, and members who write or support such provisions do not need to worry about public exposure or condemnation. A member who proposed 2,000 loopholes for ordinary people would be regarded as a nut and immediately exposed. The media would have a field day: members would fight for interviews condemning this behavior and would all make "holier than thou" speeches.

Rich people occasionally get private tax bills saving them millions of dollars. Domhoff[17] gives the example of the DuPonts, who were forced to divest themselves of the General Motors Corporation (because the courts ruled their simultaneous ownership of DuPont and General Motors was an antitrust violation and restraint of trade) but arranged to reduce their tax liability from $45 a share to $7.25 per share, paying Washington lawyer Clark Clifford $1 million for arranging this special loophole.[18] Similarly, over an eight-year period Ernest and Julio Gallo contributed $325,000 to members promoting an amendment to the Tax Code to reduce their tax liability by $27 million.[19] Members also sponsor some small-scale deals: Senator Daniel Patrick Moynihan (D-N.Y.) submitted a proposal that would have applied only to five biomedical researchers in Rochester.[20]

In a sense these examples only prove the point: the laws are made for the benefit of business and the rich. They are the ones with the power and resources to pay people to work out plausible rationales, to coerce the media not to expose these private deals, to already have (or to know how to make) the connections to powerful government officials, and to have the large-scale operations that provide opportunities for maneuverings and sheltering income through unique arrangements. Moreover, somebody has to pay the taxes; if ordinary people could get the same sort of loopholes that are routine for the rich, the government wouldn't have enough money to operate.

The notion of thousands of ordinary taxpayers each shelling out $100 campaign contributions to be exempted from taxes sounds silly, and of course it is. It's silly, however, not because the government would never agree to special give-aways nor because members of Congress would never violate tax equity for a campaign contribution. To see why ordinary individuals can't do this but corporations (and a handful of rich individuals) can, we need to examine what is involved in running a successful corporate government relations operation. Ordinary individuals wouldn't (1) know what changes were being considered or where to go to intervene effectively, (2) have the ability to get access and then craft appropriate legal gobbledy-gook to give themselves the favor they sought without opening things up for everyone, (3) know how to present and defend this rip-off as good public policy that advances the general interest or be able to defend the change through the entire legislative process. To help understand the corporate-access process, we examine each of these points in turn.

KEEPING TRACK AND KNOWING THE PLAYERS

In order to win special legislative provisions, an individual or company needs to know what is being proposed. Only rarely will special privileges be embodied in a totally independent bill; usually they are incorporated as minor parts of a general purpose bill. Based on the general sense in both the media and academia that government is a threat to business and hampers its operations, we tended to ask our questions in terms of how companies learned about threats. Almost invariably the people we interviewed would add "or opportunities"— for legislation provides many of these as well. But to deal effectively with both threats and opportunities, a company needs to know what is happening, what's possible, what other companies already have that is similar.

To keep informed, corporate government relations personnel read a host of newspapers and specialty publications, hire consultants and lobbyists, talk to members and their staffs, attend fundraisers, and constantly network in the world of Washington insiders (see chapter 6). Simplifying the task of keeping track of legislation is that in Washington things move slowly:

> It's not a tough job today because things take so long to get done in Washington, and there are so many chances to have a change made or to say to someone, "Look, you shouldn't go this way. You should go that way." A new concept that becomes law in less than five years in Washington today is pretty unusual.

The processes used to learn what issues are likely to be considered also are used to find out what members or staff people are most involved in the issue and the best way to approach these people. Reading is likely to be less important in this process; networking, informal contacts, and attending fundraisers, more important.

GETTING ACCESS AND SHAPING A SOLUTION

The PAC plays its most crucial role in helping the corporation to gain access, but even here there is no one-to-one correspondence between money and outcome. Corporate PAC officials sometimes talked as if it were normal that anyone who wanted to see a member of Congress could do so—even if the person didn't live in the member's state or district. One executive saw this as a right, not a privilege: "You want to have access to the member so you or your experts can tell your story. That's what the Constitution guarantees." At other times gaining access was presented as a significant problem and the PAC as vital to this process. Fairly typical was a company whose plant in a specific area had come under attack for environmental pollution but whose PAC officer argued that "the entire economic framework of that whole section of the country" depends on the company's plant, which therefore put the company in a strong position. Some academics argue that this alone should guarantee the company success,[21] but this executive didn't agree:

> INTERVIEWER: So does the PAC really change anything? Suppose you didn't have a PAC? You'd still have 2,000 employees and a $50 million payroll. . . .

> PAC DIRECTOR: I wouldn't have the access, and it may sound like bull-
> shit, but I'm telling you very sincerely, I wouldn't know Governor X
> to the degree that we know the governor and his staff; we wouldn't
> know Bob Y, the local congressman, as well as we know him; and we
> wouldn't know the junior senator as well.

Not everyone can get in to talk to every member, but when a
lobbyist does get an appointment, it's necessary to be prepared with a
carefully thought out proposal and supporting evidence or exhibits.
The company lobbyist can't prepare this by him or herself; many other
company officials must be actively involved.

> When legislation appears on the horizon, we send a copy of the bill to one
> of our government relations people, and he has the ability to go around
> to our different business sector units and talk to people. If it's a tax bill,
> talk to our tax department. If it's a product liability bill, talk to the legal
> department and flesh out how that bill would affect our company. Based
> on that, we might have a couple of meetings with some of the people from
> our Washington office that covers that legislation and people from the
> business sector it would affect. They'll sit down and say, "Here's what the
> bill says. We think it's great," or "we think it's terrible. We can maybe
> amend it to say this instead of that. We can live with that." And that's how
> we come up with our positions on the issues.

The PAC committee is potentially valuable here, providing contact
people in each area of company operations. However it is done, government relations cannot be isolated from company operations personnel but needs help both in identifying problems and formulating
responses.

The more carefully a company's proposal is crafted and the more
fully its arguments are supported, the more likely the member is to
accept the proposal. Congressional staffs have expanded but are still
minimal. If a small company correctly identifies a technical problem
with the proposed wording of a bill but is unable to suggest a modifi-
cation that fixes this problem without abandoning the entire bill, it is
unlikely that the member's staff would have someone with the technical
expertise needed to do so. The more effort required by the member,
the less likely he or she is to work on the problem. This becomes
a further structural factor favoring big business over most alternative groups, whether small business, the homeless, or environmental
activists.

When corporate lobbyists meet with a member or key staffer, they feel they must have full and complete information, present it honestly, explain why their alternative proposal is reasonable, and make a case that it constitutes better policy. "It's all education. That's what lobbying really is. In fact, if you do it right, it's to supply the best information you can about your side, but the information you supply cannot be so biased that it's no good to them." Lobbyists seem to be able to persuade themselves the changes they request are not just reasonable but right, honorable, and meritorious. In this they are no different from many of the rest of us who are able to see our self-interest as benefitting the general good; the difference, of course, is that they make their case on behalf of the most powerful and privileged in our society. For the most part they did not seem to be struggling with their consciences or having trouble living with themselves. It is necessary to give the member the full picture, even facts that might hurt the company's case:

> You lose your reputation for honesty and integrity, and that's it. You are finished. So as much as you might say, "Well, I'll tilt this or scratch that," or "I'll take that column out of the chart," that doesn't pay in the long run. It really doesn't.

Once information has been presented fully and accurately, the lobbyist then makes the case for the company's proposed alternative. The alternative is not presented as naked self-interest: "screw the environment; we'll make an extra $50 million if we poison the river." Rather it should be put in practical and highminded terms: "No one cares more about the environment than we at the Loot-and-Pillage Corporation. We have been moving to upgrade our facilities as rapidly as is economically practical. However, our plant in Flaming River was built before this concern with the environment, and there is no rational way to fix it to meet these unreasonable standards. If this law were passed, we would have to close that plant; the issue here is not just the effect on our bottom line, but jobs for our loyal employees in Flaming River.[22] The modification we propose would allow that plant to continue producing; the plant would improve its environmental record, and as soon as economically practicable it would meet the more rigorous standard. We have a study here showing that this would have a negligible effect on the environment and would save 1,247 jobs. If you are prepared to make this change, we'll be able to live with this bill. I realize that we don't always see eye-to-eye on all issues, but you've always been reasonable, our PAC has supported you in the past and hopes to do so in the future, we've worked together on other issues, and the change we are proposing here is totally reasonable."[23]

In some cases the member simply accepts the proposed change for any of a variety of reasons: it really does seem totally reasonable; the plant is in his or her district and the potential job loss would be serious; the member has a long-standing friendship with the corporate lobbyist, always feels that "what's good for business is good for America," or just wants campaign contributions and doesn't care that much about the environment. In many cases, however, the member has a set of tough questions and is not prepared to accept the company proposal until it is substantially modified. If the member asks, the lobbyist must give an honest and knowledgeable assessment of the likely political impact:

> PAC DIRECTOR: They [the members] say, "What do you think the steel guys will really think if I support this? Can I get away with that? Is this too tough an issue for me?" I try to give them an honest answer. If I can't give them an honest answer, then I better . . .
>
> INTERVIEWER: Is that a good opportunity for you? Is it useful when they call?
>
> PAC DIRECTOR: No, it isn't, because you've got to be honest with them. The whole thing is that they are going to call you back . . . so you've always got to be 100 percent honest with them: "You can take that issue, but it's going to kill you back in the district. That's not popular with the steel workers." Or: "I can't say that's a good issue for you because the pensioners don't like it." I'd like to say: "Support us," but you can't do that because you've got to think about tomorrow.

The nature of the friendly live-and-let-live relations between PACs and members of Congress means that if members can't accept the company's initial proposal they often ask the corporate lobbyist to help them fashion solutions:

> They say, "Here's what I think, here's what you think. Can you rework this out so I can give you a little piece of the pie and still not screw the other 93 percent of my district who want it the other way?" And we say, "Yes, if you can just do this. It doesn't change the bill, but at least it allows us to do this." It's the fun of the game.

Even if the company is reasonably sure the legislation is not going to pass this session, "You still want to get in there and shape it so as to set its character for the next session because the odds are it is going to be coming back again."

Sometimes the member of Congress is unwilling to help, and feels that the company's request is not reasonable, either because of the member's perception of good policy or because of the political realities. As an experienced politician the member is unlikely to say, "There is no way I'll ever support that." The response is more likely to be, "I would have serious difficulties with that, I'm not prepared to support it at this time, and I doubt I could support it unless you can make the changes we discussed." The company has two choices: if the member is not vital to this issue (for example, does not chair the key committee or subcommittee), the company can just move down the hall and try other members. If the member is vital or if the concerns the member expressed seem likely to be widespread, the company can modify its proposal, which probably means another round of meetings with corporate managers, experts, and lawyers. The lobbyist needs to explain the member's concerns, and then the assembled company group needs to consider alternative solutions, and see whether some of them might be satisfactory to both the company and the member.

DEFENDING THE CHANGE AND GETTING IT THROUGH

In many cases if one respected member on the appropriate sub-committee accepts the company's proposal, the committee incorporates it in the bill word for word. Other subcommittee members who ask about the change generally will accept a brief answer reviewing the rationale, and others in Congress are unlikely to reexamine the issue once it has been passed by the subcommittee and committee. Costly and far-reaching changes in areas of known controversy, however, are more likely to be challenged and examined. In these circumstances it is the company or industry's responsibility to help defend the provision by lining up other members who will support the provision or at least not publicly challenge it, thus reducing the level of controversy, and by orchestrating appropriate public relations. By the nature of the case, most of these changes do not receive much publicity: if they do, the company and the member have failed, since the aim is to present the change as minor, technically driven, and not subject to partisan disagreement. On many issues, "You don't want to get too far out in front and get tagged that you are the worst offender—the one this especially applies to."

The better the case a company or industry makes, and the more they do to build support for their proposal, the easier it is for a member to vote for them or defend them publicly. A narrowly self-interested proposal, with obvious negative consequences for the public, is much harder to defend. Much, of course, depends on the vagaries of the media and public attention. For years the savings and loan industry, and a host of its business supporters, pressured federal regulators and congressional banking committees for rulings and legislation to free them from most restrictions, while the government continued to guarantee depositors against losses no matter what stupid and crazy things the deregulated savings and loans did. Neither the public nor the media was interested.[24] When the cost of the bailout for past failures climbed into the hundreds of billions, five senators were singled out as villains, while similar savings and loan actions by other legislators received less attention, and similar relations with other industries received virtually none.

Most of the time a corporation's power, resources, and legitimacy assure that it will get its way. Other actors react to its field of power and don't oppose it. But corporations need to be willing and able to exert leverage if an opponent takes them on and push comes to shove. Procter & Gamble, for example, was targeted because its Folger's brand coffee contains beans from El Salvador. Neighbor to Neighbor, a small human rights organization, produced an ad featuring Ed Asner, former president of the Screen Actors Guild who played Lou Grant on the "Mary Tyler Moore" and "Lou Grant" television shows. The ad focuses on El Salvador's notorious abuses of human rights, including the fact that the regime has sheltered those who murdered priests and nuns. Ed Asner then calls for a consumer boycott of Folger's because it contains coffee from El Salvador. Neighbor to Neighbor bought time on a local television station at the going rate, the same as any other advertiser might do, and managed to raise $4,150 to run the ad eight times in the Boston area.[25]

Procter & Gamble's response was hardly "I disagree with every word you say but will defend to the death your right to say it." Instead Procter & Gamble fought hard to silence Neighbor to Neighbor, denying it the rights that would be conceded to a competing soap or coffee company. Procter & Gamble announced it would pull all its advertising from any television station that agreed to run Neighbor to Neighbor's ad. Since Procter & Gamble's total advertising budget is $1,506,892,000, with over $683 million of this spent for television,[26] and Neighbor to Neighbor had difficulty coming up with $4,150, television stations had no trouble making a choice. To hell with free speech, they decided, and pulled the Neighbor to Neighbor ad. Corporate pressure rarely needs to be so blatant, however, because business's field of power is known and recognized by others in our society, so reporters and others avoid direct confrontations. Nonetheless, members try to minimize situations that could lead to public condemnation. A key reason that corporations give to members representing company facilities is that those members are much less likely to receive negative publicity for doing favors for the company, since they can always argue that the action was undertaken to save people's jobs, not simply to garner a campaign contribution.

THE PAC IS ONLY A PART OF THE PROCESS

PAC money by itself is never enough to create or maintain a viable government relations operation, but the PAC is a useful, perhaps even a necessary, part of the total operation. One corporate official captured the general attitude toward the role of the PAC:

> Yes, I believe the PAC is important. But nevertheless might we have won the issue without the PAC? I think so. It made it easier with people with whom we did not have a close relationship. We went to the AA [administrative assistant, a top congressional aide] and said, "Here is a letter which Senator X is going to be the lead signer on," because he knew our company very well. "And so we'd like to ask you, John Doe, who is vaguely aware of our existence, to sign this letter. And oh, by the way, it goes without having to say, we contributed $2,000 to the senator's last campaign." It sure didn't hurt. Now would he have signed the letter anyway? I suspect he probably would have.

Even PAC officials agree that some of what they seek is dubious, but for the most part they feel they are simply seeking to improve policy:

> I'm not going to say that I haven't in the past lobbied for things that are just straightforwardly to advantage my corporation, because I have. Although more realistically, people who we employ have. I don't do a whole lot of lobbying myself. But far and away the vast majority of things that we do are literally to protect ourselves from public policy that is poorly crafted and nonresponsive to the needs and realities and circumstances of our company.

Most PAC officers insist that money alone is not enough:

I think two hours of constituent participation at a charitable event with a member of Congress, getting a bunch of employees to go to the Bowl-a-thon, the Cancer Society, is worth, I don't know how much, but a bunch of PAC money from somebody that they don't really know and whom they deal with in a strictly "business" relationship. I think the truth of the matter is, except for some major companies, any company that has more than a handful of members of Congress with whom it enjoys a genuinely close relationship, genuine mutual respect, is fortunate indeed. In the final analysis that's really all it takes. Because I'd rather have one guy who sincerely cares than I would twenty who are superficial. . . . The one that is your friend, you are going to be his primary concern. The PAC certainly is an important part of that, but only a part.

For small-scale issues or a one-time vote on a minor wording change, a strictly monetary relationship with a member might be sufficient, but if the corporation is suddenly in some kind of major trouble, the offer of a PAC contribution won't be much help. At that point no member will find it rational to assist them simply in hopes of a future donation. There has to be something more. Bringing in a check

might make the AA [administrative assistant; the top congressional aide] happy because he has to raise $10,000 that week and you walk in the door with a $3,000 check and you are a hero today at least, but I think the meaningful relationships are those that develop over time and that have many dimensions to the relationship.

Corporate government relations specialists, members of Congress, and their staffs get to know each other and become friends. Most of these people, on both the corporate and congressional sides, are extremely likeable. The proportion of warm, friendly, outgoing, genuinely nice people is about as high as you will find anywhere. It's their job to be like that, but it's clear that it is much more than that, that the job attracts people with that kind of personality. The people who aren't like that probably don't succeed at the job and tend to leave it, but whatever the reason, these are people you can't help liking. Although we have a lot more in common with academics than with corporate lobbyists, we found the corporate lobbyists were often easier to talk with, and despite the differences in our viewpoints they were friendlier and pleasanter to be with.[27] While this point is difficult to convey, it is crucial to understand how outgoing and nice lobbyists are, and that this was not a pose put on for professional purposes.

In addition to being likeable people who smooth over social situations and help put people at ease, corporate government relations personnel inhabit the same social world as members of Congress and their staffs. To a considerable degree this is true even for personnel located at corporate headquarters far from Washington, but it is overwhelmingly so in Washington. Wherever corporate headquarters are, government relations personnel have to spend significant amounts of time in Washington. Moreover, they interact with virtually all members of their home state's congressional delegation and with many other members who regularly hold fundraisers around the country. In the nation's capital, however, this is raised to a new height. Many corporate lobbyists formerly worked as congressional aides or political appointees in one or another government agency. People shift positions fairly frequently; the key person to contact may be someone you worked with not long before, or a fraternity brother, or a member of your club, or someone who serves with you on the board of a local charity. The men regularly play golf together. One PAC official interrupted our interview to take a phone call making arrangements for a golf foursome with Dan Rostenkowski (chair of the House Ways and Means Committee, the committee in charge of all tax legislation), discussing the need for a fourth with the right level of golf skills and the right personality who would make an enjoyable golf partner. Our man explained it was important that everyone have a good time, but that didn't mean you couldn't also talk a little business. Women in government relations are unlikely to be included in golf dates but may meet elsewhere, probably on the tennis courts but perhaps even at the hairdresser:

> I was getting my hair done a couple of weeks ago, and I had a very early appointment. . . . I was amazed by the women in the beauty shop . . . a number of well-known, well-connected, high-placed, high-powered women—and a lot of talk was going on.

Unplanned contacts come easily and regularly for people who live in the same neighborhoods, belong to the same clubs,[28] share friends and contacts, and inhabit the same social world. One PAC officer had car problems when driving her babysitter home and was helped by a man she didn't know. He turned out to be a member of the House Ways and Means Committee, and she has continued to have dealings with him since. In fact, as one PAC officer noted, "It's hard to quantify what is social and what is business":

I can go to lunch with people and take two minutes of their time talking about my issue, and then we can spend the rest of the time catching up on what's new. Some of those people are my best friends on the Hill. I see them personally, socially, and they're very good to me; they always help me with my issues. I don't think you have to spend two hours of somebody's time groaning and beating an issue into their heads.

WHY CORPORATIONS CAN DO WHAT OTHERS CAN'T

Legally, campaign contributors may not explicitly exchange cash for influence. Unlike the explicit exchange of an outright purchase in the market, campaign contributions are gifts based on a basic trust the gift will be reciprocated if and when it is appropriate. But these gift exchanges are always uncertain and problematic; people may not understand the rules or may not be able to negotiate the appropriate implicit understandings. The more people have in common, the more they share networks, the more they know and accept the rules of the game, the more confidence they have that things will work out. An explicit request for a quid pro quo would be not only illegal (and therefore risky to both parties), but gauche and inappropriate. An analogy can be made to a date: if a man takes a woman to an expensive restaurant and then to a major event, if he spares no expense to show that he cares about her and regards her as special, this increases the probability that she will agree to and want to have sex with him. However, were a man to propose an explicit exchange ("I'll buy you a steak if you'll spend the night with me"), the odds are high that the woman would be offended and the date a disaster. Similarly, members of Congress distinguish between being *asked* to do a favor, which they see as appropriate, and being *required* to do one in exchange for a donation, which is unacceptable:

> For [Tony] Coelho [D-Calif. and chair of the Democratic Congressional Campaign Committee], putting the official machinery of the House of Representatives to work on behalf of a $5,000 donor was no more out of line than giving him fancy luggage tags. He said he became offended only when the donor suggested an explicit entitlement to official favors. "There is a fine line," Coelho explained. "I don't mind [donors] bringing up that they have a problem [with the government]. But don't ever try to create the impression with me, or ever say it—if you say it, it's all over—that your money has bought you something. It hasn't. There's a real delicate line there, and it's hard for people to understand how we do it."[29]

Participants need to realize that sometimes friends can help and sometimes they can't. Sometimes relations balance out evenly; more often there are people to whom you have given more than you've received, but there are others from whom you've received more than you've given. What matters is not just the specific gift but a relation of trust—a reputation for taking care of your friends, for being someone that others can count on, for knowing that if you scratch my back I'll scratch yours. A month after the *Valdez* fouled the waters off the coast of Alaska, it is unlikely that many members would have regarded it as sharp political strategy to speak up for Exxon. No corporation knows when it might face a similar disaster—a company oil tanker destroying water, fish, birds, mammals, and coastline; a chemical plant emitting fumes that kill thousands; a feed additive found to cause cancer in cattle and humans; a car or a plane responsible for dramatic accidents. But it is precisely in such situations that a corporation may most need a member willing to help out—not by dramatic announcements but by stalling a resolution, amending it to remove some of the penalties, or arguing that some other forum should consider the issue first.

This culture gives enormous advantages to long-term big players. Even if a corporation hasn't contributed to the member of Congress it most needs to see, other members and other corporate officials can provide introductions and testimonials. The member knows that the corporation is a major player, has been around for a long time, and has the resources to deliver. The corporation will be able to give a PAC contribution every election for as long as the member is in Congress and do so without straining corporate resources. Moreover, the corporation will be able to draw on reserve power if need be. It is this sort of reputation that both individuals and corporations work for years to achieve. With such a reputation, very little needs to be made explicit. A wink and a nod communicate everything; even the wink and nod may be superfluous. Without such a reputation, people looking for favors are a much greater risk—that they will put the issue as an explicit exchange, thereby compromising the member (and potentially forcing a rejection of the request); that they will be more likely to double-cross a member because they don't have a reputation to safeguard; or that if asked for extra help they won't have the necessary networks to deliver.

Therefore individuals, labor unions, small businesses, or nonprofit organizations are in a different structural position than major corporations, *even if they are willing and able to contribute the same amount of PAC money.* A corporation is also able to draw on and promise access to resources not connected to campaign money. It can deliver not only a campaign contribution but perhaps also a free trip or a lecture fee or even line up campaign contributions from other corporate PACs. If a member needs information on an issue, the company has experts who can provide it. If the company has a facility in the member's district, it can provide the member with entree to its employees, it will have leverage with both its customers and suppliers, and its managers will have personal networks with other key figures in the community.

Moreover, most of the time most major corporations have a high degree of legitimacy. Even if a member of Congress is helping them to pollute the environment or evade taxes, the special benefit is still likely to be widely regarded as at least defensible and perhaps honorable. A news story, if there were one, would be a "balanced" presentation of "both sides." In part this is simply because business occupies a special place in our society, but it is also because businesses with major PACs are large operations. A tax break need not stand out; rather it will be seen as a complicated provision applying to special circumstances faced by this corporation and intended only to create fair conditions for this unusual situation.

The Social Security "notch" for those born between 1917 and 1921 helps illustrate the differing treatment accorded to nonbusiness groups. In 1972 Congress adopted a formula to ensure automatic increases in benefits for Social Security retirees to protect them against inflation. For technical reasons, however, the formula was flawed and led to greater increases in benefits than had been intended. In 1977 Congress again revised the formula, preserving the raised benefits for those who were already receiving them, but lowering benefits for future retirees and providing a five-year transition period to phase in the new benefits. The new benefit levels for those born 1917 to 1921 were intended to be 5 percent lower than the old benefits.

The new regulations, however, produced substantially more reduction in benefits than most people had expected. The "notch" in benefits for those retiring under the new law produced some anomalous results. Critics of the notch point to the example of Edith Detviler and her sister, Audrey Webb. The two sisters went to work on the same day in 1957 at the same southern California bindery, doing the same job for the same pay. "They retired 25 years later on the same day, October 8, 1982. They earned almost the same amount over their careers and paid virtually the same in Social Security taxes."[30] However, one sister was born fifteen months later than the other, in 1917 instead of 1916, and her retirement benefit is $184 a month less ($695 instead of $879, a 20.9 percent difference). More generally, if two workers each had average lifetime earnings, and each retired at age sixty-five, the one born in 1916 received $716 a month and the one born in 1917 received $592.[31]

Older Americans are not without political clout, and those born in the notch have certainly noticed the difference. When "Dear Abby" ran a column on the issue, she received a million responses—more than for any other column she has ever run. The issues director for a congressional campaign reports, "It's no exaggeration to say that during the campaign I received more calls about the notch issue than on any other subject."[32] Nonetheless, the powers that be have insisted that there is no issue. Frank Batistelli of the Social Security Administration insists that "we don't see it as a legitimate problem."[33] A *New York Times* editorial called on "responsible representatives of the elderly . . . to denounce the Notch Baby fix for what it really is: a budget-busting giveaway fired by greed, not fairness."[34] A report by the Academy of Social Insurance concluded that the problem was that prenotch retirees were receiving too much and that therefore no change was appropriate.[35] By 1991 (fourteen years after the initial law was passed) a majority of members of the House had signed on as cosponsors of a measure to change the law, but it seems unlikely the measure will pass before the notch babies are in their eighties.

Without getting involved in all the arguments, at a minimum it can be said that (1) notch babies were not aware ahead of time of the impact of the 1977 revision, (2) they made no serious effort to introduce a formula that would have led to more gradual cuts, (3) millions of people would have been prepared to support such an effort, and (4) it would have been far more justifiable and meritorious than most of the loopholes corporations win for themselves. However, the failure to be properly organized, the lack of an effective access operation at a crucial time, and the fact that older Americans do not have the same legitimacy and clout as business have meant that notch babies have for many years received lower benefits than their older brothers and sisters, and this will probably continue into the indefinite future. It is hard to believe that any corporate PAC officer who could point to such a disparity—say, in the tax rates for companies incorporated at dates a year apart—would be unable to mount a successful campaign to get the most favorable rate then prevailing.

Myth Three: Political Party Matters

One popular conception labels the Democrats the party of the common people and the Republicans the party of big business. Another common perception is that conservatives support a level playing field and want government to avoid interfering with the free market. An example from each end of the political spectrum shows this is not the case. Steve Symms is an ultraconservative Republican from Idaho; his election was supported by virtually every conservative ideological PAC, and the *Almanac of American Politics* characterized him as "one of the closest things to a libertarian in Congress: he opposes practically every kind of government program."[36] Nonetheless, in the 1986 Tax Reform Act he introduced a special provision to save Unocal $50 million. In the same bill at the other end of the (elected) political spectrum, Daniel Patrick Moynihan, Democrat of New York and rated by the *National Journal* as the most liberal senator on economic issues in 1982, sponsored special favors for a sports stadium in Buffalo, for a brokerage firm, and one that applied only to the royalties earned by five biomedical researchers in Rochester.[37]

When we began these interviews, we knew that many Democrats and many well-known liberals were happy to do special-interest favors for corporations. Nonetheless, we assumed corporate PACs would have many enemies in Congress—people who were out to get them and that they in turn wanted to defeat. We regularly asked about this in interviews and were surprised to learn that corporations didn't really feel they had enemies in Congress. Yes, there were lots of members who opposed them on any given issue, but no, there weren't any members they considered unreasonable. Essentially *all* members of Congress are at least potentially willing to help them out, to give them access, to let them make their case. One PAC official told us, "You have guys that will hold rallies right outside this building here, hold news conferences and picket lines periodically, every year," attacking the company and its policies. However, "When they go to the Congress . . . they tend to ameliorate their anti-big business or proconsumer stance." Even the people who used to lead demonstrations against the company become more open to receiving information from and entering a dialogue with the company: "I don't want to say that they are the best friends we have in government, but you can go to them."

This doesn't mean that every corporation is happy with every member, only that almost no people were regularly mentioned as hostile to business. For example, one corporation refused to contribute to Mickey Leland because they felt he was too "communistic," but another had a different attitude:

> Mickey Leland is a good example. Mickey works with us all the time. You know what he is going to do. On a social issue he is going to be a liberal. You know: Let's get arrested on apartheid. Let's try to force businesses to paint those old shacks that his constituents live in. Let's set up extra help for the food stamp programs. All that sort of stuff. But when you get down to an energy issue, he is right there with us. And that comes down to, we don't have anything against doing those things he is talking about, but that's not the purpose of this company's PAC. The purpose of this company's PAC is to pay attention to this business.

Similarly, Jim Florio was a liberal member of the House, and as governor of New Jersey instituted soak-the-rich tax and spend policies. Yet one company explicitly mentioned that "we support Florio strongly in Washington. And the reason is because he helps us on all sorts of stuff."

Only two exceptions were mentioned. One was Senator Ted Kennedy (D-Mass.), but he was mentioned only a couple of times, and these seemed vague and pro forma attempts to cite someone who took public positions hostile to business. No one volunteered any specific examples of having had trouble working with him, and people were as likely to say they had been able to work with him or had at least not found him unreasonable. The other example of a person who would not cooperate with business was Senator Howard Metzenbaum (D-Ohio), and his name came up repeatedly. Corporation after corporation mentioned that they find him a little hard to take and that while he is personally charming he is hostile to business. About one-quarter of all corporations brought him up as the member of Congress they found least willing to cooperate with them and most likely to give them a hard time. Metzenbaum plays a unique role in the Senate

> as a watchdog for legislation that in his view benefits special interests. On the floor of the Senate, he is a kind of Horatius at the bridge, putting holds near the end of the session on dozens of pieces of what he considers special interest legislation and then filibustering them if they came up. In effect Metzenbaum forces Senators backing these bills to negotiate with him, even if they had a large majority and he represented only himself. . . . Colleagues get infuriated with Metzenbaum; they vow to deny him

any special breaks he might seek; but they cannot get around him and so, grumbling, make their plans with him in mind and seek to get his approval for legislation that, before he was in the Senate, would probably pass through easily.[38]

It is perhaps worth noting that Metzenbaum is (1) a senator and needs to run only once every six years, (2) relatively old and unlikely to run for president, and (3) independently wealthy and does not need to rely on future employment by corporations. All of these factors may help explain his willingness and ability to refuse to cooperate with businesses.[39]

Not only are virtually all members accessible to business, but it is amazing how cheap it is to gain such access. On a day-to-day basis, access is apparently available for $500 or $1,000, sometimes less, or this is what records of campaign contributions appear to indicate: in 1988, the last year for which we have data, the average corporate PAC contribution to members of the House was $925 and of the Senate, $2,472. Four out of five (79.2 percent) donations to members of the House and almost half (42.8 percent) of donations to senators were $1,000 or less. These amounts have undoubtedly gone up: when we did our main interviews in 1988 and 1989, corporations complained that the cost of an average fundraiser was increasing. But they are still very modest considering that they allow corporations to gain access to members to make a case for special privileges that can save them hundreds of millions of dollars. Easy access is available even to members who are regarded as not sympathetic to business.

The fact that members and corporations deal with each other honestly is an important indicator of the nature of the relation between members and corporate lobbyists. Corporations provide full and honest evaluations of their practices even when it argues against their position because the relationship of corporate lobbyists to members of Congress is not adversarial. Congress is often portrayed (by pluralists) as a neutral arbiter between contending factions: each side makes the strongest possible case for its position, and the member then balances these out and comes to a position (believed to be) in the best interests of the district as a whole. In an adversarial situation such as a union grievance or a legal dispute, each side has an advocate who presents its case as forcefully as possible, and then the judge or arbitrator considers all the input and makes a decision. Although lawyers typically would not lie or lead their clients to lie, they certainly will make every effort to state their clients' position in the most forceful and effective way, which may mean ignoring, downplaying, or putting the best construction on key facts in the case.

The honesty displayed by corporate lobbyists when dealing with members of Congress is also, of course, an acknowledgment that they will be dealing with each other for many years to come and that the continued relationship is more important than any particular issue. However, the long-term relationship by itself is not enough to produce the honest evaluations given to members. Lawyers frequently have long-term relationships with judges, but they nonetheless are advocates for their clients; all sides understand the situation as one in which it is the judge's responsibility to be balanced, not the lawyer's.

The nonadversarial character of the member-lobbyist relationship depends on at least two factors—the legitimacy of U.S. business and the limited resources of public-interest movements. First, U.S. business is accorded great legitimacy and acceptance; the widespread notion that what's good for business is good for America is held in some fashion even by many of the critics of business. Except in rare instances where a highly visible disaster threatens lives or the environment, business is regarded as a pillar of the community—even when it argues that it should be able to pollute the atmosphere, threaten its workers' health and safety, and avoid its fair share of taxes. Business is treated as almost a part of the state, an extension of congressional staffs:

> We get a lot of calls from committee staffs who respect the company and its standards of operations. They will ask us questions on "How would this provision work?" or "How would that work?" and they know that when they do that, we give them an honest answer.

Second, although the opponents of business became much more visible and effective in the late 1960s and have retained much of their political capacity,[40] public-interest movements rarely have the resources to contest the *details* of congressional (or regulatory agency) actions. Environmental movements can and do put their issues on the agenda and manage to focus attention on a handful of the most visible corporate attempts to cripple the law by arguing for a "clean" bill without special exceptions. As such they are the main opposition corporate polluters need to worry about. But they have not been in a position to engage in hand-to-hand combat over each and every special exemption. Exposure by such movements is the main thing a member needs to fear, but there are tens of thousands of corporate special deals struck each year, and public-interest movements are lucky if they can focus major media attention on ten of these and minor attention on another hundred. Still less is the labor movement or any other organized representative of the bottom half of the income distribution able to contest corporate tax loopholes. Corporations are in a no-lose situation: no group pushes to impose extra burdens on corporations that try to win loopholes. If such groups existed and if members were frequently sympathetic to such claims, corporate lobbyists might modify their policy of honesty and full disclosure. This policy could be interpreted as an indication that members and corporations generally see themselves as basically on the same side, even if they differ on specifics—an interpretation that is further supported by the numerous occasions when members allow corporations to write the specific wording they want incorporated in a bill. To date these practices have been fully developed only at the federal level, but a number of corporations talked about branching out to the state and local levels: "Out there is a whole new field. Nobody is doing this. Taking a Washington approach to issues and coming out and trying to attack it all across. It scares the shit out of people when you do it to them. It's effective."

If corporate PACs can get the "minor" wording changes they want, then they may not care how a member votes on the roll call on the final bill. As a PAC officer explained:

> We are not big on voting records . . . because frequently the final vote on a particular bill isn't really important. . . . Probably what's more important is what's thrashed out internally in some of the important committees in Congress. And it doesn't much matter how people vote afterwards. It's what they argued for or tried to get done or stopped from happening, getting done, in those interpersonal discussions that take place.

Another corporation was willing to be understanding if a member voted in favor of the Clean Air Act: "In some cases, maybe because of local environmental people, the senator was not able to vote for [the company] on the floor, but there are a lot of ways that members can help with an issue without actually voting on the floor." Companies would like to see members vote for the company even when the heat is on, but

> ultimately we understand they are not going to vote against their own interests. If it comes down to the bottom line and the issue has gotten such public heat that it becomes their holding the job another year or [our

company], we would like to see them take the profile in courage, as they say. But we understand. We hope the issues don't get to that point. You try to defuse them ahead of time or find alternatives.

The fact that corporate lobbyists can potentially gain access to any member, that it is cheap to do so, and that when they get in the door they talk honestly, does not mean that success is automatic. If it were, corporations wouldn't bother to have PACs.

Myth Four: Business Wins Without Effort

A different sort of misconception about the access or special-interest process is held by some people on the left of the political spectrum who feel that this process operates automatically, that business is guaranteed to win with no significant effort by corporations, and in any case that the consequences are minimal. Some people believe that Congress is unimportant and that all key decisions are made by the president and executive branch. The access process described in this chapter is what G. William Domhoff calls the special-interest process, and it is the simplest and least significant of his four processes of ruling-class domination. Structural Marxists such as Nicos Poulantzas or Fred Block argue that business does not need to be conscious of its interests or to mobilize to achieve its aims and that the nature of the system requires politicians and the state to do what business wants in order to maintain a healthy economy.[41]

To some degree we agree with this reservation. The access process is not the sole basis for corporate power. The primary foundation of business power is the ability to make day-to-day business decisions unless and until the government intervenes. This, together with control over vast resources, makes it possible for a measly $1,000 to win the corporation not only access to the member but the member's support for a multimillion-dollar corporate benefit. However, access through a carefully placed PAC contribution is one component of corporate power and by no means a trivial one. A range of commentators agree that Congress has become increasingly important,[42] and any analysis of business's political problems must focus on congressional actions. In the 1960s the presidency may have been far more important than Congress, but that is no longer the case, except for foreign policy. David Vogel's analysis of business's *Fluctuating Fortunes* led him to conclude that both for the decline of corporate political power in the late 1960s and for its revival in the late 1970s, "the key to this shift was Congress."[43] The most important business group formed in the 1970s, the Business Roundtable, differed from previous peak associations in that its primary mission was *not* to develop policy behind the scenes but rather to lobby Congress openly. Nor would it be fair to interpret Domhoff's work as arguing against the importance of the processes we have been discussing. Although the access process is most centrally concerned with Domhoff's special-interest process, it also affects two of his other processes—the candidate selection process and the policy formation process. The large sums of money that flow to members of Congress willing to do favors for corporations make it difficult for any challenger to unseat them. As we argue below, the access process complicates policy formation in ways that both aid and frustrate business domination.

Corporations find it cheap to gain access, but the process also demonstrates the limits to business power and the effort corporations must make to retain their privileged position. The access process is a limited response to legislation that business would prefer had never been proposed. Corporations seek special provisions to protect themselves only because they can't totally defeat the legislation. We asked one PAC director whether his aim was generally to defeat legislation or modify it:

> I think it depends on the bill, and also it depends on the company. I think as a general statement, the business community normally goes in and says they [members of Congress] should vote against the bill. And ultimately when you get done saying that, you sit down and say, "We really would like you to consider A, B, and C." My personal attitude is that certain things are going to happen. You obviously try to make the end product as palatable as possible.

This is a pragmatic approach by someone who hardly feels in control of the process. Much of his effort has gone into fighting environmental regulations; on the one hand he has helped win many modifications, and on the other the legislation always passes by wide margins.

The limits to corporate power need to be recognized both theoretically and politically. A failure to do so leads to cynicism and despair—a sense that nothing can be done, that people can't make a difference. No question about it, the odds are stacked in favor of business, and the rest of us have to engage in massive struggles to win small victories—but victories are possible. We have won them in the past and will win them in the future. These are not only token victories either; they are real changes that bring substantial improvement. Unions have brought millions of workers higher living standards along with more dignity and respect. The environmental movement is responsible for some improvements, and some instances where we have been able to hold the line, in the struggle to preserve the earth. The fact that environmental degradation will destroy the earth and all of us with it is hardly proof that corporations would have done anything about it if left to themselves. As Marx said about the nineteenth-century movement to limit the length of the working day:

> [Capital] allows its actual movement to be determined as much and as little by the sight of the coming degradation and final depopulation of the human race, as by the probable fall of the earth into the sun. In every stock-jobbing swindle everyone knows that some time or other the crash must come, but everyone hopes that it may fall on the head of his neighbour. . . . *Après moi le déluge!* is the watchword of every capitalist and of every capitalist nation. Capital therefore takes no account of the health and the length of life of the worker, unless society forces it to do so.[44]

Even the special exceptions that corporations win for themselves require persistent effort. If members of Congress were always eager to do what corporations wanted, corporate PACs would not need to contribute to safe incumbents or establish personal connections through attending fundraisers. Corporate government relations departments wouldn't have to mount major campaigns to win their special exceptions. People can't be sure exactly how much difference the PAC makes, but there is a clear sense that it can provide a critical edge. In one interview in which a top company executive complained about problems with PACs and government relations, we asked him "What would be the consequences if you didn't do any of that?" and he answered "I'm not sure, but I'm not willing to find out."

Good PAC officers are the ones who make the right decisions, contributing ahead of time to the members the corporation later needs to see for favors. These decisions involve large measures of uncertainty, not so much in terms of who will be defeated or move to a more powerful committee, but rather in terms of what government actions the corporation may need or need to stop. A profitable company today may be in bankruptcy five years from now; today's steel or electric company may be tomorrow's oil or television company. The corporation therefore wants to build trust and relations with as wide as possible a network of members and to do so well before it has any favor to request. It is cheap and easy to make a contribution and doesn't require much effort to attend a fundraiser or make a friendly personal contact. Compared to the corporation's income and resources $1,000 is an insignificant contribution. Any individual contribution is no big deal; if in doubt, better to have contributed the money. On the other side, however, the member's actions may save the company hundreds of millions of dollars and be critical to preserving the company's very existence. Such actions probably (although not necessarily) require the member to use up some political chips, to call in favors from other members, to say "Give me this one and I'll help you out when you've got a problem." There is always a (slim) chance that this special-interest activity will be exposed and cost the member dearly in the next election. If a past history of $1,000 contributions can substantially increase the possibility that the member will be willing to offer help in a crisis, then it is a cheap insurance policy for the corporation.

But in doing so PACs sometimes find themselves coerced to make contributions they resent. Part of this is just the endemic pressure by candidates discussed in the previous chapter. Another part, however, is PACs that would prefer to be ideological,[45] to support conservatives without regard to access, sometimes find that they have to play the game and contribute to liberals who are anathema to them, in hopes of future access. Again, is this glass half-empty or half-full? On the one hand, virtually every member of Congress is willing to do favors for corporations, and virtually no members are hostile to business, able to act effectively on this hostility, and unwilling to take business money. On the other hand, the corporation is being "forced" to contribute to liberals:

PAC DIRECTOR: I give some money to some people I don't agree with merely because they are working on a bill or something, and then I'm playing access so it's not entirely ideology. There's sometimes I have to give the money: I think we've given [Representative Henry] Waxman [D-Calif.] some money, and I cringe because he's not representative of our philosophy. . . . I got a note from another guy on the PAC committee who's more conservative than I am, and he said, "Why are you giving to that turkey?" But I'm more pragmatic. I realize I've got to live with some of these people.

Now if they weren't on that committee, I'd never give them any money. Now Teddy Kennedy and Howard Metzenbaum are—one's chairman of Labor and Human Resources and the other's way up there. And yes, I need access sometimes with those people. But I just can't—they're just so far that way. Now Waxman's just so far that way—but Waxman, you're never going to get him out. He's very important to us and we may give him a modest amount of money. Now you say, is there any rationale? Well, not really. It's sort of working with the system.

INTERVIEWER: Let's take that as a contrast. You give the donation to Waxman; you don't give one to Kennedy.

PAC DIRECTOR: That's right.

INTERVIEWER: You need to talk with both of them sometimes, or the committees are dealing with things. . . .

PAC DIRECTOR: That's right.

INTERVIEWER: What difference does it make?

PAC DIRECTOR [laughing]:   Because Kennedy is usually a $1,000 minimum, and I can get to Waxman for $250 probably. So my principles—we know what we are, we just don't know what we cost.

This PAC director wasn't happy prostituting himself and his company by contributing to a member he regarded as "just so far that way," but he felt it was necessary. Since he could get access to Waxman for a $250 contribution, he was willing to do so, but drew the line at giving the $1,000 that would be needed to gain access to Kennedy.[46] In a similar instance, one Connecticut-based PAC reported it had contributed to Lowell Weicker even though "there isn't a member on my PAC committee that voted for him."

On the other hand, we don't want to push the argument so far that we appear to be agreeing with pluralists. Business doesn't win automatically, but pluralists sometimes seem to be arguing that the existence of a struggle proves it's an even contest. To us it appears a very one-sided struggle, with business clearly having disproportionate power. Take the Clean Air Act (discussed in chapter 1) as an example. Should we be impressed that after twenty years the act was revised? Or appalled at how weak the act is despite strong popular support for an effective bill? Does the Clean Air Act show corporations are too weak to stop environmental legislation? Or that even when the corporate position has virtually no popular support, corporations are still able to sabotage the legislation and guarantee it will be weak and ineffective?

LANGUAGE AND EUPHEMISM

Language reveals a great deal, not only by what is said, but also by what is not said. When something is regarded as unpleasant, embarrassing, or degrading, people develop euphemisms. The euphemism attempts to deny whatever it is about the word that's considered unfortunate. Euphemisms can help locate those activities and areas that cause strain or discomfort in a culture. Our culture, like many others, has difficulty confronting death. Thus we say that people "passed away," not that they died; we avoid referring to someone as an "undertaker" and replace it with "mortician" and then replace that with "funeral director."

A euphemism helps us deal with a problem area by removing from thought "that part of the connotation of a word that creates the discomfort."[47] Thus the euphemisms for toilet take us away from the idea of excrement and substitute the idea that we are there to bathe, wash, or rest. The language used by the people we interviewed indicates that the corporation wants only "access" to members of Congress—that it is not there to lobby or influence, isn't asking for favors, and most certainly isn't asking for a quid pro quo for a past campaign contribution. As the term *access* gains notoriety, PAC officials are searching for a new and still more distant euphemism. One PAC director we interviewed called it "courtesy": "I call it courtesy. You might call it just good manners. The opportunity to deal with staff, to meet with them to persuade them."[48]

The euphemisms used by PACs imply that the purpose of their donations to, and their interactions with, members of Congress is not to buy, bribe, corrupt, or even to influence or lobby, but rather simply to gain "access."[49] If a person goes to the "washroom" he or she may actually wash but will probably be unhappy if that is *all* he or she gets to do. Similarly, corporate PACs do want "access" to the member, but if all they get is access, they will be disappointed. At a minimum the corporation hopes to lobby and influence the member, and it is certainly willing to use money as one of the influences. However, a corporate PAC official would never explicitly say, "I've got an appointment to bribe Senator X this afternoon." Nor would a member say, "I'll do you a favor, but it's going to cost you." Both corporate and congressional officials would have a great deal to lose if they regularly used such language to describe their interactions.

The language used by corporate PAC officers is of course intended for public consumption—but not *only* for public consumption. Every group creates and nurtures illusions about itself; euphemisms are as much for the speaker as the audience. Many, although by no means all, of the PAC directors we spoke with are uncomfortable about the access process. They don't like what they do, feel it is slightly sleazy, and are embarrassed and defensive about it. Generally speaking they resent buying access and influence. The corporate government relations officials don't feel embarrassed about the policy changes they ask for and don't feel they are indefensible special-interest legislation. Their concern is that the members ought to be making better policy, and should not be giving their companies a hard time. PAC directors are uneasy that the corporation is supporting liberals that don't belong in public office. From the perspective of the people we interviewed, what troubles them is not their exercise of power—which they see as not really power at all but simply helping members to craft better public policy—but the limits to that power, the fact that they are drawn into cooperating with liberals rather than throwing the bums out. A few of the most pragmatic PAC directors didn't seem to mind this, primarily on the argument that these liberals are actually happy to cooperate and do favors for business. But many people we interviewed seemed uncomfortable contributing to what they see as antibusiness liberals. They wish they didn't have to do it but feel it is necessary to get the results they need from Washington. Corporate PAC directors often feel defensive about these donations, and most corporations respond by specifically reserving some of their money to support "probusiness" "free-market" candidates who are either running for open seats or challenging entrenched incumbents.[50]

POLICY IMPLICATIONS

One key issue about this access process is this: How much difference does it make in the end? What does it add up to? Do loopholes for business, even if there are a great many of them, actually influence the distribution of power in society as a whole? Do they change the basic thrust of the legislation? Our answer: Yes. Cumulatively these minor changes, introduced through the access process, have a substantial impact, an impact that both aids and frustrates business control of U.S. society.

The access (or special-interest) process aids business control of society in at least two interrelated ways. First, the cumulative impact of these minor changes subverts the stated intent of the policy. When "minor" change is added to "minor" change, the ultimate bill does little to reform taxes or clean the air. Thus the Internal Revenue Service is surprised to find corporations paying less tax than they had anticipated from the 1986 Tax Reform Act. Thus Barry Commoner,[51] probably our most insightful and rigorous environmentalist, concludes that regulating the levels of environmental pollutants doesn't work and that the only effective public policy is to entirely outlaw a substance. Commoner stresses this as a biological and technical problem; we see it as political. Commoner believes that limited regulations fail because all parts of the environment are linked; we believe that the way the access process operates is equally important. By the time the process is through the regulation is far from what it should have been; it fails to have much impact, but this is precisely the way it was designed and intended. There may be technical reasons why it is difficult or impossible to regulate the environment, but we've never tested those. Because of the way the process operates politically, we never have made a genuine effort to give priority to the environment and to design the regulations best suited to protecting it.

Second, the access process serves and promotes business power because it is uniquely suited to frustrating the popular will. The process introduces endless delays and complications and moves issues out of the spotlight and into the backrooms where only "experts" and power brokers are allowed. The kinds of tax regulations we quoted earlier are designed to prevent the public from knowing what is happening. The process is successful in that it keeps people uninformed and their anger diffuse. A major investigation is necessary simply to know what the government is doing. The consequence is that people without lots of time and resources get discouraged and go away.

The access process thus becomes a major weapon used to frustrate and sidetrack social movements. People become cynical and discouraged, convinced that meaningful change is impossible, that the more things change the more they stay the same, that all politics is dirty, that "you can't fight city hall." This disillusionment can serve business's purpose, since an ineffective government leaves business in control of most decisions.

Today voter anger, distrust, and resentment are high. People feel they have lost control of their government, that the government serves the interests of the few, that politicians can't be trusted. They are, of course, correct. But the access process helps incumbents direct attention away from the larger issues of principles. Frequently the key choices are made in the hidden abode of committee and subcommittee hearings or in a one-on-one meeting in a member's office. This activity is not generally subject to media scrutiny, and by the time the bill finally comes to a public roll-call vote, virtually everyone lines up on the same side.

Given a clear and understandable choice, voters do remarkably well. The aim of the political system, however, is to prevent them from having such a choice. Perhaps it is time for voters and the public to insist that key public policies be enacted in simple, clear, understandable terms that are easily available for public scrutiny. If a politician says an issue is too complicated for voters to understand, he or she is probably trying to hide something. If a bill has hundreds of exceptions and special provisions, the odds are they largely or completely undermine its stated purpose.

On the other hand, the access process also creates problems for business and indicates the limits to its power. Thousands of special deals subverting the general thrust of legislation make it difficult to develop and implement *any* coherent policy, including one that addresses the needs of business as a whole. When a rising world power has a unified and powerful ruling class, such arrangements are probably minimized. If no other group is able to effectively challenge that group's power, there is less need to pretend to enact a bill to clean up the air. The power of the dominant group and the weakness of its opposition make it possible to be more explicit and open about both intentions and consequences. Thus if an attempt is made to clean the air, both the rhetoric and the law can clearly indicate the limits to this and not pretend to do more than is actually intended. When a ruling class is most powerful, unified, and effective, companies that attempt to pursue their individual interests probably are disciplined by other businesses in a host of ways,[52] which helps ensure that policy promotes the interests of business as a whole and not those of specific companies. If the U.S. business establishment did not have to take account of alternative social movements and centers of power, and if businesses were able to more effectively unify around the principles that best supported their collective long-run interests, much of the access process would be eliminated. Although the process may help to frustrate and sidetrack popular movements, it also undercuts the effectiveness of business-dominated public policy. To pass key legislation, deals must be cut with individual businesses, which makes it difficult to develop policies in the best interest of business as a whole.

In the last quarter century the height of governmental effectiveness—of its ability to implement sweeping new policies—was probably the first year of Reagan's tenure. During this period domestic programs were cut, the largest peacetime military buildup ever was launched, and a tax cut redistributed income from the poor to the rich. David Stockman, Reagan's Director of the Office of Management and Budget (OMB), was perhaps the single most important figure in much of this activity. He began by being committed to dealing with programs and budget cuts on their merits, rather than on the amount of power a group could muster:

> "We are interested in curtailing weak claims rather than weak clients," he promised. "The fear of the liberal remnant is that we will only attack weak clients. We have to show that we are willing to attack powerful clients with weak claims. I think that's critical to our success—both political and economic success."[53]

But Stockman found this to be impossible:

> "Do you realize the greed that came to the forefront?" Stockman asked with wonder. "The hogs were really feeding. The greed level, the level of opportunism, just got out of control. . . ."
>
>   "Power is contingent," he said. "The power of these client groups turned out to be stronger than I realized. The client groups know how to make themselves heard. The problem is, unorganized groups can't play in this game."[54]

Even at the period when business was most unified and most ideological, Stockman concluded "that you probably can't put together a majority coalition unless you are willing to deal with those marginal interests that will give you the votes needed to win."[55]

David Stockman's assessment may not be particularly surprising, but it clearly indicates the vital importance of the access process: it had a major impact even with a strongly probusiness president, even at the peak of business ideological unity, even when the programs under consideration provided enormous benefits to business, even when business recognized this and wanted to support the program. Despite all this, the policy formation process was frustrated by the need to compromise with the access process. The inability to enact Reagan's budget and tax programs without dozens of special deals had serious consequences both politically and economically, undermined the programs' potential effectiveness, and contributed to public disillusionment.

Chapter 5

■■■

IDEOLOGY: DEFENDING FREE ENTERPRISE

■■■

Most corporate PACs are primarily pragmatic. They target money to incumbents to improve their chances of gaining access and then use that access to try to win special benefits for their particular company or industry. Criticism of this approach comes not only from liberals and public-interest groups but from conservatives sympathetic to business and from business leaders themselves. Conservatives complain not that business uses campaign contributions to win lower taxes or freedom from some government regulation but that business isn't bold enough—that it should fight for more sweeping benefits and should not be willing to compromise with (and support) congressional moderates and liberals. When Ronald Reagan was only an ex-governor and two-time contender for the Republican presidential nomination, he addressed the organization for corporate public affairs officers, the Public Affairs Council, and asked, "Why does half of the business PAC money go to candidates who may not be friends of business? The best thing that you can hope for by following an anti-business, incumbent contribution policy is that the alligator will eat you last."[1] William Simon, former Secretary of the Treasury and member of the boards of Dart Industries, Xerox, INA, and Citibank[2] put the point in stronger terms:

> Businessmen, too, have intensified the despotic regulatory trends by their secretive attempts to fight them—not by means of courageous open battle, but by the pathetically short-range and cowardly attempts to bribe those with political power over their destinies. . . . Business, on the whole, has been gripped by cowardly silence in the face of this consistent viola-

tion of its liberty and interests. It is its final, and possibly its worst, betrayal of the free enterprise system.[3]

Corporations that reject what Simon calls "appeasement on a breathtaking scale"[4] adopt an alternative approach, an ideological orientation supporting "pro-business, free enterprise" candidates, especially if they are *not* incumbents. Ideological corporations try to target their money to close races where a few extra dollars might change the outcome. At the present time only a small minority of corporate PACs are primarily ideological, but most corporations reserve some of their money for ideological donations. In 1988 only eight of the 309 largest corporate PACs gave more than 50 percent of their money to nonincumbents, but 85 gave at least 20 percent to nonincumbents. Even the 96 who gave 10 to 20 percent of their money to nonincumbents made a substantial number of ideological donations. (See figure 1.1 in chapter 1.)

This chapter overviews the characteristics and philosophy of ideological PACs and then provides a history of corporate ideological behavior from the 1970s to the present, arguing that it is a key factor explaining both the conservative successes of 1980 and 1981 and the limits to further conservative advances. The chapter concludes with a brief evaluation of ideological PAC behavior: is it, as many corporations (both pragmatic and ideological) seem to believe, more honorable than a pragmatic orientation?

Characteristics of an Ideological Orientation

RELATION TO LOBBYING

In the pure case, ideological corporate political action committees separate the PAC from lobbying activity. Its basic orientation and mission is to contribute money in ways that will help to make Congress be as supportive as possible of business interests in general. This means that it gives donations only during election years to probusiness candidates who are in competitive races and face opponents less sympathetic to business. PACs that are primarily pragmatic also may follow this basic approach for two, five, or ten donations each year, applying an entirely different set of criteria for these decisions than they do for the bulk of their donations.

Our focus in this chapter is on ideological *corporate* PACs. Beside them are a set of independent, freestanding, conservative (and ultra-conservative) PACs not affiliated with any other organization. Groups like NCPAC (the National Conservative Political Action Committee) and the Committee for the Survival of a Free Congress raise their money primarily through direct-mail solicitations. Because these are expensive, the costs of fundraising absorb a substantial portion of the money they take in. Executives may contribute to these groups in addition to their corporation's PAC. These PACs were important in the 1980 election and continue to exist, although their importance has declined in recent years.

Officers of ideological corporate PACs generally began interviews with statements of their goals and philosophy:

> The goal of our PAC is simple and it sounds trite, and you've probably heard it 100 times over, but the goal of our PAC is to elect probusiness candidates to Congress and keep them there once they are elected. And that's simply it.

Or as another put it:

> We are a Midwest conservative company, and yet we believe in free trade, we believe in productivity, we believe in reasonable regulation, we believe that business is good for people, business helps people, and we want the people we elect to reflect that philosophy. We don't think that business is money-gouging monsters.

Some primarily ideological PACs also articulated company-specific goals similar to those of access PACs:

> The purpose of our PAC, of course, is to support specifically the company interest and the interest of our industry in general and beyond that what we consider to be the free enterprise system.

The basic goal of ideological PACs requires that they not be involved in promoting the company's lobbying. A very few corporations make it a policy not to have any lobbying operation:

> We don't have a Washington lobbyist staff, we don't have lobbyists in state capitals. All we have is myself. I run a governmental affairs program as well as our PAC. Our governmental affairs program is more of a grass roots network. We have over 100 plants across the country. We rely on those employee relations managers, personnel managers, and the plant

managers to be our contacts, to be our lobbyists. So the goal of our PAC
is not necessarily to aid our lobbyist and to make the job that much easier.
It is more of a philosophical role. It's a very ideological role to elect
probusiness candidates.

More commonly, the company hired lobbyists but kept them at
arm's length from the PAC. One chair of a PAC committee explained
that when he went to Washington for meetings of the National Association of Business Political Action Committees (NABPAC),

> some of the people that were in this meeting with me were going over to
> their lobbyists to have dinner and then to get a list of who they were
> supposed to give money to. And that just does not happen. We don't do
> this. That kind of session would never take place. I might go see Bill X,
> who is our lobbyist there who is a friend of mine. But it would not be on
> that subject. He would not broach the topic.

Another company reported that

> I do know of cases where a legislator has done a couple of things to help
> us, voted on a couple of issues in our favor. People have asked to give
> them money, and the committee has turned them down for the simple
> reason that overall they don't match what we are looking for.

However, not all ideological PACs were able to maintain this position. As noted in the last chapter, ideological PACs are sometimes
driven to access behavior, giving $250 to Representative Henry Wax-
man (D-Calif.) and others of his ilk even though it makes the PAC
officer "cringe" to do so, or supporting Democrats despite the owner's
commitment to Republicans. Another PAC officer who articulated the
PAC's goals in terms of support for the free enterprise system nonetheless acknowledged:

> I don't like to think of the PAC as being a slush fund for the Washington
> office, but by the same token, I recognize that we are sending these people
> in to discuss issues and our positions with members of the Congress.
> . . . We like to be independent here, and yet we recognize that a PAC
> should be somewhat supportive of the Washington office. I don't think it
> makes sense to have a PAC if you aren't somewhat supportive of your
> lobbying effort.

On the other hand, some ideological PACs argued they thought the separation from lobbying might actually make things easier for their lobbyist:

> It takes the pressure off of them in Washington. For example, our office there just sent me a stack of invitations to fundraisers that must have been two feet high. What the Washington office does is call the senator and say, "I'm sorry. This belongs to the PAC. We've sent it down to Texas, and what they do is their business. We have no control over it." Then they don't have to shell out $500 to everybody in the city. I think it is to their advantage not to be tied closely to us.

This argument was, of course, self-serving for the chair of the PAC committee. It absolved him of responsibility for thinking about these issues or considering what costs the company might be paying for its ideological purity.

CANDIDATES AND RACES

Since the PAC's aim is to affect the ideological character of the Congress, money needs to be targeted to races where it can make a difference. Most incumbents are reelected—91 percent of House incumbents over the course of the post–World War II period, and 98 percent in 1988.[5] Contributing to incumbents is therefore unlikely to influence the composition of Congress, except in rare (close) elections. Moreover, most incumbents have little difficulty raising plenty of money, so an additional contribution is unlikely to have a noticeable impact on their situation. Therefore a purely ideological PAC is reluctant to contribute even to a conservative probusiness incumbent. One official summarized this position:

> The guidelines are that you've got to have a competitive race for us to make a contribution to you. You've got to need the money in terms of the sources available to your opponent. In addition to that, you've got to be meritorious in terms of public policy values that are reflected by our PAC.

It's not enough that the candidate has probusiness views; there has to be a sense that the money makes a difference. If the opponent's views are equally probusiness, it doesn't matter who wins. If the candidate's views are different from the opponent, but one side or the other is sure to win, a contribution again makes little difference. This means that ideological PACs have to be reconciled to losing much of the time:

We like to win more than we lose, but we're not in it to pick all winners. That's a pretty easy thing to do. But to give where someone's going to win with 85 percent of the vote—that's not really what we're doing with the money from our managers. In fact, that's not what we do at all.

Sometimes an ideological PAC will give to a challenger even if they are virtually sure to lose, in hopes the candidate can be competitive in a future election:

You can say it's a mistake when one [of the candidates we supported] only comes in with 35 percent of the vote, but we just have to acknowledge that ahead of time—that we know that that guy is not going to do real well. And maybe not this time but maybe next year or two years or four years down the road. Somebody has to give him the support along the way. But how can you justify giving to a candidate who already has a fund of $400,000 or $1 million and they were elected before 1980 and they are going to take it all home with them?

Despite a willingness to support some candidates who are virtually sure to lose, most of the time the aim is to contribute to competitive races:

A guy who has no chance I usually won't support, although I have a friend running in California whose chances are minuscule and I would give him $500. Some of that money I call crap shoot money, but that's less than 5 percent of our total contributions.

This means that the PAC makes every effort to determine how viable the candidate is, which requires collecting information from all possible sources, trying to get polling data, but also finding out whether the candidate has been able to attract enough money: "I get the FEC [Federal Election Commission] reports as up to date as I can to see how much money they have. That will give me an idea if they really have a chance, whether they are mounting a credible challenge." Others agree:

The other aspect of this is we try to get as good a fix as we can on money, and that's always tough. Maybe it's not necessary that the candidate with the most money wins, but it's tough to throw dollars where you don't have a chance. Although we've done some venture capital, and we don't mind doing venture capital, we're not going to do that all the time. We try to get a fix on money. We try to get some polling data.

This also means that ideological PACs generally give most or all of their money during the election year. Access PACs give the money to gain access and establish relationships, which can be done at any time, so they don't need to concentrate on the period preceding an election. Ideological PACs, on the other hand, don't want to contribute unless there is a close contest between candidates with opposing views, and that usually can't be determined more than six or eight months ahead of time:

> We don't make contributions in nonelection years. We just don't. We have discretionary money that our members have given us for the purpose of attempting to influence an election. It's a good idea to have an election if you're trying to influence it. So this idea that has now become popular, beginning to raise money five years before your election, or the moment you're elected, if you're in the House, have a fundraiser to celebrate your victory, is fine; it's a great way to take care of your children's education if you're in public life, but we don't make any contributions except in election years.[6]

This also means that such PACs don't give money to help candidates retire their debts: "We don't make any contributions after the election is over; it's extraordinarily difficult to have an effect on the election by giving money after the election is over."

A FORMULA FOR SELF-DESTRUCTION

Ideological corporate PACs are likely to emphasize the need for business to support and contribute to the integrity of the political system:

> We've got a lot of respect for the American political system, and think that American business has a tremendous stake in the American political system, and think that American business ought to try very, very hard to contribute to its integrity.

According to this view businesses undermine the integrity of the system if they contribute to candidates "hostile" to business in hopes of gaining a narrow short-run advantage for themselves. William Simon argues that "if American business consciously wished to devise a formula for self-destruction, it could not do better than this."[7] Moreover, many executives of ideological PACs identify members of Congress as enemies even if they are prepared to do favors for business. In our interviews they not infrequently labeled such members "communistic," a term they use as description and not in jest. Their implicit reasoning seems to be similar to that of neoconservative Irving Kristol: "what rules the world is ideas, because ideas define the way reality is perceived."[8] Therefore it is not enough for members to be willing to craft dozens of loopholes such that business prevails in reality. Doing so cedes control over public discussion in order to win short-run advantages. Practical control through compromise and wording change is not enough: business must define the broad terms of public debate and insist on candidates who will speak up for business and the free enterprise system.[9]

Most of the time the people we interviewed avoided open criticism of other corporate PACs. One pragmatic PAC officer thought it "nonsense" to have an ideological PAC: "If you want to have an ideological PAC, then go join AMA or the National Rifle Association or whatever the hell their cause is." In his view, ideological PACs are "a manifestation of the leadership. In those situations the boss sets the tone." A few other pragmatic executives made similar comments. Ideological PAC officers generally noted the access approach and simply said, "That's their philosophy and which we've already said we don't agree with that. That's their business." Occasionally one would explain that at one meeting or another: "I felt very comfortable talking about the way we do it versus the way they do it. They looked at me like we were a little crazy, but we think they are strange too." Ideological PAC officials reported that occasionally the pragmatics' "response was antagonistic—'Oh, so you think you're so pure.'"

One of the most ideological executives we interviewed, a member of the board of directors of his corporation, openly expressed his anger at the behavior of most corporate PACs and his inability to understand why they acted as they did:

> I think valid candidates ought to be able to wage a decent political campaign in the U.S. I believe that to be true, and I don't like a system that works in such a way that they can't. I think it is a good, good intelligent thing for American business to try to make some contribution toward that kind of a political system; because if there's anybody that's a stakeholder in the system, it's American business.
>
> And if they keep fucking around with it long enough and trying to suborn it by throwing money at it, they're going to have hell to pay. Because there doesn't happen to be another political system on the face

of the earth that is so hospitable and so good to people who like to try to make money in business, industry, and commercial enterprises.

Now that's the basis of why we're not an access PAC, and that's the basis of why we're so Goddamned dumb. And we've got all these smart sons-of-bitches that know exactly what to do with their money: find out who wins by 75 percent plus, give them a lot of money, particularly if they're chairman of a committee of importance to you.

I can't figure out what their motive is. I just look at it and look at it, and I just can't figure it out. Neither can anybody else; it's just because they like chairmen better than they like everybody else. Chairmen who don't need the money and who couldn't lose if they were caught *in flagrante delicto* with the governor's wife in the public square of the capital. And they're shoving money in there. What is their motive?

The Rise and Fall of Ideological Behavior

The frustration of today's fully ideological PACs is probably increased by the way the tide has turned against them. The conventional wisdom is that corporations are pragmatic and access oriented. That was true prior to the formation of corporate PACs and during their earliest years. By 1978 that was beginning to change, and in 1980 a great many corporations were strongly ideological. We argue this is a key factor explaining conservative successes in the 1980 elections and 1981 policy struggles. Corporate ideological commitment was dramatically reduced by 1984, and in recent years ideological PACs have become increasingly scarce.

THE IDEOLOGICAL MOBILIZATION OF THE 1970s

To understand the changing corporate mood we need to go back at least to the early 1960s. During the 1960s a series of social movements challenged many aspects of the established order. The first major movement was by blacks in the South, and within a few years a black movement in the North focused on the practices of corporate employers and city police. Riots, Malcolm X, and the Black Panther Party demonstrated that this opposition could become militant and threatening. Strong student and antiwar movements put thousands of people in the streets and led them to take over buildings. Young men resisted the draft or deserted the military. In the late 1960s the women's and environmentalist movements grew rapidly. Although most of these challenges to authority did not focus primarily on corporations, corporations increasingly felt the impact of these movements, both in the behaviors of their workers and in demands for increased social responsibility. Ralph Nader and a host of Nader-influenced "public-interest" organizations offered what was in some ways the mildest and most mainstream social movement, but it was also the one that most specifically targeted corporate practices and argued for more regulation of business.

Richard Nixon, a conservative Republican, won a narrow victory in 1968 and a landslide in 1972. But his personal preferences mattered far less than the social movements and social structure of the period, so his administration involved a host of key liberal measures on the domestic front:

> From 1969 through 1972, virtually the entire American business community experienced a series of political setbacks without parallel in the postwar period. In the space of only four years, Congress enacted a significant tax-reform bill, four major environmental laws, an occupational safety and health act, and a series of additional consumer-protection statutes. The government also created a number of important new regulatory agencies, including the Environmental Protection Administration (EPA), the Occupational Safety and Health Administration (OSHA), and the Consumer Product Safety Commission (CPSC), investing them with broad powers over a wide range of business decisions. In contrast to the 1960s, many of the regulatory laws enacted during the early 1970s were broader in scope and more ambitious in their objectives.[10]

As a result, corporations felt vulnerable and under attack. It appeared that even a conservative Republican president such as Nixon would inevitably be pushed to support more and more regulation of business and interference with the market. At meetings of top business executives in 1973, executives articulated this vulnerability: "We are fighting for our lives," "We are fighting a delaying action." As one said, "If we don't take action now, we will see our own demise. We will evolve into another social democracy."[11]

These domestic setbacks were matched by problems in the international situation. The U.S. defeat in Vietnam, the rise of OPEC, and a few years later the overthrow of the Shah of Iran made U.S. multinational corporations worry about the security of their overseas investments. Declining U.S. economic competitiveness, the rise of Japanese and European competitors, and the burgeoning U.S. trade deficit made it impossible to solve domestic problems by offering costly concessions to U.S. workers and activist movements.

Watergate and its aftermath only increased this sense that the tide was running against them, that mobilization was needed to prevent the United States from becoming a social democracy. The Democrats made huge gains in the 1974 congressional elections, adding five seats in the Senate and forty-eight in the House to what had already been secure majorities.

It would be easy to argue that business concerns reflected more paranoia than reality. Most of the new regulatory agencies were weak, lacked money for enforcement, and were inclined to go along with business. For example, in 1971 there were 47,000 commercially available chemical compounds, and the Occupational Safety and Health Administration set legal limits on concentration levels for only about 500 of them, leaving the remaining 99 percent unregulated. Most workplaces were never inspected, and if violations were found, the average fine was only about $25. Things did not change much over the next fifteen years: a 1985 study by the Congressional Office of Technology Assessment reported that the average fine for a "serious violation" was only $172—despite the fact that such violations were defined as those that created a "substantial probability of death or serious physical harm."[12] But while these regulations were often weak and enforcement minimal, they established a precedent and let public-interest movements get a foot in the door. Business understandably felt threatened, and had it not responded, these initial regulatory steps might have become more challenging.

In the mid- to late 1970s, business began its own countermobilization, operating simultaneously on many fronts. Money was shifted out of liberal and moderate think tanks and policy organizations (the Brookings Institution, Council on Foreign Relations, and Committee for Economic Development) to newly founded or reinvigorated conservative equivalents (the American Enterprise Institute, Hoover Institution, and Heritage Foundation). In 1965 and 1970 these moderate organizations had more than three times as much funding as these conservative ones; by 1975 this advantage was much diminished; and by 1980 the conservative organizations spent substantially more than the moderate ones.[13]

Advocacy advertising expanded enormously. Traditional advertising tries to sell a product: Presta-Glop cleans teeth whiter than Ultra-Goo. Advocacy advertising has no explicit connection with a corporation's products but rather promotes a political message; in 1979 David Vogel estimated that corporations were spending one-third of their advertising budgets on such campaigns.[14] The business press began the admittedly difficult task of redefining reality: "It will be a hard pill for many Americans to swallow—the idea of doing with less so that big business can have more. . . . Nothing that this nation, or any other nation, has done in modern economic history compares in difficulty with the selling job that must now be done to make people accept the new reality."[15]

Business also began to exert its muscle in more straightforwardly political arenas. One crucial step was the founding and emergence to prominence of the Business Roundtable. The Roundtable was founded in the early 1970s and differed from earlier business policy organizations in two crucial ways. First, it was open only to chief executive officers of corporations. Most earlier organizations had allowed in a few handpicked academics not to mention corporate vice presidents. Second, previous organizations focused primarily on the process of developing "appropriate" policy, which generally involved long-range study commissions and a primary focus on the executive branch. The Roundtable, by contrast, devoted most of its energy to direct lobbying activities, often focusing on Congress, the site of many of business's political losses.

The Roundtable's influence and the increasing conservative aggressiveness of business were dramatically demonstrated in the Labor Law Reform battles of 1978. Labor was the key source of both money and organizational clout for many Democratic candidates and the northern Democratic party. The Democrats controlled the presidency and had near record majorities in both houses of Congress. The Labor Law Reform bill was labor's number-one priority and involved exceptionally mild measures. A few employers had been flouting the labor laws, appealing all adverse decisions by the National Labor Relations Board and winning years of delay. Then, if necessary, the corporation accepted the very mild penalties it received when convicted. The Labor Law Reform bill prohibited such delaying tactics by providing that the decision of the NLRB would apply during the appeals process until and unless a company won an appeal. It also stiffened the penalties for violations in order to reduce the economic incentives to break the law and accept the penalties. Unions saw the bill as an attempt to isolate a few companies that had been systematically violating the law. They therefore expected most major corporations to support the bill. Given the mild nature of the bill and Democratic dominance of government, it appeared the bill would pass relatively easily.

Instead business mounted a major campaign against the law, spending more than $5 million lobbying on this one bill. In essence business used all the normal tactics of pragmatic access-oriented campaigns, but this time for the ideological purpose of defeating, rather than simply modifying, an important bill. Corporations pulled out all the stops. They cashed in their access chips so government relations personnel could meet with members of Congress and explain their opposition. Managers from legislators' home districts were brought in to state the company's case. Small business owners were called on as foot soldiers:

> Those representatives of big business who were lobbying Senator Lawton Chiles, Democrat of Florida, heard him complain that most of the pressure he had received had come from large corporations. Almost immediately, the large corporations switched tactics, abandoning the attempt to directly lobby Chiles, and instead used their corporate jets to fly small-business owners from Florida to Washington to take over the job of convincing Chiles.[16]

The business campaign was coordinated by the Business Roundtable. Big business has enormous resources, not just in the money it can spend but in its ability to mobilize others. In 1979, when Chrysler was trying to win a federal loan guarantee, it produced a list of the employment it generated in each congressional district. The list for just one Indiana Republican's district included 436 companies with sales totaling over $29 million.[17] Since the Business Roundtable included a couple hundred such companies, it was able to put enormous pressure on members. Labor law reform may have been the most important issue, but in 1978 business launched similar campaigns around consumer protection and taxes, in each case winning significant victories.

THE PAC CONTRIBUTION TO THIS IDEOLOGICAL MOBILIZATION

In 1978 business also changed its campaign contribution behavior. The change resulted from a coordinated campaign, not simply a set of isolated decisions. During the 1978 election two key letters circulated within the corporate PAC community. The first was by Justin Dart, CEO of Dart Industries and a friend of Ronald Reagan. The second mailing was sent to all members of the Business Roundtable by Donald Kendall, CEO of Pepsico and chair of the Roundtable, with an accompanying analysis by Clark MacGregor of United Technologies. Dart's analysis was framed in more aggressively conservative tones, but both communications had the same basic message: corporations should reduce their contributions to liberal and moderate (mostly Democratic) incumbents and be more "attentive to candidates' records on the broader, free-enterprise issues."[18] Kendall also decried "the, in my opinion, inflated role Washington representatives of some companies play in picking recipients of PAC funds" and implicitly urged CEOs to do more to set the direction for their PACs.[19]

These letters were circulated during the course of the 1978 election cycle. Corporations had already given many donations, and it undoubtedly took time for CEOs and boards of directors to consider them, change company policy, and then communicate this new policy to the company's PAC director and PAC committee. An analysis by *National Journal* comparing 1978 corporate contributions before and after October 1 revealed dramatically different patterns in the two periods. Up through September 30 corporate PACs gave 72 percent of their money to incumbents; thereafter, only 49 percent.[20]

The attempts to mobilize and unify the corporate community in support of ideological conservatism and an aggressive political stance began late in the 1978 election but came to fruition in 1980. As one corporate PAC director said to us:

> There was a genuine movement, the closest thing I've ever seen on the part of business in this country, almost a phenomenon that occurred in that year and a half or two years of that particular election. It was a genuine virtual fervor. Let's go out there, and we can do it, we can change the system. The Chamber of Commerce and NAM [National Association of Manufacturers] and everybody beating the drum.

Or as another put it to us: "I think we just basically kind of got with the program and did what we thought a business PAC was supposed to do at that point in time." Around 1980 "was the big, really exciting time."

The change in behavior shows starkly in data on campaign contributions. As we noted earlier, ideological corporate PAC behavior is most evident in contributions to challengers. Donations to Democratic incumbents are evidence of an access strategy. Contributions to Republican incumbents are ambiguous because they could be motivated either by the candidate's incumbency and attendant power, an access-oriented consideration, or by the person's Republican values, an ideological consideration. Open-seat donations are also somewhat ambiguous.[21]

With few exceptions, corporate contributions to challengers are based on ideological commitments. More than 91 percent of the time the House incumbent wins; in 1984, 1986, and 1988 more than 95 percent of House incumbents won. While the incumbent victory percentages are significantly lower in the Senate, they still average more than 75 percent. Occasionally an incumbent is the underdog, but for this to happen it almost requires that the incumbent has been arrested for a sexual offense or caught bribing someone. Some challengers are much longer shots than others, but contributing to a challenger is almost never a way of playing the percentages. Moreover, even if two candidates are equally likely to win, the correct access strategy is almost always to contribute to the incumbent. For example, in 1980 Al Ullman (D-Ore.) was in a tight race with Denny Smith. Ullman, however, was chair of the House Ways and Means Committee, probably the most important committee in the House and the committee of greatest importance to business. Denny Smith, the Republican challenger, ultimately won but had little power to help his supporters. Had Ullman won he would have been able to reward corporations that supported him or even penalize those that had opposed him. Contributions to challengers are thus a fairly unequivocal indication of corporate ideological commitment, a commitment strong enough that the corporation is willing to run risks and face potential penalties.

Contributions to either Democratic or Republican challengers potentially indicate an ideological orientation. Some analysts on the left have developed a theory of corporate liberalism—an argument that "liberalism has been the political ideology of the rising, and then dominant, business groups."[22] Similar analyses are sometimes put forward by extreme conservatives.[23] If these views are correct, we would expect a substantial number of corporations to give significant amounts of money to Democratic challengers. Although this is a possible ideological stance, in practice no corporation has adopted such a strategy.

Corporations may be willing to ignore political party in contributing to established incumbents, but they are only rarely willing to give to a Democratic challenger, much less a liberal one. Corporate PACs gave less than 1.5 percent of their money to Democratic challengers in every year except 1986, when they gave them 3.5 percent. In five of the seven elections from 1976 to 1988, no more than one corporation gave as much as 10 percent of its money to Democratic challengers. The peak year was 1986, when twenty corporations gave 10 percent or more of their PAC money to Democratic challengers, and four of these gave 15 percent or more.[24] (See appendix Table A.1 for a list of these corporations.) These donations hardly indicate an emerging corporate liberalism. Sixty percent of the corporate money to Democratic challengers went to just three candidates—Bob Graham of Florida, Jim Jones of Oklahoma, and Richard Shelby of Alabama. Seventy-four percent went to these three plus Tom Daschle of South Dakota and Wyche Fowler of Georgia. All of these challengers were Senate candidates, and all were incumbents—Bob Graham as governor, the other four as members of the House. Even these donations to challengers may have reflected an access strategy. For example, Jim Jones was chair of the House Budget Committee and a member of the House Ways and Means (equals "tax writing") committee. A contribution to Jones counted as money to a Senate challenger, but the corporation might have given the money at any time in 1985 or 1986 in order to get access to a powerful House incumbent working on tax "reform."

These data indicate that in theory corporations could be ideologically liberal but in practice none are (at least in terms of PAC contributions). Many corporations have made a pragmatic decision that they are willing to support Democratic incumbents, but *no* corporation shows an ideological preference for liberals or Democratic challengers. If their choice is uncoerced by pragmatic access considerations, all corporate PACs apparently exclude the left three-quarters of the political spectrum. This is an unstated, but important, ideological stance by even the most pragmatic of corporations.

Corporate ideological choices, therefore, are best assessed by examining donations to Republican challengers. Corporations that want to influence the overall composition of Congress to a more probusiness stance must contribute to Republican challengers. How many corporations have been willing to do so, and how much variation has there been from election to election? Specifically, how many corporate PACs have been willing to give 30 percent or more of their money to Republican challengers?[25] Using this as a criterion of ideological orientation, six times as many corporations behaved ideologically in 1980 as in the next closest year, 1984. Figure 5.1 dramatically illustrates these differences. (Appendix Table A.2 lists the names of all corporations that met the 30 percent criterion for any election, together with the percentage of money given Republican challengers.)

Studies indicate that campaign money influences election outcomes primarily through its effect on challengers. In order to be viable candidates, challengers must raise substantial amounts of money, and they are often unable to do so. In 1980 the large group of ideologically conservative corporations vastly increased the flow of funds to Repub-

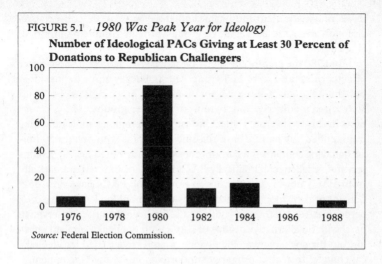

FIGURE 5.1   *1980 Was Peak Year for Ideology*

Number of Ideological PACs Giving at Least 30 Percent of Donations to Republican Challengers

Source: Federal Election Commission.

lican challengers, and many of these candidates won. The shift in business behavior was dramatic. In races pitting Democratic incumbents against Republican challengers, in 1972 the Democratic incumbents received four times as much as their challengers; in 1976, twice as much; and in 1980, the Democratic incumbents received less than their Republican challengers.[26]

The shifting character of corporate political activity can be shown in another way—through the use of a quantitative technique known as network analysis. Analysts generally agree that *if* business is able to achieve political unity, it can be enormously effective; arguments revolve around whether, when, and to what degree business is politically unified (see chapter 6). Network analysis seeks to determine whether groups of corporations display similar political behavior, and if so, the characteristics of these groups and corporations. We used one variant of this technique to analyze the overall pattern of corporate PAC donations for each election from 1976 through 1986.[27]

A significant shift takes place in the period between 1976 and 1980. In 1976 about one-quarter of all PACs were in some group with politically similar behavior. These PACs were spread among five different groups, the largest of which had only nine members.[28] Although the technique we used allows a corporation to be a member of many different groups, only one corporation was a member of more than one group.[29] Most of the groups were based on a specific industry (railroads, utilities) or geographic region (California). Two groups were more pragmatic than the norm, and three were more conservative, although even the conservative groups provided limited support to challengers.

By 1980 the picture changed dramatically. Once again one-quarter of all corporations were in a group with politically similar behavior—but this time all of these corporations were in a single group (with sixty-three members), and there were no other groups. The corporations in this bloc came from all industries and regions, indicating they transcended any narrow basis for unity. The bloc with politically similar behavior contains the corporations that contributed heavily to conservative challengers. Politically PACs in the bloc differed dramatically from PACs not in the bloc: for example, bloc PACs gave only 36.5 percent of their money to incumbents, while nonbloc PACs gave 68.7 percent. After 1980 there continued to be a single large conservative bloc, with no alternative groups of PACs with politically similar behavior, but the conservative bloc no longer aggressively tried for ideological change. Instead it primarily supported conservative incumbents.

DID THIS MOBILIZATION MAKE A DIFFERENCE?

This mobilization paid dramatic dividends. The only period when business unified around a strategy of aggressive ideological conservatism—around a willingness to challenge entrenched Democratic incumbents—is also the only period when conservatives made significant advances, including both the election of 1980 and the policy triumphs of 1981.

The dividends from the corporate conservative mobilization began in 1978, even before the 1978 election, with the defeat of labor law reform and consumer protection, combined with the passage of regressive taxes instead of the mildly progressive taxes President Carter had proposed. The election payoff was 1980—the first defeat of an incumbent elected president since Herbert Hoover in the Great Depression, Republican control of the Senate based on a twelve-seat shift, and a Republican gain of thirty-four House seats, enough to provide working control on key issues. These gains had not been anticipated by either political experts or corporate PAC directors. As one said to us: "I thought Reagan was going to win, and I thought he might carry some people with him, but sure as hell nobody thought that the Senate was going to change."

Electoral victory is one thing; the ability to turn this into meaningful policy outcomes quite another. In the period between the election and inauguration many observers were skeptical about Reagan's ability to carry through on his agenda. Reagan's campaign pledges were contradictory and unrealistic, projecting large tax cuts and increases in military spending but nonetheless promising to balance the budget by 1984. Reagan had won a landslide victory, but it was based in part on low voter participation levels: a smaller proportion of adults voted for him than voted for Wendell Willkie in 1940, though Willkie lost as decisively as Reagan won.[30] Above all, Democrats maintained control of the House, and the American system favors those trying to delay or obstruct change.

The basic contours of the drastic policy changes that were implemented have endured, structuring the political landscape for Democrats as well as Republicans. Walter Dean Burnham called it "one of the largest and most comprehensive policy changes in modern times."[31] Chubb and Peterson[32] argue that

> in 1981 the national government made decisions that sharply changed the direction of domestic and foreign policy. Major pieces of legislation reversed the course of domestic social spending, initiated the largest sustained peacetime increase in defense spending, and by creating an unprecedented budget deficit, constrained federal policymaking for years to come. These innovations are likely to be equal in their long-term significance to any associated with previous realignments.

What Chubb and Peterson gloss over is perhaps the most important of all the changes—the way the regressive tax cut, attacks on welfare, and deregulation led to the greatest increase in income inequality in the post–World War II period.[33] The increase in inequality was particularly steep at the top, where corporate executives and major shareholders are concentrated. From 1977 to 1988, real (inflation adjusted) income *decreased* for the bottom 40 percent of the population and increased slightly (from 0.2 percent to 3.0 percent) for the next 30 percent of the population.[34] For the top 1 percent, however, incomes increased by an average of 74.2 percent. The top 1 percent of families had minimum 1989 incomes of $310,000 a year and average incomes of $559,800, according to a study by the Congressional Budget Office.[35] Changes in tax policy were one key to this: "In the wake of the 1978 capital gains tax reductions and the sweeping 1981 rate cuts, the effective overall, combined federal tax rate paid by the top 1 percent of Americans dropped from 30.9 percent in 1977 to 23.1 percent in 1984. No other group gained nearly so much."[36] The number of millionaires (people with a million dollars or more in assets) increased from 574,000 in 1980 to 1.3 million in 1988. "Even adjusted for inflation, the number of millionaires had doubled between the late seventies and the late eighties."[37]

For the most part, the policy realignment of 1981 has been consolidated but has not further advanced. The failure to advance is evident in that the most notable features of Reagan's second term were an arms reduction treaty and a set of scandals concerning arms for the Ayatollah. The consolidation is evident in the Democratic acceptance of key elements of the new conservative policies. For example, the 1984 Democratic presidential nominee, Walter Mondale, did not contest the massive income redistribution introduced by Reagan but focused instead on a traditional Republican issue, the need to reduce the deficit and balance the budget. With the important but revealing exception of Jesse Jackson, no Democratic presidential candidate of 1984 or 1988 seriously challenged the basic elements of Reaganism. More than a decade after Reagan's initial triumph the policy shift of 1981 seems here to stay, but this makes it all the more puzzling that there was no second round of changes.[38]

This is not because the entire conservative agenda had been enacted by the end of 1981. Abortion remained legal and school prayer illegal. The traditional family was in trouble as huge numbers of people opted for other living arrangements. And even on narrowly economic issues, the federal government ran record-breaking deficits while U.S. international competitiveness declined.

What then can explain the lack of further policy changes? The most common explanation of why public policy changed is that the public wanted change. One might think that Reagan was more popular when first elected, and therefore more effective in carrying his message to the public. Although this is the pattern for most presidents, it was not true for Reagan: he was *less* popular than any other elected president[39] during his first year in office but was nonetheless able to win substantial policy changes. In 1985 and 1986 he was more popular than most presidents are during their second terms but was unable to win policy changes anywhere near as significant as those of 1981. This is demonstrated by Reagan's approval ratings:[40] in 1981 they were slightly lower than in 1985 (58.3 percent as compared to 60.7 percent), and 1982 was much lower (44.0 percent) than 1986 (67.4 percent). Detailed examination of voter attitudes indicates Reagan's 1981 policy initiatives for the most part lacked popular support.[41] Voters have gradually shifted to greater support of conservatism, but this *followed* the policy changes and appears to be their consequence not their cause.

THE DEMOCRATS: TAKING CARE OF BUSINESS

We believe that the shift in business behavior is a key factor that explains the different policy outcomes of 1981 and subsequent years. In 1980 and 1981 there was "a genuine virtual fervor." Far more corporate PACs gave substantial amounts to Republican challengers than in any other year. Thereafter business changed its behavior, in campaign finance and in political action more generally. Why did business change its approach after the 1980 election, becoming less aggressive, more willing to support moderate Democratic incumbents? Many factors undoubtedly contributed to this change—relaxation after enacting Reagan's first-round agenda, the 1982 recession and return of prosperity, reduced concern about government because of the implementation of deregulation, a fear of popular backlash, the difficulties of a declining world power in deciding on a coherent strategy, and undoubtedly crucial, the fact that business had succeeded in getting its most pressing needs addressed. Some of the corporations we interviewed stressed their economic difficulties in the early and mid-1980s as the reason their behavior changed: "I think we are a little bit more pragmatic now—because we have to be." As another said,

> We were making money in 1980. It wasn't until later that the companies [in our industry] started really having serious problems and we had to look for all the help we could get from anybody. I think if you look at all the [industry] companies, basically they became much less ideological and much more concerned about their own problems.

Another key factor was the Democratic countermobilization. On the left it is almost an article of faith that the Democrats can succeed only by mobilizing the unmobilized, increasing voter participation by nonvoters, and providing a program and a candidate able to mobilize and appeal to workers, people of color, women, and the poor. This may be one route to Democratic success, but it is not the only route. This is particularly the case if we realize that success for the Democratic party need not mean the capture of the presidency. From the point of view of entrenched congressional Democrats and their staffs and from the perspective of long-term state and local officials, "success" may simply mean stopping the hemorrhaging and holding on to the considerable power base they already have. This may not enact a progressive agenda, but that is hardly the aim of most Democrats, and they can and undoubtedly do remain convinced that their presence helps preserve valuable programs and prevent further cutbacks.

After the 1980 election, probusiness Democrats mobilized to persuade business that they deserved support. Tony Coelho, chair of the Democratic Congressional Campaign Committee and "perhaps the most successful Democratic fund-raiser since Lyndon B. Johnson,"[42] led this effort. Coelho went to corporate PACs and told them, "You people are determined to get rid of the Democratic Party. The records show it. I just want you to know we are going to be in the majority of the House for many, many years and I don't think it makes good business sense for you to try to destroy us."[43] Coelho is convinced that it was this kind of fundraising that helped revive the Democratic party and prevent a realignment: "What had happened, in 1980, we had our butts kicked. If the Republicans had been successful, they would have completed the job."[44]

Our data make Coelho's claim plausible: corporate PACs changed their behavior dramatically between 1980 and 1984, drastically reduced their efforts to defeat Democratic incumbents, and returned to a pattern of acceptance of the status quo. The corporate PAC director who described 1980 as "a genuine movement" also offered an explanation of why it did not persist:

PAC DIRECTOR: I think that certainly that experience has not been replicated since that point.

INTERVIEWER: Why not?

PAC DIRECTOR: For a variety of reasons, not the least of which is the impact which that election had on Democrats. [The Senator he used to work for] is a perfect example of that. Here's a guy who as a representative was conceived of as quite liberal and now is conceived of and is a genuine moderate.

INTERVIEWER: Do you think that Democrats are more moderate since the 1980 election?

PAC DIRECTOR: No question about that.

The increased conservatism by Democrats, and corporate willingness to coexist with probusiness Democrats, reduced the probability of a thorough-going partisan realignment.

For a brief period around 1980 a large proportion of corporate PACs embraced a risk-taking, ideologically conservative political strategy. Most of the corporations that did so in 1980, however, have since returned to a pragmatic strategy of supporting incumbents to gain access. Although a single case is never enough to establish a general law, the record of the last two decades indicates that the only time business mobilized and unified around an aggressive strategy of supporting conservatives, conservatives won a smashing and unexpected electoral victory. They then went on to unexpected policy triumphs that reshaped the political landscape at least for a generation. Increased government spending and regulation were once seen as the solutions to many problems; now the presumption is against them. Income has been decisively redistributed, taken from the poor and given to the rich, and no politically significant movement challenges this. The Reagan-era changes were most significant on exactly the issues of most concern to business; the pro-life, New Right, and conservative religious movements that receive a great deal of publicity did not get the same kind of policy victories.[45]

After 1980 and 1981 business and the Democratic party moved toward each other. The Democratic party changed to be more accommodating to business, and corporate PACs became more willing to give to moderate Democratic incumbents. Most Democratic members of Congress are now housebroken and do not challenge business. Corporate PACs, in their turn, are willing to make contributions to most of these members, providing they will grant access and do "minor" favors for the corporation. Today, corporations only rarely oppose moderate incumbents. As a consequence conservative Republican challengers have trouble raising enough money to be viable candidates. A few executives consider such behavior disgraceful, stupid, and shortsighted, but most prefer to live and let live. They are content with what they have won—pleased to have a system where *neither* major party challenges business and both depend on it for funding. Corporations remain mobilized, with a pragmatic conservative bloc the most unified, and the potential for strong action should they collectively feel it to be necessary.

The extent of the change is evident even in the behavior of those corporate executives who seem to have changed the least, those who remain strongly conservative in both their beliefs and behavior. Only a handful of true believers remain, and even some of these are discouraged and weakening. As one said,

> Part of it is disillusionment. We have given close to a million dollars and what good is it doing? We are losing all the time—even though I know that

we are going to keep plugging away at it because we have just got this philosophical bent and it's for the good of the country, and we are altruistic and everything else. It's not a change in direction. Not so strong as that. It's more of a tip-toeing into the realism that maybe we should support some of these people more.

Others were shifting faster. The PAC director at a major oil company reported, "We start to say 'What difference does it make to us if somebody is 100 percent labor rated when we are not a labor-intensive company?'" One of the most ideologically committed executives we talked with remains firm in his convictions, but even he has changed. He used to proselytize among other corporations, but is no longer willing to do so. In the late 1970s, he explained, "We were very, very active. We were assiduous in trying to sell our approach to the running of business PACs." However, by 1988 he had changed: "Back when PACs were first being created, I had a hell of a lot to say about it. I don't choose to do that anymore":

> I consider my convictions to be important things, and I don't wish to discuss political convictions with the people who run those corporate PACs. I think the behavior of corporate PACs is absolutely fucking disgraceful, if that's not clear. And stupid and shortsighted beyond measure.

Only one executive remained confident: "Despite the fact that we're alone and in the dark at this point in time, I'm not despondent that that's not ultimately going to pay off."

Assessing Corporate Ideological Donations

It is easy to be outraged by some of the behavior of pragmatic access-oriented PACs. Many contributions approximate bribes; while both the PAC and the member of Congress would insist that there is no quid pro quo involved, the gift creates a sense of indebtedness and obligation. Many of the changes the corporations seek, and the members enact, are special-interest favors designed to benefit a very limited group, perhaps a single corporation.

The ideological PACs that reject this approach take a stand on principle. They refuse to give money to candidates whose philosophical views they oppose, and they refuse to make contributions to gain access. The primary purpose of their donations is to influence election results, not to influence a member who has already been elected. This handicaps any lobbying effort they might make and costs their company money, but the corporation has made a decision to maintain this approach on principle. One of our companies' PAC directors felt confident she could have won the company several millions of dollars in tax breaks, but the company refused to engage in the process, feeling this to be an abuse of government.

The distinction between pragmatic and ideological PAC donations is similar to what Michael Useem[46] calls "company" and "classwide" rationality. Useem argues that some executives, and by extension some corporations, think primarily or exclusively in terms of what is good for their own company. Lower-level executives, he feels, are especially likely to see the issues in these terms. Other executives and corporations take a broader view, analyzing problems in terms of what is good for business as a whole. Useem argues that the highest-level executives, especially those who serve on the board of directors of more than one company, are an "inner circle" more likely to view issues in terms of classwide rationality.

These are not hard and fast distinctions. Most PACs follow a combination of strategies. In 1988, only eight corporate PACs gave a majority of their money to challengers and open-seat candidates, but two-thirds gave such candidates more than 10 percent of the PAC's money. The "average" corporate PAC in our sample gave five donations to challengers and eight to open-seat candidates. Only a quarter (24 percent) of the corporate PACs in our sample (with $25,000 or more in donations) gave less than five donations to nonincumbents, and a majority (52 percent) gave at least ten.[47] Most corporations thus made some donations to nonincumbents. For primarily pragmatic PACs the decision is often based primarily on opposition to the incumbent:

> I think if you have a very bad incumbent, it gets to the point where you've tried and tried and tried and he doesn't talk to you and is always going against you, undertaking causes that are clearly against you. And you realize it doesn't make any difference whether you help him or don't help him, he is not going to do anything for you anyway. So if you have the money, you try to beat him.

Another PAC officer felt that "if the incumbent is already against you, by supporting the challenger, he isn't going to be any more against you." In other respects, however, ideological donations by pragmatic

PACs were usually given on the basis of criteria similar to those employed by ideological PACs: how much difference is there in the political views of the opposing candidates, and does the candidate have a reasonable chance of winning?

Should we admire ideological donations and take them as models of the kind of corporate political behavior we would like to see? Ideological PACs clearly felt so. As one said, "It's kind of nice to feel clean about this process!" Another used the authority of BIPAC, the Business Industry Political Action Committee, to buttress its claims:

> BIPAC thinks we do an outstanding job of overcoming some of the criticisms we have heard in Washington. They think that if some of the other PACs did it the way we do it there would be less criticism.

Many access-oriented PACs seemed to agree; they felt their behavior was necessary but regrettable. One reported that "I find in most companies an annual, or even a quarterly, examination of conscience about this whole issue" of pragmatic PAC donations.

In effect, these corporate PACs are arguing that loyalty to business as a whole is more admirable than the narrow company orientation of pragmatic PACs.[48] Rather than simply advancing the interest of their own company, they aim to promote the interests of all corporations. This is a broader goal than that motivating narrowly pragmatic donations. We would also stress, however, that concern for your own class is not a particularly admirable stance if your class is already the most privileged. Business executives and owners may sincerely feel that "what is good for General Motors is good for America." In our view this is an extremely dubious proposition. Rather than supporting a reduction in taxes for one specific corporation, ideological corporations argue that all corporations should pay lower taxes. Rather than arguing that one industry or company should be able to pollute, they argue that all companies should be allowed to pollute. This politics may be broader than a narrow pragmatic orientation, but is it something to admire? Is it noble to take from the poor and weak in order to increase the wealth and power of the few?[49]

A second, closely related argument is sometimes made in support of an ideological orientation for corporate PACs. Ronald Reagan, William Simon, and Irving Kristol each in effect argued that business needed to control the terms of public debate. Simon and Kristol put their primary effort into channeling funding to conservative probusiness thinkers and writers. For example, they helped secure funding for conservative student newspapers, whose most well-known exemplar is the *Dartmouth Review*. In the 1970s it became almost the conventional wisdom that business was the source of problems and government the hope for solutions. Ronald Reagan forthrightly and articulately argued the reverse. Significantly, however, Reagan, Kristol, and Simon all made their case in the late 1970s and early 1980s. Even among corporate PAC officers, few still feel they have lost control of the terms of public debate. The executive who most forcefully argued the need to regain control of the terms of public debate feels abandoned by other corporate PACs and is embittered about it.

In the current political climate there is a tendency to think that the manager or PAC with the most conservative views is necessarily the most class conscious and far-sighted. Twenty years ago academics (at least) would probably have made the reverse assumption, that the most class-conscious and far-sighted corporations were those willing to support moderate reforms.[50] At one corporation we interviewed, members of the PAC committee regularly refer to moderate Democrats as "Communists." This is evidence of a strong ideological commitment but hardly of political sophistication. It's not clear that much political learning or thinking or self-examination takes place inside such a committee, or that these views provide the best guide to class-conscious corporate action. It is unclear what political orientation the contributors themselves prefer, but the corporation's preferences, not their own, determine the choice of corporate strategy.

Pragmatic PAC directors encounter resistance from managers who oppose contributions to liberals. One PAC director explained that he regularly contributes to a certain liberal Democrat: "The people at the refinery cannot for their lives understand why in the world we would support [this liberal Democrat]. And I will promise you, every time I do it, they raise hell." Nonetheless, he felt it important to contribute to this candidate "because he helps us on all sorts of stuff." Pragmatic PACs tend to defend their donations in the narrowest possible terms:

One reason we've been able to do it is because we are very blunt about it [to company employees]. "You do what you want to with your own money, and your own contributions and your own time. You ought to do it, and we encourage you to do it, and we want you to. When we are talking to you about the PAC, it's the well being of the corporation. And we will do things that you don't like. We are asking you to trust us to make decisions that are in the interest of this company. Because if we make those decisions, well, then we keep going and there will continue to be a company and you will continue to have jobs. What you do personally, fine." Hell, I don't like some of the people we give money to. I would never give these guys any. But that's the way it goes.

The pragmatic approach can be viewed as a narrow and short-sighted perspective. But it could also be argued that it is a sophisticated attempt to be sure that both parties and all candidates are pressured to be "probusiness":

> I don't do this for myself, I do it for the company. I don't really feel I have a party now. I think it is foolish for anybody in this business to profess an affiliation with a party. I don't think that is very healthy.

If both parties are in bed with, and in debt to, business, then corporations face a "heads I win, tails you lose" situation. When even the candidates who lead public demonstrations against a company are willing to do it favors, corporations have little to fear. If politics involved a set of clear choices between pro- and antibusiness candidates, corporations would need to worry about every election. Business is much happier creating a situation where its money, power, and influence restrict voters to choosing between two candidates—one of whom is generally and the other of whom is totally probusiness.

Why did most corporate PACs change their orientation between 1980 and 1988? One response to this question, the one given by the embittered ideological official, is that the behavior of today's pragmatic PACs is as inexplicable as it is inexcusable, that they lack both morality and the long-range vision to see the consequences of their own actions. This approach assumes that the political situation is roughly the same today as it was in the late 1970s and that in both periods the correct corporate stance is an aggressive and ideological strategy of favoring conservative challengers.

The alternative response, implicitly given by many pragmatic PACs, is that what has really changed is the character of policy debates, the way issues are framed, and the nature of political discourse. In effect they hold that because of the policy realignment of the early 1980s business is in reasonably good shape. It might be nice to win all of the time rather than simply most of the time, but the current balance of forces is acceptable—because most public debates about the issues are framed in probusiness terms, because most *Democrats* are eager to reach an accommodation with and do favors for business, because political figures who are openly hostile to business have been defeated or marginalized, with only a handful of exceptions.

Therefore pragmatic PACs have concluded that it no longer makes sense to aggressively seek a political realignment. There is comparatively little to gain, given the current level of business political dominance, but a great deal to lose. An aggressive attack by business would invite a countermobilization and the emergence of a populist response. In many ways business is better off if *both* parties and virtually all "respectable" politicians present generally probusiness positions. Better to maintain such a situation, to work with those members whose support is most problematic, and to make them dependent on business, rather than to attack them and drive them into open opposition.

Chapter 6

■ ■ ■

BUSINESS UNITY,
BUSINESS POWER

■ ■ ■

Many business apologists try to have their cake and eat it too. They admit much of what this book has argued—that businesses are enormously powerful, are not democratically run, give huge amounts of PAC money, use that money to gain access not available to other groups and advance interests different from those of the general population. Nonetheless, these business apologists deny that business has much overall impact on the political system. Rather a neat trick. How can they do it?

Their approach is to admit what they can't deny but insist that none of this matters. Pluralism is a theory that argues that a wide range of interest groups each has some political influence, with no one group dominant. While the theory has many variants, advocates of the most common form admit business has far more *potential* power than any other group. However, they argue that businesses are politically divided, so that the actions of one cancel out those of another and the *net* impact of business is minimal, perhaps nil. Chrysler might favor air bags, but General Motors might strongly oppose them. The auto companies might want steel imports to lower prices, but the steel companies would want protectionism.

For at least the last thirty years the central issue in academic debates about business political power has been whether business unifies to promote a common agenda. Many pluralist contentions have been decisively refuted, so their case now rests primarily on the claim that business has no clear and uniform political interest—that various parts of business pursue differing political agendas, one part of business counterbalances another, and business's total political impact is much less than it might be. Robert Dahl has argued that a group's power depends on *both* its potential for control (where business is very high) and its potential for unity (where business is said to be low). "Thus a group with relatively low potential for control but a high potential for unity may be more politically effective than a group with a high potential for control but a low potential for unity."[1] For pluralists, business is the quintessential example of this: "Business groups often conflict with each other as much as they do with their rivals in the labor, consumer, and environmentalist movements."[2] Eismeier and Pollock have made this point specifically for corporate PACs:

> The diverse reactions of business to the rise of the positive state have in part been the product of cleavages within the business community. Regulated versus unregulated, region versus region, small versus large, exporters versus nonexporters—these and other divisions have created a lively pluralism in business politics, often pitting corporate interests against each other as much as other groups.[3]

If the pluralist argument is correct, then business has little cumulative power. The point is vital to any claims about corporate PAC power. Since the maximum amount a PAC can contribute to a candidate is $5,000 per election (thus $10,000 if the candidate faces both a primary and the general election), and since on average winning House candidates spent $388,000 in the 1988 elections, a single PAC can supply at most 3 percent of the money needed for a congressional campaign. Since a corporation can cover only a small fraction of the cost of a candidate's campaign, a candidate can't afford to please one corporation if this reduces the chances of getting a contribution from others. If corporate PACs are pitted "against each other as much as other groups," then one cancels out the other, and no corporation can have much effect.

Unfortunately for pluralism this is another case of a beautiful theory confronting an ugly fact. Elegant as the theory may be, its factual premises just can't be supported. Congress is generally considered the area where pluralists make their best case. Here, if anywhere, each company promotes its own interests in opposition to those of other businesses. In this chapter we contribute to a long-running political and academic debate by providing additional evidence that business is usually politically unified, even in congressional activities.

Our earlier quantitative analyses of computerized records of all corporate donations indicated this was the case, but the interviews helped us understand how this unity is achieved. One of our quantitative articles analyzed donations by *all* large PACs (those that gave over $100,000 in 1984)—labor, environmental, nonconnected ideological, and trade association as well as corporate.[4] It revealed an exceptionally sharp split—a unified business-Republican group on one side and a labor-women-environmentalist-Democratic group on the other. In one sense this only confirms common sense—but it strongly refutes those pluralists who argue business is divided against itself as much as it is against labor and environmentalists. Another article examined donations by only the largest corporate PACs and showed that corporations almost always unify to support one of the two candidates in a race. In about three out of four races business can be classified as unified, giving at least nine times as much to one candidate as to the other; in one out of five races it gives predominant support to one candidate, giving him or her from two to nine times as much as the opponent; and in only one race out of fifteen is business divided (accepting a split of two to one or closer as evidence of division).[5] (See figure 6.1.) A complicated computer simulation led us to argue that PAC officers may disagree with their counterparts at other corporations, but the unstated rules forbid public disputes, and only reluctantly will one business directly oppose another.

The fundamental basis of business political unity is a set of under-

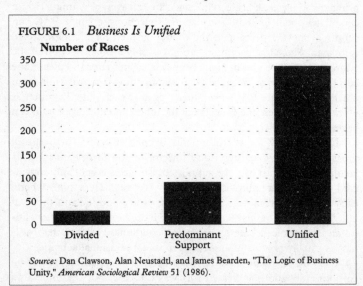

FIGURE 6.1   *Business Is Unified*

Number of Races

Source: Dan Clawson, Alan Neustadtl, and James Bearden, "The Logic of Business Unity," *American Sociological Review* 51 (1986).

lying material relations—loans from the same banks, sales and pur-
chases from each other, interlocking boards of directors, common
interests in accumulating capital and avoiding government initiatives
that might restrict their power.[6] These underlying material relations,
which are simultaneously social relations, make it possible for corporate officials to create a common culture that structures their understandings, interpretations, decisions, and actions. Corporate PACs
share information, ask each other for money, do each other favors,
work together on campaigns around specific issues, and use humor
and ribbing to coerce other corporations to maintain unity. We agree
that candidates do not need to worry about an isolated donor, even if
the company is enormous and the potential donation the maximum
legally allowed. They *do*, however, need to be concerned about "PACs
running in packs."

Business power derives in part from this ability to achieve political
unity on most issues. Even more important, however, is business's
control of the economy. We examine this often neglected source of
power and its implications in the last part of this chapter. Corporations
control a host of decisions *unless* and *until* the government specifically
intervenes. Control of the economy also gives business vast resources
to influence society in a host of "nonpolitical" ways. No campaign
finance reform proposal can realistically hope to fix the problems with
our current system unless it takes into account the vast power business
exercises in other realms.

Building Business Unity

LEARNING ABOUT ISSUES

If each company learned about congressional races and proposed
legislation separately, pluralism would be on strong ground. A few
sources of information *are* company specific. For example, sometimes
a company individually researches candidate positions on the legislation of most importance to that company. But most information comes
from a generalized "business community"—a shared network of contacts and information sources.

One basic source of information is simply that "we read constantly, till our eyes come out of our heads. We read all the dailies, and
industry publications, and news journals, and special publications, and
we are constantly looking for things." Another PAC officer emphasized newspaper reading:

> I read nine newspapers a day. I read two or three extra papers on Sunday.
> I subscribe to things like the *Political Report* put out by Stuart Rothenberg,
> which is an excellent report. I read *Congressional Insight.* I read *National
> Journal* and *CQ.* I read [several industry-specific journals].

Many of these publications are intended for a large audience, but
others are industry-specific publications or intended only for government relations specialists. Shared reading of these publications helps
create a common basis of knowledge and similar orientations.

A second source of information is the lawyers, lobbyists, and consultants whose business is to provide information, ideas, and influence
to corporations.

> Our principal outside counsel is Willkie, Farr and Gallagher, and they
> often call us up and talk about an issue and bring it to our attention. Plus
> half the law firms in Washington call us up to tell us about things because
> they want our business. We have a huge constituency of law firms and the
> like that we have worked with in the past, or that do little bits and pieces
> for us, or that hope to do so, and they tell us about things because they
> hope there will be business in it for them.

A telephone industry PAC official echoed that point:

> We have an extensive, extensive list of consultants and publishers who
> make money off the phone company. On my desk there are *Communica-
> tions Week, Communications Daily, Telephone Magazine,* and God knows
> how many others. Who are out every day with what is going on. Full-time
> reports, daily to weekly to monthly just on our industry.

Consultants and industry publications can't make money by servicing
a single company; they need to sell the same information and provide
the appropriate services to as many different companies as possible.

A paid consultant or lobbyist can greatly reduce the task facing a
corporation's government relations unit and increase its chances to be
heard:

> It's important to us to know what's happening. It's a significant part of
> any major entity's business. What happens to small businesses that don't
> get involved is they get told what legislation is and have to respond to it,
> and don't get enough time to get their input into the legislation ahead of
> time. We're trying to save ourselves the trouble of changing the system
> and rechanging it, by being involved from the beginning.

Unless you read every piece of legislation and every amendment that comes to it, you could miss something important. We could assign someone to that task full time, but it's much easier for us to contract that out to someone else. So out of 3,000 House bills I only had to read 200 and track 110.

A third source of information is communication from members of Congress and their staffs:

Members and their staffs call us up. Even if they are part of the problem, they call us to warn us, "We're planning to do this or thinking about doing that, and it might have an impact on you." We've worked with lots of these people before—we've done them favors, and we will again in the future—and they do us favors by keeping us informed. Plus many of them are friends one way or another.

This is one of the few major sources of information that is not necessarily shared. A member may have a special relationship with a particular company and call only them. Of course, members as well as consultants may want to make money out of as many companies as possible, and a sympathetic phone call to fifteen different companies in the same industry could produce a bonanza of donations from grateful PAC officers.

A fourth source of information is fundraisers. As discussed in chapter 3, fundraisers are first of all an occasion to deliver some money and get noticed by a candidate, but they are also an opportunity to meet the PAC officers of other corporations, the lawyers, consultants, and lobbyists that corporations hire, as well as other members of Congress and their staffs:

You see a staffer who you haven't seen. You run into somebody. You want him to know you have been there because you are going to try to see him. You run into one of your counterparts in another company who you haven't seen in two months, and you want to talk to him about issues. You run into people from out of town who you don't see a lot. It's a whole composite.

Most fundraisers are held in Washington, but the same principle applies to those given in other cities. We asked a PAC director based in Texas who rarely goes to Washington whether Texas fundraisers were similar to those in Washington:

Sure. You see the same kinds of people. It's a chance to not only see the candidate, whoever he is, but see your friends from other company PACs or trade associations or whatever. Every once in a while you run into one that's a little different. Sometimes it might be some businessperson has the reception in their home. It's a smaller group of people and probably a higher level of people in the business, so you get more CEOs than PAC operative-type people.

Ideological PACs, which are less tied in to the Washington fundraiser circuit, have other ways of meeting. Most frequently mentioned by our interviewees were the Chamber of Commerce and especially BIPAC (the Business Industry Political Action Committee). In our mail survey of corporate PACs about 40 percent indicated that they consult with BIPAC. BIPAC holds forums that introduce promising conservative candidates to business PAC directors and that are attended even by many unequivocally pragmatic corporations. For example, the PAC director for a highly regulated industry told us that "Bernadette Budde [head of BIPAC] does a heck of a job. I have gone in the past to her meetings, simply to know who's got a chance or what the score is." Ideological PACs were even more enthusiastic: "We support BIPAC, their educational arm. I think that's the greatest source of information that we have."

Some other groups serve many of the same purposes. A few PAC directors

rely heavily on the Republican senatorial committee and the congressional committee for their input, although that's not necessarily so helpful because, of course, they are slanted and, of course, they are biased. They have their job to do. But they would help us out a lot more if they'd be a little more objective and tell us more of a straight story.

One PAC officer, while reporting that "compared to what I am used to or compared to what I know should be, I would say we are relatively isolated," nonetheless noted that "I know all the staff members at NAM [National Association of Manufacturers]. I know quite a few staff members at the Chamber [of Commerce]." One company contributes "1, 2, 5, 20 thousand a shot" to various single-interest organizations such as the Coalition to Stop the Raid on Corporate America. For ideological PAC officers who attend few Washington fundraisers where they rub elbows with all the other PAC directors, events like the BIPAC forums provide a chance to meet with like-minded corporate PAC officials from a range of different businesses.

Fifth, finally, and above all, corporate government relations officials learn what is happening by socializing with each other and with other key players in any and every way they can. Fundraisers are one important institutional mechanism, but there are many informal ways—golf games, lunches, dinners, parties, phone calls, chance meetings in the halls of Congress, at the theater, or at a charity event. One vice president who is not based in Washington but who spends a great deal of time visiting there explained to us, "Washington is a constant networking of various levels, various circles that come together in different degrees." As another said,

Talk's cheap and worthless, and everybody's got an opinion; politics is all this town thinks about. We talk to each other all the time: "Are you giving to Henry or to Steve?" or "You ought to be giving to Henry or Steve." Obviously I call up my friends in the industry and say, "Look, if you have to give to a Democrat you ought to be supporting Dukakis instead of Lautenberg," or I'll get a call, "Will you please sign your name to a letter for Steve Symms because he was so good on the catastrophic bill. He really needs some support." So sure, I'll do that. We have meetings. I have meetings coming out my ears.

PAC officers even have an association specifically to discuss how to operate a PAC, the National Association of Business Political Action Committees (NABPAC). It seemed that practically every person we interviewed had at one time or another been on the board of directors of NABPAC:

I am on the board of directors of the National Association of Business PACs. Now nobody invents the wheel, but in this group there can be sharing of information—in terms of how to best solicit employees, brochures, things like that. What you should ask an employee—for $5 a pay period or $10 a month? What is a good number? What do top executives give? . . . So these types of things you discuss.

At some relatively early point in their careers most had evidently found NABPAC to be very helpful and continued to think fondly of it, although senior people tended not to stay actively involved.

Networking is more than simply talking to each other at events and through formal organizations. It includes lunches, golf, and phone calls to friends:

I've been in this town since 1963, and I started off working for a senator. I worked in the government doing congressional liaison—made a lot of friends, a lot of guys, and I have a lot of respect for them. There's guys I talk to, not on a daily basis but on a weekly basis, whose opinions I don't take because they are goofy, but I enjoy talking to them.

It also includes helping each other out by sharing news articles, documents, copies of bills, and the like:

People are constantly sending me articles. I try to keep up within my own purview of friends by finding as many interesting articles as I can and passing them around when I have a chance to.

PAC directors out in the hinterlands (that is, anywhere outside Washington) are expected to be experts on their region:

I have to be the source of intelligence on these races. If I know you as a PAC director in a particular state, and if I want to know the situation in that state, I would like to be able to call you and ask your opinion.

Only government relations and PAC personnel are likely to network about candidates, but people in other areas of the corporation are talking to their counterparts about actual or proposed policies. The consciousness and involvement of operating unit employees can be an important source of information:

INTERVIEWER: And how would you learn about something that specifically was going to clip your company but not, for example, Shell?

PAC DIRECTOR: Because we have an environmental department and a tax department, and it is highly likely that those kinds of things would crop up in those kinds of areas. They have networks of people that do the same things in other companies. They participate in the trade associations. They receive publications on a daily basis. I get some of this, but mine is more generic. Theirs is real specific. And so they find out about the stuff.

ASKING EACH OTHER FOR MONEY

PAC officers don't just share information and learn about the candidates and policies. They actively solicit donations from each other to help their friends in Congress. Giving a candidate money is the basic token of entry, the means of establishing a relationship. But if a member of Congress has helped you out, or if you'd like to do more than just make a contribution, the next step is to serve on the member's steering committee, which is both an honor and an obligation. Usually the steering committee's only function is to sell a certain number of tickets to the member's fundraiser. Some steering committees are much larger than others. Once asked to serve, it is important that steering committee members sell the requisite number of tickets:

> It's going back to what I didn't like to do in the beginning—that's begging guys for a lot of money. Only this time I can call the guy: "Joe can you give me $250 for Congressman X? Come on, please, he's a good guy." "Well what's good about him?" Well, you know, you spend a half hour schmoozing. Two weeks later he says: "Remember I helped you with this guy. Well, I want you to help me with this guy." "He's a terrible jerk." "That doesn't make any difference. You've gotta help me: I helped you." Then you go back to your PAC committee and say: "I need $250 for Joe Jones" and they say, "What? Why?"

Here the donation is a gift not so much to the candidate as to the other PAC. A corporation is helping another corporation to build a relationship with a member of Congress. One business can ask another for favors in ways not open to candidates themselves:

> I get calls: "Jack, we want you to give some money to Gephardt." Had this call two days ago. "Marty, I don't want to give any money to Gephardt. His failed presidential campaign—I don't want to give any money to that." "No, it's for his congressional campaign." "Marty, you've done some things for me, I'll do one for you. If it's really necessary, if you need another body there, I might." In other words, we'll do favors for one another. We're always calling each other to ask them to give.

These two comments illustrate that when one corporation's PAC officer calls another to ask for a contribution, the discussion is likely to be honest, with PAC officers raising problems that could never be discussed with the candidate. In these discussions PAC officers learn a lot about each other as individuals; about other corporations' wants, needs, problems, successes, failures; and of course about what candidates have (or have not) done for other corporations. The word quickly spreads whether a member of Congress can be trusted to deliver. In order to operate successfully, PAC officers must be willing and able to do favors for one another; any corporation that did not participate in these networks would be cut off from valuable information and would find it difficult to build a special relationship with a member. The networks of deals and obligations are such that at any given time, any major player is likely to owe and be owed favors by dozens of other corporations.

Although some people and some corporations actively seek opportunities to serve on steering committees, most consider it a necessary chore to be avoided if possible. We asked one PAC officer if he served on steering committees:

> We would like not to, and I try to avoid it as much as I can and so does everybody else in our government operation. I'd avoid it if I could get away with it, but you can't always do that. Sometimes you have to serve because the member—he's a friend of yours. He's known you for ten years, and he says he wants you to be on his steering committee. You try to say, "Well, it's a company policy not to." But there are guys who are friends of yours who won't understand your saying, "I would rather not." They'll say, "I've helped you and you've helped me, so you go out and help raise some more money."

A PAC officer could tell a member, "I'd rather not; it's inconvenient for me," but that dramatically increases the possibility that the next time the corporation wants a favor, the member will reply, "I'd rather not; it's inconvenient for me." To maintain the gift exchange network, participants have to be willing *and able* to participate and reciprocate.

A corporation can help a member even more by organizing a fundraiser for him or her:

> Senator X is a fraternity brother. Well, he's on the Y committee. He's somewhat important to our industry but not critical. He's right on the edge, so I gave a fundraiser for him. Well, I had to get on the phone and call some people.

These fundraisers are typically for an industry or other specialty group. This means that one company in the industry is getting extra credit with the member for having taken the lead and that other companies are thus helping to strengthen their competitor's position. This might not be a company's first choice, but nonetheless it is likely to participate:

> I think everybody obviously is trying to promote themselves and their companies. But most of it is cooperative things. . . . I don't say just because they are doing the fundraiser, I am not going to go. I will say this: if we belong to an association that's sponsoring a fundraiser and at the

same time one of our competitors is having one, I would say we go to the
one at the association and not to the competitor's.

This is a very moderate statement; the remarkable fact, especially from
the perspective of pluralist theory on business political competition
and opposition, is that a company is *ever* willing to attend a fundraiser
sponsored by their competitor.

Corporations support each other for many reasons. Support need
not be based on a shared commonality, such as industry, region, capital
intensity, or multinational orientation. Statistical analyses examining
these factors find they have a modest impact.[7] Corporations give in
common not only because of specific interests but because of a generalized sense of being part of the same social world, which can be
activated by any of a variety of connections. The ties between PACs
thus create a loose overlapping network, much like the interlocking
networks between boards of directors.[8] These reciprocal networks obscure any industry-based relationship that might exist. Perhaps paper
companies are particularly concerned about the Agriculture, Nutri-
tion, and Forestry Committee, while savings and loans care primarily
about the Banking, Housing, and Urban Affairs Committee. The statistical record of donations may show that both paper companies and
savings and loans gave to members of both committees, but it will not
indicate which donations were initiated by direct interest and which
were given as reciprocal favors to the other corporation.

A corporation's ability to have political influence and leverage
often *depends on other corporations as much as it does on politicians.* A
corporation that is a major participant in the traffic in donations[9] is in
a position to exercise a great deal of leverage. Such a corporation can
offer a member of Congress much more than just $5,000: it can raise
many times this much from its friends in the corporate PAC community. Equally important, it can vouch for the member and provide
introductions to other PAC officers. Obviously the member then has
to make the right moves to build a positive relationship, but the introduction is invaluable. In effect, the corporation uses its network to
evade the limits on the maximum legal donation.

Corporations don't make demands on each other: they make requests, and many of these requests are turned down. A donation is not
guaranteed just because a PAC officer calls to say, "I gave $1,000
when you asked me to, now you have to give $1,000 to the person I
pick." The candidate's characteristics are important. If corporation A
asks corporation B to contribute to a powerful probusiness candidate

such as Bob Dole, Lloyd Bentsen, or Dan Rostenkowski, corporation B's PAC is giving money to someone it is probably pleased to support. That doesn't mean that corporation A could expect corporation B to be willing to contribute to Bernie Sanders (Socialist-Vt.). The support of a respected PAC officer of a major corporation can do a great deal to advance a potentially marginal candidate such as Dick Gephardt— but Citibank itself would have trouble selling tickets to a Bernie Sanders fundraiser (not that there is any indication it's about to try). As one PAC officer said, "They give me money, sometimes I'll give them money—but not to Metzenbaum or Kennedy." Of course, most of the time a corporation is willing to ask for help only on behalf of candidates who have helped them out and are at least willing to do favors for business. Participating in these exchanges "gives us a friendly network to reach out and get funds for specific candidates we have a real interest in and anxiety to help." Other companies don't always contribute but

> more often than not they will, especially for a company of our size and reputation and the size of our PAC and our credibility. More often than not they will participate because they look to us for similar support from time to time.

Although "more often than not" corporations participate, their participation is contingent and voluntary. Several PAC officers stressed that "everybody runs their own show. Nobody outside my corporation's gigging me about how I give money." Or as another said, "We turn down a lot of fund-raising invitations from various industry-type PACs. The tail doesn't wag the dog; we make our own decisions." Sometimes the same people who told us they gave money to "some jerk" simply because another corporation asked them to do so also insisted that

> I don't think I've ever been concerned with what another PAC did about something. There's a service who will tell you what other PACs are doing, who other PACs are giving to. I don't care, and so I don't buy it. What they do in no way influences what I am going to do or anything I am going to spend.

Both sides of the coin are crucial: corporations often help each other out by donating to someone they don't care about (or actively dislike), but they do so *voluntarily,* as a *favor,* not because they are being ordered to do so.

Most favors and help result from government relations officials serving on candidate steering committees. But top executives also are involved in business networks that lead to candidate contributions, either in response to requests from other corporate executives or as the incidental product of other forms of business networking. In one interview the PAC committee chair ran through a partial list of noteworthy involvements for a few of the corporation's top executives. The CEO is a member of the Business Roundtable and of the mayor's most important commission; formerly he was president of the industry trade association. Next year another executive will be chair of a different trade association. Other executives are members of the boards of several leading charities and officers of many state and local trade associations. These executives, as well as others, are individually active in "the political arena, sometimes on the Democratic side of the aisle, sometimes on the Republican":

> All these things give you exposure to people who want you to help them financially run for public office. So our top executives are frequently requested to make contributions to political candidates individually, which they pass on to the PAC to make or consider making on their behalf. We [in government relations] frequently ask them to lend their support to get their friends to help the candidates we are interested in, and their friends in business ask them to do things like that. They are constantly asked, as are we, by our friends in other companies through our knowledge of them, through our trade associations where we work together on various legislative matters to support Jones in your state who is running for Congress.

Although the PAC normally honors requests from the top half-dozen officers, this is not invariably the case:

> Sometimes we've got a problem because one of our executive officers has been asked to be on the campaign committee to raise money for Jones and the next thing you know we have a request to give Jones $1,000. And we say right on the form, executive officer XYZ is on Jones's campaign committee to raise money for this event. And somebody says, "I don't care if he is." So we have arguments. We try to support them if we can, but there are times that we don't.

Another company with recommendations from top executives reported that the PAC is not the biggest thing on their mind. They are running a $10 billion business and not worrying about a $60,000 PAC. But when the issues tend to come up, what happens is at a cocktail party or a social function, they will bump into a congressman or a senator will hit them.

Usually it's a nuisance. They will say, "So and so asked me if we can give him something. Do you think we can do something for him?" We would hope that they will always say, "I'll get back to you" or "Call Bill or Stan" [the key government relations people]. But they don't, they say, "Oh yes, we'll do something."

So what happens is then we got to go and try to whittle down what the candidate thinks is a grand promise. Because he knows the president of the company or he met the president of the company.

So most of them, the sharper candidates, are going to realize that it's going to come back to us anyway. But once in a while you get a couple of guys who are nervous enough or anxious enough or really worried about losing that they will not take the usual kind of cool-down, so you might spend a couple grand a year that you would have preferred to spend otherwise. They don't cost us tens of thousands.

PACs also make donations because the corporation's customers have asked them to do so. One PAC officer reported that "the more serious issue, the times top executives really care, is if a client asks them to have us contribute to a candidate. I would guess about 10 percent of our contributions are at the request of a client." This is an unusually high proportion, but others report similar experiences:

> We supply [another giant company]. They'll contact our executive senior VP who heads up that business segment and say, "This is what's going on. This is real important. This issue is real important to us, and as a supplier to us it should be important to you too. Would you consider a contribution to [this candidate]?"

One of the PAC officers who told us about such donations regarded them as a form of corporate service for customers. In at least one case, however, the request to contribute to a candidate came from the CEO of the company's bank and was made directly to the company's CEO. Not only was the request made at a higher level than most of the customer requests, but the company had no legislation immediately pending and the candidate was not facing an election contest. This implies a more impressive level of business (and candidate) coordination. Presumably the corporation was first identified as a noncontributor, and then an effort was made to find the right executive to request the donation—and it's hard to imagine anything giving more leverage than a request from the CEO of the corporation's bank.

CAN INDUSTRY COMPETITORS WORK TOGETHER?

Pluralists stress the opposition that occurs between businesses. Even though companies routinely work with many other companies, a pluralist could plausibly argue that companies oppose the actions of their direct competitors. Exxon might cooperate with General Motors or Dow Chemical, but that doesn't mean it could bring itself to work politically with Mobil, Shell, or Texaco. This theory may have surface plausibility, but it is completely wrong. The companies *most* likely to work together are those in the same industry who directly compete with each other:

> In our X division, we are major competitors with a company called Y. You couldn't get more competitive. We're suing each other all the time. We hate each other, but I have a very good relationship with them down here, and often we work together on the Hill for certain bills. The [provision] in the Z bill was something we worked on together because it benefits us even though in that business they have more of a share than we do. So when we're down here, we're working on issues that impact all of our companies even though we all want to make money in competition with the other guy. But when we're petitioning the government, our interests are very similar, and that's why we have the [industry trade] association. You obviously want to work a coalition if you can. So we'll have industry fundraisers.

Important political activity takes place within and around industry trade associations, and campaigns often have both pragmatic and ideological dimensions. A company may have pragmatic reasons to fight for a change that benefits the entire industry, but a change that affects a major industry such as oil or banking has the potential to be an important issue for all of business. Industry trade associations bridge the gap between "company" and "classwide" rationality.[10] This kind of politics involves fighting for something much broader than the interests of a specific company but narrower than the interests of business as a whole. Trade associations have many functions—public relations, information gathering, research, and occasionally some kinds of marketing—but a major responsibility is certainly government relations, as reflected by their concentration in Washington.

When an entire industry mounts a campaign, its coordination and political impact can be impressive. One state had several times considered and rejected a change in its banking regulations:

> We said this is the year to do it. We've got to have an influx of capital, or the banks are really going to be in trouble. We're already in trouble anyway. The legislature is going to be more open to this than in the past, so let's form an alliance and get going.
>
> We hired a lobbyist. The [state] association hired a lobby team, one of the top ones in the state. And we let them direct us and use us as necessary. One of the things we did in conjunction, we started a survey in this company that we did in all of our offices across the state. We sent our managers a list and said, "How well do you know these legislators?" And coded it and put it in a PC so we had a contact list statewide who knew each state representative. We used that quite extensively.
>
> We went through at the beginning of that legislative session, and we assigned a contact to every legislator. We said, "Okay, you're going to be the contact. Here's some information. Here's why we're for it. Here's all the pro and con arguments." And a lot of this of course was developed by the Banking Association and other groups. It was an education process that we put our people through, and said, "Here's all of the reasons"— and some of our people, frankly, had to be convinced, people at the smaller banks, because they were saying, "Now wait a minute, that doesn't sound like a very good idea." But for the most part we did a pretty good job of that.
>
> And we used that network quite extensively to the extent of generating a typical letter writing campaign, which we did. A lobbyist might call me up and say, "So and so from X is all of a sudden undecided. She needs someone to call her up and reassure her." And I'd pick up the phone and call [a manager] and say, "Can you call [this legislator] and reassure her about it." It was a good effort, it really was.

This account mentions most of the elements of many successful business political campaigns—uniting an entire industry for a particular change, acting together through a trade association, using outside consultants and allowing them to direct and coordinate the campaign, beginning by convincing or coercing the company's own managers, using the contacts of each manager to further the change, and enjoying the ultimate success. The undecided legislator in this example probably received at least one call from each of the several banks promoting the new legislation, and many of the calls probably came from people she already knew.

One thing the account leaves out is the process whereby the industry itself came to agree on a solution. Typically this is the first step in the process. It may take some time and involve some difficult to resolve internal disagreements, but before the issues are brought into the public arena, they are resolved inside groups restricted to the business community.[11] Occasionally an industry is simply allowed to make the decision itself under parameters established by Congress. In the insurance industry, taxes on assets hit mutual companies harder, and taxes on profits hit stock companies harder:

> So what usually happens is, and it's happened now two or three times in a row when Congress wanted to change the law. This is a gross oversimplification, but the way it happened in 1959 and in the early 80s, Congress said, "look, we are getting 3 billion bucks from you guys. We want $3.5 billion. You figure out how to write the law which fairly gets it from everybody. And if you can't, we will do it, not for you, but to you."

Although industry trade associations are usually important, some of the largest companies scorn them:

> Most associations that represent those companies that are in the same business you are almost have to look at the lowest common denominator when it comes to handling issues. They have to make sure they don't offend anyone or step on anyone's toes, and very often they can't become high profile, and we need to be high profile on certain issues. We just dig our own way, and we are big enough to make these decisions. If we don't like what's going on, we go it on our own.

"Small" companies—like this oil company with sales in the billions— need to rely on the trade association, but they also have to watch out for their own interests:

> We have to depend on trade associations that we are members of to take the lead on that stuff because we just don't have the staff. What we try to watch for on the state level and the federal level are issues that affect us as a company that don't affect anybody else. Because most of the time you've got your ARCOs and Exxons out there working on the same stuff that you are interested in. But at any rate, because of the oil, most of the time that is the situation. So you have to look for little peculiar stuff that would really zap your company and nobody else.

Trade associations don't always work effectively, and the members of an industry can't always agree. One company that operates in several different industries noted that it's through the industry association that we usually take positions on public issues, as opposed to our working something out bilaterally with someone else. We would all work together to come up with an industry position if that were possible. If that weren't possible, then we would all work separately.

But this same company also reported that

it depends on the industry. In the X industry for a long time the companies were all at odds with one another, and they couldn't seem to get together on any public policy issue. There was no strong association. [Our subsidiary] walked out of the association because it had become dominated by our competitor. Now there's a new association in which the major companies are amicably working together on issues concerning the industry. So now at this point we have pretty good cooperation.

Sometimes the members of one industry agree and work together in opposition to another industry. Our interviews offered only two examples of this—the local phone companies against the long-distance carriers, and a gas and an electric utility against each other. However, these counterexamples of businesses opposed to each other appear trivial compared to the examples of business cooperation. We have tried to include *every* instance discussed in the interviews of businesses opposed to each other. These amount to one trade association that for a time functioned ineffectively because of conflict between two major companies but now has "pretty good cooperation"; a gas and an electric utility quarreling over what our informant estimates to be about $1 million a year; and disputes between the different kinds of phone companies. Opposed to this are literally dozens of examples of companies that "hate each other," are "suing each other all the time," and are each other's major competitors but that nonetheless work together well in Washington. They cooperate in promoting the same policies, sponsoring joint fundraisers, and in general behaving as a unified bloc.

BUSINESS UNITY BEYOND THE INDUSTRY

Political unity on an industrywide basis, whether or not coordinated through the trade association, is the most common form of political coalition, but corporations also unify on other bases—a similar marketing approach, form of financing, pension arrangement, source of raw material, or ultimate client:

On other types of legislation—on tax legislation affecting 936 companies in Puerto Rico—we're allies with any other 936 company. We're working with [our top two competitors]; we're not competitors then.

In the marketplace we're competitors, but when it comes to the halls of Congress or the halls of the legislatures we are allies more than we are opponents. It is bottom line oriented but it's not who has the biggest share of the market. It's all of us being able to sell our products in a healthy environment, so then we can compete for market share.

Unity need not be based on a specific shared attribute. A general sense of shared commonality is the hardest to explain and specify but perhaps the most important. Corporations have a common structural position; PAC officers share a social world and culture. The top executives of the corporation are tied together through common stock ownership, bank loans, board of director interlocks, membership in policy associations, and socialization. The government relations officers are members of the same few associations, spend their lives attending the same kinds of events and functions, and meet each other fifty times a year at fundraisers, legislative committee hearings, restaurants and clubs. They talk to each other on the phone, read the same journals and materials, and get information from the same places. Even their disagreements occur within a larger framework of ideological consensus and personal trust. The key actors are likely to have a great many friends and acquaintances in common. Years ago they may have worked for the same senator or House member, or for the same federal agency. When they want to pressure each other, they can do so through gentle kidding, using humor and comments that affirm their common position even as they express displeasure with an action:

INTERVIEWER: If you did give to Metzenbaum, would someone call you up and say "What are you doing?"

PAC DIRECTOR: Yes, they might. I've said that to other people: "Why? Why? You're cutting off your nose."

Mild humor can deliver the kind of remark that people remember. They may dread such remarks enough to avoid a course of action that might provoke further such remarks, but serious pressure or outright hostility is rare or nonexistent:

You get offhand remarks: "What did you give to that pain in the ass for?" "Your pain in the ass is my salve." You get that sometimes. Nobody's

ever called me on the phone to seriously badger us for having done
something, but you might say something in passing.

These kinds of exchanges are enforcement mechanisms that preserve
a generalized business unity. They allow one corporation to express
displeasure with another but within the context of humor.

Corporations may at times choose to go it alone—but for even the
largest and most powerful it is a considered choice, a point of pride that
they are willing and able to do so:

> PAC DIRECTOR: We've gone against the wind or against the grain on a
> number of occasions, and it doesn't cause us any particular grief. We
> supported a congressman from [state] back in the 70s and 80s by the
> name of X. It was in those days a Democratic district. We had a
> facility with almost 10,000 employees in it. He didn't particularly
> vote down the line on all issues we felt were important, but he did
> recognize we were a major employer and a force in his district and he
> always had an open mind and was very helpful to us. Sometimes if
> he couldn't be with us on an issue, he was very helpful in the proce-
> dural aspect of Congress. And as a powerful figure in Congress, he
> was influential to help out there, and we had a great deal of support
> from our employees and we supported him. I'd venture to say X
> didn't get a lot of corporate PAC money when he was in the House
> of Representatives.
>
> INTERVIEWER: Did other businesses have any trouble about that?
>
> PAC DIRECTOR: Oh yes, people will good-naturedly give you a little barb
> or a cat call. Other PACs would or sometimes candidates would.
> They would say, "What are you giving to that guy for?" but again we
> don't try to tell other people how to run their PACs. We think we
> have enough expertise and enough people who know what they are
> doing, and I guess we have enough self-confidence that if other
> people tell us how to run our PAC, that's their freedom, but we are
> not necessarily going to listen to them.

This highly pragmatic corporation was proud of its willingness to go
against the grain—to contribute to a powerful Democrat who did his
best to help them out and was highly popular with the 10,000 company
employees he represented! The grain it was going against is a generalized sense that corporations shouldn't give to liberals, and this member
was not just a moderate but a genuine liberal.[12]

These organizations and this common culture create a situation
where "it's pretty easy to see if you are in the mainstream or if you are

not." Associated with this are pressures for conformity. Usually this is the primary meaning of business unity—a generalized sense of common orientation and purpose, with subtle pressures on those who step outside the mainstream. The sense exists that businesses ought to support one another, even if the issue has no particular significance for their corporation:

> You have to put [our company] not only in [this industry and that industry] but also in the broader service sector. Occasionally there are differences between the service sector and manufacturing, but generally speaking the goals we seek are consistent with the free enterprise system. Plant closing legislation just passed. We would oppose that just as the NAM did, Chamber of Commerce—we're members of both of those—so even though manufacturing would be most heavily concerned about plant closing legislation, we too in the service sector are concerned. You will always find divergence of opinion on specifics, but generally speaking I think we are all consistent in our support of the free enterprise system.

In this case the company played a largely passive role on the issue, but in other cases corporations are mobilized to fight a key issue, and even those who would be willing to accept a proposed bill nevertheless maintain business solidarity by taking an active stance against it.

For example, in the Labor Law Reform bill fight discussed in chapter 5, unions expected most major employers to support the bill or at least to stay out of the fight. It seemed that pragmatic corporations ought to be able to live easily with the bill, perhaps after winning a few "minor adjustments." Inside the business community opinion was in fact divided, with major employers who had good labor relations arguing that business should let the bill pass without actively opposing it. The key turning point was a decision by the Business Roundtable. Its policy committee voted nineteen to eight to oppose the bill:

> Subsequently, even those corporations that had favored neutrality lobbied actively against the bill. GE, perhaps the strongest supporter of neutrality, sent its plant managers to Washington to lobby their representatives.[13]

The congressional outcome might have been different if a sizeable fraction of major corporations had supported the bill or even let it be known they wouldn't mind if it passed. Corporate success in this struggle depended on the ability of business to unify and the willingness of those on the losing end of the vote to reverse themselves and work hard for the position they had voted against.

HOW CAMPAIGN FINANCE LAWS COERCE BUSINESS TO UNIFY

The campaign finance laws are structured to encourage business unity and to limit the power of any corporation that tries to go it alone. Two features of the campaign finance laws do so. The first is simply a policy of strict disclosure. Because business has legitimacy in the larger society, its donations can be exposed to public scrutiny with little or no questioning of its activities. If General Motors or General Electric gives $5,000 to a candidate, this can be publicly reported and defended: these corporations are large enough to have legitimate reasons to give a large gift to any candidate, since they do business everywhere and have a wide range of products. It would be difficult to interest an editor in a news story about this, even if GE had contributed in this way to a great many candidates. On the other hand, if a small and failing savings and loan were to give $5,000 each to most of the members of the banking committee, this would (potentially) be news. The very largest corporations favored full and complete disclosure because it was unlikely to cause them problems, and they were happy to have the spotlight placed on any marginal business that attempted to use political influence to compensate for economic deficiencies. Thus in 1968 the Committee for Economic Development (CED), which more or less was the corporate establishment (and to a considerable degree still is),[14] issued a report arguing the following:

> Stringent disclosure requirements on every aspect of political financing must be imposed and enforced, both at the national and state levels. All candidates, political parties, associations and other organizations engaging in election activities should be required to file full disclosure statements quarterly, as well as 20 and 10 days before each primary and general election. Receipts and pledges by source, expenditure, debt, and all other commitments should be reported in detail. Moreover, each person who contributes more than $500 for all political purposes in any one year should be required to file a statement listing donations with the appropriate governmental agency. . . . All these statements ought to be open to examination.[15]

Before the next presidential election the first major campaign finance reform law had been enacted; one of the act's key features was a disclosure provision closely paralleling what the CED had recommended. This provision ensures that everyone knows what everyone else is doing and makes it more difficult for one corporation to cut a special deal at the expense of the rest of business.

The second feature of the campaign finance laws increasing the power of the organized business community is the regulation limiting individual donations to $1,000 and PAC donations to $5,000 (per candidate per election). This point is counterintuitive: why would a *limit* on the size of donations *increase* power? The answer is that a candidate cannot finance a campaign on the basis of one or two mavericks. It isn't enough to make a deal with a modern-day Howard Hughes; even if he has unlimited funds, as an individual the maximum he may contribute to a candidate is $1,000, and if he controls a PAC the maximum that it can donate is $5,000. A Howard Hughes or a Ross Perot trying to buck the corporate power structure would be unable to finance even one-tenth the cost of a candidate's campaign. Therefore, the candidate will have to get most of his or her business money from other large businesses, and the maverick won't be able to gain much political leverage. That is, under the new campaign finance laws businesses *cannot* have a major impact *unless* they act together. An individual PAC operating in isolation from other business PACs has an inherently limited impact. For maximum effectiveness, corporations need to become active parts of reciprocal networks and trade favors with other corporations.

Not only do current campaign finance laws make it impossible for a single company to buck the corporate establishment and have an independent impact by itself, but many reform proposals are intended only to provide more effective means to the same end. Charles Keating, who operated on his own, would be restricted; a mobilized and coordinated savings and loan industry would not. We are happy to see better oversight of maverick business owners, but the fundamental issue is the coordinated power of a politically unified business community.

Control of the Economy

Business's power is magnified and reinforced by its political unity. The real bedrock of its power, however, is the pervasive economic inequality in our society and business domination of the economy. Corporations do not get their political power from PACs alone. We need to examine the full range of business power in order to understand the difficulties confronting any attempt at campaign finance reform.

LEVELS OF INEQUALITY

Discussions of inequality in the United States usually focus on income, and the inequalities of income are substantial. In 1989, one out of five families had an income of less than $16,003; the average (median) family had an income of $34,210; the top 5 percent had incomes over $98,963; and the top 1 percent of households had average (mean) incomes of $559,800.[16] For every dollar in income received by households in the bottom fifth of the income distribution, $12 were received by households in the top fifth.

But the inequalities of *wealth* are far greater.[17] The top 10 percent of the nation's families control more than two-thirds (68 percent) of the national wealth. The top 1 percent controls 37 percent, more than the combined wealth of the entire bottom 90 percent of the population.[18]

These disparities are enormous not only because the wealthy have several Porsches and Mercedes while others drive Chevys and Fords. The key is that some people, wealthy people, own the factories and offices where many of the rest of us work. The very rich own productive assets as well as consumption goods. In consumption there are only gradational differences: everyone has some; the issue is simply how much. In production there are fundamentally different relationships: some people own assets and give orders, while others work for a wage and must obey orders.[19]

The primary power of the wealthy is not exercised as individuals or even as families. Power in our society is based in institutions, not individuals, and the power of wealth is channeled through corporations. There are over 200,000 industrial corporations in the United States, but all companies are not created equal: the 500 largest industrials control three-quarters of the sales, assets, and profits of all industrial corporations. More than 100 of these companies had sales over $5 billion. In the service sector as well 500 firms control a disproportionate share of the resources. The dominance of these corporations means that a handful of owners and top executives, perhaps one-hundredth of 1 percent of the U.S. population, or 25,000 individuals, have the power to make decisions that affect all our lives.[20] Collectively these people exercise enormous power, making decisions that affect our lives more than those made by the entire elected government put together.[21]

Consider for a moment those decisions that virtually everyone in our society agrees should be made by business. Consider only those decisions on which there is broad bipartisan political agreement; exclude anything that would generally be considered ethically or legally dubious or that a significant fraction of elected officials disputes as business's right. Exclude any actions that are done only through business's influence on government, and confine your attention to decisions that corporate owners and executives make in operating their businesses. Remember that any decision made by "business" is primarily determined by the 25,000 individuals at the top of the corporate ladder, since their companies control about three-quarters of *all* corporate sales, assets, employees, and profits.

BUSINESS DECISIONS

A brief and partial list indicates the scope of some of the decisions made by business:

DECISIONS ABOUT EMPLOYMENT

- Number of people employed.
- When to have lay-offs.
- Number of hours people work.
- When work begins in the morning and ends in the afternoon.
- Whether there is overtime and whether overtime is compulsory.
- Whether to allow flextime and job-sharing.
- Skill level of the jobs. Does the company make an effort to use lots of skilled workers paid good wages, or is it always trying to deskill positions and replace skilled workers with unskilled?
- Educational and other requirements for employment. Are certain educational levels necessary in order to be hired, or are they simply helpful? Are ex-prisoners or former mental patients eligible for all jobs or only some? What about the handicapped?
- Whether the firm de facto discriminates in favor of men, whites, or other groups or makes an active effort to recruit and promote minorities and women.
- Workers' rights on the job. For example, do they have free speech? A worker at a Coca-Cola plant was given a three-day suspension without pay because his wife brought him a lunch with a soda from Burger King, at a time when Burger King sold Pepsi. It is legal to penalize an employee for this or many other actions.
- Job safety. A worker was killed doing a dangerous task. Almost immediately thereafter another worker was ordered to do the same job and refused because he said conditions were unsafe and had

not been remedied. The company fired him for this refusal, and the Supreme Court upheld the firing.

- Union relations. (Within limits) whether a union is recognized, whether the union and the workers are treated with dignity and respect, how bitterly and viciously the union is resisted.

INVESTMENT DECISIONS

- Whether to expand a plant, and if so, which plant to expand.
- Whether to close down a plant and when and how to do so. Recently this right has received a very mild challenge. Many legislators were prepared (for the first time) to vote that a company should give 30 *days'* (not weeks' or months') notice before shutting down. The bill was defeated but received substantial support. However, virtually no one questioned the company's absolute right (in the United States, not in Europe) to shut down if it chose to do so, no matter what the effect on the workers and communities.
- Where to open new plants. The company has every right to bargain for the best deal it can get. Deals can include tax abatements and implicit agreements to ignore labor or pollution laws.

PRODUCT AND MARKETING

- Products produced, including whether to introduce a new product and whether to discontinue an old stand-by.
- Design, both functional and esthetic.
- Relative attention to different considerations. In a new car, how important is styling, sex appeal, fuel efficiency, safety, durability?
- Quality of the goods produced. Are they made to last, with high standards throughout, or is just enough done so they look good in the store and for the first month of use?
- Cost for which goods are sold.
- Character of the advertising used to promote the product. Does it stress the significant features of the product or distract through sex and extraneous symbols?
- Amount spent on advertising. Ninety percent of the commercials on prime-time television are sponsored by the nation's 500 largest corporations.[22]

- Places where ads appear. In left-wing journals, in right-wing journals, on television, on what programs?

COMMUNITY AND ENVIRONMENT

- Level of pollution in the workplace. Air, heat, noise, chemicals, and so on.
- Level of pollution in the outside environment. For pollution both in the workplace and in the larger community, beginning in the 1970s the government set maximum limits for a few items, but companies are completely free to do better than this. No government regulation prevents companies from setting and meeting tougher standards of their own devising. For example, in July 1991 a railroad tanker car derailed, tumbled into the Sacramento River, ruptured, and spilled pesticide. The pesticide was not listed as a regulated substance, and therefore the railroad was not required to carry it in a double hulled tanker, although it could have chosen to do so. The pesticide was unregulated, but it was strong enough to kill virtually all the fish in the river, which had been famous for its trout.[23]
- Degree of consideration for the community. Does the company make an effort to be a good neighbor? Does it contribute to local charities? Support local initiatives?[24]

This by no means exhausts the list of decisions that companies are allowed, expected, and in many cases required to make. Some regulation of business decisions occurs at the margin, with possible regulation for issues such as whether a company can pull up stakes and leave town with no more than a day's notice, dump raw wastes in the river, or make dubious claims in its advertising. For the most part, however, corporations are free to make decisions about their economic operations. If the government fails to act, big business can do as it wishes. The access process can be successful because a corporation is not usually asking for an explicit transfer of government funds but "only" to be allowed to continue to make economic decisions on the basis of its own short-term interests without regard to their effect on other members of the society. The corporation's government relations operation can succeed by winning delays, using the access process to craft special language that permits the specific corporate practice to continue, getting the regulations drafted in the way most favorable to the company, or reducing enforcement and penalties for violations.

THE PINTO GAS TANK: AN EXAMPLE OF BUSINESS DECISION MAKING

What does this mean in practice? How does business economic control interact with government relations and political action? Thousands of examples could be chosen—some of cases where business decisions appear thoroughly sensible, others where they appear problematic. Since power is most visible when it appears problematic, we illustrate business decision making with the example of the Pinto gas tank, chosen primarily because some excellent reporting has uncovered facts that usually remain hidden.

In the late 1960s, Lee Iacocca, at the time president of Ford and fresh from his triumph with the Mustang, fought to have Ford produce subcompacts. What ultimately became the Pinto was rushed into production in order to meet competition from the imports. Iacocca insisted that "the Pinto was not to weigh an ounce over 2,000 pounds and not to cost a cent over $2,000."[25] It can reasonably be argued that these limits were determined by the competitive market; in this sense, Iacocca made the decision, but it was heavily constrained. These constraints are real and important, but they still leave a great deal of room for maneuver.[26]

This point is illustrated by what happened as design and production proceeded and "crash tests revealed a serious defect in the gas tank." Dowie reports that in Ford's own tests every crash at more than twenty-five miles per hour resulted in a ruptured fuel tank, unless the car was structurally altered.

> When it was discovered the gas tank was unsafe, did anyone go to Iacocca and tell him? "Hell no," replied an engineer who worked on the Pinto, a high company official for many years. . . . "That person would have been fired. Safety wasn't a popular subject around Ford in those days. With Lee it was taboo. Whenever a problem was raised that meant a delay on the Pinto, Lee would chomp on his cigar, look out the window and say 'Read the product objectives and get back to work.' "[27]

In the "good old days" before about 1965, the odds are that no one would have learned that the Pinto had a dangerous and defective gas tank design because the dominant safety focus was on drivers. Almost certainly it would not have emerged that Ford made explicit decisions to save money by letting defective gas tanks kill people. The issue of the cars themselves simply wasn't discussed until 1965 when consumer activist Ralph Nader burst on the scene with *Unsafe at Any Speed*[28] and then led a campaign for federal regulation of auto safety. In the altered political climate of the 1970s, the federal government was supposed to regulate auto safety. Ford was no longer allowed to simply make these decisions for itself; the decisions now became a matter of public policy. In these kinds of situations the access process becomes crucial. Corporate PAC and government relations officials work to prevent the government from making "hasty" and "ill-informed" decisions. By providing Congress and government regulators with relevant information and lobbying them for "sensible" regulations, corporate government relations specialists try to limit the "damage" that government does through "inappropriate" regulations.

In this particular case, Ford and its allies delayed the implementation of gas tank safety regulations for eight years. During that period Ford was free to continue to make its own decisions, guided by its own conception of what was best. Because business makes the decisions unless and until government specifically enacts a law or regulation to limit business "freedom,"[29] Ford did not have to secure passage of the legislation it wanted, much less public support for its position. It needed only to delay, weaken, and frustrate Congress and regulatory agencies.

One of the tools Ford used was a "cost-benefit analysis" calculation of whether it made economic sense to prevent gas tank fuel leakage accidents. By Ford's calculation, safe gas tanks would save 180 burn deaths, 180 serious burn injuries, and 2,100 burned vehicles each year. Ford calculated the value of human life as $200,000 per death, $67,000 per injury, and $700 per vehicle, for a net benefit of $49.5 million from this regulation.[30] However, by Ford's estimate, the cost of saving lives and injuries was far higher: it was $11 per car or truck, and with annual production of 11 million cars and 1.5 million light trucks, the cost would add up to $137 million per year. This cost-benefit analysis (like many others) was biased and subject to manipulation. Others estimated there would be ten times as many burn injuries as Ford projected and that accidents could be prevented for far less than the $11 cost Ford used—not to mention the matter of the value of a human life. But Ford's chief "safety" official included the analysis in documents submitted to the Secretary of Transportation arguing against new regulations. This kind of memo would not be used in an advertising campaign ("Ford has a better idea: Let 'em burn") but is relatively standard fare for government relations lobbying. This cost-benefit analysis was probably the most outrageous of Ford's lobbying tactics, but Ford found many other ways to delay the regulation—by submitting reams of evidence, insisting additional studies were needed, coming up with new arguments at each stage in the proceedings, and always delaying its reply until the last possible day.

From one perspective this delay meant the needless loss of human lives, but from the perspective of corporate government relations it was an effective job of defending company profits. In retrospect Ford would probably have been better off if it had been less successful in fighting the regulation. When Ford ultimately was forced to fix the problem, it managed to do so for only about a dollar per car (not the $11 it had projected in its cost-benefit analysis). Meanwhile, the dangers of the Ford Pinto became widely known, and burn victims sued the company. Juries learned that Ford had self-consciously decided to let people burn to death rather than spend somewhere between $1 and $11 to prevent fuel tank fires. Jurors valued human life somewhat more dearly than the Ford Motor Company, and victims therefore received substantial settlements.

SPENDING THE MONEY

Direct decisions about day-to-day operations are the foundation for business power. But those who control production also receive the profits and can decide how they are spent. This implies choices about the kind of society we should have and the activities that should be supported. For example, corporate advertising expenditures were $118.05 billion in 1988.[31] This $475 per person is more than the total income per person in Afghanistan, Bangladesh, Burma, China, Ethiopia, India, Kenya, Madagascar, Mozambique, Nepal, Pakistan, Sri Lanka, Tanzania, or Zaire.[32] This $118.05 billion is more than two-thirds of total spending on public elementary and secondary education ($172.0 billion).[33]

The dollar amounts are huge, and their effect on our culture no less so. An average television viewer spends more than four hours a week watching commercials.[34] Whatever advertising's effect on sales of specific products, its continuing implicit message—buy, buy, buy; you are what you own; consumer goods can make you sexy, respected, a good parent—shapes every member of this society, whether we accept these values happily or attempt to reject them. In choosing presidential candidates, business ads on television ("Where's the beef?") provide the key lines, so that our choice of a president is influenced by a snappy hamburger ad. Many of our best minds devote their lives to promoting toothpaste and soap powder, not to mention tobacco and beer. Advertising shapes the culture when it "only" promotes the merits of Presta-Glop over Ultra-Goo toothpaste, but corporations spend increasingly large sums on advertising not tied to a product. Some of this is simply meant to convince you that Octopus Industries is a good neighbor and citizen, that you should forget the lung cancer and drunk driving associated with their products and focus instead on their support for the Bill of Rights (or the Olympics or Statue of Liberty). But much of it specifically promotes political positions. Corporations, or wealthy individuals and foundations that derive their money from business, are also primary sources of funding for many charities, for key elements of higher education, and for most think tanks. Most attempts to develop policy proposals are funded by business, and although there is no direct control over the findings of these studies, business obviously tends to support analysts with a past record of recommending the kinds of proposals business likes to see.

CONFRONTING BUSINESS POWER

A corporation's political power does not depend simply on its own PAC contributions. A member of Congress evaluating a company's request for a multimillion dollar tax loophole does not simply balance a $1,000 campaign contribution against a $50 million tax give-away. Because business is politically unified by overlapping informal networks, helping this one corporation can develop a reputation for the member as someone who is willing (and able) to help out. This reputation can lead to donations from companies (and individuals) that the member barely knows.

The member's decision whether to support the company's request is not based exclusively on campaign finance. Probably more important is the corporation's role in the economy. The member may well resent the company's proposal for a sleazy tax deal. But the company may be implicitly (or explicitly) threatening that if it doesn't get this give-away, it will close the factory and move production overseas. A similar logic applies to environmental regulations: the company may have a plausible, although suspect, analysis proving that a proposed regulation cannot be met without closing a plant. Although companies frequently lie or err in these claims, the company's control over the economy influences a field of power that constrains the member's decision more than the PAC contribution.[35]

Campaign finance proposals cannot ignore power relations in society. Many reform proposals are intended only to punish the occasional maverick, while ratifying the ability of money in general to dominate political decisions. Other reform proposals attempt to use Band-aids to deal with cancer. Even a lot of Band-aids won't do the job. We need to go another way.

Chapter 7

■■■

"THEY MIGHT START RUNNING IT STRICTLY FOR THE VOTES"

■■■

PACs are not popular. The American public doesn't like them. Even George Bush has proposed abolishing corporate and labor PACs. Reform proposals abound: dozens have been filed in the last decade, and in most sessions of Congress one or more proposals are "seriously" considered, often coming "close" to passage. Most of these "reforms," however, would do little to change the basic character of a system where those with the most money have the most access, influence, and power. Meaningful campaign finance reform *is* possible, although unlikely. Reforms that are most likely to be adopted won't solve the problems; reforms that could solve the problems are unlikely to be enacted.

PAC Directors on PACs

Many corporate PAC directors wouldn't mind if PACs were abolished. Most support the PAC system, but we were surprised how many were at least indifferent to reform:

If PACs were done away with tomorrow, I don't think we'd care too much.

■■■

I'd love to see PACs closed down.

■■■

> If we got out of the PAC business tomorrow, maybe a lot of people would say, "Great."

■ ■ ■

> The company doesn't take positions, but personally I am strongly in favor of election reforms.

But only a minority express these views. A strong majority of corporate PAC officials want PACs to be maintained and make a variety of arguments in their favor. The most persuasive is that PACs open the process to public scrutiny:

> I think it would be terrible if PACs were abolished. And the reason why I say that is because I recall the way it was before PACs. If you abolish them, you know what would happen then? It goes back under the table. And that is terrible because there will be all kinds of scandal. It is so much better now it is all out in the open. You walked in to me, and you laid out exactly what our company has been doing, who we've been giving to, and everything else. I think that that's marvelous, and that's the way it should be.

■ ■ ■

> I think the PAC system is probably as honest a way to disburse money as there is if the PACs are run on an up and up basis.

PAC directors also believe that "there's a virtue to PACs in that you are getting people involved in issues":

> I think we've gotten people involved in political activity in this country that would not be otherwise. Now you can do that without contributing to a PAC, but I think you feel a little more ownership if you've got some money invested.

■ ■ ■

> We are supportive of the system now. We believe that it's the best that can be had. We believe that there should be the opportunity to have that participation. If we don't get in there and contribute, there is going to be a void.

PAC directors differed in the extent of their commitment to the current system. They were in complete unanimity, however, in their vehement opposition to any alternative that they felt would provide advantages to their opponents, especially labor: "If you abolish PACs, you'd have to abolish them for all, including the unions."

"A TOOL AND NOTHING MORE"

PAC directors weren't upset at the prospect of campaign finance reform for at least three reasons: the PAC is only one of many ways of accomplishing their purposes; reform does not seem imminent; and even if it comes, they expect things to continue in much the same way. Their first reason for feeling sanguine is a belief that the PAC is only one of many tools available to them and not necessarily the most important:

> A lot of companies think their PAC is more powerful than it is. I dare say we wouldn't be in any worse shape if we didn't have them.

> ■■■

> We don't need a PAC. There was a time we needed it, but now business gets a fair hearing, and so we don't need PACs. We'll get a fair hearing anyway.

> ■■■

> Some PACs really get an overblown idea what it does. I always find that the type of person who is fresh out of the corporate headquarters or fresh out of the Hill thinks that PACs are more important than they are. After you get to see what they can do and what they can't do, you realize the sun does not rise or set because of the PAC system.

> ■■■

> I think PACs can do a few little minor things—help staff people like myself get entree, open doors, things of that sort which may help us do our job a little easier. But the bottom line is you still have to have your arguments and your substance correct and you do have to be persuasive.

The point that PAC directors are making here is probably *the* most fundamental fact about any proposed campaign finance reform. As the previous chapter argued, business attains its power primarily through its control of the economy and its privileged position in U.S. society. Campaign contributions are one part of the total picture. For certain purposes they are a key part, but even if business made absolutely no campaign contributions, they would still have a vast array of other resources:

Let me tell you something. If I couldn't do the job without PACs, I shouldn't be in the job. It is a tool and nothing more. But I've got all sorts of other tools. And the biggest tool I've got is experience. And also you know I talk to a lot of guys who become congressmen long before they become congressmen. You talk to them, you help write speeches for them, and other things. There's other tools to help people. Some guy might be a lot more impressed if you took him into your plant and met 5,000 workers than he ever would be if you give him $1,000. There's all sorts of ways to help guys without money. Now I'm not saying tomorrow I'm going to do away with it.

REFORMS AREN'T IMMINENT

The second reason corporate PAC directors aren't worried about reform is that they see little immediate prospect of a significant proposal passing. They hold this relaxed attitude because despite continuing reform sentiment Congress has not passed any campaign finance reform bill for over a decade. On the one hand, legislation is always being discussed and considered; on the other hand, nothing passes. For example, in 1990 both the House and Senate passed reform measures—but the conference committee that was supposed to resolve the differences between the two bills never met. Once again in 1991 the Senate and the House both passed bills but did not reconcile them, so they didn't even get far enough to be vetoed by President Bush.

This dynamic is a product of two opposing forces. On the one hand, the public strongly supports reform, so members of Congress want to be able to tell the voters that they have sponsored or supported a reform proposal. On the other hand, most members do not in fact want reform because the current system provides major advantages to entrenched incumbents, making them practically invulnerable.[1] Therefore, everybody wants to vote for reform, but almost nobody wants it to pass. If necessary, one house of Congress can pass a bill, confident that the other house will let it die. It has been some years since PAC officials seriously worried that a reform proposal might pass.

"BY THE TIME THEY CHANGE IT, IT'S TOO LATE"

The third and in many ways most interesting reason that PAC officials weren't worried is that "campaign finance reform" or "abolishing PACs" can mean different things to different people. When we asked corporate executives how they would react if PACs were abolished, they interpreted the question differently than we had intended. We meant, "What would you do if you could no longer use campaign money to influence election outcomes and member actions?" They interpreted the question to mean, "Suppose you couldn't use the PAC mechanism to funnel money to candidates. What alternative mechanisms would you use?"

> All that would happen is that a member would say to you, "I want X thousand dollars," and you'd have to get it some other way than through the PAC.

■■■

> If federal level PACs were abolished, we'd still operate at the state level. I think we would give more corporate dollars certainly. That's not something that we do a lot of now.

■■■

> It would be the pits. How many times can you show up at a $2,000 fund-raiser by going around and hitting everybody on the eighth floor for a contribution? There is a limit to what people reasonably can be expected to do.

■■■

> To me there's only two alternatives to PACs—either public financing or going back to the old system where you got the whole company together and put a whole bag of money together and brought it up to the member and said, "Here." By the way, not a bad idea—I'm not sure it was any better or any worse than anything else.

Perhaps the general reaction was most fully and articulately presented in an exchange with one quintessential "good ole boy":

INTERVIEWER: So what would happen if PACs were abolished? What would happen to your job?

PAC DIRECTOR: I'd still have a job. It would take a little different avenue, a different tack. Somebody still has to represent the company. Since you are not going to publish this,* I would suggest that my salary would go up and I would make a lot more personal contributions.

*Taken literally this seems to imply the person believed we would not publish anything. Given this remark, in order to be certain there was no misunderstanding, at the end of the interview we again reviewed the fact that we *did* intend to publish quotes, but not to attribute them to him or his corporation. He confirmed that this was his understanding as well and that in those circumstances he had no objection to being quoted.

There are ways around it. The system is dynamic. By the time they change it, it's too late. . . . I can tell you right now how I can give untold sums of corporate money to anybody in the country that I want to give it to.

INTERVIEWER: You mean you can give it to federal legislators?

PAC DIRECTOR: I can figure out a way to get it in to their phone banks. Give it to their voter registration programs. Anybody who has been involved in this process can do that. You understand what I'm saying?

In this instance, as in many others, the corporate PAC executives had a much better sense of political reality than we did. It didn't even occur to them that we were asking about a utopian system where money didn't dominate politics. They correctly focused on the changes that might actually be implemented, which would alter some specific practices but leave other avenues of influence. If PACs were abolished, they wouldn't stop using money to influence elections; they would collect individual checks from executives "and put a whole bag of money together." Their salaries would increase so they could give the extra as "personal" donations. The corporation would give more at the state level. They would find other ways around the rules—by giving money to "party building" or "voter registration drives."[2]

Piecemeal Reform Won't Work

The dominant view of how campaign finance should operate is a regulatory model. Wealthy individuals and corporations are allowed to use their money in any way they want, unless there is a specific prohibition or regulation. Anything not specifically covered by the rules is permitted. Because money can be used in a million different ways, and because it is very unequally distributed, the people and organizations trying to uphold and enforce existing rules tend to fall behind those looking for ways to evade the rules. Moreover, it is difficult to devise rules that have the intended consequences.[3]

Campaign finance could be thought of as similar to a balloon. If people and PACs pump money into it, it will expand. Regulators occasionally push on the balloon to try to make it go down. With some effort they can push the balloon down in one place—but that makes it pop out farther somewhere else. If people focus only on the area of the balloon that has been pushed in, they conclude the reform has worked.

However, if you get a look at the back of the balloon, it becomes evident that it has popped out even farther somewhere else. This regulatory model of campaign finance reform will not work. It leads to a multiplicative increase in regulations combined with an exponential increase in ways of avoiding the regulations. Some alternative strategy must be found.

The analyses presented earlier in this book indicate why some of the widely discussed piecemeal reforms are unlikely to succeed:

- *Limit the size of individual PAC donations.* The current limit is $5,000 per candidate per election, so a PAC may give $10,000 to a candidate facing both a primary and general election. The intent of both the current law and the proposed reforms is to limit the size of the donation to an amount so small that it can't influence a member's behavior.

  Our chapter 4 on access indicates the misconception underlying this proposal. Even with today's limits a single PAC donation is rarely large enough to make a member of Congress change a vote on a major, visible, contested issue. Therefore, the proposal won't change much in this regard. However, relatively small donations are enough to gain corporate PACs access to members to win "minor" wording changes that the public never hears about. The average corporate PAC donation in 1988 was $925 to House members and $2,472 to senators. Many proposed revisions would not touch these access donations. Moreover, if the limits were pushed to $500 (one-tenth of the current limit), the likely consequence would simply be an expansion of the steering committee approach discussed in chapter 6. Corporations that wanted access would join a member's steering committee, ask ten other corporations to each give the $500 limit, and earn credit with the member for raising $5,000. The total amount corporations gave and members received might not change at all.

- *Limit the amount a candidate may accept from PACs.* This restriction passed the House but not the Senate in 1979, was seriously considered by the Senate in 1986, and passed the Senate in 1991. The House limit would have been $70,000 in 1979 and $275,000 in 1990 (is there a trend here?). No one really knows how this would work out in practice. Presumably it would encourage PACs to make contributions earlier and earlier in the election cycle, so they would get their donation in before members reached their limit. This would favor donations strictly for access purposes; most members would probably reach their limit before the campaign started.

- *Totally ban corporate, labor, and trade association PACs.* This was proposed by President Bush in 1989. Assuming it withstood legal challenges—which is far from certain—its two principal effects would be to hurt Democrats (and thus help Republicans) and to cause a switch from PAC giving (relatively easily monitored) to individual giving (much harder to track).[4] Because most corporate PACs are access oriented, and because the Democrats always control the House and usually the Senate, corporate PACs give almost as much to Democrats as to Republicans. Labor union PACs, on the other hand, strongly favor Democrats. Had Bush's plan been in effect in 1988, it would have cost Democrats $76.2 million, but Republicans only $46.9 million.[5] Republicans have a substantial advantage in raising money from individuals; they hope that corporate PAC donations would be rechanneled into individual donations and that more of these would go to Republican candidates.

- *Set spending limits.* To hold down the cost of campaigns, limits could be set on the total amount a candidate can spend during a campaign. However, the Supreme Court has outlawed spending limits, unless they are part of a plan where candidates voluntarily accept public funding in exchange for agreeing to abide by a spending limit. Even if this hurdle could be overcome (and with the current composition of the Supreme Court that seems unlikely), spending limits without additional changes would turn out to be an incumbent protection program. Incumbents have important built-in advantages—name recognition, a chance to make news through their actions, free postage for congressional business,[6] over $500,000 to hire staff (some of whom will work in the district servicing constituents), and so on. Therefore, in order to beat an incumbent a challenger needs to be able to spend a substantial amount of money. If the cost of campaigns is legally limited at a low figure, incumbents will be virtually impossible to dislodge. This is contrary to what most supporters of this provision probably anticipate.

THE PURPOSE OF THE CURRENT SYSTEM

Every campaign finance system implicitly condones or encourages certain outcomes while prohibiting or discouraging others. "Every way of seeing is also a way of not seeing."[7] Campaign finance proposals draw attention to certain features of the current political system while ignoring others. The underlying basis of each proposal is an assessment of what kind of world is desirable; the variations between proposals reflect differences in people's visions of how society should be organized and governed. These visions are not necessarily articulated or conscious. The explicit rhetoric may offer a strikingly different image of the intent of the proposal. But the place to begin any examination of a campaign finance system is to consider the kind of political order it both creates and requires.

The current system has three main provisions: public disclosure of all donations larger than a certain minimum, prohibitions against any one individual or organization's giving more than a specified amount to a candidate in an election ($1,000 for individuals, $5,000 for PACs), and a limit on the total amount an individual (but not a PAC) can give during an election cycle ($25,000 in total). The limit on the size of a donation is aimed at prohibiting or severely restricting any "special relationship" between a member of Congress and a campaign contributor. Public disclosure serves the same purpose: it must be possible to check the source and use of the money in order to determine whether any special relations are being created. That is, the system does not restrict the power of monied interests to influence government. It does, however, restrict two other sorts of practices. First, it limits the power of an individual or company to control one or more members by making them financially dependent on a single donor. If the existing rules are enforced, no member can be *too* dependent on any particular donor. Therefore, members of Congress never find it in their financial interest to support a single maverick in opposition to the rest of business. This limits the ability of a maverick to use government action to override the market and the private actions of businesses.

Second, this also limits the ability of a member to extort money from a campaign contributor. Since the maximum legal donation is not large, even a donor who feels compelled to contribute can satisfy the obligation with a small amount. President Nixon demanded contributions of $100,000 apiece from major corporations; adjusting for inflation that is more than twenty times today's maximum legal donation.

More important is what this system does *not* try to do—the practices and conditions it does not attempt to regulate. No attempt is made to limit the total amount an organization may give or a candidate may raise and spend. The implicit claim is that it is possible to have enormous economic inequalities but nonetheless allow the use of money to influence politics. This can be done because it is believed that a set of rules about the appropriate uses of money can successfully ensure that inequalities in the economic realm do not influence the political process. Even though the economy is said to require and thrive on inequality, while the polity depends on equal say and representation, no conflict is seen between these two realms and the principles underlying them. We, however, believe this is the key structural contradiction that must be faced by any plan to reform campaign finance, and we therefore address the issue in our next section.

ECONOMY AND POLITY: CONTRADICTORY PRINCIPLES

Our society takes private property, the "free" market, and the buying and selling of anything and everything as givens. We accept the idea of someone owning a book, an idea (through a patent or copyright), a contract for a person's services, an animal, or a tree. With few exceptions, the people (or corporations) who own these have the right to do anything and everything they want with them. If a corporation has the patent on a process that would substantially improve a product but lower company profitability, the corporation is under no obligation to use the patent—or let anyone else use it—even if it would make the world a better place. If you buy a house with a dozen large, pleasant shade trees, many over a hundred years old, it is your "right" to chop them all down as soon as you become the legal owner, with no regard to the effect on the environment, your neighbors, or those who will come after you.

Enamored as we are with buying and selling as the best way to handle virtually any problem, and with private property and the "free" market, these concepts are not considered good policy in the political realm. "The best Congress that money can buy," to use Will Rogers's phrase,[8] is a pretty terrible Congress because some things aren't supposed to be for sale. In fact, it is illegal to sell some things (marijuana but not tobacco or alcohol), and some actions are regarded as noble if done for disinterested motives but are illegal if done for cash. Thus members of Congress are supposed to help their "friends" and constituents by shaping legislation to serve their interests but are prohibited from explicitly offering to sell either a legislative outcome or their best efforts to produce such an outcome. It is similarly illegal to offer to (directly) pay a member of Congress for such services; doing so is called bribery. In the economic marketplace the people with the most money are supposed to have the most impact, but in politics each person is supposed to have one and only one vote, and explicitly buying and selling political influence are taboo. Instead of direct buying and selling, corporate PACs give gifts to members, creating loose but nonetheless binding networks of obligation.

The disjuncture our society creates between politics and economics is at the heart of this book. Economic democracy is regarded as not just impractical but somehow immoral. It is "obvious" that people can't and shouldn't vote to determine how their workplaces are run. The only "efficient" way to operate a "private" enterprise is by having the owners have dictatorial powers; these powers are then used to create bureaucratic systems to control recalcitrant employees.[9] Economic democracy would be the worst form of socialism—hopelessly utopian, totally unworkable. At the same time most people feel it is equally obvious that democracy is the best—in fact, the only acceptable—form of government. In politics, democratic procedures are not regarded as inefficient or utopian; instead they are viewed as imposing certain short-run costs but providing enormous long-run benefits. Virtually everyone in the modern United States firmly holds *both* that the economy must be operated on the basis of "free" ownership of "private" property, with those who have the money in control of all key decisions, *and* that the polity must be based on "one person one vote" with money not allowed to exercise a disproportionate influence.[10]

No contradiction is seen between these two beliefs, held with equal firmness. We, however, argue that these two practices *do* contradict one another; it is difficult or impossible for a society with enormous disparities of wealth and income to maintain equality in politics. As long as people with money are allowed to use it to influence politics, those with the most money will have disproportionate influence both on election campaigns and on the shaping of public policy. The fiction may be maintained that everyone's vote counts equally—in fact, the people with the most wealth may insist on this loudly and vehemently—but the reality is that "money talks," and those who have the gold make the rules. This is the underlying problem that must be confronted by any attempt at campaign finance reform. If this issue is not addressed in some way, the almost certain outcome of any reform is that rather than ending the ability of money to influence politics, one specific practice will be prohibited, and one or more new practices will emerge.

WHAT SHOULD CAMPAIGN FINANCE REFORM AIM TO DO?

When PAC directors answered our question about what they would do if PACs were abolished by offering alternative ways to funnel money to candidates, we accepted those answers. In one case we pressed our interpretation of the question, however. When we finally got it through to the executive what we had in mind, his opposition was clear: "I think the members would be less accessible because I think they might start running it strictly for the votes." That, of course, is precisely the point: for us it is the hope; for him it was the fear.

We prefer a system where members run "strictly for the votes" rather than for the money and are concerned with what the majority of their constituents want, not with the wishes of big contributors. This PAC director opposes such a system, offering two contradictory arguments. On the one hand he argues that members would simply pander to their constituents:

> If members only had to play to the constituency—well, you heard, Bryce and everybody has written about the lowest common denominator in democracy. They were complaining about the same things 100 years ago that we are complaining about today.

On the other hand he argues that members would ignore everyone's wishes—that only the need for money leads members to listen to anyone:

> What happens if PACs disappear and the government pays for the campaigns? Are these guys going to close their doors altogether to the public? How'd you like to be a citizen and try to get to them? That's why guys like me exist. Right? Because Joe Blow can't get in to the guy in office.

Our proposal for campaign finance reform has four principal aims:

1. The primary aim is to do as much as possible to see to it that each individual has *equal representation*. Those with wealth and power should not be able to use this to gain extra influence. We therefore wish to create equality in campaign funding, which will make it more difficult for corporations to use campaign contributions to gain access to or influence over candidates.
2. The system should be as *democratic* as possible. If congressional incumbents are practically unbeatable, then democracy operates

only once a generation when a member dies or chooses to retire. Incumbents today are almost certain to be reelected. Of House incumbents in the post–World War II period 91 percent have won, and in 1988, 98 percent did.[11] Moreover, more than 90 percent of members have run for reelection. Combining the two effects, since the mid-1980s about 90 percent of House members have stayed from one term to the next.[12]

It has not always been so. In the nineteenth century turnover was far higher. The rate of members staying from one term to the next was below 50 percent for seven straight elections beginning in 1842, and above 60 percent for only two elections between 1832 and 1884.[13] The current popular movement for term limitations is an understandable product of this situation, an implicit admission that an incumbent who is allowed to run is virtually unbeatable. Rather than creating a competitive system, term-limitation amendments simply attempt to ensure that open-seat selection happens not just once in a generation but once in a decade.

Any reform of the campaign finance system should aim to increase the number of competitive races. Studies indicate that the problem is not overspending by incumbents but underspending by challengers.[14] In order to run a competitive race, challengers need to be able to spend enough money to get their message out to voters. Challengers who can raise enough money to do so are usually competitive; challengers who are drastically outspent can rarely make the race competitive. In 1988, in better than four out of five races (81.4 percent), one candidate spent more than twice as much as the other. Only 3.2 percent of these races were competitive (that is, decided by margins of ten points or less, for example, 55 percent to 45 percent). In the remaining one out of five races the underfinanced candidate had at least half as much money as the funding leader. A much higher proportion of these races was competitive—about four out of ten (39.1 percent). If challengers have enough money to make their case, they have a chance to make the race competitive. Therefore, a reform proposal needs to ensure adequate funding for challengers.

3. Congress should spend its time on *issues rather than on fundraising*. "Half of all senators surveyed by the Center for Responsive Politics and almost one-quarter of the House members said that the demands of fundraising cut *significantly* into the time they devoted to legislative work. Another 12 percent of the senators and 20 percent of the House members said fundraising had some effect on

legislative time."[15] Moreover, members of Congress should spend time on *major* issues, not writing individual exceptions for actual or potential campaign contributors.

4. The system should *maintain these characteristics over time*. Lots of smart, powerful, and sharp operators will do their best to subvert the system. If they are allowed to do so, they will undermine every positive feature of the reform.

Our goals for campaign finance reform are not shared by corporate executives or most members. Public statements aside, most members don't want to be in competitive races. Corporate personnel think it perfectly appropriate for wealthy individuals and organizations to use money to get additional access and influence. They want members of Congress to raise money privately because then members will provide preferential access to corporations. Senator Rudy Boschwitz (R-Minn.) institutionalized the practice. Those who contributed $1,000 or more received special blue stamps to place on their envelopes; lesser contributions entitled people to other color stamps; and noncontributors had to take their chances. Letters were opened and replied to according to the contribution level, which Boschwitz considers "a nifty idea."[16]

Public Financing

The regulatory model of campaign finance is doomed to failure. As long as our society continues to have vast inequalities of wealth, income, and power, the people with the most money will be able to find ways around restrictive rules. Virtually all current proposals are intended to limit the ways in which money can be funneled into campaigns. It is extremely difficult to do so because however many rules and barriers are erected, the ingenuity of the rich or their hirelings will always find yet another way to evade the regulations. As one PAC director said, "One of the quickest ways to find out more creative ways to spend political money would be to put PACs out of business. I guarantee it."[17] Moreover, there are virtually no meaningful penalties for those caught violating the rules. As a result, the regulators are always one step behind the evaders and shysters.

We propose an alternative approach: cut the Gordian knot of restrictions through public financing of election campaigns. This is not the appropriate place to attempt to provide a complete and detailed blueprint, but our system adds the following basic elements to the rules already in place:

1. All Democrats and Republicans who received their party's nomination to run for Congress would receive public funds for use in the general election campaign, provided that they agreed not to accept any private money and not to use their personal money. This would create more competitive races by guaranteeing that each candidate would have the same amount of money available for the campaign. A version of this system has operated successfully in presidential elections since 1976.[18]

2. The amount of public money provided to each candidate would be $250,000 for House candidates. This is a little more than *half* what was spent by the average *winning* candidate in the 1988 elections. Total spending per *race* would be roughly the same as at present, but instead of the incumbent having a three to one advantage over the challenger,[19] the two candidates would each have the same amount to spend. Incumbents will therefore spend less, and challengers more, than at present.[20]

3. Candidates would not be required to accept public funding, and if they do not take public funding the Supreme Court has said they cannot be required to abide by the spending limit. However, another provision of our proposal would make it impossible for a candidate raising special-interest money to outspend their publicly financed opponent. If the candidate raising private money raised more than the amount normally given through public financing ($250,000 for House candidates), the publicly financed opponent would be given public money to match the privately funded candidate's spending dollar for dollar. Reporting requirements would be changed to prevent privately funded candidates from collecting huge quantities in the last week or two of the campaign and using this last-minute money to buy the election.[21]

   This is a vital element of a workable public finance proposal. It guarantees that candidates who accept public financing can't be outspent by their opponent. No candidate could gain an edge through a superior ability to raise special-interest money. Without this provision, special-interest opponents of reform could simply work to see that the amount available per candidate is very low. If public financing provides less than half of what is needed to run a viable campaign, then anyone relying exclusively on public financing is almost sure to lose. Having successfully subverted meaningful public financing, business will then turn around and say this outcome proves the public opposes public financing and loves special interests.

OBJECTIONS AND ARGUMENTS AGAINST

EXPENSE. The first objection likely to be raised to such a system is expense. The easiest comparison is House general election contests. If every race were contested and every candidate accepted public funding and spent the maximum, our proposal would cost $217.5 million per election (or $108.75 million per year). How can such an expenditure be justified when deficits are high and many valuable programs are underfunded? The cost of our program is less than one-tenth the annual advertising budget for a single corporation, Procter & Gamble.[22] Alternatively, for the cost of one B-2 airplane ($865 million) we could publicly finance House elections until the year 2000.

Under our proposal total campaign spending would be no higher than it is at present. Therefore, the proposal costs nothing from the perspective of U.S. society as a whole. The issue is the effect the proposal would have in redistributing the burden from private sources to taxpayers. However, this argument cuts both ways. We would argue that in the not-very-long-run our proposal *saves* most people money by making it possible to eliminate special-interest privileges. For example, in 1955 corporations paid 27.3 percent of all federal taxes, but in 1989 they paid only 11.0 percent. The reduced contributions by corporations meant that individuals had to pay more. Total federal tax revenue in 1989 was $975 billion. If corporations had paid the same share of taxes in 1989 as in 1955, they would have paid an additional $159 billion, enough in that one year to provide public financing for both House and Senate general elections for more than 300 years.[23]

These savings could be multiplied by eliminating any of a long list of special-interest tax breaks. Moreover, as our example of the Ford Pinto in the last chapter illustrated, many special-interest benefits cost taxpayers "nothing"—at least nothing that shows up in a Treasury statement. The survivors of those burned to death in Pintos, the parents of mutilated and handicapped children, would nonetheless tell you that society paid a cost for the failure to require safe cars. Therefore, for 99 percent of the population our proposal does not cost money; it saves money.

ESCALATING CAMPAIGN COSTS. Many people feel that there is simply too much money in politics and might be concerned that our proposal would lead to spiraling campaign costs. Our proposed public funding will provide about the same amount per race as at present, but people might fear that private money will be pumped in on top of that, leading to ever higher spending levels. We have structured our proposal to prevent this from happening.

Spending levels would stay the same because almost all candidates would accept public funding and therefore would be prohibited from accepting any private money. Candidates would virtually all opt for public funding because candidates using public financing are guaranteed that they will be able to match their special-interest-financed opponents, thus undercutting most of the reason for private fundraising. Although PACs and individual donations would continue to be theoretically possible, general election candidates would not want that money because if they accepted it, they would not be eligible for public financing, and private funding would not enable them to outspend their opponents.[24] Most candidates find fundraising a miserable process, and all find that it takes time away from campaigning. A candidate that relied on private financing would face extra obstacles but gain no advantage.

TAX CHECKOFF. Some will argue that if we are to have public financing, the money should be raised through a voluntary check-off on tax returns. Experience with this system for presidential elections, it will be argued, indicates that the public does not support public financing of elections.

The voluntary check-off system is extraordinary and, in our opinion, intended to subvert public financing. The wording on the tax form makes it appear that the taxpayers must pay an extra dollar, when in fact checking the box does not raise your taxes. *Nothing* else the government funds depends on voluntary check-offs. If the B-2 relied exclusively on taxpayers voluntarily designating money, how many bombers would we build? We propose that public financing of elections be paid for the same way everything else is—out of general revenues. Let voluntary taxpayer check-offs be used for the savings and loan bailout.

RED TAPE. An objection to our proposal might be that it would involve red tape and bureaucracy. In fact, our proposal would reduce the red tape involved in the current system. At present, candidates need to keep careful records of both receipts and expenditures. Receipts are the most difficult to adequately monitor and record, but with public financing there would be no need for a record of receipts. Public funding of presidential candidates has operated successfully with a minimum of paperwork.

WOULD REPUBLICANS USE IT? For over a decade Republicans have steadfastly opposed public financing; the 1991 Senate action on this provision was by a straight party line vote. Republican opposition is important in two senses—in trying to get the proposal passed, an issue dealt with below; and in determining whether Republicans would use public financing if it were available; if they did not, the system would have a partisan character that would undercut its purposes. Experience with the presidential public finance system is reassuring. President Bush and every Republican senator opposed public financing for Senate elections. But every Republican nominee for president has accepted public financing (a total of $250 million since 1976) and Republicans have accepted federal money for their nominating conventions ($32.2 million).[25] Public pronouncements are one thing, action quite another. If the money is available, Republicans will take it.

WILL IT LAST? A final objection is that even if the system sounds good, those with wealth and power will find a way to corrupt it and evade the rules. Constant vigilance will be needed to keep this from happening, and implementation of the system would have to be accompanied by a number of "minor" changes, but the proposal also has a built-in safeguard to keep it effective.

The "minor" changes cover a host of abuses that have grown up. *All* donations to candidates and parties should have to be reported, as should *all* independent expenditures. "Bundling"—the company lobbyist collecting individual checks from executives and presenting them en masse—should be outlawed. The so-called soft money loopholes allowing unlimited contributions for "party building" should be closed. Leadership PACs and charitable organizations (under Section 501[c]3) run by members should be prohibited. Not only should *all* honoraria and speaking fees for members be prohibited, so should *all* free trips and *all* gifts over some truly minimal amount. If members object that they are unable to live on a measly $125,000 a year, they should resign from Congress and make way for someone prepared to make do on such a pittance.

The amount of public subsidy available to candidates should be adjusted for inflation. This will keep funding levels at the same place in real dollars without requiring further congressional action.[26]

So-called independent expenditures would also need to be controlled. This is money not contributed to a candidate but spent by an individual or organization in a supposedly independent effort to influence the election outcome. For example, in 1986 the American Medical Association spent over $200,000 in an attempt to defeat Pete Stark (D-Calif.), chair of the Health Subcommittee of the Ways and Means Committee and author of several bills the AMA opposed. If a candidate whose expenditures were limited confronted a massive "independent expenditure" campaign, they might in effect be drastically outspent. Rules on "independent expenditures" could be tightened in a variety of ways, as was proposed in a Senate bill[27] passed on May 23, 1991, by a vote of fifty-six to forty-two. The most effective safeguard built into our proposal, however, is simply that the candidate will have a substantial amount of money available to reply.[28]

Perhaps the most important "minor" change is a restructuring of the enforcement mechanism. The Federal Election Commission has become a joke, unwilling or unable to uphold the law. For example, presidential candidates have spending limits for each state primary. In 1988 in Iowa, the Democratic winner, Richard Gephardt (D-Mo.), exceeded his spending limit by almost $500,000, and the Republican winner, Robert Dole (R-Kan.) exceeded his limit by $306,000. It was more than three years later before the FEC completed its audit of these campaigns—long after the presidential nominations were decided.[29] The FEC is often unwilling to even *investigate* complaints.[30] Abuses need to be exposed to public scrutiny even if they ultimately go unpunished. It should not take a majority of votes to pursue an investigation but only a one-third minority.

A new system needs to be implemented where party loyalists (who invariably vote a straight party line, leading to a tie vote and no action) are replaced by people committed to upholding the law. We need commissioners prepared to take abuses seriously, act swiftly, impose penalties, and seek criminal sanctions. If corrupting Congress and the democratic system isn't a serious offense, what is?

THIRD PARTIES. Another objection to our proposal focuses on what happens to third-party candidates. Third-party candidates are a relatively minor problem, simply because there are so few. Although the campaign finance system should not erect additional obstacles to independent candidates, neither is it required to provide them advantages they have never before had. Probably the best system would simply be to say third-party candidates do not qualify in advance for public support, but if they receive 5 percent or more of the vote they are entitled to retroactive funding (as happened with John Anderson in the 1980 presidential election), and any third party that won 5 percent or more of the vote in a race is entitled to funding in the next race.

ARGUMENTS FOR

The arguments in favor of this system are more powerful but may be more briefly presented. Under this system elections would be far more competitive than they are today since the two candidates would spend equal amounts. Challengers would still have less name recognition than incumbents, but $250,000 is enough to mount a credible campaign.[31] In campaigns today, the cost of raising money is typically 20 to 30 percent of total spending.[32] With public finance there would be no fundraising costs, so the amount we propose is equivalent to $300,000 or $325,000 under today's system.

Special interests could no longer use campaign money as a way to increase their access and win benefits for themselves. Not only would members of Congress not be indebted for past donations, but members also would know they would never need to depend on a future donation and could never gain a campaign advantage by soliciting or accepting such a donation. Corporations would continue to have substantial clout based on their general wealth, power, and respectability, their ability to maintain a staff of lobbyists, their advocacy advertising, their networks, connections, and friendships. But *one* of their major special-interest weapons would have been taken away.

The guarantee of public funding for campaigns would give members of Congress more time to spend on legislation and keeping in touch with constituents who are *not* campaign contributors. As one of the two PAC directors who supported public financing said:

> I am looking to take off the back of the politician this terrible concern he has of raising money. He spends too much time raising money. He spends too much time thinking about raising money. And I think if you turn around and gave him that time back—even if he didn't use it for legislation—even if he used it to think—we'd all be better off. When I first came to Washington as a kid, Congress wasn't in from July through January.

They closed up for the whole summer months. These guys went home and got to see their people and thought a lot more about what was going on, and they came back better people for it. Now they have to spend all their time raising money. They have to spend all their time involved in enormous amounts of work that are not productive.

NEW RULES FOR PRIMARIES

Public funding for primary candidates would be much more problematic. The seemingly insuperable problem is devising a way by which only "serious" candidates could qualify for funding, so that running for office does not become a way to receive a government handout. Although full public funding for the primaries would be desirable, absent some qualifying mechanism it would be subject to abuse. Senator Mitch McConnell of Kentucky, the Republican floor leader in the battle against the Senate Election Ethics Act of 1991, argued against public funding—any public funding—on these grounds:

> If we extend [public financing to congressional] races, every crackpot who got up in the morning and looked in the mirror and said, "gee, I think I see a congressman" is going to be able to reach into the federal cookie jar and get some of those tax dollars.[33]

McConnell's complaint would be true only if full public financing were available to any candidate. Our proposal restricts funding to those candidates who not only qualify for the ballot but *win* the primary and thus a major party's nomination. Although this still includes a fair number of crackpots—as does Congress itself—it certainly restricts their number.

On the other hand, if unlimited private fundraising is allowed in the primary, this could be the opening wedge for the return of massive amounts of special-interest money. For the primary campaigns it therefore seems necessary to have a strictly regulated system of private fundraising with federal matching funds. In addition, any candidate found to have violated the rules for the primary would not be eligible for any public funding in the general election.

The fundraising rules we propose for primary candidates are a combination of measures that have been suggested by others as general election solutions:

1. No candidate may raise or accept any money until six months before the primary.
2. Contributions of $200 or less from individuals living within the election district will be matched by the federal government dollar for dollar. To be eligible for matching funds, a candidate would first have to qualify for the ballot and raise some threshold amount (say $10,000) in small individual within-district contributions.
3. In order to be eligible for public financing in the general election or for matching dollars in the primary, candidates must accept spending limits in the primary. The spending limit for *incumbents* in the primaries would be one-fifth of the general election limit ($50,000 for House races, varying amounts for Senate races depending on the state's population). Nonincumbent candidates would be allowed to spend an additional 50 percent (for a total of $75,000 in House races).[34] The reasoning is that incumbents begin with a substantial advantage in their own party's primary and therefore need to spend less. The additional spending by non-incumbents also helps increase their name recognition and thereby helps level the playing field. If this leads to additional incumbent turnover, so be it. In current circumstances, increased turnover hardly seems the greatest danger.
4. Any money left unspent at the end of the primary must be turned over to the federal treasury.

Despite all the attempted safeguards, these primary rules still make it possible for special interests to exert some leverage. However, the leverage is enormously reduced. Most viable candidates would find it relatively easy to raise $37,500 in small within-district contributions; with matching funds, that is the maximum they can spend. This is a trivial amount by the standards of today's campaigning.[35] Candidates who raised all their money in small within-district contributions would have a public relations advantage: they could argue they were not beholden to special interests. We predict most candidates would do so. Even though PACs would continue to exist, most candidates would refuse to accept their money, so PACs would have nothing to do with their funds. Candidates would hold down their spending during the primary in order to maintain eligibility for public financing in the general election.

Be Realistic

The reform plan we have proposed would eliminate or drastically reduce the impact of special-interest money and would substantially increase competitive elections and thus turnover among members of Congress. But is this realistic? Would Congress ever enact such a reform? Dick Cheney, at the time a Republican representative from Wyoming and later Bush's Secretary of Defense, offered a memorable no: "If you think this Congress, or any other, is going to set up a system where someone can run against them on equal terms at government expense, you're smoking something you can't buy at the corner drugstore."[36]

Cheney's view is probably correct: it seems impossible to get Congress to pass these reforms. But the 1960s slogan is also correct: "Be realistic—demand the impossible." The campaign finance reforms we propose here may be almost impossible to achieve, but anything less cannot realistically be expected to solve the problem. The politically "realistic" changes will provide temporary improvement but permit the rapid emergence of new abuses. It may take companies a little while to figure out some loopholes and get them regularized, but they will definitely do so.

Our proposal *is* unrealistic in the sense that at present members of Congress, political parties, corporate executives, and other power brokers are all likely to oppose it. But the proposal is far from utopian. The system actually in use for presidential elections is fairly close to what we are proposing for congressional elections.[37]

Public opinion, on this issue as on many others, is confused and contradictory. Essentially all surveys find profound distrust of PACs and the influence of money on Congress:

> A 1985 ABC News–*Washington Post* poll showed 70 percent of Americans agreed with the statement, "Most Members of Congress care more about special interests than they care about people like you." A 1985 Gallup poll found that 79 percent of those surveyed completely or mostly agreed that "Money is the most important factor influencing public policies."[38]

However, when it comes to public financing of elections, the way the issue is posed has a dramatic impact on "public opinion." The Gallup poll has consistently found more people favoring than opposing public financing, with the single exception of December 1982 (when a very small majority opposed it). Their question explicitly ties public financing to a ban on all private contributions.[39] The AMA conducted a series of polls with a question that makes no mention of banning private contributions; they consistently found a substantial majority opposed to public finance. Given the way the issue has generally been posed to the public, we are impressed that a reasonably fair question (the Gallup poll version) demonstrates consistent public support for public funding.

However, it would be a mistake to believe that on this issue, or most others, Congress will act in response to public opinion. As this book has argued, some people and organizations have vastly more power than others, and Congress responds to this power far more than it does to public opinion. Environmental issues show that even when public opinion is exceptionally strong and clear, when the public strongly backs environmentalism no matter how biased the wording of the question,[40] Congress and the president are still more responsive to corporate interests than to public views. We can hardly suppose that it will be otherwise for campaign financing.

Victory will be achieved, here as on other issues, not through the use of the access process and lobbying for minor changes, but only by the creation of a social movement that pressures power brokers through actual and potential disruptions. A losing strategy: reformers deferentially ask for appointments to meet with members of Congress, then use meetings to argue ordinary voters should receive as much consideration as the rich and powerful.[41] Far more likely to succeed:

- Guerilla theater events where poor constituents try to crash the $1,000-a-plate dinners for corporate lobbyists
- People attending a member's public appearances and reading off the names of campaign contributors, ideally accompanied by a list of the legislation and amendments the contributors are seeking
- Newspapers and periodicals running stories listing the language of amendments targeting specific companies, identifying the members who asked for the change and their relationship with the corporation or industry that would benefit

If a campaign for real reform builds major public support, business will fight back on two fronts. First, it will mount a campaign to change public opinion. Corporations will commission in-depth studies to find out what parts of the proposal have the most and least support and then will focus as much attention as possible on those aspects that make the public uneasy. Academic experts will be hired to prove that the proposals wouldn't work. The mass media will be filled with accounts explaining that public financing means that you, the taxpayer, will be forced to pay for mud-slinging and negative campaign commercials. Members will loudly insist they are happy to see anybody at anytime and will be photographed seeking the opinions of poor and middle-income constituents. Every attempt will be made to undercut support for reform through what Domhoff[42] identifies as the ideology process.

At the same time business will undertake a second approach, developing "minor" modifications that sound harmless but in practice gut the proposal. They will open loopholes that can be expanded at a later time when public attention is focused on other issues.[43] Corporations will aim to create a system where candidates need special-interest money because it provides benefits not available in any other way, either the margin of victory in a competitive election or an increase in the member's effective personal income.

Consequences

If our proposal were passed it would lead to three major changes—in the character of Congress as an institution, in the politics of the candidates elected, and in the power of business.

THE CHARACTER OF CONGRESS

The slowest and most minimal change would probably be in the character of Congress. In the current situation, Congress serves as a peculiar sort of ombuds office. Senator William Cohen estimates that "as much as forty percent of staff time is spent in casework."[44] Rather than spending their time on formulating legislation or evaluating general policy, members use political criteria—especially past or future campaign contributions—to make a host of relatively minor administrative decisions. Despite the generic use of the term *special interests*, a large majority of these decisions are made for, and at the behest of, business. In some cases the administrator at the regulatory agency or executive office is "persuaded" to adopt the member's interpretation—a persuasion that often depends on fear their agency's budget will be cut if they don't go along. In other cases what ought to be a minor administrative decision is written into law, an extremely clumsy approach that provides little flexibility to adapt to changing circumstances. This is not the purpose for which Congress was intended, and it is a perfectly awful way to decide regulatory and policy details.

A large proportion of all these political interventions into administrative decisions are made in response to (or in hopes of) business campaign contributions. If members knew they could rely on public funding, this would remove one major incentive to engage in this process. With a little luck, over time this might return Congress to the job of writing legislation and formulating general policy. At present, the typical congressional contest is decided on the basis of who is best at delivering pork barrels and putting in the fix; the edge almost invariably goes to the incumbent, whose seniority provides extra leverage. If Congress focused on policy issues rather than minor details, election contests might be decided on the basis of candidates' stands on the issues and on whether they had any fresh ideas to contribute. In this case, quite a few current members of Congress would be in deep trouble, but the country as a whole would be better off.[45]

POLITICAL CHANGE

Public financing also would lead to a change in who would win elections and in the political stands they would take. In our interviews we found corporate PAC directors believe virtually every member of Congress is prepared to "be reasonable" and "help them out." If there are members with a different view, they have either learned to keep quiet about it, or they have been effectively silenced and are generally unable to interfere with the special benefits corporations win through the access process. Members go along in order to raise money themselves and to keep corporations from sending floods of money to their challengers.

The conventional wisdom is that public funding would help Democrats and hurt Republicans. Certainly support for such proposals is more common among Democrats than Republicans, an indication of their own assessments of who would benefit. Perhaps this is so, but we would offer two important qualifications. First, the proposal we outline would do a great deal to make elections more competitive and hence to increase turnover in Congress. Since a substantial majority of members are Democrats, any proposal that increases turnover is likely to help Republicans.

Second, if Democrats were the main beneficiaries, they would not necessarily be the Democrats currently in Congress. As G. William Domhoff, Walter Dean Burnham, Thomas Byrne Edsall,[46] and others have argued, today's Democratic party has a split personality. Republicans get lots of money from business and virtually none from labor, women's groups, or environmentalists. Democrats, by contrast, get significant amounts of money from business as well as labor. In 1988, Republicans received $29.7 million from corporations and only $2.7 million from labor. Democrats received $26.4 million from corporations and $32.7 million from labor. As a consequence, the Democratic party has a split personality, and business (but not labor) has leverage over *both* major parties. The advantages of public funding would be greatest for those Democrats not able to raise money from business. Public funding would be of much more benefit to candidates like Jesse Jackson or Paul Wellstone than it would be to Charles Robb or Lloyd Bentsen. As a consequence, the character of the Democratic party might shift, and business-oriented Democrats might find themselves a beleaguered minority.

BUSINESS POWER

Finally, public funding of congressional campaigns would reduce the power of business. Not eliminate it: although campaign finance is *one* important tool business uses to influence politics, it is not the only one. If full public funding were instituted and all loopholes were plugged, establishing a level playing field for campaign finance, business would still have a privileged position. Large corporations would continue to

1. Dominate the economy and be able to make hundreds of key decisions influencing people's lives (and therefore, their votes)
2. Fund think tanks to prepare analyses and reports advancing a business point of view
3. Collect and provide information that the government doesn't have (often information that business fights to keep the government from getting)
4. Be able to hold out the prospect of lucrative future employment, for the member or key staff aides
5. Have large staffs of lobbyists
6. Directly communicate with stockholders
7. Control access to employees for political and other purposes

8. Engage in advocacy advertising
9. Frustrate policies by refusing to cooperate

And in a host of other ways, they would continue to shape the character of the society—the options available, the costs and benefits associated with them.

If corporations would continue to be so powerful, is there any point in fighting for campaign finance reform? Is it possible to win against so much might? Even if we win, would anything really change? The fact that these questions need to be addressed is one of the strongest indications of business hegemony. Once people believe that it isn't possible to change the system and that the struggle to do so can lead only to grief and frustration, the power structure has won more than half the battle.[47]

Real social change is possible. In the early 1960s, poor and vulnerable African-Americans transformed Southern race relations. Thousands of nameless people put their lives on the line; many made enormous sacrifices. Their struggles have not (yet) brought equality, but they did end the Southern racial caste system, and they brought a resurgence of black pride and awareness. A similar story could be told of the women's movement—which itself owes a considerable debt to the black movement.

A less dramatic struggle more directly linked to corporate power makes the same point. In the early 1960s auto safety was presented as depending entirely on safe drivers. Ralph Nader raised the heretical idea that perhaps cars were also a cause of accidents—and had the data to prove it. General Motors responded with a vicious campaign, even hiring detectives to dig up dirt on his private life.

Did Ralph Nader's campaign totally transform U.S. society and the power of business? No. Did it have any real effect on people's lives? Absolutely. In 1965, for every 100 million miles driven, 5.3 people died in automobile accidents. If that rate had still applied in 1988, an additional fifty thousand people would have died in auto accidents.

People sometimes argue that such reforms make the system more stable and resistant to change. Perhaps that is true in some instances. In other instances what Andre Gorz called a "nonreformist reform"[48] provides immediate benefits to people *and* makes it easier to win future reforms. Did the auto safety campaign Nader launched produce a significant change in the way people think about business? Yes. Did it make people more or less willing to consider additional reforms? Obviously much more willing.

We would argue our campaign finance proposal is also a "nonreformist reform." It proposes a reform that can be won and that if won will substantially weaken business power. By itself, will it be enough to transform American society? No. Will it have an impact? Yes. Will the end of corporate campaign contributions and the emergence of public financing make it easier or more difficult to make future political changes? Clearly easier. Will continued struggle be necessary to elect good people and to fight business power? Obviously. Will electoral politics be enough? No—business exercises power on many different fronts; that power must be opposed on every front.

APPENDIX

Table A.1   *All Corporate PACs That Gave at Least 10 Percent of Their Contributions to Democratic Challengers during the Election Cycles from 1976 to 1988.*

Name	1976	1978	1980	1982	1984	1986	1988
American Family						10.16%	
Archer Daniels Midland				11.25%		14.33%	
Beverly Health					10.19%	19.08%	
Chrysler						12.64%	
Coastal						14.49%	
Coca-Cola	10.20%					10.68%	
Enserch Corporation						10.84%	
E. F. Hutton						10.16%	
Federal Citizenship						12.47%	
First Boston						15.19%	
Florida Power & Light						16.94%	
IBP Inc.							10.50%
Jim Walter Corporation						10.16%	
Joseph E. Seagram & Sons				16.26%		12.62%	
Kerr-Mcgee						15.19%	
MCA						14.24%	
National Medical Enterprises					11.83%	12.10%	
Northwestern Bell Telephone					11.40%		
Occidental Petroleum						12.22%	
Shearson Lehman Hutton						10.27%	
Southern Bell Telephone						14.20%	
Texas Eastern			10.23%				
Warner Communication						10.18%	
Yellow Freight System					12.64%		

Source: Federal Election Commission.

Table A.2   All Corporate PACs That Gave at Least 30 Percent of Their Contributions to Republican Challengers during the Election Cycles from 1976 to 1988.

Name	1976	1978	1980	1982	1984	1986	1988
Akzona			47.88%				
Alcoa			32.74%		42.86%		
American Cyanamid			53.71%				
Amoco	33.48%		44.98%				
Armco			41.14%				
Babcock & Wilcox			31.84%				
Bechtel			44.29%				
Belden		31.15%	46.75%				
Blue Bell			51.34%				
Boise Cascade			35.20%				
Brownbuilders			47.97%				
Broyhill Furniture			34.48%				
Burlington Industries			35.47%				
Cargill			53.09%				
Carolina Power & Light			37.38%				
Cities Service			46.12%				
Clark Equipment			55.00%		55.26%		
Combustion Engineering			37.01%				
Conoco			39.34%				
Consumers Power Company			34.62%				
Cooper Industries			52.56%		38.19%		32.09%
Coors Beer	32.39%		71.63%	57.32%	46.17%		36.38%
Dart & Kraft		37.70%	59.96%				
Diamond Shamrock			51.18%				

Table A.2 (continued)

Name	1976	1978	1980	1982	1984	1986	1988
Dow Chemical #1			38.00%				
Dow Chemical #2			45.65%				
Dow Chemical #3			65.45%	34.08%	38.27%		
Dow Chemical #4			51.08%		33.12%		
Dresser Industries			39.04%				
Eaton			57.46%	36.62%	48.16%		30.61%
El Paso			33.71%				
Eli Lilly			43.49%				
Exxon			41.34%				
E. F. Hutton			43.75%				
Flowers	45.41%		70.47%	33.39%	50.11%		47.76%
Fluor			47.99%				
Georgia-Pacific			41.68%				
Getty Oil			61.27%				
Globe			43.29%				
Greyhound			34.13%				
Gulf Resources & Chemical			46.43%				
Halliburton			44.27%		31.95%		
Harris Corporation			59.03%				
Holiday Inns			36.88%				
Honeywell			54.28%				
International Harvester (Navistar)			32.94%				
J. G. Boswell			42.29%		32.14%		
J. P. Stevens							
Kennecott			42.04%				

224

Table A.2 (continued)

Name	1976	1978	1980	1982	1984	1986	1988
K-Mart			40.35%				
Litton Industries			38.88%				
L. M. Berry			64.49%	33.60%	34.86%		
McDonald's			40.02%				
Malone & Hyde			49.49%				
Mapco			38.29%				
Marriott			41.50%				
Mead			31.42%				
Merck			47.14%				
Merrill Lynch			37.75%				
Midland				31.10%			
Minnesota Mining & Manufacturing		34.60%	41.37%				
Mobil Oil			47.50%				
Morrison-Knudsen			67.11%				
Motorola			35.94%				
Mustang Oil			45.95%				
Nabisco			35.31%				
NL Industries			31.26%	33.65%	30.07%	32.57%	31.68%
North American Coal							
Occidental Petroleum			31.22%				
Olin			44.60%				
Peabody Coal Company			47.92%				
Pennzoil			35.44%				
Reader's Digest			59.10%				
Safeway Stores			80.60%				

Table A.2 (continued)

Name	1976	1978	1980	1982	1984	1986	1988
Sante Fe International			68.85%		39.18%		
Schering-Plough			51.10%				
Sears			31.65%				
Security Corporation			33.70%				
Square D			52.41%				
Standard Oil of Ohio			45.66%	33.37%			
Stauffer Chemical			44.27%				
Steak & Ale Restaurants			58.25%	32.04%			
Sun Oil	32.44%		36.40%		30.79%		
Tenneco			51.01%				
Texaco	32.20%		30.19%				
Texas Oil & Gas Corp.			88.41%	52.38%			
Texas Power & Light			33.12%				
Union Camp			34.39%				
Union Carbide			39.50%				
Union Oil	38.22%		49.65%				
Weyerhaeuser			36.02%				

Source: Federal Election Comission.

NOTES

■■■

Chapter 1. Money Changes Everything

1. Greider, "Whitewash: Is Congress Conning Us on Clean Air?" p. 40.
2. Ibid.
3. Kriz, "Dunning the Midwest," p. 895.
4. Ibid.
5. Quoted in Greider, "Whitewash," p. 40.
6. Ibid., p. 41.
7. Kriz, "Politics at the Pump," p. 1328.
8. See chapter 4 for evidence bearing on how Waxman might have been persuaded. Information in this paragraph is from Kriz, "Politics at the Pump," pp. 1328–1329.
9. Why can't industry just come out and name its groups "Polluters for Profit" or the "Coalition for Acid Rain Preservation" (CARP)? All quotes in this paragraph are from Matlack, "It's Round Two in Clean Air Fight," p. 226.
10. Babcock and Dewar, "Keating Fallout: Senators Draw Own Lines on When to Intervene," p. A17.
11. Matlack, "It's Round Two," p. 227.
12. Kranish, "House Panel to Probe Waiver for Quayle Aide," p. 17.
13. Ibid.
14. Kranish, "Quayle Aide's Firm Is Linked to Pollution," p. 4.
15. Edsall, "The Changing Shape of Power: A Realignment in Public Policy," p. 279.
16. Magleby and Nelson, *The Money Chase: Congressional Campaign Finance Reform,* p. 36.
17. Boschwitz, quoted in Jackson, *Honest Graft: Big Money and the American Political Process,* pp. 251–252.
18. Boschwitz's problem was that his large campaign fund discouraged all the credible Democratic challengers; instead he faced the incredible Paul Wellstone. Wellstone was helped by scandal in the governor's race (where the Republican nominee was accused of sexually molesting a child) and various blunders by Boschwitz. Wellstone was also able to make the

difference in campaign funds into an issue, perhaps an indication that Boschwitz erred in admitting (however secretly) he would use money as a weapon.

19. *National Journal,* "Money and Politics: A Special Report," p. 1448.

20. Ibid., pp. 1462, 1460.

21. Quoted in Jackson, *Honest Graft,* p. 244.

22. Quoted in Wilkinson, "Rules of the Game: The Senate's Money Politics," p. 33.

23. In 1976, 48 percent of House members' campaign receipts came from individual contributions of less than $500; in 1988, only 27 percent did (*National Journal,* "Money and Politics").

24. For the most definitive statement of the rules regulating PACs and campaign finance see Federal Election Commission, "Campaign Guide for Corporations and Labor Organizations" and *Code of Federal Regulations,* Volume 11: *Federal Elections.* For analyses of the history of the modern campaign finance laws see Epstein, "Business and Labor under the Federal Election Campaign Act of 1971," and Sabato, *PAC Power: Inside the World of Political Action Committees.*

25. Ahlkvist, "The Hard Facts on the Soft Money Fatcats of the 1988 Presidential Election: Rethinking Campaign Finance and Capitalist Class Conflict."

26. *National Journal,* "Money and Politics," p. 1470.

27. Ibid., p. 1459.

28. Since senators have six-year terms, they might seem more insulated from the pressures to raise money, but the advantages of long Senate terms are counterbalanced by the increased possibility of a hotly contested race.

29. A statistical measure, R squared, shows the extent to which corporate donations correlate with trade association contributions. The R squared between the amount of money general election candidates receive from corporate PACs and the amount they receive from trade-membership-health association PACs is .79. The R squared between the amount received from corporate PACs and the amount received from labor PACs is .04.

30. Quoted in Alexander, *Money in Politics,* p. 157.

31. In theory a corporation could ideologically support liberals. None of the largest did so.

32. Our research indicates that this simple measure is highly correlated with various more sophisticated measures. See, for instance, Clawson and Neustadtl, "Interlocks, PACs, and Corporate Conservatism"; Clawson, Neustadtl, and Bearden, "The Logic of Business Unity: Corporate Contributions to the 1980 Congressional Elections."

33. Clawson and Neustadtl, "Interlocks, PACs, and Corporate Conservatism"; Clawson, Neustadtl, and Bearden, "The Logic of Business Unity"; Clawson and Su, "Was 1980 Special? A Comparison of 1980 and 1986

Corporate PAC Contributions"; Neustadtl, "Interest-Group PACsmanship: An Analysis of Campaign Contributions, Issue Visibility, and Legislative Impact"; Neustadtl and Clawson, "Corporate Political Groupings:
Does Ideology Unify Business Political Behavior?"; Neustadtl, Scott, and
Clawson, "Class Struggle in Campaign Finance? Political Action Committee Contributions in the 1984 Elections"; Su, Clawson, and Neustadtl,
"The Coalescence of Corporate Conservatism from 1976 to 1980: The
Roots of the Reagan Revolution"; Su, Clawson, and Neustadtl, "Corporate PACs and Conservative Realignment: Comparison of 1980 and
1984."

34. To select this sample of 309 PACs, we sorted all corporate PACs for each
election by amount of contribution from largest to smallest. We computed
total corporate PAC contributions and then started down our list of PACs
until we had included enough corporate PACs to account for 60 percent
of all the money contributed by corporate PACs in that election. If a
corporation qualified for the sample in any one year, we analyzed its
behavior for all years, because one of the points of interest was whether
some corporations became more or less active over this period. Thus the
PACs in our sample always accounted for more than two-thirds of all
corporate PAC money in every year but 1988, when they contributed
64.7 percent of all corporate PAC money.

35. Fifty-seven percent are in manufacturing and 43 percent in the service
sector. Forty-five percent are headquartered in the Sunbelt and 55 percent in the Frostbelt. In 1984, fifty-two had defense contracts of $100
million or more, including McDonnell Douglas with $8.8 billion and
General Dynamics with $7.4 billion.

36. These PACs did not have large enough 1988 donations to qualify for our
sample, but in some previous year they contributed considerably more,
and a company that qualifies for any one year is maintained in the sample
throughout the period.

37. Most people expect corporations to heavily favor Republicans and are
surprised by the bipartisan character of corporate contributions. See
chapters 3 and 4 below for a discussion of this.

38. The manufacturing-service split was 55 to 45 percent for interviewed
corporations and 57 to 43 percent for the entire sample of large corporate
PACs. The Sunbelt-Frostbelt split was 47 to 53 percent for interviews
and 45 to 55 percent for the larger sample.

39. A further consideration in our sample selection was economic feasibility:
although we worked to include corporations from around the country, we
also tried to reduce travel costs by interviewing several corporations based
in the same region.

40. This is reasonably good for an average survey but excellent for a survey
of PAC directors. For example, Larry Sabato's highly regarded *PAC
Power: Inside the World of Political Action Committees* is based on a mail

survey with a response rate of 29 percent. A number of business associations (including the Chamber of Commerce, Business Industry Political Action Committee [BIPAC], and National Association of Business Political Action Committees) conduct a joint survey each election; their response rate is consistently under 25 percent.

41. This reluctance generally translated to being hard to reach; they were perennially "on another line" and did not return our calls. Once we managed to talk to the person, we usually were granted an interview. Almost no one explicitly refused to be interviewed, although sometimes we couldn't arrange a time that fit both their schedule and ours. They typically checked to be sure we had solid credentials and that we were not affiliated with any advocacy group. A few were happy to talk with us; most seemed reluctant but agreed to be interviewed, unless they could find a convincing reason why they would be unavailable.

42. Thus we will not reveal the names of the people or corporations interviewed.

43. For example, occasionally a PAC officer would say, "As the 149th largest corporate PAC, we feel. . . ." We might change this to, "As about the 150th largest corporate PAC, we feel. . . ."

44. Including the use of swear words; truck drivers aren't the only people who use such language. In a half-dozen cases we have created a generic statement and set it in quotation marks. All such instances are clearly identified as such.

45. Occasionally during interviews people would say some version of, "Don't quote me on that." These statements meant, "Don't quote me by name. Don't identify my company." When we were in any doubt about this, we checked this at the end of the interview. In a few instances executives asked us to turn off the tape recorder so they could make comments completely off the record. Unfortunately we can't report those remarks.

46. Their views on this, as on other issues, are sometimes complicated and contradictory, and at other points in the same interview the person might take a different position.

47. Lukes, *Power: A Radical View.*

48. Eismeier and Pollock, "The Retreat from Partisanship: Why the Dog Didn't Bark in the 1984 Election."

49. Wartenberg, *The Forms of Power: From Domination to Transformation,* pp. 66–67.

50. Ibid., p. 74.

51. Crystal, *In Search of Excess: The Overcompensation of American Executives.*

52. In Japan CEOs earn an average salary of $300,000, or seventeen times as much as workers earn.

53. Quoted in Phillips, *The Politics of Rich and Poor: Wealth and the American Electorate in the Reagan Aftermath,* p. 32.

54. Gramsci, *Selections from "The Prison Notebooks of Antonio Gramsci."*

55. Harding, "Reconstructing Order through Action: Jim Crow and the Southern Civil Rights Movement."

56. Or if talking to whites in circumstances where they felt secure in articulating their real feelings.

57. Friedan, *The Feminine Mystique*.

58. Although tenure is often understood to guarantee lifetime employment, this has to be qualified considerably. Tenure is a strong (but not absolute) guarantee against being fired for voicing unpopular views. Dismissal for cause is always possible; tenure does not protect teachers who fail to meet their classes or are convicted of malfeasance. The most serious limit to tenure, however, is (appropriately enough for this book) financial. Colleges and universities occasionally lay off tenured faculty for budgetary reasons.

59. Bednash, *The Relationship between Access and Selectivity in Tenure Review Outcomes*.

60. At highly competitive institutions, including the Universities of Massachusetts and Maryland, tenure is based primarily on publishing. Being a good (or outstanding) teacher by itself would never be enough to win tenure, unless supported by an "acceptable" level of scholarly productivity.

61. Any junior faculty member who expressed contempt for this process and refused to play the game or who publicly identified senior faculty members as outdated or ineffective would be even more likely to be terminated.

Chapter 2. Raising Money and Running the PAC

1. Thayer, *Who Shakes the Money Tree? American Campaign Financing Practices from 1789 to the Present*, p. 25.

2. Ibid., p. 50.

3. Alexander, *Financing the 1960 Election; Financing the 1964 Election; Financing the 1968 Election*.

4. Jackson, *Broken Promise: Why the Federal Election Commission Failed*, p. 40.

5. Alexander, *Financing the 1972 Election*, especially chapters 3, 12, and 13; Koenig, *Social Networks and the Political Role of Big Business*.

6. Epstein, *Corporations, Contributions, and Political Campaigns: Federal Regulation in Perspective*, p. 74.

7. *Federal Register*, vol. 40, no. 233, December 3, 1975; dissent by commissioners Harris and Tiernan, quoting the original act. Subsequent quotations are also from this dissent.

8. *New York Times*, October 15, 1975, p. 10.

9. Neither the original legislation nor FEC rules use the term *political action committee* or *PAC;* they are referred to as "separate segregated funds."

10. *New York Times*, November 8, 1975, p. 30.

11. Gale Research Company, *Contemporary Authors*, p. 517; *Biographical*

Directory of the United States Congress 1774–1989, p. 1858; *New York Times*, February 16, 1963, p. 4; December 29, 1963, p. 17; November 4, 1964, p. 4.

12. *New York Times*, November 21, 1975, p. 42; *Washington Post*, November 19, 1975; pp. A1, A7; *Wall Street Journal*, February 10, 1976, p. 1; *Newsweek*, December 1, 1975, p. 80.

13. Sabato, *PAC Power*, p. 12; Epstein, "Business and Labor under the Federal Election Campaign Act of 1971," p. 116.

14. Under FEC rules, if the prizes are available only to PAC contributors, the corporation may pay the full cost of the prizes, provided that the solicitation brings in at least three times as much as the prizes cost. Thus if a corporation offered $50,000 in prizes, it would have to raise $150,000 in PAC contributions. If it failed to do so, the PAC would have to reimburse the corporation for part of the cost of the prizes. However, in the case described above, participation in the sweepstakes was theoretically open to everyone in the corporation, whether or not they contributed to the PAC (even though the sweepstakes was closely tied to PAC solicitation). Therefore, there was no limit on the amount the corporation could spend for sweepstakes prizes.

15. That is, it is illegal to have a system where union member donations go into the PAC unless the member specifically requests this not happen.

16. Corporations may legally solicit nonmanagerial employees, but in practice virtually no corporation does so since such solicitations are subject to a number of additional regulations and restrictions. Many corporations do not even solicit all managers: some began by soliciting only top officers, and a number solicit only those earning over a certain amount, such as $50,000.

17. Dalton, *Men Who Manage: Fusions of Feeling and Theory in Administration;* Kanter, *Men and Women of the Corporation*, pp. 59–67; Lorber, "Trust, Loyalty, and the Place of Women in the Informal Organization of Work"; Smith, *Managing in the Corporate Interest.*

18. The person interviewed was proud of his company's record and insisted that it "did not use more, shall we say, persuasive techniques" the way some companies do.

19. Note that these are the participation rates for those actually solicited. Companies that solicit only top managers often have very high rates. Another company with an equally high rate among top managers might also solicit all lower-level managers, have a low participation rate among that group, and therefore report a midrange overall rate, even though it was raising more money than if it solicited only top managers.

20. Corporations could also bypass the PAC mechanism and give directly out of their treasuries. Although it is illegal for corporations to directly contribute their own money to candidates for federal office, in many states it is legal to give to candidates for state and local offices. It is also

legal for corporations to use their own money to contribute to political parties.

21. This is the amount raised by the PAC divided by the total number of corporate employees, although virtually all corporate PACs solicit money only from managers. Therefore, companies where managers are a high proportion of total employees will tend to have higher scores.

    This figure is understated because our data include only the amount the PAC contributed to major party candidates running in the general election. We have underestimated Seagram's fundraising if the company gave any money to third-party candidates, candidates who lost in primaries, political parties, or to other PACs (some powerful members of Congress form their own PACs, collect money, then distribute it themselves, thereby consolidating their influence with other members).

22. Nonconnected PACs generally are not democratically controlled, but they are not affiliated with any other organization and subsist exclusively on voluntary donations. They are controlled by their donors in the sense that people can give or not give to any nonconnected PAC and can "vote" by switching their money from one to another if displeased with a PAC's donations. Several New Right PACs lost most of their contributors during the 1980s.

23. Even if corporations solicited only stockholders, this would be a peculiar democracy, with each dollar, not each person, entitled to equal representation. In stockholder "democracy" a single individual with a million shares is entitled to more votes than one hundred thousand individuals with five shares each.

24. Friedman, *Teamster Rank and File: Power, Bureaucracy, and Rebellion at Work and in a Union.*

25. Siler, "Bolting the Boardroom Door at Sears."

26. A substantial proportion of PAC officers are women. In 1986, of the employees listed by the 309 largest corporate PACs in *Washington Representatives,* 23 percent of the vice presidents, directors, and managers were women. Most women advanced inside a government relations office; men are the only ones who rotate into government relations from positions as line managers. Three-quarters of the PAC officers who had been aides to members of Congress were men. See Scott, "Beyond PAC-Man: The Significance of Gender Difference in Corporate-Government Relations."

27. Based on information obtained from interviews the mail survey *under*estimates the number of senior vice presidents and above on PAC committees. We suspect that many mail survey respondents did not count top officers unless they exercise significant influence, even if the person attends and chairs meetings.

28. Useem, *The Inner Circle: Large Corporations and the Rise of Business Political Activity in the U.S. and U.K.;* Mintz and Schwartz, *The Power Structure of American Business;* Domhoff, *The Higher Circles: The Governing Class in*

America; Domhoff, *The Power Elite and the State: How Policy Is Made in America.*

29. Burnham, *Critical Elections and the Mainsprings of American Politics,* p. 82; Burnham, "The Turnout Problem," p. 126.

30. Although most new CEOs do not ask for changes in PAC behavior, their right to do so is not contested. One PAC official identified himself as a conservative Republican who attended the 1988 Republican National Convention as a delegate. Until recently his corporate PAC had followed a generally Republican orientation, but he told us that the PAC was going to become much more bipartisan due to the accession of a new CEO with strong ties to the Democratic party. As a loyal corporate employee (who wanted to keep his job) he strongly endorsed this shift.

31. His reference is to a bygone era.

32. Silk and Vogel, *Ethics and Profits,* p. 43.

33. Huntington, "The United States," p. 173. See also Dickson and Noble, "By Force of Reason: The Politics of Science and Technology Policy"; and Bowles, "The Trilateral Commission: Have Capitalism and Democracy Come to a Parting of the Ways?"

34. The company hopes for still more from their managers—that they act in their communities, both formally and informally, as advocates for their corporation and for business in general.

35. Tolchin, "U.S. May Ban PACs with Foreign Ties," p. 9.

36. Ibid.

37. Ibid.

Chapter 3. Gifts: Networks of Obligation

1. We are indebted to Bill Domhoff for proposing this idea to us, developing a number of stimulating insights, and suggesting some readings. Obviously he is not responsible for our specific formulations.

2. In fact, in most cases it would be illegitimate (and perhaps illegal) for a clerk to give you a better or worse price because you were nasty or nice.

3. See also Shakespeare's famous lines from *Timon of Athens,* quoted by Marx in the Paris manuscripts of 1844 (p. 127):

> *Gold? Yellow, glittering, precious gold? . . .*
> *Thus much of this will make black white, foul fair,*
> *Wrong right, base noble, old young, coward valiant.*
> *. . . This yellow slave*
> *Will knit and break religions, bless the accursed;*
> *Make the hoar leprosy adored, place thieves*
> *And give them title, knee and approbation*
> *With senators on the bench. . . .*

4. Hochschild, *The Managed Heart: Commercialization of Human Feeling.*

5. Gerstel and Gross, "Women and the American Family: Continuity and Change"; Bernard, *The Future of Marriage;* Folbre, "The Rhetoric of Self-interest and the Ideology of Gender"; Hochschild, *The Second Shift: Working Parents and the Revolution at Home;* Millman, *Warm Hearts and Cold Cash: How Families Handle Money and What This Reveals about Them.*

6. Scheff, *Being Mentally Ill: A Sociological Theory.*

7. Caplow, "Rule Enforcement without Visible Means: Christmas Gift Giving in Middletown," p. 1310.

8. Mauss, *The Gift: Forms and Functions of Exchange in Archaic Societies,* p. xiv.

9. Ibid., p. 1.

10. Caplow, "Rule Enforcement without Visible Means," p. 1307.

11. The text presents the general case, but several qualifications could be made: many products contain a warranty; some offer a service contract; and sales personnel almost always intend to create a friendly atmosphere that will ensure repeat business.

12. Lévi-Strauss, *The Elementary Structures of Kinship;* Rubin, "The Traffic in Women: Notes on the Political Economy of Sex."

13. Gouldner, "The Norm of Reciprocity: A Preliminary Statement."

14. Rollins, *Between Women: Domestics and Their Employers,* p. 190.

15. Wilkinson, "Rules of the Game: The Senate's Money Politics," p. 33.

16. Schwartz, "The Social-Psychology of the Gift," p. 4.

17. Mauss, *The Gift,* p. 10.

18. Schwartz, "The Social-Psychology of the Gift," p. 1.

19. For example, groups supporting gay and lesbian rights sometimes have difficulty getting members of Congress to accept their contributions.

20. Even though the media usually reserve their harshest condemnations for the members of Congress who accept the contributions rather than at the businesses that give them.

21. Mauss, *The Gift,* p. 11.

22. Cited in Stern, *The Best Congress Money Can Buy,* p. 63.

23. Ibid., p. 63.

24. *New York Times,* September 22, 1991, p. 20.

25. At one of the corporations we interviewed, all PAC contributors, not just the PAC committee members, receive copies of this information.

26. However, friendship rarely stands alone. In this case, the PAC officer sounded the candidate out about an issue crucial to the company's survival. The candidate had (understandably) never thought about the issue before but agreed to consider the issue carefully should she be elected.

27. These managers appear to be following not "company rationality" but "subsidiary rationality."

28. Cohen and Matlack, "All-Purpose Loophole," p. 2981.

29. Imagine the reaction if a Defense Department procurement officer agreed to accept $2,000 to give a speech to a company's development unit, talked about what the DOD considered most important in a new plane, and then stayed to answer questions and listen sympathetically to company suggestions.

30. Because of the popular focus on ethics, more House members were refusing fees even before the House voted to ban them: 115 did not accept fees in 1989, a substantial increase from 1988, but still less than a quarter of Congress. See Berke, "Leaders Set Pace for Outside Fees," p. D24.

31. Including fees from Citicorp-Citibank, Coopers & Lybrand, Edison Electric Institute, Equitable Financial Companies, Gannett Outdoor of Chicago, Hotel Employees and Restaurant Employees International Union, Kidder Peabody Group Inc., Kirkland & Ellis, Large Public Power Council, Merrill Lynch & Co., Patrick Media Group, Tobacco Institute, United States Fidelity & Guaranty (twice), and Wholesaler-Distributor Political Education Committee.

32. Including fees from Aetna Casualty & Surety Co., American Broadcasting Co., American Trucking Associations, Anheuser-Busch Companies, Association of Reserve City Bankers, Blue Cross & Blue Shield, Blue Cross–Blue Shield of Illinois (twice), Board of Trade of the City of Chicago, Campbell-Raupe Inc., CBS, CBS Television Network Affiliates, Citicorp-Citibank, CL Global Partners Securities, Coopers & Lybrand, Cosmetic Toiletry & Fragrance Association, Edison Electric Institute, Equitable Financial Companies, Erickson Air-Crane Co., Galen Dean Powers, General Electric, Harris Bank Trust, Hill and Knowlton, Hopkins & Sutter, Invest to Compete Alliance, Irvine Company, Kirkland & Ellis, Koll Company, Large Public Power Council, Mercer Meidinger Hansen (twice), Midwest Stock Exchange, National Association of Realtors, National Automobile Dealers, National Council of State Housing Agencies, National Retail Merchants Association, National Venture Capital Association, Newport Beach–Irvine Estate Planning Council, Petroleum Equipment Suppliers, Securities Industry Association, Squibb Corp., U.S. League of Savings Institutions, United Engineers & Constructors, and the Wholesaler-Distributor Political Education Committee.

33. Berke, "Amount of Senators' Free Travel Remains High."

34. Stern, *The Best Congress Money Can Buy,* p. 159.

35. Matlack, "On the Beach in Barbados," p. 2829.

36. *New York Times,* November 12, 1990, p. A18.

37. Jackson, *Broken Promise: Why the Federal Election Commission Failed,* p. 36.

38. It is illegal to solicit or accept campaign contributions on federal property. We doubt, however, that either the member of Congress or the PAC need fear a conviction.

39. As reprinted in *National Journal,* "Money and Politics: A Special Report," p. 1458.

Chapter 4. Access: "I Can Get to Waxman for $250"

1. Grenzke, "PACs and the Congressional Supermarket: The Currency Is Complex"; Kau and Rubin, *Congressmen, Constituents, and Contributors;* Neustadtl, "Interest-Group PACsmanship: An Analysis of Campaign Contributions, Issue Visibility, and Legislative Impact."
2. *National Journal,* 1990, "Opinion Outlook: Views on the American Scene," p. 1052.
3. Magleby and Nelson, *The Money Chase: Congressional Campaign Finance Reform,* p. 36.
4. Klott, "Senators Won Many Exceptions in Bill to Aid Specific Taxpayers."
5. Johnson, *MITI and the Japanese Miracle: The Growth of Industrial Policy, 1925–1975.*
6. U.S. Code, *Statutes at Large,* vol. 100, 1986, Public Law 99-514, pp. 2149–2150, sec. 204.
7. Given the loopholes provided by this tax bill, consider the claims made by Jeffrey Birnbaum and Alan Murray in their highly praised *Showdown at Gucci Gulch: Lawmakers, Lobbyists, and the Unlikely Triumph of Tax Reform.* According to them (p. 4), the 1986 tax reform bill was opposed by corporate lobbyists, who had expected it to fail: "It was too bold, they thought, too radical. It proposed wiping out a multitude of special-interest tax breaks in return for sharp cuts in tax rates. That would be a boon to the great mass of people who pay their taxes each year without taking advantage of these deductions, exclusions, and credits. But it would be a disaster for the many business interests and high-income individuals who have come to depend on tax favors from Congress."
8. Barlett and Steele, "The Great Tax Giveaway," special section of the *Philadelphia Inquirer* including articles that originally appeared April 10–16 and September 25–26, 1988; quotes from pp. 44, 5.
9. Barlett and Steele, "The Great Tax Giveaway," p. 15.
10. The other half of the U.S. "industrial policy" is Department of Defense expenditures.
11. Barlett and Steele, "The Great Tax Giveaway," p. 4.
12. Ibid., p. 22.
13. Stern, *The Best Congress Money Can Buy,* p. 13.
14. This is a tiny fraction of their average 1984 sales of $6.7 billion and average profits of $374 million.
15. The true cost of government lobbying is substantially higher than the amount of PAC money contributed because the corporation pays the salaries of the personnel involved and provides free rent, phones, and

travel. On the other hand, tax loopholes are only one of many benefits corporations derive from their government relations operations.

16. Assuming that the individual makes a $100 campaign contribution to reduce his or her taxes by $10,000, whereas the corporation contributes $200,000 through its PAC to get a tax loophole worth $20 million. Given how little the individual is contributing, he or she would presumably give it all to one member, whereas the corporate PAC would have to contribute to a minimum of twenty people even if it gave the maximum contribution per candidate (and, in fact, probably would contribute to 150 or more candidates).

17. Domhoff, *The Powers That Be: Processes of Ruling-Class Domination in America,* pp. 27–28.

18. Clifford has recently been in the news for his involvement with BCCI. This has been labeled a scandal. Helping the DuPonts evade taxes arising from their illegal holdings was seen as effective representation.

19. Stern, *The Best Congress Money Can Buy,* p. 40.

20. Klott, "Senators Won Many Exceptions in Bill to Aid Specific Taxpayers."

21. Block, "The Ruling Class Does Not Rule: Notes on the Marxist Theory of the State"; Poulantzas, "The Problem of the Capitalist State."

22. The company's employees and their families are probably among the people suffering the most from the plant's pollution, but the company is unlikely to mention this.

23. Note that these are our words, not an actual quote. We have and wish we could use some compelling examples, but we cannot do so without violating our promise of confidentiality to our respondents. This generic quote lacks the flavor of the originals, but because our examples are company specific, there is no way to present them while preserving our informants' anonymity.

24. Jackson, *Honest Graft: Big Money and the American Political Process;* Mayer, *The Greatest-Ever Bank Robbery: The Collapse of the Savings and Loan Industry.*

25. Telephone conversation by Denise Scott with Rob Everts, head of advertising for New England division of Neighbor to Neighbor, November 18, 1991.

26. *Standard Directory of Advertising 1990,* vol. 1, p. 180.

27. Almost the only interviews that were less pleasant and friendly were those with corporate officials that do not ordinarily engage in lobbying, either because they were too high up (they supervised the operations, but had never themselves been participants) or too low down (we somehow ended up interviewing a PAC manager who was not involved in contacts with members of Congress).

28. Membership fees are typically paid by the corporation; this is both one of

the perks of office and a sound investment by the corporation to make it easier for lobbyists to do their job.

29. Jackson, *Honest Graft,* p. 105.

30. National Committee to Preserve Social Security and Medicare, "Myths and Facts about the Social Security Notch," p. 2.

31. Rich, "Notch Babies Get Less Intentionally."

32. Noah, "Notch Babies," p. 18.

33. Olen, "Notch Babies Continue Fight for Increase in Their Benefits."

34. *New York Times,* January 13, 1988, p. 22.

35. Rosenblatt, "The Notchies March On."

36. Barone and Ujifusa, *The Almanac of American Politics 1984,* p. 313.

37. Barone and Ujifusa, *The Almanac of American Politics 1984,* p. 785; Klott, "Senators Won Many Exceptions in Bill to Aid Specific Taxpayers." People on the left identify Moynihan with his blaming-the-victim report on the black family and object to calling him the most liberal senator. We sympathize with this objection, but Moynihan is steadfastly liberal on economic issues, and this respected journal found him the most liberal on the votes it selected (the comparison is only to other U.S. senators).

38. Barone and Ujifusa, *The Almanac of American Politics 1988,* p. 915. Metzenbaum was identified as a problem by remarks that specifically singled him out and said he was antibusiness as well as by more guarded allusions.

39. What can explain why there are so few members that are a thorn in business's side? In the House, the rules don't give a lone individual much ability to be heard, much less to tie up a bill. A Bernie Sanders in the House doesn't have the same leverage as a Metzenbaum in the Senate. Therefore, a House member with the same intentions may not be able to be effective, and business therefore doesn't consider him or her a factor to be considered. Why aren't there more such individuals in the Senate, and/or a unified caucus in the House? Presumably because of the success of business hegemony.

40. Vogel, *Fluctuating Fortunes: The Political Power of Business in America;* Gais, Peterson, and Walker, "Interest Groups, Iron Triangles, and Representative Institutions in American National Government."

41. Domhoff, *The Powers That Be;* Block, "The Ruling Class Does Not Rule"; Poulantzas, "The Problem of the Capitalist State."

42. Burnham, *The Current Crisis in American Politics;* Sundquist, *The Decline and Resurgence of Congress.*

43. Vogel, *Fluctuating Fortunes,* p. 149.

44. Marx, *Capital: A Critique of Political Economy,* p. 381.

45. Discussed in the next chapter.

46. Senators expect larger contributions; $250 from a large corporation to a Senate race would be something of an insult and might make it harder rather than easier to gain access.

47. Lakoff, *Language and Women's Place*.
48. Similarly, although the term *lobbyist* is still used, many one-time lobbyists are now "Washington representatives."
49. Our use of the term *access* is thus an attempt to present the world in the terms preferred by corporate PAC officials themselves. Although this chapter argues that they actually want more than access, we have tried to make this part of our argument rather than a presupposition.
50. This behavior is the focus of the next chapter, which is on corporate ideological donations and activities.
51. Commoner, *Making Peace with the Planet*.
52. Glassberg, *The Power of Collective Purse Strings: The Effect of Bank Hegemony on Corporations and the State;* Mintz and Schwartz, *The Power Structure of American Business;* Schwartz, *The Structure of Power in America: The Corporate Elite as a Ruling Class*.
53. Greider, "The Education of David Stockman," p. 30.
54. Ibid., pp. 51, 52.
55. Ibid., p. 52.

Chapter 5. Ideology: Defending Free Enterprise

1. Quoted in Glen, "At the Wire, Corporate PACs Come Through for the GOP," p. 174.
2. Ferguson and Rogers, *The Hidden Election: Politics and Economics in the 1980 Presidential Election*, p. 42.
3. Simon, *A Time for Truth*, pp. 197, 198.
4. Ibid., p. 228.
5. Magleby and Nelson, *The Money Chase: Congressional Campaign Finance Reform*, p. 38.
6. Note that here and in the quote on the preceding page ideological PAC officials focus on members of Congress using campaign finance to enrich themselves. In fact, of course, top corporate executives make vastly more than members of Congress, and most members could earn more if they left public office. But ideological PAC officials are extremely concerned about members enriching themselves.
7. Simon, *A Time for Truth*, p. 228.
8. Kristol, *Two Cheers for Capitalism*, p. 140.
9. Jerry Himmelstein wrote an excellent set of comments on a draft of our previous chapter, made many of the points presented here, and suggested that we read Kristol and Simon. Himmelstein's comments and book—*To the Right: The Transformation of American Conservatism*—shaped the character of this chapter.
10. Vogel, *Fluctuating Fortunes: The Political Power of Business in America*, p. 59.
11. Silk and Vogel, *Ethics and Profits*, pp. 44, 45, 72.

12. Clawson and Clawson, "Reagan or Business: Foundations of the New Conservatism," p. 204. As another example, consider the risks business runs if it is careless about the way it handles hazardous materials on railroads:

> Lawrence M. Mann, an attorney who represents the Railway Labor Executives' Association, said that because of the agency's small staff and the paltry fines it charges, the railroads are under scant pressure to follow regulations.
>
> "If I'm a manager of a railroad," he said, "I know they won't see my car but once a year, and even if they do see it and find a defect, they give me a chance to correct it—and even if I don't correct it, the fine will only average $27." (Victor, "Trouble on Wheels")

13. Clawson and Clawson, "Reagan or Business," pp. 206–207.
14. Vogel, "Business's 'New Class' Struggle."
15. *Business Week,* October 12, 1974, p. 120.
16. Edsall, *The New Politics of Inequality,* p. 125.
17. Ibid., p. 111.
18. Kendall quoted in McGrath, *Redefining Corporate-Federal Relations,* p. 55.
19. See also Handler and Mulkern, *Business in Politics: Strategies of Corporate Political Action Committees;* Malbin, *Parties, Interest Groups, and Campaign Finance Laws.*
20. Glen, "At the Wire, Corporate PACs Come Through for the GOP," p. 176. Not all of this change can be attributed to the effects of the letters circulating within the business community. Corporate campaign strategies always tend to follow this pattern. Access-oriented donations to incumbents can be made equally well at any point, while ideological donations aren't made until late in the campaign when it is possible to judge which races are likely to be close and to involve significant political differences between the two candidates. Therefore, late money always tends to be more ideological.
21. In many cases open seats are the key races deciding the ideological composition of Congress, but donations to these races do not require a PAC to oppose a powerful incumbent. Moreover, some open-seat races are foregone conclusions because they are run in districts controlled by one party. Donations to these candidates may reflect an access strategy.
22. Weinstein, *The Corporate Ideal in the Liberal State: 1900–1918,* p. xii.
23. See Domhoff, *The Higher Circles: The Governing Class in America.*
24. The 1986 figures are markedly different from any other election from 1976 to the present. Even in 1986, however, no corporation gave as much as 20 percent of its money to Democratic challengers.
25. For this purpose we include only PACs that contributed $25,000 or more in the given election. Otherwise a PAC that was inactive in that election

but made a single substantial donation to a challenger could appear as extremely ideological. Exclusion of small PACs has virtually no effect on the pattern of results we report.

26. Clawson and Clawson, "Reagan or Business," p. 209.

27. Clawson and Su, "Was 1980 Special? A Comparison of 1980 and 1986 Corporate PAC Contributions"; Neustadtl and Clawson, "Corporate Political Groupings: Does Ideology Unify Business Political Behavior?"; Su, Clawson, and Neustadtl, "The Coalescence of Corporate Conservatism from 1976 to 1980: The Roots of the Reagan Revolution"; Su, Clawson, and Neustadtl, "Corporate PACs and Conservative Realignment: A Comparison of 1980 and 1984."

28. Two groups had five members, one had six, one had eight, and one had nine.

29. Significantly, this one corporation was United Technologies, the company whose government relations officer wrote an analysis urging more ideological PAC contributions. That analysis was sent to all members of the Business Roundtable in 1978 by Donald Kendall, CEO of Pepsico and chair of the Roundtable.

30. Burnham, "The 1980 Earthquake: Realignment, Reaction, or What?"

31. Burnham, *The Current Crisis in American Politics*, p. 268.

32. Chubb and Peterson, *The New Direction in American Politics*, pp. 21–22.

33. U.S. Bureau of the Census, 1986, *Money Income and Poverty Status of Persons and Families in the United States*, pp. 37–39.

34. From 1977 to 1988 incomes for the eighth decile increased by 5.4 percent, for the ninth by 7.9 percent, and for the top decile by 27.4 percent. Edsall, "The Changing Shape of Power: A Realignment in Public Policy," p. 275.

35. Reported in the *New York Times*, March 5, 1992, p. 1.

36. Phillips, *The Politics of Rich and Poor: Wealth and the American Electorate in the Reagan Aftermath*, p. 11.

37. Ibid., p. 10. Moreover "the top 1 percent of Americans' after-tax share of U.S. income rose from 7 percent in 1977 to a projected 11 percent in 1990" (ibid., p. xi). This is an enormous change; if the top 1 percent of the population had the same relative share of total U.S. income in 1990 as in 1977 (when their income per person was seven times the average), the rest of us would have more than $100 billion in extra income available every year.

38. In the 1930s the so-called Second New Deal of 1935 is probably the key policy legacy of the period. Without social security and the Wagner Act, the New Deal would be remembered very differently.

39. Since the beginning of polling on presidential approval ratings.

40. Approval ratings are taken from Gallup data for 1981 to 1986 *(The Gallup Poll: Public Opinion 1981; The Gallup Poll: Public Opinion 1982; The Gallup Poll: Public Opinion 1983; The Gallup Poll: Public Opinion 1984;*

The Gallup Poll: Public Opinion 1985; The Gallup Poll: Public Opinion 1986). Gallup does not provide a yearly average; these data are the average of the ratings for February, June, and October of each year. (Where one of those months was not reported, we took the closest month that was reported.)

41. Ferguson and Rogers, *Right Turn: The Decline of the Democrats and the Future of American Politics.*

42. Edsall, "Coelho Mixes Democratic Fund-raising, Political Matchmaking," p. 17.

43. Quoted in ibid., p. 17.

44. Quoted in ibid., p. 18. See also Edsall, "The Reagan Legacy," and Jackson, *Honest Graft: Big Money and the American Political Process.*

45. These groups may be winning more now and in the future through a conservative Supreme Court, but business received its reward immediately after the election.

46. Useem, *The Inner Circle: Large Corporations and the Rise of Business Political Activity in the U.S. and U.K.*

47. Only 22 percent gave at least twenty donations to nonincumbents.

48. An access-oriented PAC could use the classical theory of the free market to make an argument for the superiority of a pragmatic approach. The idea of a free market is that each actor pursues its own interest but that the outcome of this process is the greatest good for the greatest number. In producing and pricing goods companies are not *supposed* to consider what is best for the country as a whole but rather what will be best for them. According to Adam Smith, if each company or individual does this, and free competition prevails, the ultimate outcome will be the best resolution for the system as a whole. By analogy, in making its political decisions each company should pursue its own particular interests. Other companies, labor unions, environmentalists, and so on will do the same. The free competition among candidates should lead to the best possible policies for the system as a whole.

In fact, one might even argue that corporations that do *not* pursue their own interests thereby reduce their profits. This costs their stockholders lower dividends and reduced value for their stock. Stockholders might even be able to sue a management that reduced company profits through an ideological refusal to pursue the political strategy that would best advance the company's interests. Ideologically conservative corporations embrace contradictory notions: *economic* behavior must consider only the company's interests; *political* behavior must be based on larger interests. Such a corporation condemns environmentalists if they ask the company to consider society's interests, and corporate PACs if they consider their own interests rather than the "free enterprise system."

Our views on these issues differ significantly from those of Allen Kaufman, but our thinking has been heavily influenced by conversations and collaboration with him, as well as by his written work. See especially Kaufman, Marcus, and Zacharias, "How Business Manages Politics"; Kaufman, Zacharias, and Marcus, "Managers United for Corporate Rivalary"; and Kaufman, Karson, and Sohl, "Corporate Factionalism and Corporate Solidarity in the 1980 and 1982 Congressional Elections."

49. Note also that the internal operations of ideological PACs are generally similar to those of pragmatic PACs. That is, the PAC is not democratically run by those who contribute to it but rather is controlled by the CEO and board of directors. Moreover, employees may well be coerced to contribute.

50. Weinstein, *The Corporate Ideal in the Liberal State: 1900–1918.*

Chapter 6. Business Unity, Business Power

1. Dahl, "A Critique of the Ruling Elite Model," p. 465.
2. Ippolito and Walker, *Political Parties, Interest Groups, and Public Policy,* p. 282.
3. Eismeier and Pollock, *Business, Money, and the Rise of Corporate PACs in American Elections,* p. 6.
4. Neustadtl, Scott, and Clawson, "Class Struggle in Campaign Finance? Political Action Committee Contributions in the 1984 Elections."
5. Clawson, Neustadtl, and Bearden, "The Logic of Business Unity: Corporate Contributions to the 1980 Congressional Elections." See also Clawson and Su, "Was 1980 Special? A Comparison of 1980 and 1986 Corporate PAC Contributions."
6. Schwartz, *The Structure of Power in America: The Corporate Elite as a Ruling Class.*
7. Clawson and Neustadtl, "Interlocks, PACs, and Corporate Conservatism"; Mizruchi, "Similarity of Political Behavior among Large American Corporations"; Mizruchi and Koenig, "Economic Sources of Corporate Political Consensus: An Examination of Interindustry Relations."
8. Mintz and Schwartz, *The Power Structure of American Business;* Mizruchi, *The American Corporate Network.*
9. Rubin, "The Traffic in Women: Notes on the Political Economy of Sex."
10. Useem, *The Inner Circle: Large Corporations and the Rise of Business Political Activity in the U.S. and U.K.*
11. Domhoff, *The Higher Circles: The Governing Class in America;* Shoup and Minter, *Imperial Braintrust: The Council on Foreign Relations and United States Foreign Policy;* Whitt, *Urban Elites and Mass Transportation.*
12. Note once again, however, that even liberals are perfectly willing to help corporations, to work with them and be helpful until it comes to the final vote.
13. Vogel, *Fluctuating Fortunes: The Political Power of Business in America,* pp. 154–155.

14. See Domhoff, *Who Really Rules?;* Collins, *The Business Response to Keynes, 1929–1964;* Kaufman, Marcus, and Zacharias, "How Business Manages Politics"; McQuaid, *Big Business and Presidential Power: From FDR to Reagan;* Peschek, *Policy-Planning Organizations: Elite Agendas and America's Rightward Turn.*

15. Committee for Economic Development, *Financing a Better Election System*, p. 21; cited in Koenig, "Business Support for Disclosure of Corporate Campaign Contributions: An Instructive Paradox," p. 86.

16. Edsall and Edsall, *Chain Reaction: The Impact of Race, Rights, and Taxes on American Politics,* p. 23; U.S. Bureau of the Census, 1990, *Money Income and Poverty Status; New York Times,* March 5, 1992, p. 1.

17. Wealth consists of the total value of everything a person owns, minus the value of everything they owe. On the positive side a person would have such credits as all the money in their checking and savings accounts, the book value of their car, and the resale value of their house. On the negative side they would have such debits as the size of the mortgages on their house, what they owed on their credit cards, the balance on their car payments, the total of their student loans, and anything else they owed. It is perfectly possible, therefore, to have no *net* wealth; in fact, to have a negative net wealth. That simply means that if a person cashed in all their assets they couldn't pay all their debts. For many people this is a more or less permanent life condition. Others go through such a period in their lives: for example, 34 percent of students graduating from four-year colleges in 1983–84 had education debt of more than $7,000. See Henderson, *College Debts of Recent Graduates,* p. 5. It takes some years before their savings total as much as the balance on their student loans.

18. Phillips, *The Politics of Rich and Poor: Wealth and the American Electorate in the Reagan Aftermath,* p. 11; *New York Times,* April 21, 1992, p. 1.

19. Wright, *Class Structure and Income Determination,* chapter 1.

20. One-hundredth of 1 percent is enough to include the board of directors and top officers of the 500 largest industrials and 500 largest service companies, with room left over for several thousand top lawyers, foundation executives, consulting firms, and accountants. Even if we multiply this number by ten, we still include only one-tenth of 1 percent of the U.S. population.

21. Obviously, the elected government has the *potential* to make more important decisions. If some U.S. president decides to launch a first-strike nuclear attack, the importance of the government will, at least for a while, vastly overshadow the decisions of corporations.

22. Simon and Eitzen, *Elite Deviance,* p. 10.

23. Mydans, "Questions Linger as Spill Sits in a California Lake."

24. On average, corporations contribute only .009 of their pretax net income to charity, a smaller proportion than is given by ordinary individuals,

despite the fact that corporations are public institutions with enormous incomes.

25. Dowie, "Pinto Madness." This article is the basis for the account that follows.

26. When corporate decisions are challenged by unions, environmentalists, or public-interest groups, executives frequently argue that they had no choice, the constraints of the market required this course of action. On the other hand, these same executives justify their stratospheric pay on the basis that they are constantly required to make tough decisions, and the company's success depends on the choices they make.

27. Dowie, "Pinto Madness."

28. Nader, *Unsafe at Any Speed.*

29. Frequently even when a regulation is imposed, it leaves control in the hands of business. For example, instead of the government testing new drugs, pharmaceutical companies do so and report their results to the government body that is supposed to regulate them. A similar means is used to determine whether new cars meet emission standards.

30. Ford based its estimate of the value of a human life on a handy government study by the National Highway Traffic Safety Administration.

31. U.S. Bureau of the Census, *Statistical Abstract,* 1990, p. 557, Table 934.

32. Ibid., p. 840, Table 1496.

33. Ibid., p. 129, Table 208.

34. Average television viewing is twenty-nine hours and forty minutes a week; about 15 to 20 percent of this is commercials.

35. The surest way to limit undue corporate influence on Congress and the government would be to limit overall business power, including corporate control of the economy. We support such initiatives, but they are extremely unlikely to be implemented at this time.

Chapter 7. "They Might Start Running It Strictly for the Votes"

1. In the House; senators are at some risk though they have significant advantages.

2. This is the way Keating gave the bulk of his money to Cranston.

3. This is the quintessential liberal dilemma, which applies in most areas of government policy, not just campaign finance reform. Liberalism leaves the private sector free to control itself and operate as it wishes (with tremendous inequalities and power differences), then attempts to correct the worst consequences of the free market through various kinds of government programs. But even when the government programs move in the right direction, they are always minimal, with far too little power to do more than frustrate the basic direction of the private sector. Often, of course, the programs are corrupted even before they can be implemented, so they serve ends very different from those publicly proclaimed.

4. Thus academic studies overwhelmingly analyze PAC contributions because it is easy to identify the organization responsible. Individual contributors may mask their identities by using slight variations in their
   names, a home address one time and an office one the next, by omitting
   or providing misleading job information.
5. Magleby and Nelson, *The Money Chase: Congressional Campaign Finance
   Reform*, p. 84.
6. This is not supposed to be used for campaign purposes, but these are
   often hard to separate from official business. One telling indicator is the
   dramatic increase in the use of free mail during election years. In 1987
   franked mail cost $63 million, in 1988, $113 million.
7. Lukes, "Political Ritual and Social Integration," p. 301.
8. Stern, *The Best Congress Money Can Buy*.
9. See Clawson, *Bureaucracy and the Labor Process: The Transformation of
   U.S. Industry 1860–1920*, for an argument that this is not necessarily the
   most efficient way to organize production and that this form of organization developed to maximize profits and control.
10. Some of the people who might not agree with this are the owners and
    executives of major corporations, many of whom apparently feel that
    democracy must be kept under control and that those with extra money
    and power are entitled to extra consideration.
11. Magleby and Nelson, *The Money Chase*, p. 38.
12. Huckabee, "Reelection Rates of House Incumbents: 1790–1988."
13. Ibid. In 1842 the rate was 24 percent. From 1790 to 1896 the rate never
    reached 70 percent. Since 1896 the rate has been below 70 percent only
    four times—in 1910 (68.0 percent), 1912 (64.4 percent), 1914 (68.7
    percent), and 1922 (69.9 percent).
14. Magleby and Nelson, *The Money Chase*; Jacobson, *Money in Congres-
    sional Elections*.
15. Magleby and Nelson, *The Money Chase*, p. 140.
16. *New York Times*, July 4, 1986.
17. Center for Responsive Politics, *PACs on PACs*, p. 57, cited in Magleby
    and Nelson, *The Money Chase*, p. 149.
18. Although by 1988 the loopholes had become so extreme as to essentially
    create a new system: partial public financing combined with millions in
    unreported large donations. In the 1988 presidential race 400 donors gave
    $100,000 or more (see Ahlkvist, "The Hard Facts on the Soft Money
    Fatcats of the 1988 Presidential Election").
19. In 1988 in the House, 3.2 to 1; in the Senate, 2.1 to 1.
20. For Senate races the amount per candidate is more complicated to figure.
    It costs more to run in California (population 28 million) than in Wyo-
    ming (population half a million), but a formula based on a specified
    amount per voter also produces inequities. We do not develop a formula
    here, but the principle is the same as that for House races: the total cost

per race should be about the same as at present, but the two candidates should each have the same amount to spend.

21. Candidates raising their own funds would be required to report the amounts they had raised at shorter and shorter time intervals as the election approached—every month until September, every two weeks in September, every week through late October, and every day thereafter. See Stern, *The Best Congress Money Can Buy,* chapter 11.

22. *Standard Directory of Advertising 1990,* Vol. I, p. 180.

23. An increase in corporate taxes does not increase (or decrease) the resources in American society (at least in the short-run), it just redistributes who pays the money—but as we have argued, the same point applies to our public financing proposal.

24. As a final, more ideological inducement to stay with public financing, the rules would be structured so that candidates who raised large sums through private financing had to take responsibility for permanently raising the level of public subsidy. The amount of public subsidy available to candidates at the next election would be based on the average amount spent by candidates in the previous election, adjusted for inflation. Thus if candidates chose to take private financing so they could raise more than the normal amount, their opponent would be given the equivalent amount, they would each have spent more than the average, and this would raise the average subsidy for all candidates in the subsequent election.

25. *Congressional Quarterly,* "Senate's Struggle to Pass Limits Only Opens Uphill Battle," p. 1353.

26. Any new congressional action also means an additional opportunity to undercut the law through exceptions and "clarifications."

27. Today many "independent" expenditures are in effect coordinated with a candidate; the first change required them to truly be independent. The second rule required that the candidate being targeted be notified of such expenditures in advance and given an opportunity to buy time immediately afterward to reply. Third, the group making the expenditure was required to prominently and clearly identify itself. Finally, political committees operated by organizations that lobby Congress were barred from using independent expenditures. *Congressional Quarterly,* "Provisions: Campaign Finance," pp. 1529–1530.

28. Most voters don't like these "independent expenditures," many of which are quasi-smear campaigns. When Paul Sarbanes, Democratic senator from Maryland, was running for reelection in 1982, the National Conservative Political Action Committee (NCPAC) ran ads attacking him. Sarbanes replied forcefully, essentially ignoring his opponent and running against NCPAC, and won the election decisively.

29. Germond and Witcover, "Money May Be Democrats' Headache," p. 1762.

30. Jackson, *Broken Promise: Why the Federal Election Commission Failed.*

31. If the amount per candidate were set lower, this would in practice help incumbents, since they start out with an advantage and a challenger needs to be able to spend a substantial sum to make it a race.

32. Magleby and Nelson, *The Money Chase,* p. 172.

33. *Congressional Quarterly,* "Senate's Struggle to Pass Limits Only Opens Uphill Battle," p. 1352.

34. These are the amounts that may be *spent;* if candidates raised all their money through small in-district individual contributions they would only need to *raise* half this much because the rest would be provided through federal matching dollars.

35. Fewer than 200 donations of $200 each would be needed to qualify for maximum funding. Alternatively, if one out of every thousand people in the district contributed, they would need to give an average of $75 each.

36. Quoted in Sabato, *Paying for Elections: The Campaign Finance Thicket,* p. 60.

37. Except that in recent years Congress and the FEC have created loopholes and permitted massive violations of existing rules.

38. Magleby and Nelson, *The Money Chase,* p. 75.

39. Their question: "It has been suggested that the federal government provide a fixed amount of money for the election campaigns of candidates for Congress and that all private contributions from other sources be prohibited. Do you think this is a good idea or a poor idea?" This is close to the proposal we advance here; note that support for this would almost certainly increase substantially if the question substituted "special interest" for "private."

40. Ferguson and Rogers, *Right Turn: The Decline of the Democrats and the Future of American Politics,* p. 15, report that when respondents were asked "if they would favor 'keeping' or 'easing' regulations that President Reagan 'says are holding back American free enterprise,' " the public favored keeping environmental regulations by a forty-nine to twenty-eight margin.

41. Not to mention the fact that most corporate PAC contributions do not come from the member's district.

42. Domhoff, *The Powers That Be.*

43. Perhaps one appropriate response is to aim for a "minor" change of our own—return corporations to a situation where they can solicit from only stockholders, not managers, or require that the sponsors of loopholes be publicly identified, also identifying by name the corporations the amendment will benefit, and the projected dollar value of the benefit.

44. Cited in Waldman, "Quid Pro Whoa," p. 23.

45. Business is more responsible than any other group for these thousands of special deals, but even business recognizes the process is enormously inefficient. The company that fights for one special break for itself (which

it usually sees as only reasonable) probably also denounces the system as a whole, laying the blame at every door but its own.

46. Burnham, *The Current Crisis in American Politics;* Domhoff, *Fat Cats and Democrats: The Role of the Big Rich in the Party of the Common Man;* Edsall, *The New Politics of Inequality.*

47. Corporate campaigns against unions are based on essentially this principle. The real aim of union-busting tactics in organizing drives is to demonstrate that if workers insist on fighting for respect and dignity, the corporation will do everything in its power to make life miserable. The aim is to persuade the undecided that they can't make the company stop its tactics, so the only way they can achieve peace is by defeating the union (Fantasia, *Cultures of Solidarity: Consciousness, Action, and Contemporary American Workers*).

48. Gorz, *A Strategy for Labor.*

BIBLIOGRAPHY

...

AHLKVIST, JARL. 1990. "The Hard Facts on the Soft Money Fatcats of the 1988 Presidential Election: Rethinking Campaign Finance and Capitalist Class Conflict." Comprehensive examination paper, Department of Sociology, University of Massachusetts at Amherst, November 1991.

ALEXANDER, HERBERT E. 1962. *Financing the 1960 Election*. Princeton, N.J.: Citizens' Research Foundation.

———. 1966. *Financing the 1964 Election*. Princeton, N.J.: Citizens' Research Foundation.

———. 1971. *Financing the 1968 Election*. Lexington, Mass.: Lexington Books.

———. 1972. *Money in Politics*. Washington, D.C.: Public Affairs Press.

———. 1976. *Financing the 1972 Election*. Lexington, Mass.: Lexington Books.

———. 1980. *Financing Politics: Money, Elections, and Political Reform*. Washington, D.C.: Congressional Quarterly Press.

BABCOCK, CHARLES R., AND HELEN DEWAR. 1991. "Keating Fallout: Senators Draw Own Lines on When to Intervene." *Washington Post* (January 16), p. A17.

BARLETT, DONALD L., AND JAMES R. STEELE. 1988. "The Great Tax Giveaway." Special section of the *Philadelphia Inquirer* including articles that originally appeared April 10–16 and September 25–26.

BARONE, MICHAEL, AND G. UJIFUSA. 1983. *The Almanac of American Politics 1984*. Washington, D.C.: National Journal.

BARONE, MICHAEL, AND G. UJIFUSA. 1987. *The Almanac of American Politics 1988*. Washington, D.C.: National Journal.

BEDNASH, GERALDINE. *The Relationship between Access and Selectivity in Tenure Review Outcomes*. Ph.D. dissertation, University of Maryland, College Park, Maryland, 1989.

BERKE, RICHARD L. 1990a. "Lawmakers Accept PAC Money While Urging Finance Changes." *New York Times* (September 25), pp. A1, A8.

———. 1990b. "Lobbyist Softens Ethics Testimony." *New York Times* (December 16), p. 29.

———. 1990c. "Amount of Senators' Free Travel Remains High." *New York Times* (June 6), p. A23.

———. 1990d. "Leaders Set House Pace for Outside Fees." *New York Times* (May 30), p. D24.

———. 1991. "In S.&L. Case, 2 Dramatically Contrasting Views." *New York Times* (January 14), p. B8.

BERNARD, JESSIE. 1973. *The Future of Marriage.* New York: Bantam.

BIOGRAPHICAL DIRECTORY OF THE UNITED STATES CONGRESS 1774–1989. 1989. Washington, D.C.: U.S. Printing Office.

BIRNBAUM, JEFFREY H., AND ALAN S. MURRAY. 1987. *Showdown at Gucci Gulch: Lawmakers, Lobbyists, and the Unlikely Triumph of Tax Reform.* New York: Random House.

BLOCK, FRED. 1977. "The Ruling Class Does Not Rule: Notes on the Marxist Theory of the State." *Socialist Revolution* 7, pp. 6–28.

BORGER, GLORIA, AND STEPHEN J. HEDGES, WITH GARY COHEN. 1989. "The Man Who Tried to Buy Washington." *U.S. News & World Report* (November 27), pp. 18–24.

BOWLES, SAMUEL. 1978. "The Trilateral Commission: Have Capitalism and Democracy Come to a Parting of the Ways?" In *U.S. Capitalism in Crisis,* edited by the Union for Radical Political Economics, pp. 261–265. New York: Union for Radical Political Economics.

BURNHAM, WALTER DEAN. 1970. *Critical Elections and the Mainsprings of American Politics.* New York: Norton.

———. 1981. "The 1980 Earthquake: Realignment, Reaction, or What?" In *The Hidden Election,* edited by Thomas Ferguson and Joel Rogers, pp. 98–140. New York: Pantheon.

———. 1982. *The Current Crisis in American Politics.* New York: Oxford University Press.

———. 1987. "The Turnout Problem." In *Elections American Style,* edited by A. James Reichley, pp. 97–133. Washington, D.C.: Brookings Institution.

BUSINESS WEEK. October 12, 1974.

CAPLOW, THEODORE. 1984. "Rule Enforcement without Visible Means: Christmas Gift Giving in Middletown." *American Journal of Sociology* 89: 1306–1323.

CENTER FOR RESPONSIVE POLITICS. 1988. *PACs on PACs: A View from the Inside.* Washington, D.C.: Center for Responsive Politics.

CHUBB, JOHN E., AND PAUL E. PETERSON. 1985. *The New Direction in American Politics.* Washington, D.C.: Brookings Institution.

CLAWSON, DAN. 1980. *Bureaucracy and the Labor Process: The Transformation of U.S. Industry 1860–1920.* New York: Monthly Review Press.

CLAWSON, DAN, AND MARY ANN CLAWSON. 1987. "Reagan or Business:

Foundations of the New Conservatism." In *The Structure of Power in America: The Corporate Elite as a Ruling Class*, edited by Michael Schwartz, pp. 201–217. New York: Holmes & Meier.

CLAWSON, DAN, AND ALAN NEUSTADTL. 1989. "Interlocks, PACs, and Corporate Conservatism." *American Journal of Sociology* 94: 749–773.

CLAWSON, DAN, ALAN NEUSTADTL, AND JAMES BEARDEN. 1986. "The Logic of Business Unity: Corporate Contributions to the 1980 Congressional Elections." *American Sociological Review* 51: 797–811.

CLAWSON, DAN, AND TIE-TING SU. 1990. "Was 1980 Special? A Comparison of 1980 and 1986 Corporate PAC Contributions." *Sociological Quarterly* 31: 371–388.

CODE OF FEDERAL REGULATIONS. vol. 11, *Federal Elections* (revised as of January 1990).

COHEN, RICHARD E. 1990a. "Closed-Door Negotiation on Clean Air." *National Journal* (February 17), p. 405.

———. 1990b. "Leading the Senate on Clean Air Bill." *National Journal* (March 31), p. 797.

———. 1990c. "When Titans Clash on Clean Air." *National Journal* (April 7), pp. 849–850.

COHEN, RICHARD E., AND CAROL MATLACK. 1989. "All-Purpose Loophole." *National Journal* (December 9), pp. 2980–2987.

COLLINS, ROBERT M. 1981. *The Business Response to Keynes, 1929–1964.* New York: Columbia University Press.

COMMITTEE FOR ECONOMIC DEVELOPMENT. 1968. *Financing a Better Election System.* New York: Research and Policy Committee of the Committee for Economic Development.

COMMONER, BARRY. 1990. *Making Peace with the Planet.* New York: Pantheon Books.

CONGRESSIONAL QUARTERLY. 1991a. "Provisions: Campaign Finance" (June 8), pp. 1529–1530.

———. 1991b. "Senate's Struggle to Pass Limits Only Opens Uphill Battle" (May 25), pp. 1351–1353.

CORN, DAVID. 1990. "Dirty Bookkeeping." *New Republic* (April 2), pp. 14–16.

CRYSTAL, GRAEF S. 1991. *In Search of Excess: The Overcompensation of American Executives.* New York: Norton.

DAHL, ROBERT A. 1958. "A Critique of the Ruling Elite Model." *American Political Science Review* 52: 463–469.

DALTON, MELVILLE. 1959. *Men Who Manage: Fusions of Feeling and Theory in Administration.* New York: Wiley.

DICKSON, DAVID, AND DAVID NOBLE. 1981. "By Force of Reason: The Politics of Science and Technology Policy." In *The Hidden Election: Politics and Economics in the 1980 Presidential Campaign*, edited by Thomas Ferguson and Joel Rogers, pp. 260–312. New York: Pantheon.

DOMHOFF, G. WILLIAM. 1970. *The Higher Circles: The Governing Class in America.* New York: Random House.

———. 1972. *Fat Cats and Democrats: The Role of the Big Rich in the Party of the Common Man.* Englewood Cliffs, N.J.: Prentice-Hall.

———. 1978. *Who Really Rules?* New Brunswick, N.J.: Transaction.

———. 1979. *The Powers That Be: Processes of Ruling-Class Domination in America.* New York: Random House.

———. 1990. *The Power Elite and the State: How Policy Is Made in America.* New York: Aldine Gruyter.

DOWIE, MARK. 1977. "Pinto Madness." *Mother Jones* (September/October), pp. 18–32.

DWYER, PAULA. 1990. "Dialing for Dollars, Cranston Style." *Business Week* (December 31), pp. 44–45.

EDSALL, THOMAS BYRNE. 1984. *The New Politics of Inequality.* New York: Norton.

———. 1985. "Coelho Mixes Democratic Fund-raising, Political Match-making." *Washington Post* (December 1), pp. A17–A18.

———. 1988a. *Power and Money: Writing about Politics, 1971–1987.* New York: Norton.

———. 1988b. "The Reagan Legacy." In *The Reagan Legacy,* edited by Sidney Blumenthal and Thomas Byrne Edsall, pp. 3–50. New York: Pantheon.

———. 1989. "The Changing Shape of Power: A Realignment in Public Policy." In *The Rise and Fall of the New Deal Order 1930–1980,* edited by Steve Fraser and Gary Gerstle, pp. 269–293. Princeton, N.J.: Princeton University Press.

EDSALL, THOMAS BYRNE, WITH MARY D. EDSALL. 1991. *Chain Reaction: The Impact of Race, Rights, and Taxes on American Politics.* New York: Norton.

EISMEIER, THEODORE J., AND PHILIP H. POLLOCK III. 1987. "The Retreat from Partisanship: Why the Dog Didn't Bark in the 1984 Election." In *Business Strategy and Public Policy,* edited by Alfred A. Marcus, Allen M. Kaufman, and David R. Beam, pp. 137–147. Westport, Conn.: Quorum Books.

EISMEIER, THEODORE J., AND PHILIP H. POLLOCK III. 1988. *Business, Money, and the Rise of Corporate PACs in American Elections.* New York: Quorum Books.

EPSTEIN, EDWIN M. 1968. *Corporations, Contributions, and Political Campaigns: Federal Regulation in Perspective.* Berkeley, Calif.: Institute of Governmental Studies.

———. 1980. "Business and Labor under the Federal Election Campaign Act of 1971." In *Parties, Interest Groups, and Campaign Finance Laws,* edited by Michael Malbin, pp. 107–151. Washington, D.C.: American Enterprise Institute for Public Policy Research.

FANTASIA, RICK. 1988. *Cultures of Solidarity: Consciousness, Action, and Contemporary American Workers.* Berkeley: University of California Press.

FEDERAL ELECTION COMMISSION. 1986. "Campaign Guide for Corporations and Labor Organizations" (September).

FEDERAL REGISTER. 1975. vol. 40, no. 233 (December 3).

FERGUSON, THOMAS, AND JOEL ROGERS. 1986. *Right Turn: The Decline of the Democrats and the Future of American Politics.* New York: Hill and Wang.

———, eds. 1981. *The Hidden Election: Politics and Economics in the 1980 Presidential Election.* New York: Pantheon.

FOLBRE, NANCY. 1988. "The Rhetoric of Self-interest and the Ideology of Gender." In *The Consequences of Economic Rhetoric,* edited by Arjo Klamer, Donald N. McCloskey, and Robert M. Solow, pp. 184–203. Cambridge: Cambridge University Press.

FRIEDAN, BETTY. 1963. *The Feminine Mystique.* New York: Norton.

FRIEDMAN, SAMUEL. 1982. *Teamster Rank and File: Power, Bureaucracy, and Rebellion at Work and in a Union.* New York: Columbia University Press.

GAIS, THOMAS L., MARK A. PETERSON, AND JACK L. WALKER. 1984. "Interest Groups, Iron Triangles, and Representative Institutions in American National Government." *British Journal of Political Science* 14: 161–186.

GALE RESEARCH COMPANY. 1979. *Contemporary Authors. Vols. 77–80.* Detroit: Gale Research.

GALLUP, GEORGE. 1982. *The Gallup Poll: Public Opinion 1981.* Wilmington, Del.: Scholarly Resources.

———. 1983. *The Gallup Poll: Public Opinion 1982.* Wilmington, Del.: Scholarly Resources.

———. 1984. *The Gallup Poll: Public Opinion 1983.* Wilmington, Del.: Scholarly Resources.

———. 1985. *The Gallup Poll: Public Opinion 1984.* Wilmington, Del.: Scholarly Resources.

———. 1986. *The Gallup Poll: Public Opinion 1985.* Wilmington, Del.: Scholarly Resources.

———. 1987. *The Gallup Poll: Public Opinion 1986.* Wilmington, Del.: Scholarly Resources.

GERMOND, JACK W., AND JULES WITCOVER. 1991. "Money May Be Democrats' Headache." *National Journal* (July 13), p. 1762.

GERSTEL, NAOMI, AND HARRIET ENGEL GROSS. 1989. "Women and the American Family: Continuity and Change." In *Women: A Feminist Perspective,* edited by Jo Freeman, pp. 89–120. Mountain View, Calif.: Mayfield Publishing.

GLASSBERG, DAVITA SILFEN. 1989. *The Power of Collective Purse Strings: The Effect of Bank Hegemony on Corporations and the State.* Berkeley: University of California Press.

GLEN, MAXWELL. 1979. "At the Wire, Corporate PACs Come Through for the GOP." *National Journal* (February 3), pp. 174–177.

GORZ, ANDRE. 1967. *A Strategy for Labor.* Translated by Martin A. Nicolaus and Victoria Ortiz. Boston: Beacon Press.

GOULDNER, ALVIN W. 1960. "The Norm of Reciprocity: A Preliminary Statement." *American Sociological Review* 25, (2): 161–178.

GRAMSCI, ANTONIO. 1972. *Selections from "The Prison Notebooks of Antonio Gramsci."* Edited and translated by Quintin Hoare and Geoffrey Nowell Smith. New York: International Publishers.

GREIDER, WILLIAM. 1981. "The Education of David Stockman." *Atlantic Monthly* 248 (December), pp. 27–54.

———. 1990. "Whitewash: Is Congress Conning Us on Clean Air?" *Rolling Stone* (June 14), pp. 37–39, 146.

GRENZKE, JANET M. 1989. "PACs and the Congressional Supermarket: The Currency Is Complex." *American Journal of Political Science* 33: 1–24.

HANDLER, EDWARD, AND JOHN R. MULKERN. 1982. *Business in Politics: Strategies of Corporate Political Action Committees.* Lexington, Mass.: Lexington Books.

HARDING, SUSAN. 1984. "Reconstructing Order through Action: Jim Crow and the Southern Civil Rights Movement." In *Statemaking and Social Movements: Essays in History and Theory,* edited by Charles Bright and Susan Harding, pp. 378–402. Ann Arbor: University of Michigan Press.

HENDERSON, CATHY. 1987. *College Debts of Recent Graduates.* Washington, D.C.: American Council on Education.

HIMMELSTEIN, JEROME L. 1990. *To the Right: The Transformation of American Conservatism.* Berkeley: University of California Press.

HOCHSCHILD, ARLIE RUSSELL. 1983. *The Managed Heart: Commercialization of Human Feeling.* Berkeley: University of California Press.

HOCHSCHILD, ARLIE, WITH ANNE MACHUNG. 1990. *The Second Shift: Working Parents and the Revolution at Home.* New York: Viking.

HUCKABEE, DAVID C. 1989. "Reelection Rates of House Incuments: 1790–1988." Congressional Research Service Report for Congress, March 16.

HUNTINGTON, SAMUEL P. 1975. "The United States." In *The Crisis of Democracy: Report on the Governability of Democracies to the Trilateral Commission,* edited by Michel J. Crozier, Samuel P. Huntington, and Joji Watanuki, pp. 59–118. New York: New York University Press.

IPPOLITO, DENNIS S., AND THOMAS G. WALKER. 1980. *Political Parties, Interest Groups, and Public Policy.* Englewood Cliffs, N.J.: Prentice-Hall.

JACKSON, BROOKS. 1988. *Honest Graft: Big Money and the American Political Process.* New York: Knopf.

———. 1990. *Broken Promise: Why the Federal Election Commission Failed.* New York: Priority Press, a Twentieth Century Fund Paper.

JACOBSON, GARY C. 1980. *Money in Congressional Elections.* New Haven: Yale University Press.

JOHNSON, CHALMERS. 1982. *MITI and the Japanese Miracle: The Growth of Industrial Policy, 1925–1975.* Stanford, Calif.: Stanford University Press.

KANTER, ROSABETH MOSS. 1977. *Men and Women of the Corporation.* New York: Basic Books.

KAU, JAMES B., AND PAUL H. RUBIN. 1982. *Congressmen, Constituents, and Contributors.* Boston: Martinus Nijhoff.

KAUFMAN, ALLEN, MARVIN KARSON, AND JEFFREY SOHL. 1987. "Corporate Factionalism and Corporate Solidarity in the 1980 and 1982 Congressional Elections." *Journal of Political and Military Sociology* 15: 171–186.

KAUFMAN, ALLEN, ALFRED MARCUS, WITH LARRY ZACHARIAS. 1987. "How Business Manages Politics." In *Business Strategy and Public Policy: Perspectives from Industry and Academia,* edited by Alfred A. Marcus, Allen M. Kaufman, and David R. Beam, pp. 293–312. Westport, Conn.: Quorum Books.

KAUFMAN, ALLEN, LARRY ZACHARIAS, AND ALFRED MARCUS. 1990. "Managers' United for Corporate Rivalry: A History of Managerial Collective Action." *Journal of Policy History* 2 (1): 56–97.

KLOTT, GARY. 1986. "Senators Won Many Exceptions in Bill to Aid Specific Taxpayers." *New York Times* (June 6), pp. D1–D2.

KOENIG, THOMAS. 1979. "Social Networks and the Political Role of Big Business." Ph.D. dissertation, University of California at Santa Barbara.

———. 1987. "Business Support for Disclosure of Corporate Campaign Contributions: An Instructive Paradox." In *The Structure of Power in America: The Corporate Elite as a Ruling Class,* edited by Michael Schwartz, pp. 82–96. New York: Holmes & Meier.

KOSOVA, WESTON. 1990. "Cranston Wiggling." *New Republic* (March 19), pp. 24–25.

KRANISH, MICHAEL. 1991a. "Quayle Aide's Firm Is Linked to Pollution: Official Works on Emission Rules." *Boston Globe* (November 20), pp. 1, 4.

———. 1991b. "House Panel to Probe Quayle Waiver for Aide." *Boston Globe* (November 21), pp. 1, 17.

KRISTOL, IRVING. 1978. *Two Cheers for Capitalism.* New York: Basic Books.

KRIZ, MARGARET E. 1990a. "Turbulence Ahead for Clean Air Act?" *National Journal* (January 27), p. 223.

———. 1990b. "Politics at the Pump." *National Journal* (June 2), pp. 1328–1332.

———. 1990c. "Dunning the Midwest." *National Journal* (April 14), pp. 893–897.

LAKOFF, ROBIN. 1975. *Language and Women's Place.* New York: Harper & Row.

LÉVI-STRAUSS, CLAUDE. 1969. *The Elementary Structures of Kinship.* Rev. ed. Translated and edited by James Harle Bell, John Richard Von Sturmer, and Rodney Needham. Boston: Beacon Press.

LORBER, JUDITH. 1989. "Trust, Loyalty, and the Place of Women in the

Informal Organization of Work." In *Women: A Feminist Perspective,* edited by Jo Freeman, pp. 347–355. Palo Alto: Mayfield Publishing Co.

LUKES, STEVEN. 1974. *Power: A Radical View.* New York: Macmillan.

———. 1975. "Political Ritual and Social Integration." *Sociology* 9 (2) (May): 289–308.

McGRATH, PHYLLIS S. 1979. *Redefining Corporate-Federal Relations.* New York: The Conference Board's Division of Management Research.

McQUAID, KIM. 1982. *Big Business and Presidential Power: From FDR to Reagan.* New York: Morrow.

MAGLEBY, DAVID B., AND CANDICE J. NELSON. 1990. *The Money Chase: Congressional Campaign Finance Reform.* Washington, D.C.: Brookings Institution.

MALBIN, MICHAEL J. 1980. *Parties, Interest Groups, and Campaign Finance Laws.* Washington, D.C.: American Enterprise Institute.

MARX, KARL. 1844/1959. *The Economic and Philosophic Manuscripts of 1844.* Moscow: Progress Publishers.

———. 1867/1977. *Capital: A Critique of Political Economy, vol. 1.* Introduction by Ernest Mandel, translated by Ben Fowkes. New York: Vintage Books, 1977.

MATLACK, CAROL. 1990. "On the Beach in Barbados." *National Journal* (November 17), p. 2829.

———. 1991. "It's Round Two in Clean Air Fight." *National Journal* (January 26), pp. 226–227.

MAUSS, MARCEL. 1925/1967. *The Gift: Forms and Functions of Exchange in Archaic Societies.* Translated by Ian Cunnison. New York: Norton.

MAYER, MARTIN. 1990. *The Greatest-Ever Bank Robbery: The Collapse of the Savings and Loan Industry.* New York: Macmillan.

MIDGET, WARREN. 1988. "The High Price of Advice," *Forbes* (May 28).

MILLMAN, MARCIA. 1991. *Warm Hearts and Cold Cash: How Families Handle Money and What This Reveals about Them.* New York: Free Press.

MINTZ, BETH, AND MICHAEL SCHWARTZ. 1985. *The Power Structure of American Business.* Chicago: University of Chicago Press.

MIZRUCHI, MARK S. 1982. *The American Corporate Network.* Beverly Hills, Calif.: Sage.

———. 1989. "Similarity of Political Behavior among Large American Corporations." *American Journal of Sociology* 95: 401–424.

MIZRUCHI, MARK S., AND THOMAS KOENIG. 1986. "Economic Sources of Corporate Political Consensus: An Examination of Interindustry Relations." *American Sociological Review* 51: 482–491.

MYDANS, SETH. 1991. "Questions Linger as Spill Sits in a California Lake." *New York Times* (July 21), p. 14.

NADER, RALPH. 1966. *Unsafe at Any Speed.* New York: Pocket Books.

NATIONAL COMMITTEE TO PRESERVE SOCIAL SECURITY AND MEDICARE. [N.D.] "Myths and Facts about the Social Security Notch."

NATIONAL JOURNAL. 1990a. "Money and Politics: A Special Report." no. 24 (June 16).

———. 1990b. "Opinion Outlook: Views on the American Scene." vol. 22 (April 28), p. 1052.

NEUSTADTL, ALAN. 1991. "Interest-Group PACsmanship: An Analysis of Campaign Contributions, Issue Visibility, and Legislative Impact." *Social Forces* 69: 549–564.

NEUSTADTL, ALAN, AND DAN CLAWSON. 1988. "Corporate Political Groupings: Does Ideology Unify Business Political Behavior?" *American Sociological Review* 53: 172–190.

NEUSTADTL, ALAN, DENISE SCOTT, AND DAN CLAWSON. 1991. "Class Struggle in Campaign Finance? Political Action Committee Contributions in the 1984 Elections." *Sociological Forum* 6: 219–238.

NOAH, TIMOTHY. 1986. "Notch Babies." *New Republic* (December 1), pp. 18–21.

OLEN, HELAINE. 1991. "Notch Babies Continue Fight for Increase in Their Benefits." *Los Angeles Times* (July 25), p. A5.

PERROW, CHARLES. 1984. *Normal Accidents: Living with High-Risk Technologies.* New York: Basic Books.

PESCHEK, JOSEPH G. 1987. *Policy-Planning Organizations: Elite Agendas and America's Rightward Turn.* Philadelphia: Temple University Press.

PHILLIPS, KEVIN. 1991. *The Politics of Rich and Poor: Wealth and the American Electorate in the Reagan Aftermath.* New York: Harper Perennial.

POULANTZAS, NICOS. 1969. "The Problem of the Capitalist State." *New Left Review* 58 (November–December): 67–78.

RICH, SPENCER. 1988. "Notch Babies Get Less Intentionally." *Washington Post* (March 25), p. A23.

ROLLINS, JUDITH. 1985. *Between Women: Domestics and Their Employers.* Philadelphia: Temple University Press.

ROSENBLATT, BOB. 1989. "The Notchies March On." *New Choices for the Best Years* (February), p. 12.

RUBIN, GAYLE. 1975. "The Traffic in Women: Notes on the Political Economy of Sex." In *Toward an Anthropology of Women,* edited by Rayna Rapp Reiter, pp. 159ff. New York: Monthly Review Press.

SABATO, LARRY J. 1984. *PAC Power: Inside the World of Political Action Committees.* New York: Norton.

———. 1989. *Paying for Elections: The Campaign Finance Thicket.* New York: Priority Press Publications.

SCHEFF, J. THOMAS. 1966. *Being Mentally Ill: A Sociological Theory.* New York: Aldine.

SCHLOZMAN, KAY LEHMAN, AND JOHN T. TIERNEY. 1986. *Organized Interests and American Democracy.* New York: Harper & Row.

SCHUMPETER, JOSEPH ALOIS. 1942/1950. *Capitalism, Socialism, and Democracy.* New York: Harper.

SCHWARTZ, BARRY. 1967. "The Social-Psychology of the Gift." *American Journal of Sociology* 73: 1–11.

SCHWARTZ, MICHAEL, ed. 1987. *The Structure of Power in America: The Corporate Elite as a Ruling Class.* New York: Holmes & Meier.

SCOTT, DENISE. 1991. "Beyond PAC-Man: The Significance of Gender Difference in Corporate-Government Relations." *Sociological Practice Review* 2 (4) (October): 252–263.

SHOUP, LAURENCE H., AND WILLIAM MINTER. 1977. *Imperial Braintrust: The Council on Foreign Relations and United States Foreign Policy.* New York: Monthly Review Press.

SILER, JULIA FLYNN. 1991. "Bolting the Boardroom Door at Sears." *Business Week,* pp. 86–87.

SILK, LEONARD, AND DAVID VOGEL. 1976. *Ethics and Profits.* New York: Simon & Schuster.

SIMON, DAVID R., AND D. STANLEY EITZEN. 1990. *Elite Deviance.* Boston: Allyn and Bacon.

SIMON, WILLIAM E. 1978. *A Time for Truth.* New York: Reader's Digest Press.

SKOCPOL, THEDA. 1980. "Political Responses to Capitalist Crisis: Neo-Marxist Theories of the State and the Case of the New Deal." *Politics and Society* 10: 155–201.

SMITH, VICKI. 1990. *Managing in the Corporate Interest.* Berkeley: University of California Press.

STANDARD DIRECTORY OF ADVERTISING. 1990. vol. 1. Skokie, Ill.: National Register Publishing Company.

STAROBIN, PAUL. 1990. "Foggy Forecasts." *National Journal* (May 19), pp. 1212–1215.

STERN, PHILIP M. 1988. *The Best Congress Money Can Buy.* New York: Pantheon.

SU, TIE-TING, DAN CLAWSON, AND ALAN NEUSTADTL. 1991. "Corporate PACs and Conservative Realignment: Comparison of 1980 and 1984." Unpublished manuscript.

SU, TIE-TING, DAN CLAWSON, AND ALAN NEUSTADTL. 1992. "The Coalescence of Corporate Conservatism from 1976 to 1980: The Roots of the Reagan Revolution." In *Research in Politics and Society,* edited by Gwen Moore and J. Allen Whitt. Greenwich, Conn.: JAI Press.

SUNDQUIST, JAMES L. 1981. *The Decline and Resurgence of Congress.* Washington, D.C.: Brookings Institution.

THAYER, GEORGE. 1973. *Who Shakes the Money Tree? American Campaign Financing Practices from 1789 to the Present.* New York: Simon & Schuster.

TOLCHIN, MARTIN. 1990. "U.S. May Ban PACs with Foreign Ties." *New York Times* (July 4), p. 9.

U.S. BUREAU OF THE CENSUS. 1986. *Current Population Reports: Money Income and Poverty Status of Persons and Families in the United States,* series P-60, no. 157.

———. 1990a. *Statistical Abstract of the United States. 1990.* 110th edition. Washington, D.C.: U.S. Government Printing Office.

———. 1990b. *Current Population Reports: Money Income and Poverty Status of Persons and Families in the United States,* series P-60, no. 174.

U.S. CODE. 1986. *Statutes at Large.* Public Law 99-514, vol. 100, pp. 2149–2150, sec. 204.

USEEM, MICHAEL. 1984. *The Inner Circle: Large Corporations and the Rise of Business Political Activity in the U.S. and U.K.* New York: Oxford University Press.

———. 1990. "Business Restructuring, Management Control, and Corporate Organization." *Theory and Society* 19: 681–707.

VICTOR, KIRK. 1990. "Trouble on Wheels." *National Journal* (May 26), p. 162.

VOGEL, DAVID. 1979. "Business's 'New Class' Struggle." *Nation* (December 15), pp. 609ff.

———. 1981. "The Public Interest Movement and the American Reform Tradition." *Political Science Quarterly* 95: 607–627.

———. 1989. *Fluctuating Fortunes: The Political Power of Business in America.* New York: Basic Books.

WALDMAN, MICHAEL. 1990. "Quid Pro Whoa." *New Republic* (March 18), pp. 22–25.

WARTENBERG, THOMAS. 1990. *The Forms of Power: From Domination to Transformation.* Philadelphia: Temple University Press.

WASHINGTON REPRESENTATIVES. 1986. 10th ed. Washington, D.C.: Columbia Books.

WEINSTEIN, JAMES. 1968. *The Corporate Ideal in the Liberal State: 1900–1918.* Boston: Beacon.

WHITT, J. ALLEN. 1982. *Urban Elites and Mass Transportation.* Princeton, N.J.: Princeton University Press.

WILKINSON, FRANCIS. 1991. "Rules of the Game: The Senate's Money Politics." *Rolling Stone* (August 8), pp. 31–34, 96.

WRIGHT, ERIK OLIN. 1979. *Class Structure and Income Determination.* New York: Academic Press.

INDEX

■■■

Abdnor, James, 60

Abortion, corporate contributions and, 69

ACA (Americans for Constitutional Action), 66

Academy of Social Insurance, 113

Access: to Congress, viewed as a right, 101; costs of gaining, 116; defined, 75; as euphemism for lobbying, 124; at fundraisers, 82–83; as goal of corporate PACs, 1; obtaining, and shaping solutions, 101–5; reverse, 75, 194. *See also* Access PACs; Access process

Access PACs: basic orientation of, 12; bribery and, 90, 152; buying votes and, 90; concern of, with company, 115, 155–56; contribution decisions of, 63–65; contributions to liberals by, 155, 178; criticism of ideological PACs by, 136; criticized by business leaders, 129–30; criticized by ideological PACs, 136–37; defending policy in narrow terms, 155–56; dominance of, 13; donations to challengers by, 153–54; donations to opposition members by, 64; free-market rationale and, 243*n*48; mail contributions by, 85–86; minor wording changes as aim of, 91–92; political party and, 67–69; ratings and, 66–67; and regret of actions, 64. *See also* Access process; Corporate PACs; Ideological PACs; Lobbyists and lobbying

Access process: aims of, 2, 4, 88; cooperation of all members of Congress with, 114, 216; corporate discomfort with, 125; defending provisions against challenges to, 105–7; to delay regulations, 185, 187–88; to destroy campaign finance reform, 215; facilitated by prior contributions, 122; impact of, 125–28; as only one form of business power, 119, 185; publicity for changes and, 105, 118. *See also* Lobbyists and lobbying

Acid rain, 3–5, 64

ADA (Americans for Democratic Action), 66

Advertising, 77, 138, 184–85, 188–89

AFL-CIO, 66

Alexander, Herbert, 28

Almanac of American Politics, 63

AMA (American Medical Association), 136, 214

American Council of Highway Advertisers, 77

American Enterprise Institute, 139

American Medical Association (AMA), 136, 214

Americans for Constitutional Action (ACA), 66

Americans for Democratic Action (ADA), 66

Anderson, John, 210

Asner, Ed, 106

AT&T, 15, 98, 99

Atwater, Lee, 22

Auto industry, 5, 158

Auto safety, 186–87, 206, 218

Ayres, Richard, 4